Loving LIES

Linda Kage

OMNIFIC PUBLISHING
LOS ANGELES

Omnific Publishing
1901 Avenue of the Stars, 2nd floor
Los Angeles, CA 90067
www.omnificpublishing.com

First Omnific eBook edition, September 2014
First Omnific trade paperback edition, September 2014

The characters and events in this book are fictitious.
Any similarity to real persons, living or dead,
is coincidental and not intended by the author.

Library of Congress Cataloguing-in-Publication Data

Kage, Linda.
  Loving Lies / Linda Kage – 1st ed.
  ISBN: 978-1-623421-29-8
  1. New Adult Romance — Fiction. 2. Forgiveness — Fiction.
  3. School Shooting — Fiction. 4. College — Fiction. I. Title

          10 9 8 7 6 5 4 3 2 1

Cover Design by Micha Stone and Amy Brokaw
Interior Book Design by Coreen Montagna

Printed in the United States of America

This one is for Alaina Cayenne, and no one else,
because no one pushed me as hard as she did to get this story finished,
and also because I'm really, really sorry
I forgot to type her name
in the acknowledgments of that other book!

Chapter One

It was a good day to be a good person.

As Tess Simpson strolled toward the entrance of Granton Regional Medical Center, she drew in an invigorating lungful of February air. Of course, not everyone shared her opinion. Next to her, her best friend grumbled about the frozen breeze blowing through her coat. Bailey yanked a pair of gloves from her pocket and pulled them on without finesse. Then she cast the clouds a petulant glare before flipping up her hood.

"I cannot believe you talked me into doing this. You hate me, don't you?"

"Actually," Tess said as she cheerfully bumped her elbow into Bailey's, giving her an exaggerated wink, "I love you so much I want to be with you always. You complete me."

The teasing remark made Bailey snort, but Tess decided to ignore her lack of enthusiasm. Nothing was going to burst her bubble. Humming to herself, she applied a layer of Mighty Mango lip gloss before slipping the tube back into her purse just as they approached the front doors, which swished open to welcome them inside.

"And these outfits are ridiculous," Bailey ranted on. "I mean, *really?* Who makes their volunteers wear true candy striper costumes anymore?"

"Oh, come on. The auxiliary who trained us explained the uniforms. With so many students pouring in lately to help out, they needed an easy way to distinguish the true nurses from the volunteers."

Bailey sent her a sideways frown, full of dry impatience. "Gee really, is *that* why?" With a sniff, she rolled her eyes. "I went to the training sessions too, you know. You don't have to repeat everything the auxiliary said back to me verbatim."

"Well, you don't have to act as if you've forgotten what she said either." Tess was used to her friend's cranky attitude, but Bailey was on a roll today.

Not that she was going to let that bother her either. She just wouldn't.

"I'm just sayin'. I feel like I'm in a jail cell."

Only Bailey would think of jail from seeing *red* and white stripes.

"Psht!" Tess snapped her fingers over Bailey's mouth, squishing her lips together and successfully shutting Bailey up. "This is for a good cause. We're needed. Just think of how much of a better person this'll make you feel."

Bailey batted Tess's hand away. "Yeah right. This ain't goodness I feel oozing out of my nose." She pulled a tissue from her pocket and pretended to blow her nose. Then, in a voice crammed with as much nasal blockage into it as possible, she whined, "I think I'm coming down with a cold."

"Oh, you are not. Faker." Tess pressed the button for the elevator before she set her hands on her hips and stared Bailey down with a determined arch of the eyebrows. "Don't you dare flake out on me. You *said* we could do this."

"Well, remind me to never agree to anything you suggest again," Bailey muttered. She stuffed the tissue away. "And by the way, we are so *not* needed since there are already other student volunteers just — " she made air quotes " — *pouring in*. Your words. We'll probably be in the way."

The elevator dinged, and a pair of silver doors yawned open to their left. Grabbing Bailey's arm to force her along, Tess swept them into the car. "Too bad. You already promised. A deal's a deal. We're doing this."

With a little moan of resigned acceptance, Bailey folded her arms over her chest as Tess pushed the button for the third floor. When Bailey didn't complain after the doors shut, Tess grinned and opened her coat to smooth her hands over the outline of her red and white striped apron.

"And I like the outfits. They remind me of candy canes, not jail cell bars." With a wiggle of her butt, she grinned and added, "Plus I look good in mine." As Tess twerked against her friend's leg, determined to coax a smile out of her, Bailey only snorted again and elbowed her away, though Tess swore she saw the corners of Bailey's tight lips tugging up.

"That's because your apron conforms to the shape of your body. You have a little waist to go with your curvy hips and big boobs. I'm sporting a straight line of blob over here. Looks like I'm hobbling around in a potato sack made of freaking jail-cell candy canes."

"Oh, whatever. You look cute too." Unable to help herself, Tess bumped her hip into Bailey's one last time. "Maybe not as cute as I do, but you'll pass."

"Witch," Bailey grumbled as the elevator stopped and let them out, but this time she was definitely hiding a smile as she spoke.

"Grump," Tess playfully volleyed back, smacking Bailey on the butt as she floated into a tiled vestibule. When said grump didn't follow, she had to reach back, catch Bailey's arm, and yank her along. "This way, dear."

As soon as they stepped forward, a harried-looking woman in scrubs descended upon them. Panting, she bent at the waist to rest her hands on her knees. "Oh, thank goodness. More volunteers. I am so glad to see you two. It's been one of those days. We'll take all the help we can get this evening."

Tess sent Bailey a told-you-so smirk, to which her best friend scowled and moodily shoved her hands into the pockets of her candy striper apron before pointedly lifting her chin and glancing away.

"I need one of you to deliver this cart of flowers to all the room numbers written on their cards. And I need the other to help the boy in room three-twelve eat his dinner."

"Oh no." With a gasp, Tess pressed her hand to her chest, her heart going out to the poor darling needing help. "He can't feed himself?"

That was so tragic. Tragic stories made her emotional.

Before Tess's sympathy bug bit her right in the tear ducts and she had to ask Bailey to spare her a clean tissue, the nurse gave a moody harrumph and glared at room 312, an open door not too far from them. "Oh, he can feed himself all right. He's just being stubborn, as usual. He refused breakfast *and* lunch. But he needs to stop fooling around and get some sustenance before he makes himself really sick." Mumbling under her breath, she added, "I wish we could put the obstinate ass on a feeding tube and be done with it."

"Do you know *why* he refuses?" Tess asked, her brow furrowed with worry. She wanted to fix this as soon as possible.

The nurse scowled, obviously irritated by the question. Then she let out a reluctant breath. "Jonah woke up with amnesia. He can't remember anything. And what's worse, no one's come to claim him, so he takes it out on all us nurses."

"Wait. *No one?*" Tess shook her head. That couldn't be right. "What about his family? His friends? Classmates? Surely, someone—"

"No one," the nurse cut her off with no room to argue.

Tess gulped and glanced sympathetically at the opened door to room 312. The poor, poor boy. She'd lose her appetite too if no one came to visit her and she couldn't even remember who to miss.

"How the heck do you even know his name if he has amnesia?" the ever-practical Bailey wanted to know.

Hmm. Good question. Tess hadn't thought of that; she'd been too worried about his feelings. See, this was why she'd made Bailey volunteer with her; Bailey always considered things that didn't even occur to Tess, and Tess considered things that didn't occur to Bailey. They really did complete each other.

"Because his student ID was on him when he was brought in. All we know is that his name is Jonah Abbott and he's attended Granton for three years."

Tess brightened. "Well, surely you could contact the university to find his—"

"We've called once. They never called back. And if you haven't noticed, we've been a little swamped around here." The nurse splayed out her hand to clue Tess and Bailey in to the chaotic atmosphere surrounding the third floor of Granton Regional Medical Center. "If you want to play Nancy Drew and find his next of kin, be my guest. No one here has the time to dig too deeply. We'll get to it when we get to it. Right now, we're more concerned with keeping everyone *alive*."

"Well, I'd be happy to find them for you." She didn't understand how no one had found him yet, but the world honestly had turned upside down in the past few weeks. She guessed anything was possible.

The nurse arched her eyebrows as if doubting Tess's sincerity. "Just keep in mind that if someone really cared about him, they would've come for him by now."

She sort of had a point. Exactly fourteen days had passed since the Granton school shooting. If someone were truly worried about Jonah Abbott, they certainly would've located him days ago. She winced, pity flooding her chest until it felt crammed full. Aside from trying to regain his memories and heal from a gunshot wound, he probably felt completely abandoned.

And Tess knew he had to be a victim from the shooting, because everyone on this floor was supposed to be; that was why she was here. Since this atrocity had happened on their home turf, the students of the university had wanted to help as much as possible, so the hospital had let them sign up for volunteer services to assist the harried medical staff with caring for other students who'd suffered in the shooting.

Tess had volunteered herself as soon as she'd come across a sign-up sheet, and of course she'd coaxed Bailey into joining her, since they did everything together.

Glancing at the open door of room 312, she ached for Jonah Abbott. She could only imagine the horrors he'd survived.

After hooking her arm determinedly through Bailey's and giving her a bolstering squeeze, she smiled at the nurse with absolute reassurance. "We'll make sure he eats, get the flowers delivered, *and* we'll find his next of kin. No problem."

But no sooner did she speak than a boom and clanging crash resounded from behind her. Ducking instinctively as the reverberation vibrated up the backs of her legs and spine, Tess let go of Bailey to duck and cover.

It wasn't gunshots, however, and she felt stupid for reacting so impulsively when no else around her had. Flushing, she dropped her arms from over her head and brushed her hair out of her face, trying to look cool and unaffected, when actually her heart was trying to pound itself out of her chest. Twisting to see what had happened, she wondered if someone had knocked over a cart.

But it was worse. Way worse.

Disbelief widened her eyes as she stared at a broken plate of food dripping down the door of 312 where the patient inside had obviously heaved his supper.

If that was all the food he was allotted for tonight, she was screwed.

"Yeah. I'll take flower duty." Bailey popped forward and latched her hands around the cart full of vases and potted plants.

Before Tess could call after her and argue that they should do their tasks *together*—since she tended to lose all her courage without her trusty BFF at her side—Bailey took off down the hall in the opposite direction of Jonah Abbott's room.

Great. What the heck was she supposed to do now? Biting her lip, Tess glanced helplessly at the nurse.

The nurse patted her arm with a commiserating sigh. Offering no words of advice, she said, "Good luck. You'll need it." Then she too fled.

Tess balled her hands into fists as she gaped after the escaping orderly and finally lost a tendril of her good mood. "Thanks a lot," she muttered. "Just leave me standing here with no clue what I'm doing."

Oh, well. She'd just wing it, then.

With a huffed breath, she shoved her sleeves up to her elbows and got to work. The first order of business was getting Jonah another tray of food. But hunting up someone to help with that proved impossible. As soon as she mentioned his name or the dreaded number 312, everyone suddenly became too busy to assist her.

The jerks.

Were they so heartless they didn't care that he was going through hell right now?

Fed up with everyone *and* their best friends, she took matters into her own hands. A quick visit to the Tex-Mex fast food restaurant across the street later, she was marching back into the hospital with a contraband bag of take-out hidden in the depths of her enormous purse.

"This'll taste better than boring old hospital food anyway," she assured herself, ignoring the growl in her stomach as the tantalizing aroma of beef, refried beans, cheese, and signature sauces teased her nose. Her mouth watered, reminding her she'd yet to eat supper, but she refused to steal even one taco from poor Jonah. He needed all the nourishment he could get.

She was going to take care of him so well. Her thoughtfulness would no doubt induce him to eat every last bite. It'd cheer him up in no time and—

She slowed to a stop to watch a guy with a balloon and bundle of flowers ease into another room down the hall. Her insides balling with sympathy, she realized no one had brought Jonah flowers.

No one had cared enough to buy him a balloon, or get well card, or anything. No one cared at all.

God, who was she kidding? He wasn't going to eat the food she'd brought him. He thought he'd been abandoned. Unless...

The idea that hit her was so brilliant she clasped it whole-heartedly without another thought. She would make him feel cared for and loved. And since he couldn't remember anything anyway, he wouldn't know the difference. Tess just couldn't handle knowing someone was miserable.

Glancing around to make sure no one was paying her any attention, she slipped her candy striper apron over her head and wadded it into a ball before stuffing it behind a nearby trash can. Then she smoothed down her blouse, finger combed her hair, and snatched up her purse before strolling into room 312 as if she actually had the nerve.

Only to jerk to an immediate halt.

Holy crap. She'd expected to find a thin, frail, dork of a guy, with glasses maybe, and a big nose stretched across a face full of acne. Yeah, with a high forehead, greasy hair, and a long, gangly neck. A loner college geek no one wanted to visit, working toward a degree in rocket science, or whatever degree college geeks worked toward when they wanted to become rocket scientists.

Okay, actually, she hadn't really been expecting that either. She had no idea what she'd been expecting. But the muscled-up beefcake with long, thick eyelashes, a rugged five-o'clock shadow, midnight black hair, and a wounded soul peering out from gorgeous brown eyes was definitely not on her list of top one hundred expectations. Even with his skin blanched with sickness, bandages on his head and around his chest, and a cast on one arm, he looked too yummy to be real.

Dear God, this was not good. Hot guys made her nervous. And when she managed to actually form words to talk in the presence of one, she usually blurted out the worst things to say, ever. Without Bailey here to ground her, this was going to bad. So horrifyingly, disastrously bad.

Jonah Abbott took her in from head to toe, his intense gaze making her uncomfortably warm and fluttering the muscles in her belly, uncaging the butterflies. Then he wrinkled his brow with confusion.

"Who the hell are you?"

When hope filled his sleep-bruised eyes, she bit the inside of her lip to keep from crying. He needed someone who cared—who really cared—to be with him so much right now.

"I—" Tess licked her lips and told herself to explain that she was a concerned classmate who'd come to see how he was doing because they'd become good friends over the last semester. But for the life of her, she couldn't spit out a course to name. Why couldn't she come up with *one* class? Damn it, she was going to kill Bailey for abandoning her.

Her brain was frozen, she couldn't think, couldn't concoct a good lie. She could only blurt forth the worst thing to say, ever.

"I'm your girlfriend."

Chapter Two

Jonah winced as he shifted his torso on the cramped, crinkly hospital mattress, trying to find a comfortable spot. A dull throb arced from the gash on the side of his head and down his body to all three of his bullet wounds.

He could do with another dose of morphine. But when he eyed the button lying by his hip to pump himself full, he didn't push it.

The ache was welcome. It let him know he was still alive.

God, he hated this. Hated the helplessness, the fear, the confusion. Slippery sweat dripped down his temple as the sterile scent of the infirmary burned his nostrils.

He wanted out of here so bad. He wished he had another plate of food to throw, helping him vent some of his frustrations. Fisting his hands at his sides, he gritted his teeth and jerked his good leg as if he could shake his bed enough to shimmy himself free. But the sudden movement only brought pain. He nearly howled aloud from the white-hot waves that sluiced through him.

Concentrating on working his lungs until the needlepoints of agony abated, he blinked away his spotty vision when something filled his doorway. Long past the point of expecting visitors, he glanced over and blinked some more. But it didn't matter how sharply he tried to bring her into focus, a girl remained standing in *his* doorway. A real, live redheaded girl.

She couldn't be a nurse; she wasn't wearing scrubs. And she wasn't a volunteer either; she didn't have on one of those stupid red and white striped prison aprons.

Jonah gawked openly.

"Who the hell are you?" he asked, startled to hear the deep baritone coming from his throat. It killed him that he didn't even recognize his own voice.

"I—" She was a tiny thing, with wide blue eyes that made his gut clench with something he couldn't distinguish. Looking scared out of her mind, she finally rushed out the words, "I'm your girlfriend."

"Girlfriend?" A jolt ricocheted through him, and he gnashed his teeth from the resulting flood of pain. But even as he winced, his heartbeat clanged in his chest with hope.

Finally. Someone had come for him. He wasn't alone after all. But the bitter resentment that had been clinging to him for the past week roared its ugly head.

Narrowing his eyes, he shook his head. "No. No, I don't know you."

"I—I know." Her eyes watered as she blinked repeatedly. "They told me you had amnesia. That's so…awful."

She had a unique look. Huge bubbling red curls sprouted out around her head, bouncing as if excited.

Wait. Excited hair?

He frowned. His mind must be wigging out on him again.

When she stepped hesitantly into the room, another jolt of adrenaline skipped along his veins. He might not remember her, but the idea of her coming close gave him a strange kind of high. Was someone really here to see him? Was she honestly his girlfriend?

It didn't seem possible. He didn't want to hope it was true.

He remembered pretty much nothing, but a gut instinct told him curvy, short redheads with wild hair weren't his type. Not that she didn't appeal to him. She totally did. An inherent need rose within him, wanting her to move close enough that he could touch her and find out if her skin was as soft as it looked. But still…this just felt… off. Deep in his being, he sensed this pretty, ethereal creature simply couldn't belong to him.

Which was too bad. Her blue eyes were so full of concern, like she really did care.

"Are…are you okay?" Reaching out, her fingers went for his hair. "I've been so worried."

He hated how much he wanted her to touch him and soothe his scattered fears, so he shied his face away, unable to trust it…to trust anything.

She immediately flinched back and sent him an apologetic cringe, tucking her hands together against her chest. "Sorry. I forgot. You don't…know me."

Squinting, he studied her hard. Why couldn't he recognize her? Why couldn't he recognize *anything?*

"What's your name?" Maybe a name would spark something inside him.

"Oh, right. Of course, you don't—sorry. Tess. I'm Tess. Well, Contessa Anabelle Simpson, actually. But everyone just calls me Tess."

When she gave a nervous laugh and fluttered her hand in the air around her like the beating of hummingbird wings, Jonah found himself focusing on her slim fingers. How many times had he touched those fingers? How many times had they touched him?

Could she really be his?

"What do *I* call you?" He had to know.

Her laughter died, and she went suddenly sober. "Tess," she whispered as her slim little hand crept up to rest at the base of her throat. "You call me Tess."

He shook his head. "I don't…I don't remember. I'm sorry, but I can't—"

"Hey, no. It's okay. It's fine." Those active fingers he was quickly becoming obsessed with now reached out to clutch his good arm, bare skin to bare skin. The contact pierced him deeper than he was comfortable with. His muscles flinched in surprise. "Don't worry about any of that right now. Your memory will come back when it's ready. Just concentrate on getting yourself better, okay? That's what's most important right now."

She sent him a tremulous smile, and his obsession grew to encompass her full red lips as well as her pretty hands.

"Which reminds me," she rattled on, letting go of him so she could dig into the huge purse draped over her shoulder. When she lifted out a paper sack with the logo of a familiar pink and purple bell on it, she sent him a huge grin. "They said you weren't eating, so I brought your favorite."

His favorite? That didn't seem right. Yet as she set the bag on the tray by his bed and opened it to pull out some wrapped tacos, his mouth watered.

"Two chalupas, a beef burrito, three crunchy tacos, and a caramel apple empanada."

Gaze shifting from between her and the food, he asked, "That's what I usually get?"

She busied herself by pulling out each item. "Mm-hmm." It hurt that she wouldn't look him in the eye, like she couldn't stand to see him so broken. Just how bad did he look? "So…which one would you like to start with?"

Overwhelmed by the choices, he eyed the food in her arms and damn near panicked. Shit. He didn't know where to start. He wouldn't even know his own name right now if someone hadn't told him what it was. How the hell was he supposed to know which kind of burrito to eat first?

"I don't—" He choked on a hoarse sob that had been trapped in his throat. Humiliated for letting his anxiety show, he balled his hand into a fist while oxygen sawed through his lungs at a crazy speed.

"Oh, God. I'm sorry." Eyes going wide, Tess let all the burritos and tacos tumble from her arms and onto his food tray so she could reach for him again. "Don't worry. It's okay. I'm sorry. I didn't mean to upset you." As if realizing she'd touched him again, she quickly pulled her fingers back, leaving him bereft. "Here." She snatched up a plain taco and began to unwrap it. "Crunchy tacos are always a safe place to begin a meal." Once she had half of it uncovered for him to eat, she gave him an encouraging smile and gingerly brought it to his hand.

His fingers reflectively clamped around the bottom portion and he grew transfixed by how different his hands were from hers. His fingers were huge and beefy with rough leathery skin full of calluses.

What had made them so tough? Was he a factory worker? A carpenter? A farmer? He had no clue. They'd told him he was a college student, but these didn't look like a student's hands.

"Do you want me to lift the back of your bed some more so you can sit up, or is this a comfortable enough angle for you?" Tess flicked open a folded napkin as one might snap open a clean sheet to spread over a bed. After it floated down onto his chest, she tucked a corner into the neck of his hospital gown.

Jonah stared. For the life of him, he couldn't imagine dating a girl who mothered him. He didn't feel like the pampered type.

When she caught him gawking, she paused. "Are you okay? What's wrong? Jonah?"

He shook his head. Jesus. No wonder why he couldn't picture himself with her. His own freaking name sounded foreign to him. Why wouldn't everything else?

"I just don't understand," he choked out. "This doesn't add up."

Alarm filled her eyes. "What…what do you mean?"

"They said I've been here two weeks."

She crinkled her nose as if confused. "They said? Don't you *know* how long you've been here?"

He shook his head. "I've only been awake from the coma for a few days."

"You were…" Tess's eyes widened as she pressed her hand to her heart. "Good God, no one mentioned a *coma*. Oh…" She turned away slightly. "You've been through…more than I originally thought."

Watching her closely, he took in the fine tremor of her fingers as she brushed at her cheeks. She really did care about him, didn't she? Which only made him more curious.

"Why did it take you so long to come?" The words he'd been waiting days to lash out at someone rumbled from his chest in more of a sob than the harsh demand he intended it to be. He clenched his teeth to keep his chin from wobbling.

Her big, scared blue eyes blinked. "What?"

He didn't care for her pathetic attempt at stalling. It only made him think there was something big she was hiding from him. But it did help him regain some of the anger he wanted to keep.

"If I've been here for *two* weeks, and you're my *girlfriend*," he growled, snarling each word, "then why the hell did it take you so long to check on me? Why has it taken so long for *anyone* to check on me?"

Her eyes watered as her mouth opened. "Jonah," she rasped, his name cracking on her lips as they pleaded with him to understand.

He shook his head, more confused than ever. "Just *tell* me."

"I...I...I'm so sorry." She covered her mouth for a moment as if needing to collect herself before she dropped the big explanation bomb. "Everything's just been...crazy. Ever since—" Breaking off suddenly, she bit her lip. "What all do you know about...what happened to you?"

He swallowed drily. "Not much. The nurses told me there had been a mass school shooting at the university I attend. And I was one of the victims. After being shot three times, I hit my head on the corner of a table when I fell, which I guess put me in the coma. When I woke up, I had no idea who or where I was."

"Th-*Three* times?" Tess went ashen as she cradled her belly. "You were shot three times? Oh God. I had no idea. You're so lucky to be alive."

"Yeah," he muttered. He felt *real* lucky. When a thought struck him, he sucked in a breath. "Were you...were you hurt too?" Maybe that was why she hadn't been able to get to him sooner. Maybe she'd been hospitalized and—

But she shook her head, her face full of guilt. "I...I...no. I was in my dorm room when it happened. I watched it all on TV. They had this one aerial shot from a helicopter they kept showing over and over again. We could see a figure lying on the ground in the middle of the street. It never moved. I think I cried all day for that one person, hoping whoever it was had survived." Her eyes flashed to him. "I prayed it wasn't you. And I...I called, but you never answered your phone."

Turning away slightly, she lifted a hand to tuck a stray red curl behind her ear. "They sequestered us to our dorm rooms and wouldn't let us out. I kept waiting for you to call back. But you never did. I was sure—" When her words broke off, he could see the torment in her entire being. Shaking her head, she looked back at him and whispered the last part. "I was too scared to check the fatality list. I couldn't...I just couldn't. I'm so sorry. I was scared."

His throat worked. She still looked scared. Before he knew it, his anger slipped. The urge to ease her fears overcame him until he had to clench his hand into a fist and glance away. But as he took in his broken body covered by a thin white hospital sheet, the view reminded him why they were both here.

Brows wrinkling into a slight frown, he choked out, "How many died?"

She swallowed. "Eleven."

Jonah's body went cold. He cleared his throat and closed his eyes. "I hadn't been able to…I hadn't asked anyone that yet."

"Twenty-one people who were wounded survived, though," came her optimistic answer. "My friend's boyfriend, Logan, was one of them. He caught a bullet in the chest when he stepped in front of her and saved her life."

Opening his eyes, Jonah looked up. "Logan?" He shook his head. "I don't…Do I know him too?"

"I — " She began to answer but stopped abruptly. "Of course. Of course you know Logan. Sure."

He nodded, even though the name Logan didn't resonate with him in the least.

"Who *did* die?" he asked. "Anyone I know?"

When her gaze darted away, grief filled him. Oh, God. Who had died? He hated that he couldn't remember the names of anyone truly important enough to ask about. He hated that she was keeping things from him. He hated this entire confusing, fucked up situation.

"You know, why don't you just focus on getting yourself better right now? We can worry about what happened in the shooting later when you're healthy and you get your memory back. The nurse I talked to was worried about you. She said you hadn't eaten breakfast or lunch today, so you really need to eat. Okay?"

Jonah shook his head and glanced away. "I'm not hungry."

"But — "

"*No*, God damn it," he roared, winding back his arm. "I don't want *food*." After he launched the taco across the room, it splattered against opened door, adding to the mess already plastered to the surface. "I want to know what the hell is going on. Why are you the only person who's come to visit me? Where is my family? My friends? I have family and friends, don't I? What *aren't* you telling me?"

"I…I'm sorry." Trembling visibly, Tess scurried to pick up the meal she'd brought him and stuffed everything back into its takeout bag. "I don't know why I did this. I shouldn't have come here like this. This was a big mistake."

"Why?" he demanded, the panic rising in his chest as she fumbled in her haste to collect her things. She wasn't just going to leave him, was she? "Are we no longer together? Did I cheat on you? What's going on?" When she didn't answer, he latched his hand around her forearm and exploded, "*Tess!*"

She jumped and lifted her eyes.

He immediately wanted to apologize for scaring her, but God, he needed answers. He needed *something*.

"You can't...you can't just leave me like this." To his mortification, his voice wavered, magnifying his fears enough for her to see and dissect every weak particle of his existence. "You're the only link I have to...to anything."

Her shoulders rose and fell sharply. More tears trembled at the edge of her eyelashes. Closing them, she opened her mouth. But before she could speak, a nurse barged into the room.

"What is all this yelling and commotion about in here?" Her lips pinched together as she eyed the door. "Mr. Abbott, did you throw more food? Just who do you expect to clean this mess up?"

"I will," Tess said quickly. "I was about to get right to that."

Leaving Jonah's side, she hurried to the door to pick up the shattered dinner tray and stack the pieces. As the mollified nurse sent him one last lethal scowl before turning on her heel and storming from the room, he frowned at his girlfriend. She was a definite people pleaser, wasn't she?

"You shouldn't do that," he grumbled. "A nurse or one of those volunteer people will get to it eventually."

She paused before sending him an unreadable glance. Then she shrugged and went back to work. "I don't mind."

Once again, Jonah wanted to apologize for yelling at her. But his overwhelming emotions had been boiling inside him since the moment he'd woken in the hospital bed. Not knowing anyone—himself included—and no one claiming to know him was taking its toll. The fear had built hour after hour.

Since Tess Simpson had walked through the door with the closest thing he had to answers, he couldn't stop the bitter taste of frustration when she only left him with more questions.

He stewed in his regret until he realized she'd finished scrubbing his mess. Then he only felt guiltier because she'd been the one to clean up after his temper tantrum.

"Thank you." He spoke quietly and humbly, not quite able to look at her. A ball of shame formed in his throat; it took him two tries to swallow it down.

"It's no problem."

She forgave too easily, which worried him. Was she the type to let a person walk all over her? Jonah hoped to God *he* had never walked all over her.

"But I'd really like it if you ate." When he glanced at her, she fluttered her lashes and sent him a begging smile. "Please. For me?"

He nodded, ready to do anything to get back into her good graces. He must've been crazy about her before the accident. No matter how frustrated he was or how many questions he felt the need to strangle from her, the desire to keep her happy seemed ingrained in him.

Jonah was starving, but he didn't have an appetite. That didn't make a lot of sense, he knew. The pangs in his stomach were cursing him to fill it already, except nothing sounded enticing enough to keep down.

Since Tess had brought him Tex-Mex, though, he reached out and slowly slipped the still-warm bag onto his lap. Her eyes lit with hope as he pulled out the first thing his fingers found and unwrapped it.

As soon as his teeth sank into the crisp breading of the chalupa, he closed his eyes and moaned, his craving for food thankfully roaring to life. "God, this is good." He took another bite, filling his cheek.

Tess let out a large breath, her eyes sparkling with relief as she grinned. "Better yet?"

She must know him well if she knew eating helped calm his moodiness. He muffled out his answer and took another bite. "Mmph. Much."

Smiling, she sank slowly into the chair beside his bed and watched him quietly as he polished off one taco after another, not even letting his broken arm slow him down. He stared back, still stunned someone was here, visiting *him*.

"Do you need a drink?" she asked, lifting the cup of ice water from his bedside tray as he began to eat the empanada.

Since she was already handing it over, he accepted with a nod and sucked heartily from the straw. He didn't want to admit it, but the nurses who'd been badgering him all day to eat had been right. Eating freaking helped.

Or maybe it was the redhead with the too-kind blue eyes who truly helped.

Tess took his cup back as soon as he finished drinking. "Thanks." He watched her set it carefully on the tray, and questions once again flooded his brain. "There's so much I want to ask, but I don't even know where to start."

She gave him a tremulous smile as she folded her hands in her lap and began to wring them as if nervous. "Look, I swear to you, I'll find your family. You won't be here alone for long. Okay?"

He blinked at her, wondering why she didn't know where his family was already, when another idea struck. Shit! She'd definitely worded that as if she didn't consider them a couple.

"So we're *not* together anymore," he murmured with a wince. He might not remember her, but he already knew he didn't want to lose her. God, what asinine thing had he done to push her away and make her break up with him?

She didn't answer, which pretty much confirmed his suspicions. Just what kind of guy was he if the only person who bothered to visit him in the hospital after he'd nearly died was his *ex*-girlfriend?

"Um...I'm going to go ahead and take off," she said, glancing longingly toward the exit.

She made it sound so final, as if this was goodbye forever. Jonah's stomach clenched, threatening to upset all the food he'd just eaten.

"Will—" When his esophagus closed and his voice went hoarse, he cleared his throat. "Will I ever see you again?" He wanted to beg her to come back. Hell, he wanted to beg her not to leave in the first place.

She looked away for a moment, and he almost lost it. She was going to tell him no, and he was going to return to being all alone again.

Forsaken.

But obviously, her too-kind heart had her rasping out, "Of course. I'll be back tomorrow as soon as...after all my classes let out. So just..." She finally turned back to him, showing him a wealth of pain in her beautiful eyes. Damn, he must've hurt her bad. "Just take care of yourself and eat everything the nurses bring you, okay?"

With a slight nod, he whispered, "Okay."

She forced a smile, but with the tears clinging to her lashes, it only made him ache with regret and the need to apologize for whatever he'd done to hurt her.

"Okay," she repeated as if bolstering herself.

This time, when she reached for his hair, he didn't flinch away. He closed his eyes and breathed in a relieved breath as soft fingers brushed his bangs across his forehead. When he opened them, she leaned in with her lips pursed. He could tell her target was his forehead, but he needed more than that. He needed an intimacy he'd been craving since he'd opened his eyes days ago. He needed to know someone cared. So, he tilted his face back, readjusting just in time for her to catch his mouth against hers.

Plus, he had to know what it felt like to kiss her.

Realizing what he'd done, she pulled back, looking startled. "Oh! Uh…" Her gaze raced over his, and her fingers fluttered back to her throat. "I was actually aiming for your hair because I thought you'd be uncomfortable with…" With a noisy swallow, she zipped a quick glance at his lips. "Since you don't remember me at all. But… um…okay."

She darted back in and stamped her mouth to his with a quick, impulsive peck. He barely had time to digest what had happened. But the scent of peaches remained as she pulled away.

Lifting his face to stare at her, he watched the color rise to her cheeks. Strangely, it didn't throw the redness of her hair off balance. In fact, her blush and those scarlet locks complemented each other, giving her a glowing kind of angelic effect.

He wanted her to kiss him again, longer this time. And not because there was something comfortable and familiar about her. But because her lips had felt new and exciting.

In fact, if she hadn't claimed to be his girlfriend, he would've sworn that had just been their first kiss together, ever.

Chapter Three

Tess needed to escape this room before she had herself an honest-to-God heart attack. Her pulse raced a million miles per minute, and her cold skin was slick with nervous sweat.

She hated lying, and every word that had spewed from her mouth since she'd stepped into this room had been coated, dunked, and outright punctured with lie after lie. But with each fib that fell from her tongue, she'd been forced to layer another on top of it.

It was obvious Jonah Abbott needed someone in his life right now who "knew" him. He had to be experiencing every kind of pain there was to experience. Physical, emotional, mental. Hell, probably even metaphysical. And knowing he had no one could only hurt him more. So, she'd struggled to keep up the lying game for his own good.

Trying desperately not to flush but feeling her face heat anyway, Tess glanced away after kissing him. "Well." She blew out a breath and licked her lips. She could still feel the soft press of his mouth against hers and taste caramel apple from the empanada he'd eaten.

Her cheeks burned hotter. "Okay, then. I guess...I guess I'll see you tomorrow." Forcing an overly bright smile, she risked a quick glance his way.

He didn't answer, simply watched her as if trying to figure her out. Darting her gaze away, she gave a jerky, embarrassed wave, grabbed her purse, and sprinted toward the door.

"Tess," he called, his voice edging toward panic. But she'd already hit the hallway, and no way could she go back, not without telling him the truth. Right now, she didn't think the truth would help him.

Covering her mouth, she hurried down the hall and veered blindly around the first turn she came to, only to get rammed in the gut by an empty cart.

She didn't even feel the pain in her abdomen. She closed her eyes and moaned. "I'm sorry." Lifting her hand in apology to the cart pusher, she whirled away to run in the opposite direction.

But Bailey's voice had her screeching to a halt and spinning back. "Tess?" From the other side of the cart, her friend blinked at her as if she'd lost her mind. "What the hell? Are you okay? Did someone hurt you?"

Like a balloon deflating of air, all the pent up misery and guilt rushed from her system. "No." Tess charged toward Bailey and grabbed her arm. "We need to go. Right now."

"Wha—" Bailey stumbled along behind her. "What happened? Oh, shit. You didn't kill the poor bastard in three-twelve, did you?"

"No. But I'm going to have a panic attack if we don't find an exit soon." When she hurried them around another corner, she whimpered. "Where the hell are all the elevators in this freaking building?"

"Good Lord." Bailey let out a huff, grabbed Tess's hand, and led her the other way until they exited the hall and those magical silver doors came into view.

Beyond grateful, Tess rushed to them and started jabbing buttons. She didn't speak until the doors opened and she and Bailey were safely sealed inside alone. When the floor began to drop, making everything in her stomach dip as well, she wrapped an arm around her waist and turned to her friend.

"I think I just made the worst mistake of my life."

Bailey blinked. "Well? What happened?"

Tess sucked in air, so much that she became lightheaded. "I—I—I felt so bad for him. No one had come to visit him, he'd been shot three times, and he'd just come out of a coma. A *coma*, Bailey, a freaking coma. And now he has amnesia. He was so alone and afraid and upset. And his eyes. Oh, my God. His eyes seemed to hold all the pain in the world. I just couldn't…he needed to know *someone* cared, so I…so I told him…"

"You told him what?"

With a wince, Tess buried her face in her hands and peeked between the gap in her fingers. "I told him I was his girlfriend."

Bailey's jaw dropped. "You did *what?* Holy shit, Tess! Why would you say *that?*"

"I just told you why!"

"But his *girlfriend?* Why would you go that route? Couldn't you have just said you two shared a class together or something?"

Tess began to wring her hands. "That was the original plan, but I…I froze. He was just…he was so hot. Like…an eleven hot. Like mouth-wateringly gorgeously hot."

"*Oh.*" Bailey rolled her eyes. "Jesus, what is it about a guy with a pretty face that brings out your stupid gene?"

"I don't know," Tess wailed, gripping her hair. "But I wish it'd just go away and quit afflicting me because it's going to get me into deep trouble one of these days."

"You mean like it just did."

Tess dropped her hands to scowl. "You're not helping."

"Well, what the hell am I supposed to do? You got yourself into this one, babe."

"You weren't supposed to let me get into it in the first place, *babe.* I thought we were going to do all our assigned jobs *together.* But you just raced off, leaving me standing there by myself to deal with him alone."

Bailey shrugged. "Hey, you should've told me that. I didn't know you wanted us to tag team our duties."

"I *couldn't* tell you! You were halfway down the hall before I could even open my mouth." She fisted her hand and punched her friend in the arm, right at the shoulder joint. "Thanks for deserting me, by the way."

When the elevator doors opened, she marched into the foyer, leaving Bailey behind. But Bailey caught up to her soon enough and quietly kept pace as Tess stormed outside and all the way to Bailey's car. Her friend silently clicked the car unlocked on her key fob, and Tess yanked open the passenger side door.

Neither of them spoke until Bailey started the engine. Putting the gear into reverse, she briefly glanced over and bit her lip, scowling at Tess.

Bailey might be the braver of the two, but she was always the first to cave after an argument. Letting out a groan, she mumbled, "I'm sorry, okay?"

And Tess was always the first to forgive. But this time she sniffed, folded her arms over her chest, and turned to stare out the passenger side window.

Another mute minute passed.

Finally, Bailey asked as she pulled out of the parking garage, "So, what are you going to do about this amnesiac guy who thinks you're his girlfriend now?"

Just thinking about Jonah's situation made her want to bawl for him. "I have to go back tomorrow."

Bailey stomped on the break at a red light. "What? Are you crazy?"

She sounded so incredulous, Tess turned to scowl at her. "I can't not go. I *told* him I would."

"Oh, my God, Tess. You lied about everything else. Why start being honest now?"

Stomach knotting with guilt, Tess bit her lip. "I have to go back. He needs me."

She said it so quietly, she kind of hoped Bailey hadn't heard her because she knew her friend would jump all over that one. But apparently, Bailey had elephant ears.

"He *needs* you?" This time she punched the gas as she zipped into traffic. "Oh, brother. You talked to him for, what, ten minutes? How could he possibly need you?"

"He doesn't have anyone else. You don't understand. You didn't see him."

"So, you're just going to keep lying to him, telling him you're his girlfriend, then?"

"Yes. I think I have to. Until he gets his memory back, anyway. Then he'll have his life returned to him, and he won't need me anymore."

Bailey shook her head and muttered to herself, "There is so much wrong with everything she just said, I don't even know where to start."

Then speaking directly to Tess, she lifted her voice. "And you don't think he'll be pissed about the fact that you've been *lying* to him once his memory returns?"

Swallowing down her dread over that very possibility, Tess shrugged. "He might be. Or he might be grateful I was there to befriend him. That's just a chance I'm willing to take."

"Oh, brother," Bailey grumbled again. She paused at another stoplight and glanced across the car. "He's going to ask questions, you know. Questions you can't answer."

Tess groaned and sank lower in her seat. "He already has."

"And?" Bailey cocked an eyebrow.

"And I only made him more frustrated by evading the answers. He ended up concocting some idea that we'd broken up before the shooting and he somehow did something really bad to upset me. That's why he thinks I'm so…standoffish, or whatever, toward him."

"Well, actually that might work." When the light turned green, Bailey tore through the intersection. "Wow, the amnesiac came up with a good backstory lie for you already. Right on." She lifted her hand for a congratulatory fist bump, but Tess scowled at her.

"This isn't funny."

Bailey rolled her eyes and dropped her hand back to the steering wheel. "Then maybe you should tell him the truth."

"No." Tess shook her head and turned away. "I have a better idea. I'm going to find his family and friends and, once they go to him, he'll see someone he actually recognizes, get his memory back, and end up *thanking* me for helping him. Or at the very least, he'll be so happy to be back in the arms of people who *do* care for him, he'll forget all about me."

"Except you're overlooking one detail."

Tess frowned and glanced over. "What's that?"

"There's a very real possibility *no one* cares." When Tess opened her mouth to argue, Bailey spoke over her. "No one's come to see him yet."

"I'll find someone," Tess said, her jaw firm with more confidence than she felt. "Someone has to care about him. That's all there is to it."

Determined to find someone who cared about Jonah Abbott, Tess Googled his name as soon as she and Bailey made it back to their dorm room. When over eighty-one thousand results popped up, she winced. Glancing briefly over the few pictures at the top of the search engine, her shoulders slumped when she didn't immediately spot his face.

Revising her search, she typed in his name along with *Granton University* and hit pay dirt.

"He's a football player," she said aloud, clicking on the first link, only to lift her eyebrows. "A really good one. Wow, he's already broken university and state records."

"Really?" Bailey plopped down beside her on the bed, gnawing on a Twizzler stick, to read the screen over Tess's shoulder. "A football player, huh? Which position?"

Tess arched a brow and glanced at her. "As if it matters. You don't know the difference."

"What?" Bailey shrugged. "I was just being polite."

Snorting out a laugh, Tess shook her head. "You would be polite if you were asking *him*. But you're asking me, who doesn't know the difference either, so it's a moot point."

"Ahh. A tight end," Bailey said with a smug sniff as she motioned toward the words near the top of an article.

Tess clinked on the link. It was a small-town newspaper piece from the city of Bristol and had been written three years before, talking about one of their seniors—Jonah—receiving a football scholarship to Granton.

"He's from Bristol," she murmured, growing more excited by the second. In self-congratulations, she ripped the Twizzler out of Bailey's hand, tore off of a piece with her teeth, and handed it back. "I honestly didn't think it'd be so easy to find information about him. But Bristol. That's, what, less than an hour from here, right?"

"An hour and fifteen minutes," Bailey, Miss Numbers herself, corrected, polishing off the rope of candy.

"Whatever." Tess rolled her eyes and typed in a search for his name, adding the word Bristol. When she came across a five-year-old obituary for a Paul Marsch, she discovered Jonah had been one of Marsch's surviving grandsons. "The only other survivors for this guy who lived in Bristol were his daughter and son-in-law, Ted and Phyllis Abbott. That must be Jonah's parents. Don't you think?"

Letting out a squeal of excitement, Tess almost expected to be led to a link with their address, phone number, and map of how to get to their house when she searched for Ted and Phyllis Abbott of Bristol. But she encountered a snag when Paul Marsch's obit ended up being the only thing tied to them online.

"Have you tried the school directory yet?" Bailey asked, pushing from Tess's bed to wander across the room and flop down on her own mattress so she could hunt up another Twizzler stick. Her voice was bored as she took a bite, picked up a fashion magazine, and flipped through the pages.

"That's a good idea." Leaving her search engine, Tess logged onto the university's Web site. When she saw a link for the Granton massacre's memorial page, she paused. She'd visited this page before, but now it felt different. Each deceased victim of the shooting had been named with their picture and a small eulogy of their accomplishments attached to it.

Of the eleven who'd been killed — twelve counting the shooter who'd committed suicide at the end of his rampage — more than one had been a football player for the university. Tess shuddered and clicked onto the page before she could stop herself.

Dorian Wade, the star quarterback had actually been murdered in his dorm room two nights before the shooting. But since he'd been killed by the same person, he was added among the list of victims. Being a football player himself, Jonah would know Dorian. She gulped and hit print, listing out everyone who'd died. Amnesia or not, he had a right to know who was gone. Didn't he? Or would it only frustrate him more to see a list of people he couldn't remember?

After her small desk printer kicked into gear and started spitting out pages, Tess finally typed Jonah's name into the *Find People* section of the university's search engine. When her query immediately brought up results, she fisted her hands into the air. "Jackpot! We have a permanent *and* local address. And…oh, my God."

Bailey paused her reading to lift her face. "What?"

"His dorm room's in Grammar Hall." Tess glanced over at her roommate. "How could he live in the same building as us for a full semester and we've never seen him before?"

Her friend shrugged. "Well, being that I didn't see him tonight, maybe I *have* seen him before."

Tess scowled. "Don't be silly. I know everyone you do. And we have definitely never seen this guy before."

Bailey sniffed but didn't respond to that. "What's his room number?"

"One-eighteen," Tess answered distractedly as she searched for more links with Jonah's name. But the only thing she could find now were articles about football stats, which might as well be Arabic to her poor, sports-ignorant eyes.

"Well, that explains it." Bailey flipped a page on her magazine. "He's on a completely different wing and floor than us. I'm sure there are plenty of people living in that part of the building we've never met or seen before."

Experiencing the itching need to physically do something for Jonah, Tess pushed her laptop off her knees and stood up. "I'm going to his room. Maybe he has a roommate who's willing to visit him at the hospital." She arched her eyebrows. "Want to come with?"

She honestly thought Bailey would hop to because they always did everything together, but Bailey surprised her by snorting. "No." She wrinkled her face into a look that told Tess she shouldn't have even bothered to ask. "And why are *you* going to so much trouble? I'm sure the proper authorities will eventually locate his next of kin."

But it had already taken them two weeks...and Jonah was suffering.

"Because..." She shrugged helplessly. "I'm his girlfriend. This is what girlfriends do."

"His *fake* girlfriend," Bailey reminded her with a concerned wrinkle in her brow. "Tess, you do remember you lied about that part, right? I mean, you're kind of going a little over the top here. You don't know the first thing about this guy. You don't *owe* him anything."

"I know. I just...no one deserves to be alone, Bailey. And he's *alone*. Totally, completely, utterly alone. How would you feel if you woke up and didn't know anyone, *yourself* included? I'd be completely freaked out right now."

"God, he must be *really* hot." Bailey shook her head and went right back to reading.

Tess scowled at her. She didn't want to confirm it—though, yeah, Jonah had been super, gorgeously hot—because that was not why she was doing this. Huffing at her friend for her lack of support, she slipped on some flip-flops and left their room. By herself.

She shuddered as she hurried along the hall toward the wide stairs at the main entrance of the dormitory. Rubbing her arms, she glanced behind her to make sure no one was following. She hated walking alone through this corridor. Watching eyes seemed to shadow her every step. Ever since the shooting, she'd been doubly freaked to go *anywhere* on campus by herself. Thankfully, she and Bailey were nearly joined at the hip, and her best friend was the fearless type. Tess rarely had to worry about anything with Bailey around. Without her buddy, however, her heart pounded and anxiety reigned.

Trying to calm her breathing, she skipped down the main steps and shivered again, almost expecting Einstein, the creepy boy genius, to pop out from under the stairwell.

Whenever Tess had left the building with her suitemate, Paige, Einstein had always appeared out of nowhere to puppy-dog Paige around. Tess swore he'd practically lived under those stairs, waiting for Paige to pass by.

But Einstein was dead now. Sixteen years old, a junior in college, and he'd gone off the deep end, killing eleven people and then himself in the Granton University Massacre.

When she passed the shadowed nook he used to haunt, the ghost of his creepy self seemed to slither out toward her with a waft of cool air. Tess muffled a small squeak of fear and skipped into a terrified run until she was panting down the hall, a good thirty feet from the staircase.

"God…" She hugged herself again, hoping she wasn't the only person skeeved by the memory of him always hanging out there.

Realizing she wasn't paying attention to room numbers, she lifted her gaze to find she was almost to her destination. But when she found the door to Room 118 covered by yellow police line tape, she slowed to a stop and gaped. After checking the entire hall in front and behind her, she noticed no other room had the same adornment.

"What the heck?" she whispered. Jonah couldn't be the only person from Grammar Hall who'd been hurt in the shooting. Could he?

No, of course not. Einstein was gone too. And he'd lived somewhere here on the first floor, she was sure.

So, why had the police cordoned off only Jonah's room?

When a door across the hall and two rooms down opened, Tess jumped. A lanky guy exited and pulled to a surprised halt when he saw her gawking.

She sent him a tense, guilty smile and pointed toward Jonah's door. "Do you know why that tape's there?" she asked, hoping she looked sweet and timid enough not to appear intrusive.

A shuddered, troubled expression immediately clouded the boy's face. "Because it was *his* room," he mumbled and brushed past her rudely as if he found her question insulting.

She turned to watch him hunch his shoulders in a defensive manner, letting her know he clearly didn't want to talk about it.

But she had to know. Crinkling her brow with confusion, she called, "Whose room? Jonah's?"

He stumbled a step as if not expecting that inquiry. Then he glanced back briefly. "No. Well, yeah. His too. But it was also *his* room." When Tess only blinked, he rolled his eyes and whispered, "Einstein. It was *Einstein's* room."

Chapter Four

Her stomach full of knots, Tess chewed on a hangnail as she watched Bailey haphazardly sling books and papers into her bag. Tess had been ready to go for ten minutes. Physically ready, at least. Mentally, she was absolutely not ready at all.

For the first time since the shooting, the campus was beginning their regularly scheduled classwork again.

She hadn't known anyone who'd died in the shooting. Well, except the quarterback, Dorian Wade, but she'd only spent, like, half an hour in his company, and she'd been too drunk most of that encounter to remember much about him.

Oh, and Einstein. She'd kind of known Einstein. But she refused to go there.

To say the least, she hadn't known anyone enough to really *mourn* their loss. That didn't stop her from feeling really freaked out about attending classes, though. Her level of security had plummeted in the past two weeks. She glanced around most places she went, on the lookout for some crazy person with a gun, knife, baseball bat, or even a threatening leer.

Some days, she was able to push those unsettling feelings down and let her usual perky self take over. But today was not one of those days.

"Ready?" Bailey asked, zipping up her backpack and slinging one strap over her shoulder, apparently unconcerned by what they were about to do.

Tess scowled at her, really hating it that her best friend had to be so utterly fearless. "Aren't you freaked out *at all?*" she demanded.

Bailey gave a clueless blink. "'Bout what?"

"Oh my God. Dozens of people were shot down mere days ago, Bailey. It's like a...a *war zone* out there. We're going to be trampling over ground where people were slaughtered. How can you act so blasé, like it's just any other day?"

"I'm not acting. It really *is* just another day. Geesh, you big coward. Nothing is going to happen."

"I bet you thought that two weeks ago too." Tess fiddled with the strap of her bag, loath to sling it over her shoulders. After her first class with Bailey, she had to go her own way. By herself. She didn't want to do anything by herself today.

"Seriously, sweetie. The campus is probably safer today that it's ever been. I bet we'll see a campus cop or some kind of uniform as soon as we step out the front door."

And they did, too, damn it. Bailey sent her a smug, told-you-so smirk as they exited their dormitory and saw a handful of men in army fatigues just outside the entrance of Gibson Hall, the main cafeteria.

"Shut up," Tess muttered, even though Bailey hadn't said a word.

With a laugh, Bailey bumped their hips together and started up a conversation about homework assignments, which helped drag Tess from her anxiety. But as soon as they reached their Psychology room, a note taped to the entrance told them their professor had cancelled class for the day.

"Geez Louise." Bailey scowled as if offended she couldn't learn all about physiological and neurobiological processes. "I wonder if *every* professor is going to cancel today. I wouldn't have gotten out of bed if I'd known we weren't having class."

Too relieved to answer, Tess turned with her friend and followed her back toward their dorm.

"Want to hit up Gibson and get some breakfast while we wait around?" Bailey asked as soon as they dumped their bags on their beds.

Tess shook her head. She couldn't eat now if she tried. "I'm not very hungry." She'd never been much of a breakfast eater.

"Well, I'm starving. This break in my schedule has me all out of whack. I'm going to go stuff my face." Bailey paused at the door and glanced back at Tess. "You going to be okay?"

No. Tess didn't feel as if she'd ever be okay again. Her world was no longer the safe, protected haven she'd always thought it was. Bad things happened. People went crazy and killed strangers for no plausible reason. Innocent bystanders died horrible, awful deaths just for being in the wrong place at the wrong time. And she could've easily been one of those unlucky bystanders.

But she bit her lip and nodded. "I'm good."

Bailey rolled her eyes, letting Tess know she totally didn't believe her, but she pulled open the door anyway. "Okay then, liar. See you later. Love ya."

"Love you too." As the door closed, Tess slumped down onto her mattress next to her backpack and picked at a chip on her fingernail polish. She hadn't repainted her nails since the weekend before the shooting, when her family had gone snow skiing with Bailey's family.

Everything seemed to be timed for before and after that day. She hated how important it had become.

When noises from the room next door told Tess her suitemate was home, she blew out a sigh of relief and padded through her bathroom to knock on the door on the other side. One of her suitemates, Mariah, had dropped out of Granton the day after the shooting, just as quite a few other students had. The other suitemate—

"Come in," Paige's voice called.

"Hey, sweetness." Tess bulldozed inside. "Bailey went out for breakfast, so I'm all alo—" She gasped to a halt when she realized Paige had company. "—lone," she finished lamely.

She still wasn't used to Paige having a boyfriend. And Logan Xander just had to be one of those hot specimens that rendered her brain-dead.

"I...I'm sorry." She backed her way into the bathroom and hooked her thumb over her shoulder. "I didn't realize you—"

"It's okay." Paige smiled, waving her back. "Come on in. We're just kicking back for a minute."

She sat cuddled on her single-sized bed with Logan as they held hands. With his arm in a sling, he looked tired and pale as he rested his cheek on Paige's shoulder. He'd only been out of the hospital for a few days, but Tess wondered if he'd left too soon. He didn't look well at all. She hoped he was getting enough sleep and eating right. The first step toward good health was making sure to take care of the basic essentials.

Not that she'd ever have the courage to say any of that to Logan's face.

"Did your first class of the day get cancelled too?" Paige asked.

Tess dragged her gaze away from the yummy mess that was Paige's boyfriend and nodded. "Yeah. You guys?"

They both nodded. Logan closed his eyes and sank closer to Paige while she idly sifted her fingers over his short hair. "Want to keep us company?" she asked, glancing toward Tess.

"Umm..." Tess shook head. "No thanks. Actually..." An idea struck her. "Actually, I need to do a little research. Have either of you heard of a football player named Jonah Abbott?"

"No, I haven't," Logan answered, opening his eyes just enough to glance up at Paige. "You?"

She wrinkled her brow and murmured, "No. I don't think so, but that name sounds kind of familiar for some reason. Maybe...no. Sorry, I just can't place it."

Tess didn't dare tell her about his association to Einstein. Paige had been the only person to try to befriend Einstein, and it was anyone's guess what bringing up his name would do to her. Actually, Tess just feared speaking his name aloud, period. Bad juju and all that. She hadn't even been able to tell Bailey that *he'd* been Jonah's roommate when she'd found out last night.

It still sent a spooky shiver up her spine every time she thought about it. No way would she be able to tell Jonah himself he'd roomed with the very boy who'd tried to kill him.

"Well, Jonah was shot three times in the...in..." Tess stumbled when both Logan and Paige winced. Logan's hand flitted toward his own healing bullet wound on his chest. "Anyway, I met him yesterday when Bailey and I volunteered at the hospital. And I guess he hit his head pretty hard when he fell after being shot. He was in a coma for a week or so, and when he woke up, he had amnesia. None of his family or friends have come to visit him. I was trying to find out as much about him as possible so I could, I don't know, give him a file of information about himself to maybe help jog his memory."

"Well, that's sweet of you," Paige murmured. "But, wow, that poor guy. It's hard to believe he hasn't had *any* visitors."

"You said he played football?" Logan asked, squinting. "Maybe you could talk to his coaches or other players. I'm sure one of them would want to see him."

Tess bit her lip thoughtfully. Talk to hot jock guys? Yeah, that would be unlikely. "That's a good idea," she said, sending Logan a stiff smile. "I have his parents' address, too. When I have some free time…" Her words drifted off as she realized she probably had time now. "Oh! You know, with all the professors cancelling classes today, I think I'll go see if I can talk to them right now. They don't live that far away. Will you guys let Bailey know where I went, if you see her?"

Tess hated GPS navigation systems. When she needed their guidance the most, they led her out into the middle of a cornfield. Literally. Gritting her teeth, she pressed the gas until she came to the next intersection with a county mile marker, telling her she was indeed on the correct road.

Hmm. That was odd. Going straight, she drove on until she reached the next house another half a mile down. Squinting at the mailbox, she saw that the freaking navigation system had been right. Tess pulled Bailey's car into the driveway and turned around to head back the way she'd come. When she didn't see another house for two more miles, she decided Jonah's permanent address should lie between this house and the last one she'd passed, which just couldn't be, unless the university had had the wrong information posted.

Frustrated and not sure what to do now, she started back home. Passing through the small town of Bristol, she stopped at their one stop light and waited for it to turn green as she tapped her fingers on the steering wheel. Talk about a total waste of the day.

When the light changed, she pressed the gas and rolled through the intersection. But as she passed a convenience store, she pulled in. There might be one more option she could try before leaving town. After the three-hour round trip this was going to take, she wanted to be absolutely certain she'd tried every possibility before giving up hope on Jonah's family.

She filled up Bailey's car, since Bailey didn't mind if she borrowed it as long as she topped it off with gas. Then she went inside to pay. The clerk behind the counter had a phone book, thank God, and he was kind enough to let Tess borrow it. Thirty seconds later, she found the address and phone number for Ted and Phyllis Abbott. And it had been nowhere near the address in the school directory.

Which made everything even stranger.

"Excuse me." She smiled hopefully at the clerk. "Do you know where Whispering Pines Road is?"

He scowled, looking slightly confused. "I know where the Whispering Pines *trailer park* is." He winced and raised a hand to rub the back of his neck, then used his free hand to point and give her general directions to the trailer park.

"Thanks." Giving him a grateful grin, she handed the phone book back. "And you should try a new pillow."

Blinking, he said, "What?"

"Your neck." She pointed to his hand as he continued to massage his nape. "It's bothering you. The same thing happened to my dad. He went to chiropractor after chiropractor to fix his neck problems. But it turned out he just needed a new pillow."

"Huh." He shook his head and grinned. "I never thought of that. Thanks."

"No problem."

After leaving her simple advice and returning to Bailey's car, it didn't take much for her to find the trailer park where Jonah's parents lived. The trailer in question seemed to need the most repairs. Since it was still winter and the grass was dead, it wasn't long and seedy, but she could already picture the yard overgrown and neglected. The blue and white paint had long ago bleached down to show patches of rusted metal underneath. Both windows in the front were broken and duct-taped together, and the front screen door hung at an angle from one hinge.

She would've assumed the place was abandoned if she hadn't heard muffled music coming from within.

Tess paused when she reached the steps. They looked too rotted to hold her weight. So, she bit her lip and strained to reach past them, balling her hand and giving a hard knock.

Immediately a dog, a little one from the tenor of his high-pitched yip, began to bark inside.

"Shut that damn mutt up," a man roared.

Seconds later, the barking ceased, and another second after that, the door cracked open a few inches.

A timid feminine voice squeaked through. "We're not buying anything. Sorry."

Arching onto her toes, Tess leaned forward until she saw a haggard face with a dark purple bruise circling one eye. "Oh, I'm not selling anything. But...Mrs. Abbott?" She went out on a limb and said, "I'm actually here about your son. Jonah?"

She hoped Jonah was their son. Or at least she hoped this woman would somehow be related to him, or at least know who he was, to correct her.

The door opened a few more inches revealing stringy gray-blond hair and a hopeful expression creasing her already wrinkled face. "You know Jonah?" Brown eyes that looked identical to her son's lit with excitement. "You've seen him?"

"Yes." Tess bobbed her head, growing a little excited herself. "He—"

The door flew open wider. Phyllis Abbott flinched and clutched the Chihuahua close to her breasts as a barrel-chested man with wide shoulders like Jonah's appeared behind her, nudging her not-so-politely out of his way.

"Who the hell is it? And what's this yap about the kid?"

He had evil eyes. Not at all like his son's.

Unable to control her reaction, Tess slunk a step back. "Yes, I—" She cleared her throat, stiffened her spine and lifted her chin. "I'm Jonah's friend." *Don't kill me, please don't kill me.*

Ted Abbott loomed above her as he shook a grease-stained finger threateningly. "You tell that little shit if he shows his pie hole around here again, I'll kill him."

Tess sucked in a breath. "I...um..." She took another step back. "Actually, I'm here to inform you he almost died." Then she added, "He still might," just to get some kind of reaction from him. "He's in the hospital right now. I don't know if you saw the report about the Granton school shooting on the news—" and they would most likely be the only two people in America who hadn't if they said no "—but he was a victim in that and was shot three times. He has amnesia and was in a com—"

But Jonah's dad only smirked. "Good. Serves the little fucker right. Just don't expect me to foot any funeral or hospital bills if he keels over."

Tess blinked. "Ex-Excuse me?"

"I told him when he left I was done with him. And I meant it. He's probably legal age by now, anyway. I'm not responsible for none of his bullshit."

Before she could even think about responding, he slammed the thin metal door in her stunned face.

Well.

At least that explained why Jonah's family hadn't gone to visit him.

Chapter Five

J onah sat at a table outside of a diner.

Tucking his chin deeper into the collar of his coat and redistributing his weight from one hip to the other so the cold metal chair under his butt could soak through his jeans and freeze the other cheek for a while, he sent his best friend a glare as he rubbed his bare hands together.

"I hate you right now. We could be sitting inside at a warm, comfortable booth if you didn't have to freaking smoke. Those things'll kill you, you know."

"Nah." Sean smirked and blew a lungful of nicotine toward him. "I'm sure something else will take me long before cigarettes do."

With a sputtered cough, Jonah waved his frozen hand in front of his face to clear the air. "Thanks, asshole. Thanks a lot."

Sean smirked. "Just sharing the lung cancer, my friend."

"Yeah, well next time you feel like dying, don't take me down with you."

The waitress bustled outside, carrying two red plastic baskets loaded with greasy burgers and curly fries. Dropping Jonah's meal in front of him, she huffed out a disgruntled breath. "Anything else?" she asked, dragging a bottle of ketchup and mustard from her apron.

"Yeah, I need a refill." Sean lifted his empty cup, rattling it so she could hear the lonely ice tumbling around inside. She gritted out a sigh that caused a vapor cloud to escape her lungs and mix with the cigarette smoke hovering above their table.

"Sure." She forced a totally fake smile as she jerked the cup from his hand, though it ended in a narrowed-eye snarl when she added, "Be right back."

As she stormed away, Jonah hooked a thumb over his shoulder, pointing at her. "You're pissing off our waitress, too. She doesn't want to come out in this weather to serve us. Probably spit in our food."

"Then they should let us demon smokers eat inside. Damn." Sean continued puffing as he scowled at his food. "Besides, the cold is good for people. Teaches 'em to be sturdier."

"I don't think that girl's main goal in life is to be sturdy." Pausing for that first juicy bite, Jonah sank his teeth into the sesame-seeded bun and moaned, closing his eyes in ecstasy as the flavors hit his tongue. God, he loved eating here, frozen ass or not. Nothing on earth beat a good old-fashioned cheeseburger.

"Yeah, I can see you're real torn up about my choice of restaurants."

The euphoria of the moment ruined by Sean's dry tone, Jonah opened his eyes to scowl. "So, what's up?"

Sean had called him this morning to meet here for lunch, saying he wanted to discuss something important.

"I'm gay," Sean said.

Jonah choked on his hamburger. As his best and only friend calmly kept smoking, he managed to get his bite the rest of the way down with a couple painful swallows. His face was no doubt ten tones of red as he picked up his drink to take a hefty gulp.

When he had his digestive system back under control, he slammed the cup down and focused on Sean. "What?"

"I'm gay," Sean repeated, his expression refusing to alter. He looked so blasé about his announcement he might as well have pointed into the air and said, "There's the sky."

"What the hell," Jonah demanded. "Are you fucking with me?"

"No, I'm dead serious."

Shaking his head, Jonah realized he wasn't going to clear the chaos filling it. "But…since when have you been gay?"

Sean shrugged. He calmly pinched off the smoking cherry of his cigarette before tossing it into the ashtray and picking up his chicken salad sandwich. "Since birth, I guess." Then he took a healthy-sized bite.

*Lifting both his hands and stunned out of his mind, Jonah gaped.
"How can you be gay? You date women all the time."*

*Jonah teased him relentlessly about being a man-whore, actually.
With his blond-haired, blue-eyed, pretty-boy looks and easy smile, Sean
had women flocking to him constantly. And he rarely turned them away.*

*Instead of cracking one of his easy smiles now and saying he was just
joking, Sean sighed. "They were all a front."*

*"A front? But…" Jonah stared at him hard. When he realized Sean
was telling him the honest-to-God truth, he shook his head once again,
denying it. Seriously, though, how could he not even suspect something
like this of his very best friend on earth? He'd had no clue at all.*

*How much more didn't he know about Sean? Jesus, did he really
know the guy at all?*

*Feeling betrayed and abandoned, he worked his mouth a few mo-
ments before managing to ask, "So…Jesus, why're you telling me this
now? We've known each other for twenty years."*

*Sean screwed up his mouth thoughtfully. "Fifteen, technically. We
didn't meet until kindergarten."*

"You know what I mean, asshole!"

*Finally beginning to look unsettled, Sean grumbled something under
his breath and shifted in his seat. Jonah noticed it then: the fear in his
friend's eyes.*

*"Look. You're not exactly the most accepting person when it comes to
someone who's not…you know…like you. I didn't want you to drop me
flat when you found out. So, I've been keeping it under wraps for the
past couple of years."*

*"The past couple of— Christ, Thompson! You're the only fucking
friend I have. Did you honestly think I was just going to write you off
because you decided you prefer cock over pussy?"*

*Ditching all pretenses of casual, Sean stared dead into Jonah's eyes,
and Jonah could see just how much it was taking his buddy to drop this
bomb on him.*

"Yeah, actually, I kind of did."

*Hissing another curse under his breath, Jonah wiped a hand over
his face. "Well, fuck you, then. Your faith in me is astounding, you know.
Holy shit."*

"Look, I…I'm sorry. I just thought— "

"Oh, shut up." Scowling, Jonah waved him silent. "You are like a brother to me. The only family I have. I would stand beside you no matter what. And if anyone gives you shit about this, I'll be the first person in line to ninja kick them in the face. Got it? Nothing is going to make me drop you. You idiot."

When Sean nodded and blinked as if he was about to start bawling, Jonah sighed and rolled his eyes. Time to scale the drama down a notch.

"But seriously," he grumped. "Did you have to go and make your big reveal here, today, in this frozen-ass weather?"

Shoulders loosening, Sean grinned and leaned back in his chair to recapture his cool, collected front. "Sorry, bud. But I met someone, and I don't want to hide my relationship with him. Besides, I thought bloating you full of your favorite food first would help ease the shock. I know how food calms you down."

Jonah made a face of understanding. The man had a point. With cheeseburgers in his belly, he really couldn't stay pissed. But then something about Sean's explanation struck him. Mouth flapping open, he gawked. Sean had been spending all his time lately helping the drama department get ready for their big end-of-the-year play.

"Wait, you met someone? Oh, God." He moaned out his biggest fear. "You met someone recently? Please don't tell me he's some artsy-fartsy douchebag from the drama department."

Sean let out a loud belly laugh. "Why, yes. Yes, he is. He's an actor." When his guffaws tempered to a snicker, he taunted, "You're going to totally hate him."

Oh, hell. Jonah moaned, unable to stop frowning. "Thanks, dickbreath. Thanks a lot. If you're going to turn gay, couldn't you have at least fallen for someone I could actually get along with? Like another athlete, maybe. I've heard gay baseball players are pretty bad-ass."

He didn't want to have to play nice with some freaking actor who probably dramatized every wordy sentence he spoke. Good Lord, the agony of that very thought made him shudder. For Sean, he'd gag his way through it and play nice with an actor, but he'd hate every second.

"Too late," Sean announced, looking entirely too pleased with himself, his chest all puffed up with pride. "I'm already in love with this one. Aubrey is…amazing."

Jonah lifted a non-impressed eyebrow. "Aubrey?" Geez-uz, the guy even had a freaking actor's name.

Could his day get any worse?

Apparently, it could.

"Hey, Abbott," a voice called from across the street, interrupting his coming-out-of-the-closet conversation with his best friend.

Jonah glanced over to see a familiar figure marching his way. Einstein, the kid genius—a.k.a. the bane of his existence—waved once before dropping that hand and lifting his other to show off what he held. "Thanks for letting me borrow your gun."

Mouth falling open, Jonah looked wide-eyed at the rifle Einstein bandied about as if it were a water pistol.

Surging to his feet, he roared, "What the hell?" How had that little pissant gotten his gun? He'd had it locked in its case under the backseat of his locked truck. Taking a step toward Einstein to snatch his property from the idiot's careless clutches, he skidded to a halt when the end of the barrel swung his way without warning, aiming at the center of his chest.

"Eins—" He started to yell the warning, but the sixteen-year-old college student had already pulled the trigger, and surprisingly, the kid had found bullets and loaded it too, because it fired.

At first, he had no idea he'd been hit. Something slammed into his leg, and he felt like he was in one of those dreams where he wanted to move but couldn't. Then a sharp needle dug its way into his gut.

Confused, he glanced toward Sean to see if he found everything to be all wonky, slow motion, and dreamlike too. But he no sooner looked at Sean than Sean's head exploded like a melon.

As he watched his only friend—his family and a man he thought of as an extension of himself—die, a scream pierced his ears. The waitress who'd just stepped outside the cafe with Sean's refill dropped the cup, spilling soda all over the ground. She spun around to race back into the diner when another blast ripped through the air.

Jonah finally began to topple over then. As he fell, he watched a bright red spot appear and grow on the waitress's back as she, too, fell.

The world veered sideways.

Right before he landed, the third bullet entered him. This one burned and screamed through his organs until everything went blank.

Jonah jerked awake with a gasp. Body tense and mind racing, he stared up at the ceiling of his hospital room until he could orient himself. Tears filled his eyes, and dry pain crowded his throat. He shoved the damp moisture off his eyes before one of his hateful nurses came in and found him sobbing like a baby.

He hated sleeping these days. Bad dreams always came whenever he lost consciousness. Haunting memories he refused to grasp. Filling his chest with more hospital air, he pushed the disturbing images from his mind and tried to focus on the here and now, which honestly wasn't all that much better.

When he couldn't help it a minute longer, he glanced over to check the time on the wall.

Fuck. She'd lied to him.

The little redhead had completely deceived him. Jonah had actually believed her when she'd told him she would come back today. He'd even eaten all of his breakfast, lunch, and dinner to please her. But with dusk filling the sky outside, reality told him she wasn't going to show. It didn't matter that he'd waited and watched for her all day. Didn't matter that he'd kept his promise and eaten all his food just as she'd asked him to. She obviously wasn't going to keep *her* promise.

Damn it. He was such an idiot. He'd seen it in her eyes; she hadn't wanted to come back. The girl was a terrible liar. So, why had he anticipated her return so much?

Probably because she'd been the only thing to give him any kind of hope since he'd woken in this bed. He didn't even care that he knew she hadn't told the truth. The parts about her that had been honest were just so…honest. Pure. Heart-felt. It made him wonder why…but then the whys of it really didn't matter now. She wasn't coming back.

Clenching his teeth, he fisted his hands and muttered, "Screw it."

Frenchie, his physical therapist, had told him not to try to stand. Jonah hadn't walked yet because his damn PT had only worked and stretched his muscles every time he'd stopped in to check on Jonah. He wasn't even planning to allow Jonah the opportunity to try until he returned in another two days.

Well, Jonah didn't want to wait two days. He didn't want to just lie here with his heart cracking open because some tiny, blue-eyed redhead had lied to him. He just wanted to get away for a few minutes. Escape.

Blowing out a deep breath to bolster himself, he tried to swing his legs over the side of the bed to set them on the floor. But he'd grown so numb just lying there that it felt like he was moving two concrete blocks. Clenching his teeth, he ignored the heat rising to his face as he strained, ignored the pain exploding from every bullet hole in his body, ignored the nurse who walked into his room, carrying more medicine.

She skidded to a halt. "Hey! What do you think you're doing?"

"I'm going for a walk," he grated out, glaring at her from narrowed eyes and clenched teeth. "I need to walk."

"The hell you do." She hurried forward to set the tiny cup of pills down before turning to him, arms already raised to restrain him. "You're not supposed to get out bed yet, Mr. Abbott."

"Well, I am anyway. I need—"

"No." She grabbed his arms. "Before your therapist left today, he said you could try on Wednesday with the walker. That's soon enough."

He glared and batted her away. "Let go," he warned. "I'm trying this. Now."

"No, you're not. There aren't enough people in here to help if you can't do it."

When he ignored her and attempted to stand anyway, she pushed him right back down. He growled and resisted, causing a jagged pain to shoot up his leg. He gasped but kept struggling. "I just want to try. I *need* to try."

The damn nurse didn't seem to care what he needed. "And you will. In *two* days when your therapist and a roomful of assistants are here to help you."

"I don't want to wait. I don't need help. I just want—"

"And I really don't care what you want." Well, at least she was being perfectly honest with him. No one in this hospital seemed to care what he wanted. "You're *waiting*."

"God...damn it!" Using his feeble strength to break free of her, he failed miserably, only hurting himself more with each twist of resistance. "Let me go!"

"I need some help in here," she yelled toward the doorway.

"You *need* to back off." Jonah's IV tore from the flesh in the back of his hand as he struggled. He just about had the upper hand when the wild-eyed nurse dug her nails into his thigh wound, subduing him.

He roared out his pain as a handful of people in scrubs flocked into the room, pile-driving him onto the bed.

Half a dozen voices screamed at him, telling him what they wanted him to do, and he hollered right back, trying to tell them he just wanted to be left alone. All the while, his body turned into one huge ball of shrieking, throbbing agony, each nerve ending pulsing unyieldingly. But he was so mad and scared and hurt, he continued to fight against the bodies holding him back, against the voices telling him what he couldn't do.

He knew he must look wild, and he knew he was acting crazy, but he couldn't help it. He had to escape. He needed to be free from all this. Everything became about the fight, the will to not give up.

Bowing up his back while both of his arms and legs were being pinned down, he lobbed his head back and forth, cursing the entire room full of orderlies as he caught sight of one nurse sucking a syringe full of juice from a tiny clear bottle and then pulling it free before turning his way.

"No! Don't you fucking get that thing close to me. *Just leave me alone.*"

"Hold him steady," Needle Nurse demanded of her cohorts, and she approached, the gleam in her eyes scaring him shitless.

Jonah did not want that shot. Managing to wiggle his arm that was bound up in a cast free from its captor, he slapped the syringe away. As it flew across the room, pretty much every person holding him down groaned and cursed.

They recaptured his arm, using so much force this time the pain actually paralyzed him. His mouth opened in a silent scream as another needle was filled.

When someone else filled the doorway, he jerked his attention that way, to tell whoever it was to fuck off. He didn't have another body part left for a new tormentor to restrain anyway. But when he saw who had arrived, the fight instantly drained out of him.

It must've startled his captors into thinking they'd killed him or something because as soon as his body went limp, about fifty hands jerked off him as if refusing to take culpability for his death.

Sinking deeper into the bed with his newfound freedom, he stared at the redhead frozen, petrified in the doorway, her blue eyes wide with shock as she gaped at him over the hands she held against her mouth.

"You came back," he croaked, his voice so hoarse it barely cleared the air. Then a sob seized him, and it didn't matter how much he blinked, he couldn't see her through all the wetness clouding his vision. But he knew she was there.

She was *here*. Nothing else mattered. He needed her to draw him back away from all the fear.

He mopped at his face with trembling fingers. "You came back."

She dropped her hands and took a hesitant step forward. "Of course I came back." Her gaze skipped to the nurse with the half-filled syringe. "What's going on?"

The nurse's lips pinched thin with disapproval. "Who're you? Are you family?"

"Yes," Jonah rasped before Tess could answer. His hand trembled as he reached for her. "Yes. She's family."

As if sensing his need, she rushed the last few feet and gripped his fingers. He couldn't take his eyes off her, was even too afraid to blink for fear she'd disappear if he closed his lashes for even half a second. She was like his angel, showing up just in time to save him from the very brink of despair.

"Are you okay?" she asked, worry lining her beautiful eyes. "What happened?"

"I just wanted to walk," he confessed. And, damn it, his eyes were no longer just moist. Now they were streaming, and his burning hot cheeks were flooded.

"He's not allowed to try that yet until his physical therapist comes in on Wednesday," Needle Nurse announced haughtily while the others in the room made a mass exodus for the door.

Tess wiped his tears away with her bare fingers before she glanced at the nurse. "What do you mean *try?* Isn't he capable of walking?"

Jonah glanced at the nurse, wondering that himself. He'd never come right out and asked because he'd been afraid of hearing the answer. And his orderlies had never been very forthcoming with updates because he wasn't the most model patient.

In his opinion, the woman still wasn't being very helpful when she answered, "The bullet that hit his thigh broke his right femur. And since it took so long for a medical team to get into the area after the shooting, and then transport him to a hospital, and *then* work on his more life-threatening injuries first, it didn't get set properly. He has two pins holding it together."

Jesus Christ. Did that mean he was going to be able to walk or not?

"Dear God." Tess turned back to him, and damn, it looked like she was going to cry any second too. A heavy ache bloomed in his chest as she tightened her grip on his hand — which helped keep him from having a panic attack — only to frown and lift their bound fingers with a gasp. "He's *bleeding*."

The nurse glanced over and grumbled something under her breath. "He must've jerked his IV free when he was fighting us." Sniffing with disdain, she sent Jonah a dirty look. "Are you going to behave and let us patch that up?"

"Wow," Tess said, not sounding impressed in the least as she raised her eyebrows at the bitchy nurse. "*Really?* Don't you think you could give him a little leeway here and not treat him like a criminal? I mean, he's only been awake from his *coma* for a few days, has no idea what his own name is or who his friends are, has three bullet holes in his body, and now he doesn't know if he'll *walk* again. I'm sorry, but excuse us if he isn't the cheerful ball of optimism you think he should be."

Though his face was still wet from bawling, Jonah felt like laughing. As sweet and passive as she'd been yesterday, he never would've thought this blue-eyed, redheaded angel would have the backbone in her to get so defensive on his behalf. But there she stood, defending him like a pro.

So very glad she'd come back, he lifted her hand to his mouth and kissed it gratefully. He might not know the first thing about her, but he was going to cherish every second of her company.

Chapter Six

Tess was pleased when Jonah's nurse transferred her glare from him to her. He didn't need to be glared and bickered at right now. He just needed a little tender loving care, proof taken from the way he kissed her hand in thanks, stirring a warm tingle inside her.

The nurse narrowed her eyes ominously before muttering, "I'll be right back with the supplies," before she spun away and stalked from the room.

Tess waited until Nurse Ratchet was gone before she turned her attention to the boy on the bed with the silent tears streaming down his cheeks. She blew out a breath and forced a smile. "Well, *she's* certainly pleasant."

Jonah didn't smile at her joke. His chest still heaved from the nervous breakdown she was sure he'd just adverted himself from having. But at least his breaths were coming more easily now. And no new tears welled in his eyes.

"None of them like me. I think I'm the worst patient in the entire hospital."

He sounded so apologetic and regretful about that fact that her heart went out to him. She began to reach for his hair to soothe him, but he lifted his face to look at her. Feeling caught in the act, she dropped her fingers unobtrusively.

"I can't believe you came back," he said, his voice full of awe.

"I said I would." She tried to stay upbeat, but with the tragic way he stared at her as if she was the only thing keeping him together, she had to bite her lip and glance away again. "I didn't mean to get here so late, but I drove to Bristol and…" Her voice trailed off as she peeked at his face for any sign of recognition. "Does that name mean anything to you?"

He squinted as if running the word through his head. "Bristol?" he repeated. When she nodded, he shook his head. "No. Is it a town?"

She nodded again. "Yes. It's your hometown. I found your parents and went to tell them what happened to you." Wincing, she glanced away. "And now I know why you never talked about them."

His eyes widened with panic. "Why?"

Tess blew out a breath. Man, this was going to be hard to report. But she wanted him to know. "The permanent home address you have in the school directory is false, so obviously you didn't want to be tied to these people in any way. Except I found them in a phonebook once I reached Bristol. They live in a trailer park called Whispering Pines." She paused to study his face. "Does that ring any bells?"

Jonah blinked once, then twice, before he slowly shook his head.

She shrugged, not really expecting him to have a bright flash of clarity but kind of hoping he might. "Well, that's where they live. Ted and Phyllis. Those are their names."

He puffed out a sudden, harsh breath. "You talked to them?"

After a pregnant pause, she sighed. "Yes, I did."

His face paled as if he already knew he wasn't going to like what she had to say, but he asked anyway. "And?"

"Well…" She eased into the chair beside him. After tucking a piece of hair behind her ear, she dropped the bomb. "They didn't…" Oh man, how was she going to word this? "Apparently, you had a big falling out with them years ago or something. I'm not sure. But it was probably before you were eighteen, because I don't…Well, your dad said something to make it sound as if he hadn't seen you since you'd become a legal adult. Anyway…" She fluttered out a hand as if it wasn't an important detail. "I don't think they're going to make it down to see you."

The air exhaled from his lungs. He stared at the wall over Tess's shoulder. "Okay."

She bit her lip again. "I'm so sorry." When she covered his hand, he turned his over so they lay palm to palm and their fingers interlaced.

"So, *both* of them want nothing to do with me?" he asked. "My dad *and* my mom?"

She wrinkled her face into a look of indecision. "Well, mostly. Your dad was the biggest jerk, telling me…Well, anyway, I have a feeling if I'd caught your mom by herself, she might've responded differently."

He glanced at her, hope flaring in the depth of his intent gaze. "How's that?"

"She…" Tess shook her head. "I don't know how to say this, but I think…I think maybe he beats her. Her eye was bruised, and she just acted…you know, submissive. Abused. She looked concerned about you until *he* showed up in the doorway. And then she just… shut down and went blank."

Jonah stared for the longest time before he blinked and glanced away. "I don't know how to feel about that."

Her fingers tightened around his. "It's okay. Without your memories, these people don't mean anything to you. I can only imagine how hard it is for you to learn…well, what you just learned."

He nodded, his face still vacant of emotion. "I wonder if I still love them."

"Of course you do." She rose up so she could kiss his forehead. "All children love their parents, even if they're crappy, awful parents that don't deserve it. They gave us life; we just can't help it."

Glancing at her, he sent her a thoughtful smile. "Thank you. Even though it was a wasted trip, thank you for what you did. Thank you for trying. I don't…I have a feeling not a lot of people would've gone to that much trouble for me."

Her smile was soft. "It was my pleasure." In the span of a few seconds, but very significant seconds, they stared at each other as he ran his fingers along hers. Then her eyes widened. "Oh, that reminds me. I printed some pages off the internet, hoping maybe one of them might help jog your memory."

Jonah crinkled his brow. "What kind of pages?"

She shrugged. "Oh, just things about you. Mostly football stuff. Stats and numbers. Things like that."

"Football?"

Lifting her eyes, she gave him a full grin. "Yeah. You're a football player. Does that help you remember anything?"

A brief, haunted expression filled his face before he glanced away. "No."

"Well, you are. And a damn good one too. Best tight end in the division," she announced before giving a small frown. "Not that I know what a tight end does, exactly."

An amused smile flickered over his lips as he turned back. "He does whatever he needs to do from blocking, catching a pass, or protecting the quarterback."

Her eyes widened. "You remember that?"

His gaze went just as wide. Then he blinked. "Yeah," he said slowly. "Yeah, I guess I do remember that."

She smiled her bright, joy-filled smile again. "That's great. Here. Maybe this will help some more."

When she thrust a stack of papers at him, he accepted, even though he looked a little overwhelmed by the quantity. What he read from the headline on the first page made his eyebrows arch.

"Wow. I'm *not* half bad, am I?"

"I know." Excited to share all his glowing accomplishments with him, Tess perched herself on the edge of the bed to sit by his hip. "You've broken two state records and are working toward the national level. And some NFL scouts have even come to a couple of your games to watch you, even though you don't graduate until next year. Isn't that exciting?"

"Yeah," he muttered, his eyes flickering with bitter regret. "Unless I never walk again."

Tess winced and bit her lip as she sliced her gaze to his leg. "Right," she said. "I forgot about that."

Well, crap. His entire future was on the line now. She'd come here, hoping to reassure him and let him know he had a life beyond these four sterile walls. But instead, she'd only added to his misery and layered on something else for him to worry about.

"What's this?" He lifted a sheet near the back of the pile.

When she glanced over, her eyes widened. "Oh, I wasn't going to show you that." She went to reach for it, but he pulled it back, keeping it in his possession.

"What is it?"

"It's—" She cleared her throat. "It's a fatality list of all the people who died in the massacre. Kind of a memorial."

His hand holding the paper began to tremble and a bead of sweat slid down his temple. "Who do I know?"

Tess reached for the list again with no success as he pulled it away from her. "Maybe you should wait until you have your memory back before you look at it. It's not going to mean anything to you right now anyway."

He ignored her and focused on the list, his fingers curling tighter around the edges of the sheet the longer he scanned it. She had no idea what thoughts filtered through his brain as his gaze shifted over each obituary, but his jaw was tense and his eyes bright. When he stopped dead three-fourths of the way down, his throat worked and his expression froze, but otherwise he didn't react.

"What?" Tess asked, moving to the head of his bed so she could see the list over his shoulder. "Do you recognize a name?" God, she hoped this wasn't how he got his memory back. Focusing in on the area where he was centering his attention, she murmured, "Sean Thompson?" Tess turned to study his face. "Did you know him?"

He set the page down and stopped looking at it to rub his eyes. "This is giving me a headache."

"I'm sorry." She slipped the sheet out of his hand and folded it quietly before tucking it into her purse, out of sight. "I didn't mean to overload you. I just thought I could help you remember."

He didn't respond, but his lips trembled before they opened as if he was going to say something. Then he shut them and dropped his hands to his waist, squeezing his eyes shut one last time before opening his lashes to look at her.

"Can we—" He paused and glanced away, sucking in a deep breath.

She set her hand on his forearm, encouraging him to say whatever he wanted to say. "Can we what?"

He blew out the breath and met her gaze once again, his brown eyes almost desperate. "I think pushing the memories to come like this is making it worse. I just…I was wondering if we could not force them tonight. Instead maybe we could try something differ-ent, like, I don't know…" He pulled his bottom lip in between his teeth. "Maybe we could pretend we've never met before." Rolling his eyes, he added, "Not that I'll have to pretend there. But if we acted like we were meeting for the first time, I could...I could get to know you better."

Tess caught her gasp, not expecting this request. "Oh." She cleared her throat. "Um...sure. Yes, definitely, we could do that. No problem. If that's what you want."

He looked at her with such intensity that when he said, "I do." She gulped from the impact of it.

"Okay, then." She eased into the chair at his bedside and folded her hands in her lap. "What do you want to talk about?"

"You."

Her eyebrows shot up as alarm flooded her. "Me?"

"Yeah. We can't exactly talk about me since I don't know anything about me. So...I want to know everything there is to know about you."

"Oh. Um...okay. Well..." She blushed and tucked another stray piece of hair behind her ear. "Let's see. My name is Tess, as you already know."

The damnedest thing happened next. He grinned. Jonah the grumpy amnesiac from room 312 *grinned* at her. "No," he teased. "Actually, I don't. We just now met." Then, for the love of babies and cute, furry small animals everywhere, he winked. "Remember?"

She gulped dry air. Overcome by the sheer magnetism of his amused smile and the twinkle in his brown, brown eyes, she gaped at him with awe.

Oh, God. He was going to drag out her stupid gene again. Who knew what she was going to blurt out *this* time. Probably that his baby had just kicked inside her.

"I'm really awkward around guys," she said, rushing the words. "Around, like, really hot guys. Like your-level-of-hotness guys."

He laughed, and that only made him more attractive, because, *oh man*, the richness of his chuckle sounded amazing. An echo of it raced through her, thrilling every sensitive nerve ending inside her.

"Okay," he said, seemingly amused by her outburst. "I'd ask how we managed to hook up in the first place, then, but since I'd have to break the rules of this pretend *first* meeting to do that, I guess I'll just leave that question for another day. But tell me more, Tess who is awkward around guys who are as hot as I am."

She flushed and glanced away, even though she couldn't help but smile by the teasing inflection in his voice. He actually seemed to be enjoying how much of a complete fool she was making of herself.

"I attend Granton University," she said, trying to breathe through her nose to calm herself. "I'm a freshman. My major is…undecided. And I room with my best friend, Bailey, who is going to be an electrical engineer."

"Bailey," he murmured the name as if trying to remember if it meant anything to him.

Tess nodded. If there was one thing she could talk about with complete ease it was her best friend. "She and I can be complete opposites sometimes. She knows exactly what she wants out of life. I'm completely clueless. She's brave. I'm a chicken. She is a total slob, and I'm a neat freak. She thinks with her brain while I think with my feelings. And she isn't afraid to say whatever is on her mind whereas I always bite my tongue, worried I'll say the wrong thing or accidentally offend someone…unless my stupid gene has been unleashed, in which case, I blurt out all kinds of asinine things."

Realizing she just said a lot of things without reservation, she paused to gauge his reaction. Still watching her as if fascinated by everything she had just exposed to him, he murmured, "We may have to agree to disagree about your last comment. But aside from that…keep going."

She exhaled a quick breath. "But…but in a lot of ways Bailey and I are practically the same person. Our taste in things like music and books and movies is identical. We're both student workers at the library. We completely complement each other in that I like to follow and she likes to lead. I love her open honesty, and she loves that I forgive her for being so blunt with her open honesty. Oh, and we were both raised by widowed fathers and older brothers. And we—"

"Widowed father?" Jonah cut in, his forehead wrinkling with sympathy. "Your mother died?"

"O-Oh." Tess stumbled over her own tongue. "Yeah. A long time ago when I was five. She had cancer and went slowly. But the entire family was with her, holding her hands as she passed. We all got to say goodbye. When I think back on her, I have nothing but fond memories, like how she always made smiley faces on the beef patties with the ketchup and mustard when she cooked hamburgers. She'd fashion a pickle slice to give it a nose, or sometimes cut the tomato in half to hang floppy ears over the side. I've never seen anyone do that to a hamburger since she was alive. More people should do that, you know."

With a smile, she glanced at Jonah only to realize how personal she'd just gone. "See? There's goes my stupid gene again."

His expression clouded with confusion. "What do you mean? You didn't say anything stupid."

"Yes, I did. If we technically just now met, then I shouldn't have told you so much about myself. Talk about TMI."

He glanced down at his hands that were sitting idly in his lap. After looking thoughtful a moment, he smiled and turned back to her. "Well, my name is Jonah, and I was shot three times in a school massacre. Then I fell into a twelve-day coma, only to wake up with amnesia." Grinning proudly, he asked, "How's that for TMI on the first date?"

A small part of her soul melted at his thoughtful consideration. She returned his engaging smile with one of her own. Cheeks scorching hot from pleasure instead of embarrassment, she answered, "Okay. You win."

He chuckled and held his hand out toward her. She hesitated, not sure what he wanted. But when she slowly reached out and took his fingers, he seemed pleased and interlaced their grip, letting his thumb strum over her knuckles.

Oh, hell, he just wanted to hold her hand for nothing other than the pure pleasure of holding her hand. Should that affect her as intensely as it was affecting her?

"I like your TMI," he murmured. "Can you give me some more, please?"

Breathless and a little dizzy by the fact that someone—and a superhot *male* someone at that—actually enjoyed her bumbling, stupid-gene ways, she blew out a strained breath. "Well, there is one thing I've always wanted to unload on someone."

He arched interested eyebrows. "Really? Do tell."

She nodded. "Yeah. It's about Bailey, actually. She was riding in the car with her mom when they got into an accident, and I guess she was trapped for a really long time before help finally arrived. I think...I think she was forced to see her mom die an awful, grue-some, painful death. She might've even died slowly." Gulping, she glanced away. When Jonah's fingers tightened on hers as if offering her support, she sent him a small, appreciative smile.

"The thing is, Bailey was seven when her mom died. And I was five when my mom died. But I have memory upon memory of my mother. Bailey is completely blank when it comes to hers. I think the accident was so traumatic she's just blocked it out completely. She blocked her mother completely. Her dad didn't want her to suffer unduly, so he told her her mom died when she was young, like two or three years old. She has no idea she was there when it happened. And I—"

Tess focused on the strong masculine hand holding hers. "It really bothers me that I have to keep that from her. I mean, Bailey is my absolute best friend on earth. We have no secrets from each other. Except *this*. But her dad doesn't want her know; he's too afraid of what it'll do to her. And with good reason. She was a complete zombie for months after it happened. I was afraid she'd never be the same again. If she knew, she might have a major setback."

"So, you knew her back then?"

"Oh, we've known each other since birth. Our mothers were best friends and got pregnant with us at about the same time. I think Bailey and I have been mandatory companions since the womb. But that's okay. I love her to death. And she shows it in different ways, but I know I'm one of the most important people in her life, too."

"I can tell how close you guys are." Jonah drew her hand to his mouth and lightly kissed the backs of her fingers. "I think you've told me more about her than you have about yourself."

Tess sputtered, realizing she had. "Geez, I'm sorry. I just—" God, she was going to blush the entire night away, wasn't she? "Sometimes, I feel like we're an—I don't know, an extension of each other. No matter how irritated we may get with each other, we always stick together."

"As all best friends do," he murmured, a sad far-away look on his face.

"You sound like you know exactly what I'm talking about," Tess said. "Do you have a friend like that too?"

He blinked and focused on her, his skin suddenly ashen. "I don't..." Glancing away as if ashamed, he mumbled, "I don't know."

"Oh my God." Tess gasped. Smacking herself in the forehead, she said, "I am so sorry. For a minute, I totally forgot about your amnesia. It really was like we were getting to know each other for the first time."

His smile was small as he studied her face. "Let me guess. We never opened up like this before the coma, did we?"

Now Tess had to glance away. The lies ate at her stomach like acid. "No," she said quietly. "We never did get this deep into personal conversation before." Because they'd never gotten into a conversation at all.

His eyes held hers as if he regretted that, as if he wanted to take their talk even deeper, make it more personal. Then he flushed slightly and gave a small laugh. "There I go again, breaking the rules of our pretend first meeting. I'm sorry."

She shook her head. "No. Don't apologize. You made the rules; you're allowed to break them if you want to."

Yet she hoped and prayed he didn't. She liked how this first-meeting discussion was going. And she especially liked that she didn't have to lie so much this way.

"No," he murmured. "I don't want to break the rules quite yet. I like learning about you."

Warmth stole through her. "Now I feel guilty about hogging all the conversation and centering it around myself."

"Don't feel guilty. I like this." His words were so soft and sincere; she had no idea how to respond.

So, they just studied each other, a content silence filling the room until he smiled. She couldn't help it, she smiled back. She wasn't sure what they were smiling about, but she couldn't seem to stop. She just felt…happy. And he seemed to share the joy.

She bit her lip, and his grin spread. Dear God, he knew exactly what he was doing to her, and it tickled him. Tess rolled her eyes to let him know he was getting a little too cocky. In return, he gave a low chuckle.

"You are so God damn adorable," he murmured, lifting her knuckles to his mouth to kiss them a third time.

Absolutely glowing under his compliment, Tess shook her head. "And you are too handsome for your own good."

Smile spreading, he used his grip on her hand to tug her just a little bit closer. "You keep telling me how good I look."

Cheeks burning hot, she smirked before bashfully admitting, "Well, yeah. Have you *seen* yourself lately?"

He looked thoughtful for a second before saying, "Actually, no. I haven't. I've been too afraid to look, worried about how bad the damage is."

"Oh." Right. The amnesia. Why did she keep forgetting about that tonight? "Well, you don't look bad. I mean, the *damage* isn't that bad. There's a green ring around one eye where you have a fading bruise, and you have a patch of gauze on one side of your head. Then your arm…" She motioned toward his cast. "Well, you can see your arm. But other than that, you look—"

When she didn't go on, too busy scanning his flawless features, he quietly asked, "How do I look?"

"Well…" She shrugged. "You look perfect. Your hair." Unable to help herself, she reached out so she could curl a thick brown lock around her fingers. "It's thick and dark and really, really soft. It's straight but pliable enough to make it move however I want. And the color is…amazing."

"What color is it?"

"Brown…but so much more than brown. It's like…those commercials where they show dark chocolate in a liquid form. Then blend in a couple streaks of caramel, and there you have it."

"Sounds…delicious."

Yeah, Tess would definitely agree he had yummy hair. Yummy *everything*.

"It matches the color of your eyes as well as the beard growing along your jawline." Her nails briefly tracked his five-o'clock shadow. "You have a very strong, proud jaw. Masculine. And your lips. Wow, you have those full, really soft-looking lips."

"Damn," he breathed. "I *am* gorgeous."

Tess laughed even as she blushed hard, realizing just how much she was gushing.

His own smile smoothed into a serious expression before he opened his mouth, but a nurse—the same one who'd promised to mend his hand earlier—entered before he could say whatever it was he was going to say.

"We forgot to take our meds, Mr. Abbott," she started, only to slow to a stop when she saw Tess. Her eyes narrowed slightly. "Visiting hours were over half an hour ago, miss. You're going to have to leave."

Jonah's hand tightened on hers as he scowled at the nurse. But Tess gasped as she glanced at the clock. "Oh my God. I hadn't realized it had gotten so late." She stepped aside to let the nurse in next to him and hand him a cup full of pills. "You never did come back to see about his bloody hand and torn-out IV, either."

The nurse glanced at the dried blood on Jonah's skin and winced. "That's right." Instead of apologizing, she nodded. "I still have a little bit of time before my shift ends. Let me just…I'll be back with the supplies I need." She hurried from the room again, Tess frowning after her.

"Are you always treated like this?" she demanded, whirling to Jonah.

He shrugged. "I'm not exactly a model patient, so it's not like I expect five-star service."

"But—"

"It's okay," he said, reaching for her hand again. "As you can see, I did just fine without her for a couple hours."

And it really had been a couple hours. Knowing she needed to get Bailey's car back to campus, Tess took his fingers but only to squeeze them in farewell. "I better get going."

He nodded, his expression taking on sorrow. Then he forced a small smile. "Same time tomorrow?"

Hearing him say aloud that he wanted to see her again filled her chest with a crazy, amazing sensation. Blushing madly, she nodded. "You bet."

Like she was going to turn down a chance to see him again.

The sadness fled as his brown eyes twinkled with hope. Crooking the finger on his free hand, he beckoned her close as if he wanted to tell her a secret.

With a curious, confused grin, she leaned in, cocking her ear toward his mouth.

"Closer," he whispered.

Her stomach swirled with excitement at the word. Really intrigued now, she lowered down to almost within an inch of his lips. "Yes?" Breathless and giddily light-headed, she waited for him to say something.

Instead of talking into her ear, though, he touched her chin and tilted her face around toward his.

"This might be presumptuous for our first date, but…" He set is mouth against hers.

Tess's mind blanked out as her eyes flared wide. Then his lips brushed by hers again, lingering this time, and her senses took over. She held her breath, wanting it to last.

It did. His palm stroked her jaw and glided around her neck to cup the back of her head. Then his mouth opened under hers, and his tongue took over. Swept along by the overwhelming pull of his coaxing touch, she kissed him back, closing her eyes and meaning it from the bottom of her soul.

He didn't pull away at once but bit by bit, easing his touch, slowing the drag of his lips, nuzzling his nose to hers until there was just enough space between them again for him to say, "I had an amazing night tonight."

"I…" Her mind still hadn't returned from its trip into euphoria. After drawing in a deep breath, she slurred, "I did too."

He smiled, his brown eyes warm with tenderness and affection. "So…same time and place tomorrow?" he repeated with enough hope in his voice that she nodded without a thought to how much trouble she was getting herself into.

When his nurse re-entered the room, toting a cart full of supplies to patch Jonah's hand, Tess jumped back guiltily.

The nurse arched a censorious eyebrow. "Still here?"

Tess gulped. "I was just leaving." She darted a farewell glance at Jonah. When his eyes glittered with something warm and affectionate, she waved and turned away, hurrying for the exit. She tried to hurry away from the all the feelings he was stirring inside her, but it didn't matter how fast she moved, they followed her wherever she went, growing at a crazy speed.

Chapter Seven

Tess had no idea why she tiptoed when she entered her dark dorm room. She already knew Bailey was the lightest sleeper known to mankind. As soon as the hallway light flooded into the chamber when Tess opened the door and slipped inside, her roommate stirred in her bed across the room.

The light flickered on.

"You had my car *all* day."

Tess slumped her shoulders, shut the door, and leaned against it, feeling drained. "I know. I'm sorry." Biting her lip, she offered Bailey an apologetic wince before she fished into her huge purse to pull out Bailey's car keys and toss them across the room. "But you've never minded before."

Bailey caught the keys with both hands and cradled them against her chest. Her eyes narrowed as her forehead wrinkled. "Because I've always known what you were doing before. Now...now you're like hiding things from me. And what is up with that glow on your face? Did you just win the lottery or something? Oh my God, are you drunk?"

"No! I'm not drunk. I—" Tess's face burned hot as she lowered her gaze to the carpet. "I was at the hospital," she mumbled into her chest.

She pushed away from the door and busied herself by setting her purse on her desk and shrugging off her coat.

"You…" Bailey groaned and tossed her keys to the floor beside her bed. "Please don't tell me you're still obsessed with that amnesia guy. *Tessie*…"

Hearing an approaching lecture in Bailey's voice, Tess hurried to add, "And before that, I drove to Bristol to find his parents."

"What! In *my* car?"

Tess pulled her shirt off, preparing herself for bed. "I filled it back up with gas."

"That's not the point." Slapping her hand to her forehead, Bailey let out a miserable groan. "The point is that you're worse off than I thought. Look, I know you want to make the world a better place, but some people's messed-up lives are better off—"

"And he was Einstein's roommate," Tess added with a whisper and cautious glance toward their bathroom door as if Paige might be listening at the lock and could hear everything.

Bailey's mouth snapped shut. Then she blinked. "What?"

After wiggling out of her pants, Tess slipped on a large old comfortable shirt she'd stolen from one of her brothers and crawled into her bed.

"I found out last night when I went to his room. Some guy from across the hall told me who had lived there. There was yellow police tape stretched across the door and everything." She shivered and hugged herself, burrowing deeper under the protection of her blankets. "It was really creepy."

"Oh man." Bailey breathed and then wrinkled up her face and scowled at Tess. "I *knew* you were keeping something from me when you came back last night, all quiet and thoughtful. Why didn't you tell me then?"

Tess shrugged. "I don't know. I don't even know what it means."

"Well, I'd say it means your fake boyfriend must've been a pretty crappy roomie to get himself shot up three freaking times by his own roommate."

Another quiver of dread ran up the back of her spine as Tess shuddered again. "Can you just imagine? Realizing the very person who's been sleeping in the same room with you for an entire semester is crazy enough to go on a shooting spree." She paused to give Bailey the stink eye. "Wait. You haven't been feeling any overwhelming urges to—"

"Whatever." Bailey threw a pillow at her. "You've known me way too long to even ask that."

Tess laughed and tossed the pillow back, only to turn serious again. "There was no way I could tell Jonah about it. He was already on the edge of having an emotional meltdown when I showed up tonight. I just don't think he's ready to hear anything like that." Casting another cautious glance toward the door that led through the bathroom and into Paige's room, Tess lowered her voice. "The real question is do we tell Paige?"

"Are you insane?" Bailey squawked. "She goes deathly pale whenever I even make a *reference* to the shooting. Mentioning little psycho boy's name will probably send her over the edge." Giving her own little shake of horror, Bailey rubbed her arms. "No, there's no reason to tell her your fake-boyfriend was Creepy's roommate." Narrowing her eyes, she pointed an accusing finger at Tess, "Which reminds me, you just totally changed the subject and diverted me from my lecture. Meaning you didn't tell *Jonah* the truth tonight. Did you?"

Tess fell back against her pillows, yanked her covers over her head, and let out a small whimper. "I couldn't." Especially after learning his parents wouldn't be counted on to be there for him. She'd made no plans to tell Jonah the truth when she'd driven to the hospital tonight. And now, she really didn't want to fess up.

Because she kind of liked being the only person he had, which was bad, but she just couldn't help herself. Tonight had been so—

"He's going to find out eventually. You know that, right?"

Tess closed her eyes and kept the blankets over her head. "Maybe." Or maybe, if God wanted her to be blissfully happy, Jonah would never regain his memory, and she could just keep being his girlfriend.

"It would be best if you got it out of the way and did it now. Band-Aid quick. Just tell him. At this point, he still might forgive you."

Or he might throw her out of his hospital room and refuse to ever see her again, in which case, he'd be left with no one to visit him and her heart would shatter into a million pieces, and God…she'd gotten herself into quite a pickle, as her mom used to say.

"If you're that hard up for a boyfriend—I mean, a real one—there's this party on Friday—"

"No," Tess said before Bailey could continue. "You know how I get at parties." She typically turned so nervous she started shooting whatever alcohol was on hand, just to loosen up and avoid any stupid-gene comments spilling from her mouth. But then she ended up getting blitzed to the point that her stupid gene made an appearance anyway.

"So, you'd rather just fake it with the amnesiac?" Bailey demanded.

"Yeah." Tess's voice was soft as she remembered "faking" it tonight. Except it hadn't felt that fake at all. "I would," she murmured, touching her lips and remembering their parting kiss.

As if she could see Tess's actions under the blanket, Bailey said, "Is there something you're not telling me? This just feels so...I don't know. I'm not trusting this. I don't trust...him."

With a scowl, Tess flipped the blanket off her head, and sat up to aim the irritation at her roommate. "How can you not trust him? He doesn't even remember who he is."

Bailey shook her head. "I don't know. It's just a feeling."

"But...you didn't even meet him. You can't possibly get a feeling if you don't even know the person you're...getting feelings about."

"Oh, yes, I damn well can. I'm seeing *your* reaction to him. And you're not acting like...you. You're all..." She waved out her hand and made a face. "Well, I have no clue who you're acting like, but it's not like my friend Tess *at all*."

Guilt slithered into her conscience. Tess glanced away, wondering if Bailey knew how much she couldn't stop thinking about Jonah, or if she suspected they'd kissed. She wasn't completely sure why she hadn't already spilled all the details about those few kisses she'd shared with him. Probably because Bailey was already overreacting about her merely visiting him. If she knew Tess was growing a crush on her fake boyfriend, she'd completely freak. She'd probably break out another tell-him-the-truth lecture and completely burst the euphoric little bubble Tess had going.

She decided to cling to her bliss for just a little while longer. Her time with him was too special to go spreading around like some kind of dirty locker room gossip, anyway. Those memories were hers to keep in a private, hallowed place inside herself.

Across the room, Bailey's sigh was disappointed, but it told Tess she was giving up on her argument for the rest of the evening. "Fine.

I'll drop it. For tonight. Too tired to think straight anyway." Seconds later, the lights were extinguished. "Night."

Tess blew out a breath and lay down, bringing her blankets up to her chin. "Good night."

Staring up at the dark shift of shadows across her ceiling, she wanted to apologize, but she wasn't sure why. She just knew she was wrong. And Bailey was right. She hated being wrong, especially when Bailey was right. But she couldn't stop her wrongness in this situation. Thinking of him alone in the world, without her, hurt too much. And after getting to know him a little better tonight, she felt even more invested. She was beginning to get…close.

Jonah Abbott was like a drug, and she wanted to go back for more. Even now, the itch to crawl out of bed and drive to the hospital consumed her. She wondered how easy it would be to sneak past the nurses and slip into his room. Would she surprise him? Would he be happy to see her? Annoyed or uncomfortable?

Would he want to kiss her again?

Touching her lips once more in the dark, Tess smiled goofily. If she had her way, she'd definitely be kissing those lips again.

"Okay, now I can't sleep." Bailey's voice across the room stopped Tess's grin short. "I saw the cowboy today."

"What?" Tess sat up and fumbled until finding the string for the light over her bed. Giving it a hard tug, she twisted to face Bailey as soon as brightness filled the room. "Why didn't you say something sooner?"

Bailey had been obsessed with "the cowboy" since last semester when they'd met the stranger in Paige's room. He'd stop by to pick up Paige's roommate for a date, and that had been it for Bailey. She'd wanted him. Bad. They didn't even know his name.

Tess was glad her friend had returned her obsession back onto the cowboy. Bailey had recently gone on a couple dates with a guy from back in their hometown, but Tess had never liked him. After the school shooting, he'd grown annoying to Bailey, too, asking too many questions about what had happened, so she'd dropped him.

"I don't know." Squishing up her facial features with disappointment, Bailey shrugged, folded her arms behind her head, and stared moodily up at the ceiling. "I forgot all about it when I saw that look on your face as soon as you came through the doorway." She glanced over. "What was that about, anyway? You looked way too happy for a miserable hospital visit."

Tess waved her hand to brush that topic aside, still not ready to talk about that. "Did you talk to him?" she demanded. "What did he say? What's his name?"

"No," Bailey muttered, her scowl at the ceiling deepening. "I didn't talk to him. I just saw him across the courtyard when I was walking to class."

"Well…did you try to track him down?"

"Of course." Only Bailey would say *of course* to that question. Tess never would've had the nerve.

"And?"

"And he walked into Ferdinand Hall. I followed, but as soon as I stepped inside, he had completely disappeared."

Tess grinned and turned her light off. "So, you're totally going to stake out Ferdinand Hall now, aren't you?"

Bailey's snort told her she needn't have even bothered to ask. "Oh, you know it."

"Are you sure it was the same cowboy, and not some random dude wearing a cowboy hat?"

Tess scraped the last of the polish off her thumbnail and went to work on her pointer finger. Students streamed by her, a couple bumping into her with their book bags or arms. She stepped off the sidewalk to let them through, surprised that Ferdinand Hall, which housed the English department, was such a busy place.

"It was definitely the same guy," Bailey said from beside her, avidly scanning every face that passed.

"But how do you know?"

"I just know. It was him."

She didn't know. Tess could tell by the little wrinkle between her eyes she always got whenever she wasn't sure about something but totally wanted to be.

Tess heaved out a dramatic sigh. "Class starts in ten minutes."

Bailey sent her a piercing scowl. "If you're worried about being late, go ahead and go. I'll get there when I get there."

No way was Tess abandoning her. Best friends just didn't do that. When one went on a super-crazy mission, like stalking a complete stranger outside a college building, the other was obligated to stupidly follow along out of pure loving loyalty.

And anyway, Tess still didn't want to travel anywhere on campus by herself. She'd learned last night that when she wasn't on Granton school grounds, she didn't freak out. She'd been fine by herself at the hospital, and even when she'd traveled to Bristol and back. But as soon as she'd parked Bailey's car in the lot outside their dormitory, the creepies had immediately invaded her. She was only cool when her best friend was at her side. So, she was not leaving her best friend's side as long as she could help it. This campus was haunted with too many memories for that kind of courage. And Tess was in no way courageous.

"Do you think he's an English major?" Tess wondered idly as she watched another handful of people pile through the doors of Ferdinand.

Bailey snorted. "I highly doubt it. True cowboys do not major in English. It's probably a required credit he had to take."

Tess opened her mouth to start a lecture about judging people when a more pressing thought struck her. "Hey, do you think *I* should major in English?"

"No," Bailey said without even thinking it through.

After deliberating the possibility herself, Tess shrugged and agreed. She might love to read her fiction books, but grammar and writing were so not her thing. "Yeah," she murmured aloud. "Probably not." Clearing the polish from her pointer finger, she moved to her middle, only to pause, deciding to leave the flecked pink paint there. In case she needed to flip someone off—which she'd never done before, but hey, you never knew when it might be a good time to start—she at least wanted it to be a colorful bird. "So, what do you think I *should* major in?"

"Science." Bailey answered without missing a beat.

"Really?" Tess wrinkled her nose. "Science?" She'd never thought of herself as a science nerd before.

Bailey stood on her tiptoes and craned her neck looking out into the main courtyard. "You've always gotten better scores in science than I have. It's downright freakish how well you memorized the name of every muscle in the body."

"Hey, that's not freakish." Lifting her chin, Tess gave an offended sniff. "It's just the sign of a good memory."

"And yet you can't name the capitals of all the states, you constantly mess up your times tables, especially the sevens and eights, and you still can't recite the Lord's Prayer."

Tess dropped her hands to her hips and scowled back. "Hey, you botch up the Lord's Prayer just as badly as I do, babe."

"But I don't know the name of every freaking muscle in my body either, now do I?" Looking as if she might start bawling, Bailey shoved her chin-length, multi-colored hair out of her face and took a deep breath. "I don't think he's coming here today. We're wasting our time."

Opening her mouth to snip something acerbic back about how well Bailey knew strange electrical terms, Tess took in the distress on her friend's face and wisely stayed quiet. "We might as well get to class, then," she answered, adding a commiserating sigh.

Bailey had been right, though; she'd loved the anatomy and physiology chapter they'd covered in her Life Sciences course they'd taken together last semester. The inner workings of humans intrigued her so much. Learning each part of the body and how it worked had been like piecing together the most complex and interesting puzzle ever.

"Yeah, we should go," Bailey mumbled. "I doubt any professor will cancel classes today, not after that nasty bulk email the administration sent out yesterday, scolding them."

She looked so depressed, Tess wanted to give her a hug to cheer her up. The world just wasn't the same when her buddy wasn't making a sarcastic observation about life. She was tempted to blurt out a really asinine comment just so Bailey could pounce all over it like she usually did.

But a commotion at the entrance of Ferdinand stole their attention.

"Hey," someone called loudly and almost rudely. Both Bailey and Tess turned to watch some lanky dark-haired guy pause in the opened doorway where he was about to exit. He pointed up at a hulking blond boy who was trying to enter. "I know you, don't I?"

Obviously not wanting to engage anyone in conversation, the blond lowered his chin as if trying to shield his identity. He mumbled some answer, but Tess couldn't hear what he said. When he tried to shoulder past the boy leaving the building, the dark-haired guy set a hand on his chest to keep him there.

"No. I know who you are," he insisted, his eyes narrowing ominously. "You're one of those assholes who used to pick on Einstein."

Instant apprehension prickled Tess's scalp. It felt as if every red hair on her head curled in a different direction. She gulped and subconsciously eased closer to Bailey until Bailey grasped her hand and unobtrusively backed them away from the main doors of Ferdinand.

Everyone else who was gathering to enter or exit the building paused to glance at the blond in question.

A muscle in his jaw ticked before he gave a quick negative shake of his head. "You got the wrong guy," he mumbled as he tried to step around the brunette.

But the boy talking to him wasn't about to let him pass so easily. "No. I remember you. You were there that night a whole group of you ran Einstein up a tree."

Tess gasped and covered her mouth, vaguely remembering that night. She'd been a little under the influence — or as Bailey had called it, totally plastered — and she, Bailey, and Paige had gotten a ride back to Grammar Hall from the designated driver who was now Paige's boyfriend. When he'd pulled to the curb, they'd found a dozen guys picking on Einstein, and the bullies had cornered him up a tree. Paige had chased them off and accosted the lead bully by twisting his finger and taking him to the ground.

"Is he the one Paige went ninja on?" Tess murmured quietly to Bailey, squinting as she focused on him now. She remembered so little of that night.

"No," Bailey whispered back. "That guy had dark hair."

"Oh."

"So, how does it feel — " the lanky boy kept pushing at the blond's chest, taunting him " — being responsible for tormenting a scrawny little sixteen-year-old boy until he tumbled right over the edge of insanity and *killed* eleven people? You feel like a big, strong, tough guy *now?*"

Though the blond was easily twice the size of the brunette, he lifted his hands and backed away from him. "Man, just leave me alone."

"I knew two people who died that day."

"And I didn't kill them," the blond insisted.

"Yeah, well, you might as well have. Their blood is on *your* hands."

The blond whimpered out a tortured sound. Instead of trying to enter Ferdinand Hall again, he whirled around and took off running, bulldozing right past Bailey and bumping into Tess, shoving her out his way. She stumbled off balance, and Bailey's grip tightening on her arm was the only thing that kept her from tumbling to the ground.

Stunned, she gaped after the blond as he raced off. She'd caught a glimpse of a full-colored tattoo of the Roadrunner on his forearm when he'd shoved her. And by the way he was speeding now, she could almost see his legs turning like blurred wheels the way the cartoon character's did.

"Coward!" someone shouted after him.

But he didn't answer; he just kept running.

"Well, that was...intense." Bailey grabbed Tess and hurried them away from the scene.

"That poor, poor boy," Tess said, glancing after the fleeing Roadrunner. "They didn't have to make him feel so bad."

Bailey snorted. "Are you freaking kidding me? The jerk had it coming. He and that entire crowd picked on Einstein like—"

"Can you *please* not say his name," Tess hissed, rubbing her arms as her skin prickled with unease. "Gives me the creeps every time I hear it."

"What? Einstein?"

Tess shuddered and sent her friend a glare.

Bailey rolled her eyes. "You are such a sissy. What do you think's going to happen? His ghost is going to come haunt you if you speak his name aloud?"

"Maybe," Tess challenged, only making Bailey laugh. She poked her buddy in the ribs. Hard. "Now, hush."

"Ouch." Bailey stopped laughing and scowled as she rubbed her side. "In any case, I can't believe you're feeling sorry for a *bully*."

"I didn't say I felt sorry for him, exactly. I just don't think bullying him right back is the answer. I mean, what if he goes off the deep end next and starts another rampage? The way he and his crowd treated... you-know-who was absolutely wrong. But you have to admit, the kid *was* super weird. I don't know how many times he insulted me, and I always went out of my way to be nice to him."

"Yeah." Bailey nodded. "He was strange. No doubt about it."

"I bet all those bullies feel bad enough as it is. There's no reason to rub it in or start a whole new cycle of bullies to pick on them. It needs to stop somewhere."

Shrugging as if she was going to agree to disagree, Bailey appeared thoughtful for a moment. "You know, I haven't seen much of anyone from that crowd since it happened. They all just kind of went into hiding. Especially that head bully."

Tess wrinkled her nose. "What head bully? I don't remember a head bully."

"Sure. He was the one Paige took to the ground the night you got all drunk with — "

"Yeah, I remember *that* part." Remembering *who* had gotten her drunk sobered her up immediately. Not only had Dorian Wade been the first person killed by Einstein, but he'd attacked Paige a few nights before his death. If any name was taboo to mention aloud, it was probably his. What was worse, Jonah had to have known Wade since they'd both been on the football team.

She hoped the two hadn't been close. How creepy would that be?

Tess cleared her throat, trying to blot Dorian Wade from her memory. "But I don't remember what this *head bully* you're talking about looked like, so…I have no idea if I've seen him around campus or not."

"I bet he dropped out of school." Bailey nodded as if that had to be the only conclusion. "I totally would if I were him. Because seriously, he's got to be the most despised student on campus these days."

Chapter Eight

Someone was in his room.

Jonah woke drowsy and disoriented, much as he always woke from his midday rest. He usually hated his afternoon nap, but today he was loath to open his eyes. He'd actually been having a good dream for once. A *really* good dream that left him aroused and aching.

Though he was awake, he kept his eyes closed, willing himself to fall back to sleep. But his Spidey sense tweaked back to life, telling him he wasn't alone.

He opened his eyes and rolled his face to the side to glare at the nurse who he was sure he'd find taking his vitals.

But seeing red hair and big, beautiful blue eyes instead made him catch his breath.

He woke a little more quickly and licked his dry lips. "You came back."

She gave him an angelic smile. "Of course." Then she winked. "It's time for your sponge bath."

His eyes flew open wide, and his body was more awake than it had been in a month. He began to sit upright, because the thought of her stroking his bared flesh with a wet sponge was just too—

She gave a husky laugh. "I'm just kidding. I can't believe you fell for that."

His disappointment was almost more painful than the ache from his wounds. He closed his eyes and collapsed back onto his mattress with a groan. "You're absolutely cruel, do you know that?"

She laughed again, this chuckle more angelic. "Are you really that upset that I'm not going to wash you?"

The look he sent her should've told her how crazy he found her question, but he went ahead and growled, "*Yes!*"

Flushing, she bit her lip and glanced away. "Oh."

He adored her shy side. Her blush and the way those perfect white teeth bit into her bottom lip drove him mad.

"God," he groaned, shifting on his bed. "You are such a tease. Keep doing that to your lip, sweetheart, and my next dream starring you will be even dirtier than the one I just had."

"*What?*" Her teeth immediately lost their grip on her lip as her mouth gaped open. "You were dreaming about me? Just now? Really?"

He nodded. "Oh, yeah."

"Wow." She inched closer, her blue eyes alive with wonder. "What was I doing?"

Tossing out a lazy grin that was still full of the sleep he'd just enjoyed, he slid his gaze over her face. "You sure you want to know?"

"*Oh.*" She rolled her eyes and stopped easing toward him. "It was one of *those* dreams. Seriously, what is it with you guys and sex dreams?"

His smile merely grew. "Best dreams ever."

She blushed. "So…" Glancing down at her fingernails, she began to pick at the chipped pink polish on her pinky. "Was I any good?"

Jonah arched an eyebrow. He hadn't thought she'd ever ask him anything like that. He liked the unexpected question.

"What do you think?" Reaching out, he took her hand, making her stop messing with her fingernails. When she lifted her face, he drew her hand toward him.

Her eyebrows lowered in confusion. "What're you—"

When he set her palm against his lap and pressed down just enough for her to feel the hardness underneath, she gasped. "Jonah!

What're you—oh, my *God*." She surprised him again when she didn't immediately jerk her arm away. Instead, she sent a wide-eyed glance toward the opened door of his room. "What if someone walked in?"

"I don't care." He knew he should stop. He knew he should feel guilty. But he couldn't bring himself to accomplish either. Tess was back, and he was going to enjoy every minute of every one of her visits. Before it was too late. The world could be falling down around them, and he still wouldn't care. As long as she didn't take her fingers away, life was amazing.

"This is the first wood I've had since I woke from the coma. I'm so freaking glad *that's* not broken too."

Her eyes softened with sympathy. Keeping her palm against him, she darted another quick, guilty peek toward the open door and bit her bottom lip, looking tempted enough to get his hopes rising. "We shouldn't do this," she whispered right before she applied just a bit more pressure to his groin.

Jonah ignored the risk, half closing his eyes because her warm fingers felt so good against him that he could barely keep them open, but his lashes parted just enough so he could continue to see her in all her glorious innocent excitement.

"I could walk," he told her. "In my dream. I could walk and stand, and I didn't have any bullet holes in me. I was standing there, taking you against a wall."

She gasped and tried to remove her hand from his junk, but he caught her wrist and brought her back. And she allowed it, though her fingers began to tremble. If he was reading her right, he'd say she wanted this as badly as he did but was just too timid to take it. Which blew his mind.

Why? Why would she want *him?* What was she doing here? When had he ever done anything decent enough to deserve her company?

Fuck, it didn't matter. She was here. And he was going to cherish this stolen time with her.

He let out a soft sigh. "Your legs were wrapped around my waist, and every time I thrust deeper into you—"

"Enough," she whispered, her face so red, he was a little worried she might physically burst from her embarrassment.

But he was still juiced up from the vision to drop it completely. "I want that dream to come true. I want to be able to stand and walk and be with *my girlfriend* as soon as I get out of here." He managed a tender grin. "It doesn't even have to be against a wall. Just…however you want it."

She licked her lips. He could see the rapid beat of her heart ticking against the tender skin along her neck. And it only stirred his body more to know she was just as affected as he was.

So, when she said, "You will," in a low, throaty tone that promised him the world, he groaned aloud. Hot damn.

"Promise?" he asked, watching every nuance of her face, searching for those little tells she gave away when he'd figured out she was lying.

She blushed harder and glanced away, even as she nodded her affirmative. Jesus. No tells. No lie.

A loud clang in the hall followed by the ripe curse of an orderly had Tess yanking her hand away from his lap.

Jonah almost sobbed from the loss of her warmth, and even more from the loss of their moment, but he was still so overwhelmed that it had all really just happened that he couldn't even regret the end of it.

"I can't believe we did that," Tess whispered, looking completely scandalized. A person would've thought she'd actually shimmied her hand under the blanket and touched him skin to skin.

Her eyes were so wide and blue, and her mouth had dropped open so far, Jonah wanted to kiss the shock right off her lips just to see how it tasted.

"What?" He grinned uncontrollably, forcing his voice to go innocent even though his damn smile vibrated out every pore of his body and he must look one hundred percent ornery. "Don't tell me you've never touched me there before."

Okay, fine. He asked that just to make her blush. But, Jesus, it worked. A pink tinge spread down her cheeks, her neck, and disappeared into the opening of her collar. He wondered how far down that amazing color went.

Glancing away, she mumbled, "Not in public like this where someone could catch us any second."

"Do we do it a lot?" he pressed, fishing for another reaction. "Like, all the time?" When her eyes flared wide, he couldn't help himself. He had to tease her. Flashing a wolfish smile, he snagged her hand again. "I bet you can't keep your hands off me."

"Jonah." She choked out his name, looking stunned to the core. When she pushed her wild red hair out of her face, showing him just how scarlet her cheeks had become, he tugged her closer to the bed.

Alarm filled her face. He chuckled, too happy to feel any kind of regret. "Don't worry, Contessa Anabelle. I won't make you touch me there again." Then he winked. "At least not in public where someone could catch us at any second."

"I'm not…" She bit her lip and tightened her grip on his hand. "I'm sorry. I don't mean to be such a prude. I've just…I've always been ultra-conservative in…*this* department."

He lifted his eyebrows. "Even with your boyfriend?" He caught his breath and held it before he added, "With me?"

She cleared her throat tactfully. "Well…you might have coaxed me out of my timid shell a time or two."

"Really?" Still tugging on her fingers so she'd have to move closer yet, he grinned. "Now this sounds interesting. What's the kinkiest thing I ever got you to do?"

Her embarrassment kept growing. He hadn't thought her cheeks could get any more crimson than they already were. But they did.

She glanced away. "I don't know."

He knew he should drop the inquisition, but he couldn't seem to stop himself. After she'd left him last night, he hadn't been able to get her off his mind. And now that she was back, he wanted to push their relationship and somehow cement it into place so nothing could rock its foundation. Not even the truth.

"When was our first kiss? And don't tell me you don't remember that either. *I'm* the one with amnesia here."

She rolled her eyes as she turned back to him. "I know that. I just—"

"Don't want to talk about what we were like together…before?" he asked quietly. He should stop with this line of questioning, but he was realizing he learned more about her when she answered him, from how she reacted to what she said…and didn't say.

Shaking her head, she sent him an irritated frown. "No, that's not it at all."

If she said they weren't together, he wasn't sure what he'd do. He was even more worried what *she'd* do. If she left now…Shit, he wasn't going to think about that. But even as his skin went cold with dread over the very possibility, he pressed, "We *are* broken up, aren't we?"

"No," she growled, her glower gaining strength. "Will you just hush and let me talk?"

So relieved by her answer, and a little surprised by the force behind it, he spiked his eyebrows up. He was coming to realize she didn't lose her temper easily, but when she did, she knew how to stand up for herself. He liked that.

He zipped his thumb and index finger across his mouth and sent her an angelic smile.

She rolled her eyes. "Thank you. Now, where was I?"

He shrugged, refusing to speak. She gave a long, suffering sigh and leveled him with a dry look. He figured anything he did right now would get on her last nerve, so he simply kept smiling innocently.

Finally, she gave in to a reluctant grin. "First kiss, huh? Well, it happened on our…third date. After one or your football games. We went to this frat party and…and you taught me how to take a JELL-O shot."

Jonah lowered his brow at the picture she painted. Jesus, that was the worst lie she'd made up yet. "So, I liquored you up and took advantage of you?"

She flushed again and ducked her chin. "It wasn't like *that*. And I certainly didn't mind your…advances."

Lie or not, his chest swelled with an arrogant kind of pride just to hear her brag about his prowess. "So, you approve of my kissing abilities, huh?" He waggled his eyebrows, hoping she might praise his accomplishments a little while longer or maybe let him give her another sample of them.

"Well…" She glanced at him from under a veil of her long lashes. "I'm still with you, aren't I?"

"Yeah," he murmured. "You seem to be."

Her shoulders fell. "Oh, my God. You *still* think we're not together anymore, don't you?"

"You have to admit," he confessed on a shrug, "it seems a little too good to be true that you're really mine."

He liked the pleasure that bloomed on her face. He liked the way her breathing kicked up and her pulse fluttered in her throat.

Jonah told himself he needed to compliment her more often, because looking at her like this was downright intoxicating.

"Well, I guess I'm going to have to *prove* to you that we're really together." Tess touched his face, thrilling his skin with the slide of her soft hands. Then she leaned down. When she kissed him, he was a goner.

Her lips were perfect and plush. Soft with just the right amount of suction. And he clung to them even as she slowly pulled away.

Those long lashes of hers lifted enough to show him a spark of sensuality in her blue eyes as she met his gaze. "So, what do you think now?"

Though his throat was dry, he managed to croak, "I think I'm the luckiest damn bastard on earth."

She laughed and rolled her eyes. "Says the man lying in a hospital bed with three bullet wounds and a coma under his belt."

"Like I said, luckiest damn bastard on earth." Then he hooked his hand around to the back of her neck since she was still close and tugged her back for another round.

Taking control of this one, he thrust his tongue into her mouth, causing her to gasp and then moan. Her fingers curled into his shoulders, a couple catching at a tender pocket of flesh at the edge of his cast, making him flinch. But it was the best kind of pain ever. He wanted her to clutch him like that forever.

Breaking her lips away from his, she pressed their foreheads together and stayed molded to him a moment as if she needed to catch her breath. "You sure are in a frisky mood tonight."

He slipped his fingers through her hair, relishing this moment of contact with her. "That's because you're here. It's easy for me to forget about all the bad shit when you're here."

She swallowed loud enough to tell him how profoundly his words affected her. Then she pulled away and straightened to her full height, tucking a lock of hair behind her ear. "I think that's actually the amnesia making you forget."

Since he knew she wasn't ready for any serious declarations, he made a silly face. "Oh, yeah. I forgot."

Laughing, Tess nudged his shoulder. "Honestly, what's gotten you into such a good mood?"

He frowned. "Honestly, I just told you. *You* did. And that dream." He let out a refreshed sigh. "It was a really awesome dream." And it had been the only non-nightmare he'd had since waking up from his coma. The woman literally took his nightmares away.

Tess lifted her eyebrows. "I guess."

Needing to touch her, and still grateful he had someone here to see him, he caught her hand and brought it to his mouth to kiss her knuckles. But when he tugged her skin close to his nose, he drew in a deep whiff only to pause.

"Why do you smell like French fries?" Damn, French fries sound good.

Flushing, she tried to jerk her hand back, but he wouldn't let her go. Testing his theory, he popped her index finger into his mouth. Mmm. Yeah, there was definitely French fry salt on her.

"Jonah!" she gasped, immediately yanking the digit free.

"You *taste* like French fries too!"

"Okay, fine," she grumbled. "I may have stolen a couple of your fries."

"Did you say *my* fries?" Now he was downright intrigued. After turning away, Tess came back around with her huge purse in her grasp. When she unzipped the top, the smell that came wafting out made his mouth water.

She pulled out a familiar paper bag with a red-headed girl on the front, and he damn near whimpered.

"Hamburgers?" He reached out with both hands. "Oh, my God, you didn't." He ripped the sack from her clutches and dumped the contents into his lap. "Oh, my God." He moaned again. "*French fries.*"

He consumed a handful of fries before he turned his attention to the burger. He nearly didn't push down the wrapper in time before he sank his teeth into the meat and breading mixed with onions, cheese, and tomatoes. The groan that followed was probably too carnal to be motivated by food alone, but he didn't care.

It tasted so frigging good.

"Ohhh…kay," Tess said, watching him with big eyes. "I'll take that as a thank you."

With his mouth full, he answered, "If I could get out of this bed right now, I'd kiss the ground you walk on. So, yeah, *thank you.*"

She flushed and ducked her chin. "Well…you're welcome." Clearing her throat, she turned away.

He watched her wring her hands behind her back in a fretting-type manner as she wandered around his room, inspecting all the medical gadgets hooked up to him.

"So, your therapist comes tomorrow to test your walking, huh?" she said suddenly, her expression hesitant as she glanced back at him.

Just like that, his good mood plummeted. He wished she hadn't remembered that. The hamburger went dry in his throat, and he found it very hard to swallow. After taking a large drink, he nodded and focused his attention on his food so he wouldn't have to meet her eyes.

"Yeah. Tomorrow."

She nodded as well. "So...is it numb or can you actually *feel* anything down there?"

Hardening his jaw, he glanced away. "I can feel everything." A little too well.

"Well, that's good."

"Sure." His voice was so bitter she whirled around to send him a concerned glance.

"What's wrong?" she asked, drifting closer.

Stuffing his mouth with the last third of his hamburger, he shrugged. "Nothing."

But she didn't drop the issue. Setting her hand on his arm, she asked, "Are you scared?"

Wow, how had she nailed it on the first guess? Since that truth wasn't something he could confess, he looked away and kept chewing somehow through clenched teeth.

"I know I would be." When her soft fingers touched his hair, he closed his eyes tight and swallowed the rest of his food. "It's okay, you know, if you are scared. You don't have to be tough and strong. Everyone experiences fear, Jonah."

When she lightly brushed his bangs across his forehead, he opened his lashes and looked up. Something warm and powerful squeezed in his chest. He let her play with his hair for a while before he spoke again.

"Can we do what we did last night and get to know each other some more?"

The way her face lit up and she sucked in a breath told him the night before had been meaningful to her too. The pressure inside his ribcage grew hotter.

Biting her lip, she whispered, "Sure."

He grinned—beamed really—and scooted to the far edge of the bed, patting the open space as he went. "Well, then crawl up here, sweetheart, and let's get started."

"Wha—" Her expressive eyes grew wide before she glanced at his face and then the doorway of the room. "We didn't do *that* last night."

Her innocence was going to be the death of him. Honestly! He loved how shy and yet totally sensual she could be. "But I want you close." He put on the begging eyes, and by damn if that didn't work.

She glanced toward the door again, telling him how tempted she was.

"What if I bump something? Your leg. Aren't you in pain?"

"Na." He lifted his morphine button. "See this little doohickey here? That's my pain reliever. If anything hurts, I push it, and bam, just like that, no more pain."

She looked so intrigued by the morphine pump, he didn't have the heart to tell her he hated pushing that button because it always knocked him out and gave him horrific dreams.

"Are you sure I'll fit?"

"As tiny as you are?" He snorted and patted the bed again. "Of course. Now get your cute tush up here, woman, before I start crying. You don't want me to cry, do you?"

When he puckered out his bottom lip and feigned a pout, she rolled her eyes and grinned. "Oh, my God. You look ridiculous."

"B-B-But, Tess." He sniffled as if he was going to start bawling any second. "I need you close, right beside me."

"Oh, all right," she said, her face about ten shades of scarlet. "If it'll make you hush and stop looking so pathetic."

His grin was instantaneous. "It will."

"You are such a faker." She grumbled as she set what was left of his French fries on the side cart and gingerly climbed onto the hospital bed with him. But he just smiled and reached out his good hand to assist her up.

Being as large a guy as he was, there really wasn't room for two people, but he didn't care. To have her stretched out beside him, he'd make room.

"There," he murmured once she was crowded in with her body squished right up against his. Oh, yeah. It was perfect. He smiled at her. "Comfy?"

She laughed. "No. Not at all."

"Here." Tucking her even closer, he turned and shifted her just enough so that they were facing each other, her cheek was resting against his chest and one of her legs had been wedged between his. "Better?"

Her gulp was so audible, he actually felt it in his own throat. When she lifted her face from his heart and looked up at him, the stiffy she'd given him when he'd first woken to her in his room paled in comparison to what his body experienced this time around. The heat that swirled through him consumed him from head to toe.

"How's that?" he asked, ignoring how hoarse his voice had gone.

"Jonah." Her voice wavered with anxiety. "We shouldn't be doing this."

"Why?" No way was he letting her off the bed just yet. "Aren't you comfortable?"

She nodded. "Yeah. A little *too* comfortable."

He grinned. "No such thing." Then he bent his head and kissed her.

Chapter Nine

The nerve endings in Tess's brain went on overload and fried out. It was impossible for her to process the fact that she was lying face-to-face on a hospital bed with a complete hottie as he kissed her like he meant it.

His hands tangled in her hair and tightened their grip, forcing her to tip her head up and meet his mouth more firmly. Then his tongue swept in, and she was a complete goner.

She knew she should stop him, but she found her fingers curling around the thin material of his hospital gown and urging him closer. He cupped her face, and she arched her body up until she could feel his erection through all the cloth separating them. When he slid his casted arm around her back and applied pressure at the base of her spine to bring them even tighter together, she broke away with a gasp.

"What're we...this can't be...I thought..." Whew, it was still hard for her to think. "I thought I was coming up here so we could to get to know each other better."

He grinned, looking a little too full of himself. "You did. And I'm getting to know you *a lot* better. You taste really good."

She groaned and closed her eyes before leaning forward to rest her forehead on his shoulder. Why had she let this get so far out of hand? This was so wrong. He wasn't her boyfriend; he was a complete stranger, and she was totally deceiving him, completely taking advantage of his lack of memories.

But she felt so safe and warm snuggled up against his chest, as if she *did* know him and trusted him implicitly. Lord, she'd already trusted him with some of her deepest secrets last night.

"Jonah..." she started, knowing she'd gone way over the line with this whole charade. He wasn't hers. She wasn't his. And she was probably worse than his parents for slotting herself into his life when he didn't know any better. She gulped. "I need to confess something to you."

Band-Aid quick Bailey had called it, right?

She opened her mouth to spill everything but he whispered, "Don't."

Tess's eyebrows furrowed. "Don't what?"

His brown eyes flooded with panic as he shook his head. "Don't confess anything. Please. It's not like I'll know any different until I get my memory back, anyway. Right?"

"But—"

He kissed her gently, effectively silencing her. Then, pulling back just enough to catch her gaze, he said, "I don't like the look in your eyes. It's telling me I'm not going to like what you have to say. So, don't say it. If you cheated on me—or whatever—I don't want to know tonight. Okay? I like how this is going. I don't—" He squeezed his eyes closed. "You have no idea how much your visits help me. Just...Every time you walk through that door, I feel..." Shaking his head, he opened his lashes. "You don't even know."

Tess's lips parted. She really needed to tell him now. If he was growing to depend on her like this, it was only making what she was doing to him that much worse.

As if he knew her mind, he caught a piece of her hair and gently tucked it behind her ear. "You can always tell me tomorrow. One more night won't hurt anything."

Damn, his powers of persuasion were much stronger than her conscience, and she always followed her ever-nagging, potent conscience.

But one glance into Jonah's Abbott's eyes, and she caved. "Okay," she said. "Tomorrow, then."

His relief was palpable. The kiss he planted on her melted the rest of her resistance. Tess curled into him, arching closer without realizing what she was doing until he hissed out a breath of pain and broke his mouth from her to grimace.

"Oh, my God." She pushed against his chest. "I'm so sorry. Let me up."

"No," he gasped, tightening his grip on her.

What? Was he insane? "But I'm hurting you."

His casted arm didn't budge. "It'll hurt more if you leave."

"Jonah," she begged, beginning to panic because the muscles in his face hadn't loosened yet, telling her loud and clear that he was still in misery. "Don't do this to me. You're in pain. God, at least push your morphine button."

He shook his head stiffly. "Hate that stuff. It always knocks me out and gives me nightmares."

"But you said—"

"Some things are more tolerable than others. This is tolerable. Losing the rest of my time with you tonight is not."

She sighed. "At least let me get off the bed so I won't—"

"No."

If both her arms had been free to do so, she would've thrown them up in the air in frustration. "You are so freaking stubborn, do you know that?"

He just grinned and nuzzled his face into her neck. "But I'm going to get my way, aren't I?"

Oh, now he was just rubbing it in. Not cool. "Yes," she grumbled, then quickly added a "probably" so it wouldn't sound like she was a complete pushover, even though she was.

"Good." His mouth pressed against the pulse in her throat. "Now... what were we talking about again?"

"We weren't." She giggled because, geesh, his lips kind of tickled when he hit a sensitive spot right behind her ear. "You were demonstrating to me how frisky you were tonight."

"Good plan. Let's keep doing that."

With another laugh, she nudged him in the shoulder. "*Jonah.* What if someone walks in?"

"They'll just have to settle for watching, because there's not enough room on this bed for a third person."

Her scandalized gasp made him chuckle.

"God, I love shocking you," he confessed. His warm touch soaked through the cotton of her shirt as he skimmed his hand from her hip and right up her ribcage until he toyed with the edges of her bra.

Tess totally didn't mean to encourage him, but she bowed up her back, thrusting her chest firmly against his. Groaning, he slid his palm over her until he was cupping her through her clothes. When he began to knead her, she clamped her thighs around his leg and clenched her teeth to keep in all the feelings wanting to break free from every pore in her body.

"Jonah," she gasped, gripping his shoulders.

"Damn," he breathed, kissing the tip of her chin as she arched her neck back. "The way you say my name makes me want to be this guy you seem to think I am." Then he kissed her jaw and next her throat. "Let me be that guy, Tess."

The serious, heartbreaking tone in his voice made her glance at his expression. She wasn't sure what had shifted him from playful to somber so quickly, but she was ready to take that trip with him, wherever he needed to go. Cupping his face in both her hands, she sent him a soft smile.

"You can be anything you want to be."

He blinked, and in that one swish of the eyelashes, his brown eyes seemed to fill with tears. "What if I get my memories back and realize I'm horrible?"

Her chest clenched as if she were feeling his worries right along with him. This had to be a common one for amnesiac patients: fearing who they really were, wondering if they'd even like themselves.

"You're not." She kissed his cheek, even though her mind went back to his parents' trailer, taking in the contempt in the father's eyes. What kind of person did you have to be to make your own father despise you? Then again, Ted Abbott hadn't exactly been the kind of person she would seek out for a character reference.

It didn't really matter what Jonah had been like before. Right now, he was one of the most amazing people she'd ever met. He made her pulse race and, despite how gorgeous he was, he'd eased her nerves enough that she could open up to him and be herself.

He wasn't a bad person.

"Seriously," she teased, rubbing her nose against his. "Would I date a jerk?"

He studied her a moment before giving a reluctant smile. Interlacing his fingers with hers, he tipped their foreheads together. "I just want to be good enough to deserve you."

Tess had no clue how to respond to that. To her, she wasn't good enough for *him*. She was the one lying.

She was still wondering what to say when her stomach growled. Tess bit her lip, hoping he didn't hear. But, dang it, Jonah arched an eyebrow.

"Either you're hungry or your stomach just told me it wanted some personal space."

It definitely didn't want personal space. "I haven't eaten since lunch," she admitted, and she waved her hand to signal that it was no big deal. "But it's fine. I'm just one of those people who doesn't miss a meal…if you can't tell."

A scowl lit her fake boyfriend's face as if she'd offended him. "No. I *can't* tell," he growled. "You're so tiny I'd say you need to eat more meals."

She sniffed. "I'm short. But I wouldn't exactly call myself tiny."

An ornery grin lit his face just before he smoothed his hand around to grasp her bottom and squeeze gently. She gasped, and his smile only grew.

"If you're talking about this, I feel the need to state that men prefer a little curve to their women. And you are curved—" his hand wandered over to the next cheek "—to perfection."

No one had ever been so free with her body. She knew Jonah didn't know any better—he probably thought they did things like this all the time—but his boldness kind of turned her on. Okay, fine. It *really* turned her on, like, a lot.

"I'll make you a deal." His eyes sparkled as he grinned and kept stroking her bottom. "For every fact you tell me about yourself, I'll share one of my beloved French fries with you. That way, you won't have to starve, and I'll still get to know you better."

She nodded, tickled he still wanted to learn more about her. "But what should I give you for every fact *you* share about yourself?"

His face went briefly shuttered. "But I don't know any facts about myself. Remember?"

Waving her hand, she rolled her eyes. "I meant about your new self."

"I don't know what you mean."

"You can always have an opinion about something, whether you have memories or not." When an idea hit her, she grinned. "For instance. You can have an opinion of whether you prefer kisses on the cheek…" She paused to set her lips softly against his scruffy start of a beard. "Or on the lips."

When their mouths touched, he made a growling sound in the back of his throat. "Lips," he said against hers. "Definitely the lips."

She grinned. "I thought so."

He cupped her face so he could kiss her some more. "I also have an opinion of where I most like you to touch me."

Tess rolled her eyes. And here returned frisky Jonah. "Let me guess." She lowered her hand to his lap and pressed it against his ever-present bulge.

He sucked in a breath. "Damn, you know me too well."

Biting her lip, she watched him grit his teeth and close his eyes as she stroked the length of him, learning his shape.

She couldn't believe she was doing this. It probably wasn't all that bold of a move comparatively speaking, what with the blanket and his hospital gown separating them from direct contact. But this was as bold as she'd ever gotten with any man, going where no Tess had ever gone before. Her heart thumped like mad in her chest, and her breaths sawed a little faster through her lungs.

"I kind of like touching you here too."

Jonah lifted his lashes to smile at her. Then he leaned in toward her so he couch reach for something behind her on his bedside tray. She glanced over her shoulder to see that he'd grabbed the carton of French fries. He pulled one free and held it up to her mouth.

She glanced at the fry and then him.

He rolled his eyes. "I told you I'd give you a French fry for every time you told me a fact about yourself. And the fact that you like to touch me there might be my favorite fact yet. So…have two." He pulled another one free and held them both to her mouth.

Tess paused before she shrugged and took the fries from his fingers with her teeth. As she chewed, he grinned with pleasure. "Thank God you supersized. I have a lot of fun facts I'd like to draw out of you."

She swallowed and licked the traces of salt off her lips. "Your turn to share a fact."

The grin he gave her should've warned her what he was going to say next, but it still tugged a blush to her cheeks. "I'd like you touching me there even more if your hand was inside the blanket instead of outside."

Her fingers paused. Biting her lip, she wondered if she should dare. His suggestion was crazy, but God, she kept on considering it.

His eyes went wide. "Holy shit, you're tempted. Aren't you?"

She glanced toward the doorway, wondering how risky it would be. No one had come to check on him since she'd been here but—

A nurse walked into the room. Tess yelped and jerked her hand off Jonah's crotch. The nurse stopped in her tracks, her tennis shoes squeaking against the floor because she halted so fast.

"What're you doing on that bed with him?"

Embarrassment flooded her as she scurried to crawl off the mattress. "I'm sorry. I—"

"Don't you realize how many staples and stitches and casts are holding that boy together? Haven't you ever heard of MRSA? If you jostled him too much and opened a healing wound—"

"Hey," Jonah cut in roughly, glowering at the nurse. "She's fine. She didn't hurt me."

But Tess had already bowed her head in shame. The nurse was absolutely right. She could've hurt him badly.

"She needs to know the repercussions," the nurse hissed right back.

"She did nothing wrong," Jonah said. "I *asked* her to come up here and—"

"You know what," Tess broke in, about to panic herself into tears. Worried Jonah and the nurse might actually come to blows, she waved her hands, surrendering. "It's okay. I knew I shouldn't have. And I'm sorry." She glanced at the nurse and made eye contact to show her sincerity before turning back to Jonah and choking out, "I'm sorry."

His jaw tensed. "You don't have to apologize," he said moodily, shifting his glare to the nurse. "I made you do it."

When his chest started to heave as if he was about to work himself into a tizzy, Tess reached out and calmly took his hand. His warm fingers immediately clamped around hers and turmoil swirled in his brown eyes as he looked up at her.

"It's okay," she assured him with a small smile. After a quick glance at the nurse to make sure her back was turned and she was busy reading the numbers on his monitoring machine and jotting them down in a clipboard, Tess leaned down to Jonah and whispered into his ear. "Next time, we just won't get caught."

She straightened quickly when the nurse glanced their way. Face flushed because she was sure the other woman had heard her, Tess offered her a weak, guilty smile. But the nurse turned away and scribbled something else, giving no indication that she'd heard anything. Finally, Tess risked a peek at Jonah.

His face glowed with joy, and a smile spread across his face, making his tired eyes glitter with more life and vitality than she'd ever seen in them before. Then he winked at her and squeezed her hand in a conspiring way.

She rolled her eyes, blushing harder.

Tess stayed another half hour after the nurse's check-in. But she didn't get back on the bed with Jonah, no matter how much he tried to cajole.

The boy was proving to be a lot more enticing than she bargained for. After just a few days — mere *days* — of knowing him, she felt…

Honestly, she had no idea how she truly felt, but it was a lot stronger than she knew she should feel about a virtual stranger. Her emotions didn't seem to care, though. He needed her, and she was too drawn to him to stay away now.

She didn't leave until nearly forty-five minutes after visiting hours were over. Not that she really tried all that hard to escape. Every time she'd look at the clock on the wall and mention how she should go, he'd grip her hand and put on the begging eyes, telling her he wanted her to stay.

How was a girl supposed to resist that? Honestly.

So, she didn't. She stayed until the door to his room opened. Diving behind his bed so she wouldn't get caught and in trouble with yet another nurse, she hid out until his check-in was complete and they were the only two left in the room. There'd been a moment in there she was tempted to kick Jonah's bed because he'd started to snicker about her lame hiding technique. But, hey, no one had caught her so she figured she'd done just fine.

After that, she didn't let his big brown begging eyes get to her. Well, not completely. She only stayed five minutes longer, most of which was spent kissing each other goodbye. His mouth was becoming downright addictive, which was probably going to be another problem.

But she'd worry about that later.

It wasn't until she was sneaking out of his room that she realized her hiding technique truly did suck.

"Hey!"

She had no idea why she'd been easing out of his room back first, maybe so she could face him and see him for as long as possible before she was in the hall. But at the sharp call, she yelped out a muffled scream and whirled around.

"Oh, my God," she gasped as the nurse who'd scolded her for being on Jonah's bed marched toward her. Pressing her hand to her heart, she winced, bracing herself for a new lecture. "I'm sorry. I'm so sorry. I totally lost track of time and—"

The nurse waved her concerns aside. "Are you his girlfriend?" she asked, not really sounding accusatory but not sounding all that friendly either.

Oh, boy.

Tess barely controlled herself from wincing. "Um…" For some reason, lying to a nurse felt about as bad as lying to a priest. So, instead of admitting anything verbally, she merely gave a vague nod of her head.

When the nurse's face bloomed into a bright smile, Tess was instantly befuddled. "I'm Kari," the nurse said, sticking out her hand. "And I just wanted to thank you for being here for him. You cannot imagine how much your presence has helped him in the past few days. Before you came along, he was—" she blew out a breath as if relieved that time was over "—completely unmanageable. No one wanted to deal with him. But now he actually has a couple of friendly moments between all the crabbiness."

Tess blinked at her, not sure what to say. It was hard to believe she'd had that much influence on anyone. But beyond the disbelief was warmth and tenderness…and a load of guilt. Despite how much she was doing this for a good cause, she didn't want to deceive him anymore. And yet, hearing the nurse say what she'd just said, she was convinced more than ever that she should stay on this dishonest path.

"I…" When her voice cracked, she licked her lips and tried again. "Thank you."

Nurse Kari's smile was sincere when she patted Tess's shoulder. "But, seriously, don't bother hiding the next time you stay late. I saw you the moment I walked in. And do be careful when you crawl on the bed with him again. He's still very fragile. The risk of him getting an infection truly does exist."

Tess wisely shut her trap, cleared her throat, and nodded. Face flaming hot with embarrassment, she waved goodbye to Kari and darted toward the exit.

Chapter Ten

Jonah's stomach wouldn't stop swirling over the indigestion he was giving himself. The day he would learn whether he could walk had finally come. Though he'd been impatient for it to arrive, now that it was here, he wouldn't mind waiting awhile longer.

What if it ended up he couldn't walk? What if—

He shook his head, refusing to think about that. He was going to have to walk. That was all there was to it.

The door to his room swung open. He schooled his expression to hide all the panic and anxiety crowding through his system. People had been popping in all morning to make sure he was ready. And with every visit, his apprehensions rose. The last visitor, a nurse, had told him his physical therapist had arrived and had decided to put Jonah last on his rounds so he could spend more time with him. Jonah was sure he was about to hyperventilate.

His face already felt tense when he glanced up, but seeing Tess stroll into his room sent him over the edge. *Shit.*

"What are you doing here?" he demanded, utterly alarmed. She might calm him down and cheer him up every other time she visited, but today...today he didn't want her here. He didn't want her to watch him fail. She'd be more likely to leave a failure behind and never come back.

She jerked to a stop, looking surprised and a little hurt by the harshness in his voice. And he immediately wanted to kick himself. He hadn't meant to hurt her.

"I...I...couldn't stay away. I had to know how you did today."

He tried to calm his tone. "But...don't you have classes?"

Her shoulders relaxed, and a soft smile lit her face as she snorted. "As if I'd actually be able to concentrate in any of them while you're here, doing this. This is the only day I've skipped, anyway. One day can't hurt anything."

"You..." But he couldn't think of anything to say. It just threw him totally off balance to know she cared enough to be here while he experienced one of the biggest, possibly most life-altering moments of his life.

Giving up on words, he held out his hand. She skipped forward, her face filled with joy, and suddenly, he was glad she was here, relieved he had a hand to hold as he waited. "Thank you for coming."

"Of course."

He gazed at her, continually amazed that she returned every day, just to see him, to be here for him. Emotion filled his throat, but he swallowed it back down. Dropping his gaze, he watched his thumb move over her soft knuckles.

"You painted your fingernails," he said, needing to talk about something totally unrelated to the trials that awaited him.

Tess sent him a startled glance. "Yeah. I figured it was time."

He wasn't sure what that meant, but he assumed it was a good thing because the smile that blossomed across her cheeks was blinding in its beauty. "I like the color," he went on, smoothing his finger over her glossy red nails. "Reminds me of your hair."

Groaning, she leaned closer to him, driving him crazy by the flowery smell her proximity brought him. "Please don't tell me you like my hair next. I *know* better than that. This mop is completely ridiculous."

Jonah smiled as he looked up to her curling red locks. "No. I don't like your hair." He let go of her hand so he could wind a brilliant strand of scarlet around his index finger. "I'm hopelessly in love with your hair."

When she sucked in a breath, he knew he'd said the right thing. Tugging gently on the lock he held, he drew her closer. "So, are you going to give me a kiss for good luck, or what?"

Her blue eyes glittered with a glee that did all kinds of amazing things to him. "Jonah, if you just wanted me to kiss you, all you had to do was say so. You didn't have to toss in all that 'for luck' stuff."

"Tess," he said, towing her in even closer. "I just want you to kiss me."

She laughed, but he cut the sound short with his mouth. She had to catch her hand in the mattress by his head to keep from losing her balance. Burying both of his hands in her amazing hair, he cupped her face and urged her mouth open so his tongue could curl around hers.

Being with her, like this, did things to him, pulled emotions from him, until he pressed his forehead to hers the moment their kiss ended. "I'm scared out of my mind that I won't be able to—"

"Well, well, well." Someone broke into his whispered confession, thank God, keeping him from spilling his soul to her. "What do we have here?"

Tess jerked guiltily upright and spun toward the doorway as Jonah's physical therapist strolled into the room.

"There's a new face." Striding forward, he focused on nothing but Tess as he held out his hand and sent her a big, goofy grin. "You must be my man Jonah's better half?"

She appeared momentarily flustered but finally nodded and shook his hand. "I'm Tess."

"It's good to meet you, Miss Tess. Call me Frenchie."

Frenchie had always been annoyingly cheerful when he came to inflict pain on Jonah three days every week by stretching his muscles. He looked like a computer geek with pasty, pale skin, frail frame, and thick black horn-rimmed glasses, but he talked more like a salesman, yapping on, usually in a one-sided conversation. Jonah was typically too bitter to engage him, though, so he kind of preferred it being one-sided.

Today, however, he scowled at his PT because the man was making his girl blush.

"So, I'm the physical therapist," Frenchie rambled on. "And today is this big boy's special day to finally try getting up on his feet. But I assume you already knew that, and that's why you're here. To watch the show."

"If that's okay," Tess answered with a nod.

"Sure, sure. The more cheerleaders coaxing him on, the better." Turning to Jonah, he waggled his eyebrows. "You ready to get this party started?"

Hell, no. But Jonah drew in a deep, bracing breath, glanced at Tess, and nodded.

"All right, then. First we're going to do our routine stretches to limber you up, and then we'll call in some help for the walking part."

Realizing they weren't going to get straight to attempts at walking set Jonah's nerves on edge even more.

When Frenchie had him sit up and draw his legs over the side of the bed, his stress blossomed through every limb, making them quake. His muscles strained as he shifted his hips around. Frenchie assisted him, grabbing his legs until he was sitting upright on his own with his sock-covered feet actually pressing against the floor. He couldn't believe it. This was probably the first time in weeks that the soles of his feet had touched a floor.

But Tess's gasp stole some of his wonder. "Oh, my God. You have clothes on."

Both he and Frenchie glanced at her, all of their eyebrows lifted. She immediately blushed and slapped her hand over her face. "I mean…" She waved frantically at his outfit. "You changed clothes. You were still wearing your hospital gown last night. I, uh, just now noticed you're not in it anymore. And your I.V.'s gone too."

Her flustered expression was adorable. Jonah grinned, and Frenchie snickered. "Yeah, you did seem a little too preoccupied to notice what he was wearing when I came in."

After sending his therapist a brief scowl, Jonah glanced back toward Tess. "One of my nurses went to the store this morning and picked me up some street clothes."

"We can't have our boy walking around the hospital with his tushy hanging out, now, can we?" Frenchie laughed, making Tess blush and Jonah roll his eyes.

The gray T-shirt was actually a little snug and the pants too short. A lump bulged from the right side of his stomach where his bullet wound was taped together under his clothes. But he was so relieved he wouldn't have his bare ass on display when he tried to walk today, he didn't care. Short and tight clothes were better than no clothes.

"We'll start with the knee joint," Frenchie was saying as he grasped Jonah's leg and started bending and stretching.

Jonah clenched his teeth and focused on breathing through the pain. Every once in a while, a muscle would stretch over a sensitive spot, and he'd nearly black out from the agony.

"Does this actually help him?" Tess asked, edging in closer to watch the show over Frenchie's shoulder. "He looks like he's in a lot of pain."

"Of course it helps. I wouldn't torture him without a good reason." Frenchie grinned up at her, explaining the reason behind each stretch. Tess looked so fascinated by it all, Jonah's PT actually scooted aside to let her work his second leg, talking her through the procedure, step by step.

Jonah watched her, endeared by how seriously she took the task and how closely she listened to each one of Frenchie's instructions. Her soft hands felt much better than Frenchie's, too, and it didn't hurt nearly as much when she pulled on sore muscle tissue. After she finished with his knee, she actually looked reluctant to step aside and let Frenchie finish. Jonah couldn't take his eyes off her as she concentrated on every part of the process.

After working his hip joints, ankles, and feet, his PT dusted his hands off on his hips. "And with that, I think we're ready for the main event." He winked once at Tess and turned back to Jonah. "Let me go grab a couple more hands, and we'll be good to go."

When he jogged from the room, Tess immediately moved closer. He glanced at her warily, hoping to God she didn't try to feed him any sappy words of encouragement. He didn't think he could take that right now. Felt like he might throw up as it was.

But instead of a boosting "*You can do it,*" she wrinkled her nose. "That was kind of fun. Is Frenchie his first name or last?"

"Uh." Jonah blinked and chuckled, glad she was still stuck on what she'd just done. "You know, I have no idea." He'd never thought about Frenchie's name before, because he'd been too bitter and rude to care before. But with Tess here, his bitterness had drained away. If only it hadn't left behind an emotional time bomb. He wanted to yank her into his arms and sob against her shoulder because he was so scared right now.

"You really look different in those clothes."

She blushed over her confession, causing a thrill of arousal to spark through him. Sitting upright in regular clothes with his feet against the ground, Jonah *felt* different. He felt like someone who might actually have a life outside this building.

His mouth spread wide as he caught her hand and tugged her closer. "Good enough to kiss?"

Tess licked her lips. "Oh, much better than that."

At his urging, she shifted between his knees so her hips were braced by his thighs. But when Jonah bent his head to kiss her, a tongue clucked disapprovingly from the doorway.

"There you two go again. I swear, you guys are like magnets." Frenchie grinned at them as he swept into the room, leading two nurses.

Tess backed away, and Jonah wanted to dive after her, tugging her back to his side. But Frenchie was already positioning her to stand behind him as he sat on a rolling stool in front of Jonah and slid a walker between them. His two helpers flanked them on either side.

Jonah lifted one eyebrow as he glared at the contraption. "A walker?" Jesus, he was going to feel like an eighty-year-old trying to get around with this thing.

"Hey, don't knock it." Frenchie stroked one of the metal railings as if to soothe its insulted feelings. "This baby is going to help you work a miracle, my boy."

Under the PT's instructions, two nurses helped him upright by the arms. Frenchie remained sitting in front of him and gripped him around the waist, talking him through each step and telling him how everything was going to work...or not work.

As Jonah hovered above the ground, not yet putting his full weight down on his legs, he glanced toward Tess where she stood with her hands clutched together by her mouth as if in prayer.

Worried blue eyes took him in, and he immediately forgot what he was about to do.

"God, you're tiny," he said. He had no idea she was so much shorter than him. He'd always had a thing for petite girls.

With an immediate frown, she slapped her hands to her hips. "No, I am not." Though clearly, she barely came up to his shoulder. "You're just...mammoth."

He grinned. He was so busy smiling at her that he didn't notice how the orderlies had put his hands on the walker until cool aluminum filled his palms. His smile fled and dread filled the pit of his stomach. Somehow, he just knew this wasn't going to end well.

"Now, gradually," the therapist instructed him, "let out the weight in your good leg. Don't put any pressure on the broken one."

Jonah nodded, following the instructions. His knee trembled, but he felt as if he was actually holding himself up with his one leg, even though his weight seemed to settle on the wound in his gut instead of his hipbones.

The hands holding onto his arms began to ease up on their hold. Jonah instinctively put the weight down on his bad leg as well, to brace himself.

And he nearly blacked out. With a choked cry of pain, he crumpled, agony splitting through every atom in his body. Tess gasped and lurched forward. But the nurses had already caught him and were easing him back onto the bed, while his limp noodle legs dangled uselessly over the side.

"It's okay. It's fine," Frenchie's soothing voice reassured him. But Jonah knew it wasn't. He couldn't walk.

They tried for about ten minutes—though to Tess, it felt like hours. Jonah kept growling to keep at it, and they'd go again until Frenchie finally murmured, "No. That's enough for today. You've lost what little strength you had."

"No. One more—"

"No," Frenchie repeated firmly. "This is enough."

Tess's shoulders slumped with relief. She'd tensed up so much in the last couple of minutes, it physically hurt to watch Jonah go through this. Every muscle in her body ached for relief.

Her misery had to be nothing compared to his, though. Not only was it physical torture for him, but she could see it breaking down his emotions and pounding his morale into submission as well.

She was so ready for everyone else to leave so she could pamper him for a while, until he smiled up at her with that smile of his she so adored.

But as the two nurses helped him lie back on his bed, the expression on his face devastated her. He looked hopeless. Beaten. What if she couldn't make him smile?

Frenchie bent slightly to speak confidentially into Jonah's ear, and the entire time Jonah lay unnaturally still without responding. She glanced away and concentrated on breathing through her nose, but her sympathy kept rising up in her, wanting to consume her.

When she turned back, she caught the therapist watching her. He cast her a weary half-smile before he patted Jonah's shoulder and told him he'd be back Friday so they could try again. Then he strolled from the room.

Once Jonah and Tess were alone, she hurried to his side. But he closed his eyes and turned his head aside, away from her.

"I'm kind of tired," he said, his voice so low he rasped the words. "I think I'll take a nap."

"Okay. That sounds like a good idea." She touched his hair, but he only flinched from her fingers.

Dropping her hand, she watched him rest his hand by his head and breathe slowly. She knew he was still awake, but he refused to open his eyes.

Knowing he didn't want her there, she gave up and trudged reluctantly from the room.

She didn't collapse until she pushed open a door and found herself in an empty, quiet stairwell. Then she pressed her back to a wall, slid to the ground, and hugged her legs so she could sob into her knees.

After a good five minutes of tears, she'd calmed herself enough to dig her phone from her purse and send Bailey an SOS text.

Thirty seconds later, her friend responded, calling her phone directly. "What's wrong? Are you okay? Who do I have to kill?"

"I…I'm okay. But can you come to the hospital and pick me up?"

Bailey was quiet a second. "If you're at the hospital, why don't you have my car already?"

Tess sniffed back a stray tear. "You made it sound like you didn't want me to use it anymore, so I took a bus here."

"Christ, Tessie, you know my car is your car. But, yeah, sure. Give me a couple minutes to sneak back into class, grab my things, and ditch. Then I'll be right there."

"Good. I need you." Closing her eyes, she blew out a relieved breath. She could always count on Bailey.

Chapter Eleven

"I'm sorry you had to ditch class for me."

Bailey sighed as she turned down the street leading to Grammar Hall. "Ditching class for you is the least of my worries. Why the hell were *you* ditching class?"

Tess didn't answer. She already knew Bailey had figured out the truth. God, why hadn't she listened to her best friend's advice the first night she'd met Jonah? Why hadn't she just come clean and told him everything? Maybe she wouldn't have grown so close to him. Maybe she wouldn't have stuck around to see his absolute heartbreak today. And maybe she wouldn't feel like she was being ripped in two right now.

Sniffing as more tears flooded her cheeks, she tried to wipe them away with the back of her hand. But they just kept falling.

"Jesus," Bailey muttered, reaching past her to open the glove compartment. She yanked out a handful of fast-food restaurant napkins and thrust them at Tess. "Here. Take care of yourself. I can't—" She blew a breath and shook her head. "I can't handle seeing you this upset."

"Thank you." Tess had her face dry by the time Bailey parked.

After killing the engine, Bailey didn't move except to rest her hands on the steering wheel and clutch it with a white-knuckled grip. "You have to stop this, you know." Her voice was low and void of her usual sarcasm. "This guy has made you cry more than once, Tess. He's not—"

"Jonah has never made me cry. It's the situation he's in that's heartbreaking. I'm crying *for* him, not because of him."

"I don't care," Bailey muttered, shaking her head adamantly. "My best friend does not cry this much. She smiles and laughs and always finds the good in life. She's optimistic, happy, and blissfully carefree."

Yeah, well, lately, Tess's world had been filled with fear and heartbreak. Ever since the shooting, finding something to smile about had become a lot more difficult.

"That's it." Bailey ripped her keys from the ignition and shoved open the driver's side door. "Come with me."

As she marched toward their dormitory, Tess scurried to follow. Her friend stormed all the way into the building and up the stairs, and then down the hall toward their room. Once they were inside, Bailey grabbed her arm and tugged her through the bathroom and into Paige's room.

"I'm calling an intervention," she announced loudly as soon as she stepped inside without knocking. "Right now."

Tess jerked to a halt when she glanced around Bailey's shoulder and caught sight of Paige and Logan on the bed, curled up together where they'd obviously been making out. Poor Paige's lips were swollen, and Logan's face was flushed. Tess tried to retreat, but her bestie yanked her forward again.

Catching the apprehension in her gaze, Bailey rolled her eyes and hooked her thumb toward the door. "But hot guy's got to go first."

Paige immediately scowled, pushing upright into a sitting position even as she straightened her shirt. "Hey, don't tell him to—"

"It's fine," Logan cut in, setting his hand on Paige's arm. "I don't do girl talk all that well, anyway. And they obviously need to…girl talk." Kissing her cheek, he rose to his feet, saluted to Bailey, sent Tess a sympathetic glance, and turned toward the exit.

As soon as the door shut behind him, Bailey lit in. "Jeez Louise, did the doctor *sew* you to him when he got his bullet hole patched back together? I haven't seen you guys apart since the shooting."

Paige flinched at the word *shooting*. "Hey, we're no more attached than…than you and Tess are."

Bailey made a face as if she was going to argue, but then she shrugged. "Touché."

Scowling with irritation at Bailey, Paige tried to smooth out her tousled hair. "So, what's up?"

Or maybe it was sexual frustration clouding Paige's face. Tess totally understood that excited yet unsatisfied gleam in her suitemate's eyes. She'd been experiencing some of the same sensation herself lately, pretty much every time an interrupting nurse walked into Jonah's hospital room.

"Tessie's lost her damn mind, that's what's up." Without grace, Bailey flopped onto Mariah's abandoned, stripped mattress to sling and arm over her head. "I don't know what to do for her."

When Paige lifted her eyebrows and glanced at Tess, Tess hugged her waist and cowered in the bathroom doorway, the situation making her extremely uncomfortable.

"She's overreacting," she said. The changes to Paige's room didn't help ease her anxiety either. Without her old roommate's large screen TV, microwave, or cluttered bedding and clothes, the room looked stark and lonely, adding to Tess's discomfort, reminding her how much the world had recently changed.

"Am not," Bailey shot back. Pointing to Tess, she spoke to Paige. "Just look at her eyes. Can you even imagine how long she had to cry to get them that red and swollen?"

Sympathy filled Paige's face as she finally scooted off her bed and went to Tess. "What happened?" she asked, enfolding Tess into a sisterly hug.

Bailey might be her best friend on earth and Tess would always choose her over their suitemate, but Bailey wasn't exactly the touchy, huggy type. Tess latched onto Paige's hug and started weeping all over again into her shoulder.

"Oh, for the love of God," Bailey exploded, letting Tess hear the underlying panic in her voice. "Here we go again. Just make it stop, Paige. Make her happy again. Tess is not meant to be this miserable."

Paige Zukowski truly had a talent for cheering people up. Not five minutes after Tess and Bailey had invaded her room, she'd led Tess to her bed, set her down, and had her spill everything. Well, maybe not everything. Tess kind of excluded exactly *how* close she and Jonah had grown. She'd probably go to Best Friend Hell for that one, but she just couldn't kiss and tell. Those stolen moments with him had meant everything. Bailey would only try to morph it into something bad and wrong. And it hadn't been.

It just couldn't have been.

"So, Tess tells some guy no one knows, even himself, that she's his girlfriend to make him feel a little better while he's in the hospital and she grows a little too close him," Paige said, summing up the past week in one sentence. Glancing at Bailey, she asked, "But what I'm confused about is why you're so worried about this?"

Bailey's mouth fell open. She jabbed her pointer finger toward Tess. "Because!" she exploded. "The guy has amnesia. He doesn't even know who he is. How could *she* get to know him at a time like this to know for sure whether or not he's worthy of her? And let's not forget that the entire foundation of their relationship is a *big fat lie*. He's going to get his memory back someday, and then what?"

Paige smiled patiently. "Well, I'm sure Tess has already thought that scenario through and has a plan to explain the truth to him." She glanced to the topic of their conversation. "Right?"

Tess bit her lip, feeling a little sick to her stomach. "Um…"

"See." Bailey popped to her feet and began to pace the room. "She's got nothing. She's going into this totally blind, and she's going to end up hurt. And I just can't allow that."

"Then I guess we'll have to help her come up with a reasonable explanation to give him whenever she feels it's time."

"But there is no reasonable explanation except that her ridiculous stupid gene comes out every time she's in the presence of a hottie. And I'm not just calling her names; I know for a fact how this evil gene affects her. It's like Tess's very own scientifically proven disease. But how exactly do you explain it to a clueless guy?"

"Actually." Tess blushed furiously when Paige and Bailey glanced at her. "He already knows about my stupid gene. I mean—" she flailed a nervous hand "—I told him about how I blurt out crazy things in the presence of men who attract me."

"You did?" Bailey blinked and blindly sat down on Paige's bed next to them. "How the hell were you able to confess a thing like that?"

"It was kind of in the middle of one of my stupid-gene, blurt-it-all-out moments. But surprisingly, after that, I felt a lot better and could actually relax around him and, you know, be myself."

"Holy shit." Covering her mouth with her hand, Bailey gaped badly until she dropped her fingers and let out a huge grin. "That's it," she said with finality. "He's never allowed to get his memory back again. This guy is good for you. I can't believe you…you mean, you can seriously be yourself with him? One hundred percent Tess?"

Tess bobbed her head, grinning big time, her chest swelling with joy as Bailey grinned back.

"Oh, my God," Bailey wailed, wiping away a mock tear…or maybe it was real. "My baby's got her first boyfriend. I'm so proud." Then she threw open her arms and hugged Tess hard.

Tess was so startled by the enveloping squeeze, it took her a moment to hug her best friend back. Before she knew it, they were laughing and hugging each other some more, swaying back and forth over the momentous occasion.

Until Paige discretely cleared her throat. "Um, not to be a spoilsport or anything. But maybe we should get back to working on a plan to tell this guy the truth. Especially in light of recent events."

"Screw that," Bailey said. "I'm all for sneaking into his hospital room tonight and bashing him over the head again to make sure the amnesia stays permanent. You know, keep him her clueless boyfriend forever."

Tess immediately frowned at that idea. Anything that involved him and more pain was not a good plan.

Next to her, Paige sighed. "Five minutes ago, you were ready to accuse him of being a serial killer."

Bailey just snorted and waved her hand. "That was before I knew he was perfect for my Tess. Seriously, Paige. Relax. She was able to open up to him. She doesn't just do that for anyone, you know. She's got senses like a dog or something; it's as if she can smell evil on a person. If this guy got past her shy zone, then he's fine."

Flattered by Bailey's complete faith in her, Tess reached over and squeezed her friend's hand. "Thank you." But now she was even more worried because—

What if her dog senses were all out of whack? Just how well could she trust herself? Because when it came to Jonah Abbott, she always reacted the way she knew she shouldn't.

"In that case, then," Paige said, "I think we *really* need to come up with a good game plan to keep him around after his memories come back."

Tess's shoulders slumped. What if they never came up with a way to make Jonah want to stay with her? And just how had she gone from simply wanting to help a stranger feel loved to wanting to make her fake boyfriend a permanent one?

Tess couldn't sleep. Listening to Bailey's heavy breathing, she pushed the covers off her and rose from her bed.

After she'd spent most of the day talking about Jonah with her two friends, she couldn't get him off her mind.

Hours into their discussion, Logan had shown up with pizza, so Paige had invited Bailey and Tess to stay and eat with them. The four of them talked and even managed to laugh over a few jokes. But they never really came up with a feasible strategy of how to best explain her lies to Jonah. And that worried her. There really would be no way to explain it, would there? He'd either forgive her or push her away. And the uncertainty of what he'd choose terrified her.

"Did you ever talk to his coach?" Logan had wondered at one point. Tess had to admit she hadn't yet.

In fact, since the moment she realized she wanted him all to herself, she'd stopped trying to contact anyone on his behalf. And that couldn't be good. The entire point of this was to help him find someone who cared and who would keep him company until he got his memory back so he didn't feel alone.

Guilt swamped her. She really did need to approach Jonah's coach the first chance she got.

She knew she'd grown too close to Jonah, and she was pretty sure he'd grown just about as close to her. But would he change his mind once his memories returned? As soon as he knew who he was, would he return to his old life and abandon her?

In that case, maybe it would be best to tell him everything now, while he was still the Jonah she'd come to know, not the one neither of them knew. Gaining his forgiveness now might be easier than it would be later…when he was someone else.

But thinking about him being someone else, someone she didn't know, alarmed her. She could only imagine what that same uncertainty did to him.

God, the poor guy was dealing with so much; he had "tangled mess" written all over him. All she'd wanted to do was somehow help him unravel a few of the knots so he could begin to sort his life out again. But she'd managed to somehow get herself tied up right along with him until she felt tethered to him and caught in the middle of his issues just as deeply as he was.

She needed to be close to him now, more than she'd ever needed to be with anyone. She dressed in the dark. Barely daring to breathe so she didn't wake her roommate, she tiptoed to Bailey's desk, found her car keys by feel, and left the dorm room.

Pausing in the hall, she waited thirty seconds just to make sure Bailey didn't follow. But Bailey must've been in the deepest stage of sleep. She didn't wake up.

Jonah was also dead asleep when she snuck into his hospital room twenty minutes later. Tess felt as if she'd been holding her breath since the moment she'd stolen Bailey's keys. But the air rushed from her lungs now, in a strange kind of relief, as she stared at his peacefully dreaming body, a blanket draped over him all the way up to his chin.

Lifting the sheet, she eased into his bed, only to realize he was wearing nothing but the jogging pants he'd had on earlier when he'd tried to walk. His chest was bare and smooth, gleaming in the dim lights around the room. A four-inch patch of square gauze was taped to his lower torso on the right side.

She touched the area gently as she laid her head next to his, facing him.

He woke with a jerk, sucking in a startled breath.

"Sorry," she whispered, touching this face. "I didn't mean to wake you." Or maybe she had. She was so messed up right now.

She moved her fingers over his beautiful features as he blinked her into focus.

"Tess?" he mumbled, his voice full of sleep and eyes heavy-lidded. "What're you—" He shook his head as if he needed to clear it and glanced around. "What time is it?"

"A little after two."

He squeezed his eyes shut and then drug them back open. "In the morning?"

She winced. "Yeah. I'm sorry, I should go."

When she moved to roll off the bed, though, he curled onto his side and into her, so they could fit more fully together.

"No. Don't go." He slid his arm around her waist as if it was the most natural act in the world.

She froze, holding her breath again. "Okay."

Jonah nuzzled his face into her. "What're you doing here, though?"

"I couldn't sleep," she admitted and leaned forward to kiss his chin full of dark stubble. "I was sad. I needed my boyfriend to make me feel better again."

Worry filled his tired eyes as he cupped her face. "What happened? Are you okay?"

She shook her head. "No, I'm not okay. I was completely shut out by this guy earlier today who was trying to walk. And it broke my heart because I couldn't do anything to help him while he was going through the worst turmoil of his life. I felt so worthless and helpless. I even cried a little. It reminded me of when my mom was dying. I just stood by her bed, unable to even ease her pain."

"Jesus." He squeezed his eyes closed and buried his hand deep in her hair so he could shift their foreheads together. "Baby, I'm sorry. I'm so damn sorry. I know I was a dick. I just—"

She set her hand over his mouth and adamantly shook her head. "It's okay. You don't have anything to apologize for. You were completely within your right to—"

"No." He grasped her hand to remove it from his mouth. "I was wrong. And I know it. I just couldn't—" Gritting his teeth, he let out a harsh laugh. "I wanted to do it for you. I wanted to get right up and walk to show you I could, that I was capable and worthy and—"

"Jonah, you didn't have to show me anything. I don't need—"

"Well, I *do* need! I needed to do it for you. For my girlfriend. If I'm going to keep you, I needed to be strong and capable."

Guilt and pain clogged her throat. She wondered what he'd do if he knew she wasn't really his girlfriend. How could she ever tell him now? How could she tell him they weren't really as close as he seemed to think they were, as close as she wanted them to be?

Squeezing her eyes shut, she rested her cheek against his heartbeat. He deserved the truth. But that wasn't what she wanted to tell him. She wanted to tell him she was heartbroken for him because he hadn't done what he'd hoped to do today. She wanted to encourage him and beg him not to give up just because he hadn't succeeded his first try. There was so much she wanted to talk about with him, about what they'd both been through today.

But instead, she said, "I'm scared."

He must've been expecting her to start up on the walking issue too because he pulled back slightly as if surprised by her admission. Then beautiful brown eyes filled with sympathy. He cupped her face with one hand.

"What're you scared of?"

"Everything," she admitted before gulping. "It feels like my entire life has…changed. I've been so coddled and sheltered from all the bad things in the world. My dad and brothers never let anything happen to me. Even my best friend goes out of her way to make sure I'm shielded. But this shooting has me shaken. Nothing—" she had to pause to take a breath "—I mean, *nothing* is as it used to be anymore. I feel like I'm right out there, exposed to everything, with no clue how to defend myself. I see danger everywhere I look, and I hate it. I hate this panicky, helpless feeling that every time I turn around, some big evil will—"

"Shh." Stroking her cheek, he leaned forward to gently set his mouth against hers. "I know. I know exactly how you feel. When I was growing up—"

Before he continued, he cut himself off abruptly. She lifted her face, eager to hear about his own experience with fear, but he shook his head, dismissing whatever he was going to say.

"There's a lot of bad shit in the world, Tess. But if you let it get to you, it'll drag you under until you just can't breathe through it, until it takes you down, too."

She searched his face, already feeling comforted and safe just being here in his arms, listening to him understand her phobia. "How do you stop it from getting to you?"

He laughed softly. "I don't know, exactly. You just keep on keeping on, I guess. Look for every ounce of happiness, laughter, silliness, and hope in the world, and you cherish those moments."

Gazing into his eyes, Tess fell. Hard. "I'm happy," she whispered. "Right here, just like this. With you. I've never felt this kind of happiness before."

He swallowed. Then his gaze fell to her mouth before he swooped in to kiss her. She clutched his shoulder, and he turned his torso in toward hers so he could roll half on top of her. But he sucked in a curse and winced, breaking the kiss so he could fall back onto his side and writhe.

"Oh, my God." She clutched his good arm. "Are you okay? I didn't mean to hurt you. Let me get off the bed so you can—"

"No!" His hand shot out and caught her hip so she couldn't leave. "We've been over this. You know I'd rather you stay."

"But the nurse was right. I could make things worse."

He leaned into her with a teeth-gritted smile. "Then I'd die with a smile on my face. Besides, my girl came here to be cheered up. I take that shit seriously. Now...let me cheer you up."

Chapter Twelve

It had taken Jonah forever to fall sleep. He'd felt like crap from the moment he'd turned his back on Tess and she'd walked out of his room earlier today. He'd wanted to call her back, but what would he have said? *Sorry for letting you down, for being a complete failure?*

But now that she was here, in his bed, at two o'clock in the morning, none of that mattered. She'd come back, despite everything, because he was the one she wanted to be with. So, he made it his new life mission to give her what she'd asked for: a smile.

"Let's see here," he murmured against her throat and had to kiss the warm, soft, great-smelling skin a couple times. "How to cheer up Tess? Hmm. There's got to be a happy button on you somewhere, I'd think." Being as silly as he could, he picked up her hand and pressed on her bright red thumbnail as if punching a real button. After gauging her reaction, he made a face. "No. No, I don't think that was it."

When she smiled, finally realizing he was playing, he arched an eyebrow. "Or was it?" He pressed on her thumbnail again. She shook her head and laughed, so he made a fascinated sound. "Interesting. It seems we've located one happy button, but I'm curious to know if the subject has more."

When he lightly squeezed the tip of her nose, she chuckled some more and ducked her head. "You're being ridiculous."

He merely grinned. "Isn't that the point? To be silly and make you smile?"

With a sad twitch to the lips, her shoulders sagged. "I shouldn't have said that to you."

"Yes, you should have. And I'm glad you did. There should be no other goal in the world than to make someone important to you smile." He slid his hands down her sides until he reached the hem of her shirt, finding his way under the cloth, he smoothed his fingers back up, skin against skin across her abdomen.

She drew in a taut breath, and he grinned, gently rubbing his thumb around her belly button. "Now what about here? Do you feel any happiness when I touch you here?"

Tess nodded without saying a word. Her lashes fell closed, and it took everything he had not to kiss her perfect lips. *Oh, the hell with it.* He leaned in and set his mouth against hers. The kiss was slow and powerful, tugging all kinds of emotions out of him.

For the first time in his life, he didn't want to be anywhere else than where he was. He was home. Tess was his home.

His fingers continued to forage a path under her shirt, exploring her warm, soft belly until he needed to feel more. He stroked upward, and she arched with him, her body encouraging him.

"That's definitely a happy button," Tess admitted breathlessly when he cupped her bra.

Jonah paused with his hand on the underside of her breast. Blinking down at her, he stared with clueless abandon. "Huh?"

Her smile brightened her entire face. Drowning in her absolute beauty, he could only gape dumbfounded as she murmured, "And the amnesia strikes again." She swept a lock of hair out of his face. "Have you already forgotten that you're looking for happy buttons?"

A pang of guilt hit him. Right. Happy buttons. Amnesia. For a minute, he'd forgotten all about that. About everything but Tess. Nothing else had mattered. But now that she'd pulled him back to reality, he skimmed his hand out of her shirt and patted her clothes back into shape.

Her eyebrows wrinkled in confused. "What's wrong?"

He shook his head. "I don't want to go too far. Not here. And if I kept on with those particular happy buttons, I'm not sure I could stop."

She laughed. "Of course you could stop. We're in a hospital, for God's sake. Like we actually would've —" When she caught sight of his face, she must've seen exactly what he was thinking. She gulped. "Oh."

Yeah. Oh.

Nothing would've stopped him if he'd gone too far. Not any of his wounds or pins or casts. Not their location or the fact they could've gotten caught at any moment. If Tess was willing, he would've continued with no concern for the future. And the future might be very concerning. For both of them.

"I don't want to go too far until—" He stopped talking with a regretful wince.

Tess touched his shoulder, her brow puckered with worry. "Until what?"

God, she always looked so worried about him, always paid attention to everything he said, as if he really mattered to her.

He looked down at his hands. "It's just...I know you now. More than you know about me. And I want to wait until the amnesia thing is over, and you can get to know the real me before we...do anything."

She looked stunned before something flickered across her face. "But if...I already know the real you, Jonah. I'm your girlfriend, remember?"

He just looked at her. After a slight nod, he said, "Yeah. I guess you're right. In which case, I guess *I* want to get to know who the real me is before we do too much."

Tess nodded immediately. "That's fine. I didn't mean to pressure you. You don't have to—"

He touched her lips and grinned. "You're definitely not pressuring me. In fact, any type of pressure you want to put on me would be entirely welcome. I just want...I want to do this right. I don't think I could lose you, so we're going to wait until...We're just going to wait a little while, all right?"

"All right." Biting her lip, she gave a single nod. When her attention fell to his throat, she let out a long sigh. "I never did get to tell you what I was supposed to tell you today."

A ripple of apprehension stole through him. "Well, it's already tomorrow, so that was actually yesterday you were supposed to tell me." He gave a small, helpless shrug. "I guess you lost your chance."

She rolled her eyes. "Jonah."

"Besides, aren't we supposed to be ridiculous and fun for the rest of the night? How the heck did we get so serious?"

"I really should tell you—"

He placed his fingers over her lips. "Tomorrow."

"You said that yesterday."

With a grin, he kissed her nose. "You the mean the day before yesterday?"

"Oh my God. You're seriously trying to confuse me, aren't you?"

He chuckled and kissed her again. When she went with it and kissed him back, he deepened it just a little more, until they were right back where they'd been before, his hand up her shirt and her back arched in sublime offering.

"Damn, I really need to stop getting us worked back up to this point." He kissed his way down her throat, and she mewled out a sound that drove him crazy. "Maybe it's because I really, really like this point."

"I do too," she panted back.

"Do you want to touch me, too?" he blurted before he could think through what he was going to say. Then he internally cursed himself. "Never mind. I shouldn't have asked that." He really didn't want to go that far, and besides, only a jackass asked a girl to pleasure him. Right? "Just wipe that question from your—"

"Here?" Tess asked, gingerly placing her fingers on his warm abdomen and making the skin jump from the unexpected contact.

Umm...not quite. But he was glad she misunderstood and didn't touch him a few inches lower. Besides, it wasn't like her soft touch didn't feel like heaven right where it was.

He sighed out his pleasure. "Yeah. Right there."

Her gaze followed the path of her hand as she barely grazed her fingernails over every dip and groove on his stomach. "You are so...beautiful."

He wanted to wince, or maybe crack a joke to gainsay her. Guys weren't beautiful. But the awe in her voice and the captivated gleam in her blue eyes made him feel beautiful. Like a beautiful person.

Leaning in to press his forehead to hers, he closed his eyes and soaked in the beauty of the moment.

"The first time I saw you," she whispered, "my stomach dropped into my knees and did a thousand somersaults, I swear."

Choked by her confession, Jonah cupped the back of her head and kissed her hair. This had to be the sweetest moment he'd shared with anyone. He wanted to capture it and somehow keep it forever.

Grazing his cheek down alongside hers, he drew in a breath, breathing her in.

"When did you realize I was boyfriend material?" he asked.

She dipped her face to kiss his throat. He made a sound of satisfaction deep in his throat.

"Probably the moment I first looked into your eyes. You have very expressive eyes."

"Do I?" He closed them so she couldn't see how profoundly that affected him.

"Mmm. Yes. I could see how much you needed to be loved and accepted."

Since that was the utter truth, it hit a little too close to home. Pulling her close, he kissed the corner of her mouth and kept his eyes closed. "That sounds pretty altruistic of you. Didn't you get anything out of it?"

He opened his lashes just in time to watch her smile. "Yes. I got to feel needed. And helpful. Being the only girl in my family, I was always so pampered and put on this stupid pedestal. Everyone treated me as if I was too fragile to touch. After my mom died, it was even worse. But with you…" Her fingers skated up his ribcage and over his heart. "I feel…I don't know. Like I have a purpose. Like I'm needed, just me, and no one else. It feels powerful."

"You *are* useful, Tess. And I do need you. Only you. You are so special; I don't even know how to tell you. Just this week alone, you have helped bring me back from this dark place I thought I could never return from. You're the kind of person who makes the world a better place."

She blinked some mist from her eyes, and he touched her cheek to make sure it stayed dry.

"Wow," she choked out. "I wasn't fishing for compliments, but… thank you. Really. Thank you."

"I wasn't trying to compliment you. I just wanted to let you know how much I appreciate everything you've done for me." He glanced away, fearing the future, fearing what would happen between them. And she must've read his expressive eyes because she hugged him.

"Jonah? What's wrong?"

He lowered his face and rested his forehead on her shoulder. "Everything," he whispered. "The future. Losing you. Everything."

Had he mentioned everything?

"You are not going to lose me. I'm not going anywhere unless you tell me to leave."

He lifted his face and took in the intensity in her expression. "But what if you learn I'm not worth staying for?"

Taking his face in her hands, she smiled. "Except I already know you *are*, so it's a moot point. Remember, you're the one who's forgotten who you are. I haven't. And I'm telling you, you're definitely worth loving."

Loving? His insides seized. Had she just admitted that she loved him? Or was she saying the potential was there? Did she expect him to say it back? Did he *want* to say it back?

"So are you," he said instead, because it was true.

She smiled, her face lighting up. He knew he'd said the right thing, and he kissed her lightly. With her soft, warm hands running over his torso, he groaned out a sound and had to fist his hands not to do the same to her.

But then she had to go and pull back from his lips to ask, "Do *you* have any happy buttons?" which sent all kinds of fireworks through certain parts of his anatomy.

He arched his brow, and she rolled hers eyes. "Don't be perverted; you know what I meant."

Jonah grinned and kissed her jaw. "Hey, you started it."

"No. I believe you started the whole happy button thing."

"Oh, yeah. Damn, I'm brilliant."

She gave a low laugh as her fingers trailed down his chest, lower than they'd been before. But still not quite low enough. He sucked in a breath as she stopped just above his waistband.

"What about here?" she asked. "I've found one or two bumps that might be considered buttons."

"Six," he growled, tickling her until she yelped. "There're six bumps there, woman. Don't go downsizing my six-pack."

"Six?" she lifted her eyebrows as if she didn't believe him. "Are you sure?"

"Well, let's check your counting skills." Taking her hand, he made her smooth her fingers over every sculpted ab muscle he had, counting aloud as she passed over each one.

"Wow," she murmured, tracing them again. "I can't even imagine how much football training you had to do to get all these. And how healthily you had to eat." Abandoning his stomach, her curious hand found his arm and began to investigate the rock hard muscles there.

"Whatever. Sneak me in a Snickers bar, and I'll show you just how healthily I *don't* eat."

Tess grinned. "Craving chocolate, are we?"

He actually whimpered. "Like you wouldn't believe."

"Gee, I don't know." She let out a low whistle. "Chocolate contraband is a much heftier fine than burritos or hamburgers. You might have to owe me big time for a Snickers."

He loved the teasing glint in her eyes. "I'll do anything," he swore, placing his hand solemnly against his heart. "For chocolate, I'll be your slave for life."

"Hmm." Tapping her red-painted nails against her chin, she studied him for a moment, silently deliberating before she nodded. "Okay, then. I'll take it. I hereby command you to kiss me. Like you mean it."

"Yes, ma'am," he murmured and went in with purpose. Jonah could never kiss her enough. Their mouths seemed like they had been made to fit together. So, he kissed her, on and on. And he touched her with reverence, keeping it as clean as possible, even though in his mind, their actions kept getting dirtier and dirtier. She reciprocated, learning each and every inch of his bared chest as she kissed him back.

Sometimes they'd take a break, just to lie against each other and talk about anything and everything. And sometimes they'd kiss some more. Exhaustion wore him down, but he was afraid to fall asleep. He didn't want the night to end. And yet, a time came when he grew too tired to kiss and too tired to talk. He rested his face against hers and soaked in the feel of her body against his as sleep stole into his foggy brain.

"Thank you for coming back tonight," he slurred, needing to say it before it was too late.

"Thank you for not getting mad at me for coming back."

"Mmm." God, even the feel of her hands running through his hair was drugging him unconscious. "I'll always welcome you back," he promised before he remembered nothing else.

When he woke briefly to catch a nurse checking in on him, he tightened his arm around Tess, prepared for a fight to keep her. But the nurse said nothing about his bed companion, and he sighed out his relief as she left the room. Tess slept on, so he closed his eyes and joined her.

The next time he woke, sunlight streamed into the room, and she was gone.

Chapter Thirteen

"Let's go bug Paige at The Squeeze. Bet we can sweet talk her into giving us a free latte and muffin."

When a distracted Tess didn't immediately answer Bailey's suggestion, but yawned instead, Bailey bumped their shoulders together. "Besides, it looks like you need a caffeine pick-me-up. Seriously, what is wrong with you? You got plenty of sleep. Hell, you went to bed before I did last night."

Tess winced. She felt crappy for not telling Bailey about her midnight visit. But it was something special between her and Jonah.

"I'm fine," she mumbled. "And I don't really want to go into the food district quite yet." That was where the massacre had taken place. She wasn't sure if she'd ever be able to walk over that ground again. She couldn't believe Paige could go in to the coffee shop she worked at each day, either, though that probably had more to do with the fact she worked with Logan and got to see him there.

Bailey let out a depressed sigh. "Yeah, I had a feeling you'd shoot that idea down. So, how about that ice cream parlor on Lincoln and Pine? It's completely off campus and has the best frozen mocha drinks." When Tess didn't immediately answer, Bailey growled. "Oh, come on. It's beautiful out, neither of us has to work this afternoon, and we've just gotten out of our last class for the day. How can you say no?"

"I just…" Tess sent her friend an apologetic cringe. "I kind of wanted to head over to the sports complex and see if I could talk to the head football coach for a minute."

"Oh." Bailey let out a groan and rolled her eyes. "So, this is about Jonah…again."

"Sorry, but I—"

"No, no. I get it. I'm out. Hunky football player's in. Let's head over to the sports complex already. You never know, maybe my cowboy will be jogging laps around the track or something." She snorted, obviously not believing her own suggestion.

But Tess brightened anyway. "Really? You'll come with me?" That was so un-Bailey-like.

"Well, obviously, if I ever want to spend any time with you again, I guess I better."

Looping her arm through Bailey's, Tess grinned and skipped them along the sidewalk in a faster walk. "You're the best, do you know that?"

"Yeah, yeah, yeah. I'm a damn saint. Now let's get this over with before I get a cramp just stepping inside that dreaded building of exercise."

It didn't take them long to find Coach Whitely's office in the sports complex, but a crabby secretary made them sit in the outer office for a good half hour before she let them in. And even then, he was talking on the phone so they had to wait another ten minutes, sneaking bored faces at each other until he hung up.

"What's up?" he asked as soon as he disconnected, his tone harried to let them know he didn't want his time wasted. He opened a notebook on his desk and began to leaf through it, not even glancing Tess and Bailey's way.

Tess licked her lips and sat forward. "Jonah Abbott is still in the hospital from the school shooting, and I was wondering if you could take the time to visit—" he looked up at those words, his eyebrow arched, and she gulped and more hesitantly finished "—him."

With an irritated sigh, he closed his notebook. "Let me get this straight. You want to me drop everything to go see some sick kid?"

His smug, arrogant attitude made Tess bristle, but it made Bailey snort. "Oh, whatever. It's not even football season. How busy can you be?"

Coach Whitely seared Bailey with a narrow-eyed glare. "Little girl, this team lost three of its best players. So, yes, I *have* been that busy, trying to figure out a new lineup for next year while I'm setting up memorials for the ones I lost. Too busy to worry about the ones who're doing just fine."

"But he's not *just fine*," Tess jumped in, leaning forward in her seat even more. "Sir, he may never walk again."

That seemed to get the man's attention. "Who're we're talking about again?"

"Jonah," she said. "Jonah Abbott. He's a first string tight end and just beat the state record for —"

He held up a hand to stop her. "Yeah, yeah. I know who Abbott is." Eyebrows furrowing, he muttered, "Well, that's a damn shame." Blowing out a long, harassed breath, he shook his head sadly. "That one might've actually made pro, too. He was a good player. Yet, as I recall, none of his teammates were very fond of him. Not very personable, if you know what I mean."

Actually, Tess had no idea what he meant. Jonah seemed plenty personable to her. To her, he seemed amazing.

She wrinkled her nose. "How does his personality matter? He's one of your players. You should feel some kind of responsibility toward him. He's in room three-twelve at Granton Regional. And he needs someone to visit him. Badly."

The coach merely sniffed. It was more than obvious he didn't like being told what he should and shouldn't do. "As I see it, if he can't walk, he can't play. So, that makes him *not* one of my players, now doesn't it? If you ask me, *some* people get what they deserve."

Tess's mouth fell open as he turned away. What a total bastard.

"What the hell does that mean?" she demanded. Her own voice kind of startled her. She'd never spoken so rudely to someone in authority. "How can you be such a pompous, self-serving son of a —"

Bailey slapped a hand over her mouth before she could say anything else. Smiling stiffly at the douchebag coach, she pulled Tess up to her feet, even as she firmly kept her quiet.

"Thank you for your time, sir. We'll be on our way now."

She didn't release Tess's mouth as she dragged her backward toward the door. Wanting him to know clearly what she thought of him, she lifted her hand, showing him the new sparkling red polish on her middle finger. His eyes narrowed as Bailey shoved Tess into the hall and slammed the door.

Tess scowled and pushed away from her. "What did you do that for?"

Folding her arms over her chest, Bailey answered, "You're welcome."

"For *what?* I was just getting started."

"Oh my God. *Who are you?* You were just about to get us both in trouble. I saved your butt."

"Whatever. That jackass was a complete moron who doesn't know an amazing guy when—"

"Shh." Bailey tapped her lips to hush her. "Something fishy is going on here. No one's visited your boyfriend since he's been in that hospital, and the people you tell he's there don't give a shit. What do you think that means?"

"That the world is full of some truly crappy, insensitive people?"

She opened her mouth to rage on, but Bailey glanced at a picture on the wall and hurried to it, ignoring her. She scanned the four-foot panoramic picture of the entire football team until she murmured, "There." Pointing, she pressed her finger against the chest of one, specific player. "Is that him? Is that your Jonah?"

Squinting, Tess leaned forward until she was staring at a mini-portrait of her fake boyfriend. "Oh my God. How did you…?" She turned slowly to stare at Bailey with wide eyes. "Who is he?" she whispered. Dread chilled her skin.

"That right there is the head bully, the one who always led the race when people were chasing Einstein down the halls. He's the one Paige took to the ground with a single twist of his finger the night you got plastered."

"No." Tess shook her head and took a step away from the large photo, unable to believe it. "No. He couldn't be."

"He is." The sympathetic look on Bailey's face proved she wasn't joking. "I'm sorry, but that is definitely the guy."

"But…" Covering her mouth with both hands, Tess shook her head a little bit more adamantly.

Jonah wasn't a bully. He just wasn't.

"Tess—" When her friend took a step toward her and reached out as if to comfort her, Tess threw up her hands.

"*No!* He's not." No way. Impossible. The Jonah Abbott she knew couldn't be a bully if he tried. And yet her insides twisted with misery even as she denied it. Clenching her teeth, she scowled at Bailey, blaming her for all of this. "Why would you even say that?"

With a sad sigh, Bailey shook her head. "I can't believe you don't remember him at all. Every time we saw Einstein running from a group of people, he was right there, yelling the loudest. He was the worst of them, the—"

"No. Don't even. Did you actually ever see him *hurt* Einstein?"

"Well, no, but none of them physically ever really touched him, Tess, and he still lost his damn mind and shot up half the campus."

"But…no. Not Jonah. You're wrong. You're just—" Tess huffed out a frustrated breath. "You're just jealous."

"*Jealous?*" Bailey propped her hands on her hips. "Of what?"

"Of…of…of all the time I'm spending with him. You don't like that there's someone else important in my life, taking up my time and attention."

"Oh my God." Tossing her hands into the air, Bailey spun in a circle before coming around and muttering, "Will you listen to yourself? *Important?* Shit, Tess, this guy is a complete stranger. You've known him less than a week, and what you know is that he remembers nothing about himself…if that's even true. Hell, if I were him, I'd conveniently lose my memory too."

"Oh, no you did not. Take that back."

"Take what back? That I think he's faking his amnesia? Wouldn't you if you were responsible for twelve people's deaths and I don't know how many—"

"He is *not* responsible! Jonah is completely innocent. He would never…he'd never…" Not sure what else she wanted to argue, she narrowed her eyes and sucked in a long breath. "Who was it last night that said he was perfect for me?"

Bailey growled. "That was before I learned he was the head freaking bully of Granton University. The guy's bad news. He's practically Satan's little brother."

"No, he is a *good* person. And I'm going to prove it."

With that, Tess spun away and marched off. Bailey called after her, but she ignored it. She wanted to be pissed. She wanted to rage and yell at Bailey some more, but somewhere inside her, she knew her buddy was coming from a good place, so she just couldn't release any of her fears and anger on her. But the growing concern in her swelled until she began to tremble.

Knowing Bailey wouldn't like it if she took her car for another Jonah visit, she found the nearest public transportation pick up spot and waited nearly an hour before she found a ride to the hospital. Her emotions had settled themselves enough that she didn't want to scream and cry at the top of her lungs anymore, but she couldn't stop shaking.

No way could she tell Jonah what he used to be. He wasn't that person anymore, and it seemed impossible that he ever could've been.

Besides, lots of people came out of amnesia to turn into someone totally different than they were before. Didn't they? Or was that only in books and movies?

It didn't matter. Jonah wasn't a bully, and she knew that to be true from the core of her being. Breathing out a steadying breath, she stopped by a convenience store to buy a Snickers bar. She'd promised him one, after all. Tucking it snugly into her huge purse, she marched into the hospital to see her boyfriend. Okay, fake boyfriend, but over the past week, it didn't seem so fake anymore.

As soon as she stepped off the elevator and onto the third floor, she turned toward room 312 only to catch sight of someone else entering it. Someone not wearing scrubs.

With a gasp, she jerked to a halt and stared until she recognized the back of Coach Whitely as he opened the door and strolled inside.

He'd come. He'd actually come!

Thrilled she'd somehow managed to convince Jonah's coach to visit him, she took off sprinting and was out of breath by the time she reached the door and yanked it open.

Flying inside with her wild hair streaming behind her, she was full of smiles until she saw who else was already in Jonah's room with him and his coach. With their backs to her, two uniformed officers stood next to Coach Whitely, surrounding Jonah's bed.

"On the date in question, do you remember—"

"What're you doing?" she burst out, making all four males in the room swivel their attention her way. "You can't ask him questions. He has amnesia. He doesn't remember anything."

The coach huffed out a breath and crossed his arms over his chest, rolling his eyes while Jonah grew very pale. Both cops studied her a moment before they turned back to Jonah.

"Is that true, Mr. Abbott? Do you have amnesia?"

Jonah stared at the one who'd asked him the question for an overly long moment before he licked his lips and quietly said, "No. I don't have amnesia. I remember everything."

Tess covered her mouth with one hand and used to other to reach out and catch the wall to support her. She wasn't sure how she remained standing. It felt as if her legs gave out and crumpled to the floor, but somehow she stayed upright.

Jonah didn't look at her even though she willed him to with all her might to send her one glance, any signal: a wink, a smile, an apologetic wince. Something.

But he didn't.

"And who's this?" The other cop asked, motioning to her. "She your girlfriend?"

Still, he didn't look her way. "No," he said, ripping her heart from her chest. "She's just some volunteer they had come in to keep me company. I never met her before I ended up here."

"If you wouldn't mind stepping out into the hallway, then, miss. This is official police business."

She nodded, but felt too numb to move. When Coach Whitely glanced at her with a searing glare, she finally stumbled into reverse and pushed into the hallway. But the door remained open and didn't fall shut. It let her stand there, just out of sight, and listen to everything being said inside.

"Did you know it was *your* gun that was used in the Granton school shooting, Mr. Abbott?"

This time her knees really did give out. Pressing her back to the wall, she sank to the floor in dazed shock as Jonah's rough, choked voice answered with a terse, "Yes. I knew."

She gulped, not certain she could sit here and listen to this, and yet unable to move as she soaked in every word.

"Did you *give* Anthony Morris the gun?"

"What?" Jonah exploded. "No! Hell, no."

"Did you know he *had* your gun?"

"Yeah." From his bitter tone, Tess could picture Jonah glaring at the officer who'd asked the question. "About two seconds before he *aimed* it at me and pulled the trigger. And I have no clue where he found bullets. It wasn't loaded."

Her chin trembled, and a tear splashed against her cheek.

"So, you didn't give it to him, let him borrow it, show it to him at all?"

"No," Jonah snarled. "I didn't even know he knew I had one. I never brought it up to my room. He must've...I don't know...he must heard me talking about it on the phone or something. Or broken into my truck and found it. I don't know! But I had it locked in a case under my back seat inside my locked truck."

"If it was locked away so securely, then how could he have gotten to it?"

"Probably because he was my *roommate*. I hung my keys on a hook by the door. *Both* keys were on the same key fob. He could've taken it any time I wasn't looking."

"What the hell were you doing on campus with a gun anyway?" his coach demanded. "School policy implicitly prohibits firearms on campus. There are signs everywhere—"

"I target shoot," Jonah cut in moodily. "Okay? I compete in target shooting competitions. And I usually keep my gun at a friend's house. But I'd been to a competition recently, and I kept forgetting to drop it off again. I had honesty forgotten it was back there."

"So, you're saying Anthony Morris *stole* your gun?"

It was still so bizarre to hear Einstein called by his real name. Tess had only known him as his nickname until he'd gone crazy. Then she'd heard his real name spread all over the news and that helped ease the shock. She could almost pretend someone she'd never met before had done all that horrific damage.

"He had to have," Jonah said, "because I did not give it to him. I would've never let that kid near it."

A buzzing started in Tess's ears. Huddled on the floor, she hugged herself and tried to digest everything that was happening. But it hit her like a tidal wave. She couldn't believe he had his memory back; he remembered *everything*. Did that mean—?

She closed her eyes and tipped her head back to thump it against the wall behind her. With every kiss and touch and shared intimacy, he'd known she wasn't really his girlfriend. Why had he played along then? Why—?

"Am I going to be arrested for owning that gun?"

His voice floated into the hall, the hint of panic tainting it. She couldn't believe it had been his property that had killed so many, that had been used to try to kill him. What must he be feeling about that? She wished she had a glimpse into his head so bad right then, because it was a complete mystery to her.

"No. You won't be arrested or charged as an accessory or anything. By your wounds, I'd say it's fairly obvious you didn't willingly let him have your gun. Thank you for your time, Mr. Abbott." There was a pause and shuffling of feet before the officer added, "Hope you get better soon."

A second later, the policemen strolled through the opened doorway and walked right past Tess without noticing her. Scrambling to her feet, she popped into Jonah's room before she realized his coach was still inside. Jerking to a halt in the entrance, she watched Coach Whitely's back stiffen as Jonah glanced warily up at him.

"For bringing a firearm onto campus, which directly led to the death of twelve of our students, I came to let you know you're off the team, the university is revoking your scholarship, and you are hereby expelled from Granton University permanently."

His dark eyes bright with a ring of red around them, Jonah stared at his coach for a moment before lowering his gaze. "I understand." He sounded so gruff and broken that Tess's chest tightened with sympathy even as her heart broke from all the lies he'd told her this past week.

The coach turned on his heel, only to pull up short when he caught sight of Tess in the doorway. "And thank you, young lady, for telling us exactly where we could find Mr. Abbott. The police had just contacted me about him right before you showed up."

Jonah jerked his head up to pierce her with a look full of shock and betrayal.

Face flooding with color, she shook her head, horror filling her veins. "But I didn't—"

Coach Whitely strode right past her and was gone as quickly as the police officers had disappeared. Frozen to the core, she risked a wide-eyed glance at Jonah.

"You told them how to find me?" His voice was low and full of accusation.

She closed her eyes for a brief second before she turned the tables and countered, "You have your memory back?"

He ground his jaw and lifted his chin. His hard gaze dared her to contradict him. "Yeah. I do."

Pressing her lips together hard to keep her jaw from trembling with unfulfilled tears, she choked out, "Since when?"

"Since I woke up from a nap right before the second time you visited me. It all came back," he snapped his fingers, "just like that."

"Just like that, hmm?" Fury, betrayal, and pain as she'd never imagined before whiplashed through her. Storming to his bedside, she growled, "How dare you?"

Winding back her hand, she slapped him hard across the cheek, making him jerk his face to the side. The immediate mark in the shape of her palm that remained looked extra red against the white of his hospital sheets, reminding her why he was there and what he'd been through.

Gasping when she realized what she'd just done, she covered her mouth with her hand.

He rotated his jaw, touched his cheek briefly, and slowly looked up at her. "How dare I?" he said in a low voice, his eyes flaring with anger. "How dare *you?* You started this, Contessa. The first words out of your mouth when you stepped into this room were a fucking lie."

"Wha…" She clutched her stomach at his brutal tone. "Okay, fine. I started the first lie. I will admit that. But why didn't you say something to contradict me as soon as you knew?"

"Are you crazy?" he growled. "Some girl I didn't know was coming into my room and claiming to be my *girlfriend.* Trying to get close to me. I had to find out what your ulterior motive was."

"Ulterior motive?" Instantly shaking her head, she said, "But I didn't have any—"

"*Stop lying already!*" Breathing hard after his shout, he shook his head. "I knew who you were. I'd seen you before. With *her*, with Einstein's little protector."

Tess frowned in confusion before it hit her. "Paige? But…but what does she have to do with anything?"

"There's only one thing you could want from me. Revenge."

This made no sense. He was making no sense. Tess shook her head some more. "I don't understand. Revenge for what? I didn't even know who you were before I walked into this room."

"Oh, please. You can drop the innocent act. I can guess exactly why you've been lying to me this entire time. I know what you're thinking, that it's *my* fault all those people were shot and killed. I'm the big bad bully who pushed Einstein over the edge, I provided him with the fucking weapon to do it, and you wanted to see me pay for that."

"That's ridiculous." She stomped her foot and glared at him. "I didn't even know you were the one who led the bullying against him until today. And I sure as hell didn't know about the gun until *just now*."

He looked up at the ceiling and gave a hard laugh. "Well, please excuse me while I don't believe you. Your track record with honesty isn't exactly stellar in my book."

"Oh my God!" She threw her hands into the air, still just as confused and frustrated and enraged and hurt as ever. "I've never done anything to hurt you, Jonah."

"Never?" He glanced at her as if he truly hated her. "What about when you contacted my football coach today so he could come straight to my hospital room to kick me out of school? I'd say that's a pretty decent revenge."

Tess's mouth fell open, momentarily too shocked by his accusation to defend herself.

He snorted. "Or what about…what about coming in here every day and making me think you cared? Pretending like you were the perfect, devoted girlfriend. Yeah. You found a way into my head to attack on a totally different battlefield."

"No." She shook her head. "You're wrong. I do care. And I didn't… I only went to Coach Whitely to tell him where you were so he'd visit you and you wouldn't feel so alone."

"Bull…shit."

She groaned out a growl of irritation. "Why won't you believe me?"

"My God. Why do you think? Because everything you've ever said to me has been a lie."

"Not everything. Not when I opened up my soul and told you all my secrets, even the stuff I can't tell Bailey." Tears filled her lashes. "Not when I kissed you. Oh…God!" She gasped when an idea struck her. "All those times we…and you knew I wasn't your— " She set her hand over her mouth while tears streamed down her cheeks. "You totally took advantage of me."

He flinched and turned his face to the side. She watched him draw in a breath as if he was in physical pain.

But she was experiencing her own misery. "If you honestly thought I did all this just to wreak revenge on you, then why? Why would you kiss me like that? Touch me, flirt with me like you really thought we were—" Her voice choked out on her when she began to remember everything they'd done.

"Oh, God." Poleaxed, she slid her hand down to cradle her stomach, which churned with dread. "Was that your way of paying me back for what you thought I was doing to you? Pay the awkward, shy redhead a little attention to make her think you really meant all that sweet bullshit you said, then crush her fragile ego by admitting it was all a hoax. Was that your way of exacting revenge before you thought I was going to?"

When he just closed his eyes and refused to answer, she gagged on her own horror. "You are an awful, awful person."

Staring at him one last time, she realized how much of a coward he was because he couldn't even open his eyes to let her see his guilt. Pathetic. With a sniff, she turned around and walked from the room.

Chapter Fourteen

Tess returned to campus, but she didn't return to her room. The thought of facing Bailey right now revolted her stomach. Not only had her best friend been right about everything, but she'd been right about *everything*, even the idea of Jonah faking his amnesia.

A dramatic I-told-you-so was more than she could take right now, so she wandered into the food district instead. Feeling wild and defiant, she marched through the center of the walkway, despite all the fear ambushing her, and even entered The Squeeze where Paige worked to order a drink. Thank God, her friend wasn't on duty; she didn't feel like talking. Still needing to face her fears over this place, she then found a bench at the edge of the district, sipped her latte, and thought about all the horrors that had happened within these few blocks.

Would Einstein have gone insane and started a killing spree if he hadn't taken Jonah's gun? Would he have even felt the need if Jonah hadn't harassed him into it? It was impossible to say. He'd always been unhinged. Anything could have triggered it. But Jonah's involvement was so deeply entangled with everything that had happened, she thought she should feel like blaming him. And yet she didn't.

She should probably hate him right now, too, but she couldn't do that either. She'd lied to him just as much as he'd lied to her. They'd both crossed the line. And besides, thinking about how all the motives behind the intimacies he'd shared with her had only been a lie still hurt too much for her to feel the full force of her anger quite yet. She just couldn't believe he'd only been playing along to cast his own revenge for the revenge he mistakenly thought she wanted to get.

Some lies she could handle, but that wasn't one of them. Knowing he'd faked his feelings crushed her.

"Tess?" a hesitant male voice called from a couple yards away, startling her.

Swiping her arm over her face one last time to hide all traces of her crying spree, she looked over to see Logan closing in, concern written on his face.

"Paige and Bailey have been looking everywhere for you. They're pretty worried."

She drew her knees up to her chest to hug them. Focusing her gaze on a stone sculpture of a lion, the Granton mascot, she said, "I'll go back soon."

Logan nodded, but he surprised her by joining her as he eased himself onto the opposite end of the bench. Silently, they sat that way, staring off at the lazy afternoon of the campus around them. Then he let out a breath.

"I did a little research on your friend at the hospital, hoping to help you find some of his acquaintances. But I'm guessing you already know what I found."

She nodded slowly. "I know who his roommate was, and who he used to pick on."

"Yeah," Logan said softly. "I'm sorry. I know you had higher expectations from him."

Wiping at her face and glad to find it dry, she nodded. "I am too. I mean, I didn't even realize I did expect anything from him, but after today…" She shook her head, still keeping her legs tucked up against her chest. "He faked his amnesia."

Logan winced. "Ouch."

"And, oh, my God. I just realized he totally let the truth slip last night. He said, 'When I was a kid,' and then cut himself off. I didn't even catch it because I was so stupid and enamored and…I'm not even sure if I'm allowed to be upset about this. I mean, I lied to him first, right? He was just protecting himself, playing along so he could find out what my ulterior motive might be, because God forbid someone to be nice to him and help him for no other reason than to be nice and helpful. But I get that he didn't know that. Still… Did he really have to do some of the things he did, and say some of the things he said? He made me feel like…"

Pressing a hand to her chest, she choked out a humiliated sob and gritted her teeth as the tears came again.

"Why would he act like he wanted me to keep coming back to see him? Why would he tell me things, such personal things that made me think he cared? Why…why would he be such a total sweetheart to me, with no bullying tendencies whatsoever, and then turn a complete one-eighty, telling me this was all about *revenge?* I don't…I just don't understand. Any of it. It makes no sense. It doesn't fit. I… it can't be true. If only I had one minute inside his head to know what he was thinking, how he was feeling, or why he was doing any of this, I'd just…I don't know. I'm so confused. And hurt. And mad. I'm so fucking mad."

When she turned and focused on Logan's face, she realized how far off the deep end she'd gone. But at least now she could admit she was mad, too, not just hurt.

"And why I am I talking so much to you?" she demanded. "I don't talk to super-hot guys. I'm, like, physically incapable of it. But since meeting Jonah, I can…Dear God, what the hell has he done to me?"

"Well…" Logan scratched a spot behind his ear and cleared his throat. "Okay, I have no idea what happened between you two. But I know a little of what he's done, and I know what he's been through. From my own personal experience, I know doing something that is unforgivably wrong, something that not only affects your own life but the lives of many others, will change you. I have no doubt he is a completely different person now than he was on the day of the shooting. But I'm also pretty sure *he* has no idea who he is, either. If he's anything like I was, he's pretty upset with himself right now. And remorseful, and scared, depressed. Guilty. I'm sure he's full of a lot of uncomfortable emotions he doesn't want to feel. And I bet he's grasping for something to save him, but he's even more afraid to reach for it because he knows he doesn't deserve it."

Glancing at her, Logan smiled softly. "I bet anything his meeting you did help him, until the truth came out. I'm still just guessing here, but I doubt he liked realizing you finally knew all his imperfections.

My biggest fear was always worrying about people finding out what I'd done. Now that he knows that you know, he could be ashamed and pushing you away so he can't see any negative reaction you'll have to the real him. Or maybe he doesn't think he deserves you."

"So, you're saying I should go back and give him another chance?"

With a shrug, Logan sighed. "I'm not saying everyone deserves a second chance, but I do know not everyone throws them away either. Some of us actually appreciate them and work our asses off to justify them."

His words made sense. Out of all the confusion brewing in her head, his common sense felt like a light at the end of a long, black tunnel. She could actually find her way out of the dark now.

"Thank you." Going with the urge claiming her, she sprang forward and threw her arms around him for a hard hug. "You have no idea how much that just helped me."

"Oh, uh…yeah." He patted her back awkwardly. "You're welcome."

He smelled good. Tess took a moment to inhale his spicy male scent. For some reason, it reminded her of Jonah. He had his own unique aroma, and the thought of possibly never smelling it again made her nearly sick to her stomach with anguish. It didn't even matter that she shouldn't want to smell him again. He had used and hurt her. But, God, just one more sniff would be—

No. No, she wasn't going to go there. Returning her attention to Logan, she pulled away to give him a watery smile. "Paige is a lucky girl to have such a wise man."

Logan shook his head. "Actually, it's the other way around. I'm lucky to have her. I'm lucky she gave me a chance when she had no reason to whatsoever. Her forgiveness and acceptance saved me in ways you can't even imagine."

Tess nodded. "I think I understand. I'll definitely think about that." Then she blew out a breath and returned to her side of the bench. "I don't think I've ever heard you talk so much."

With a soft chuckle, Logan sent her an amused sidelong glance. "Ditto."

Logan escorted Tess back to Grammar Hall. They walked in silence until she unlocked the front door and pulled it open. The stairs Einstein used to hide under were the first thing to come into view.

Jonah used to chase him here and throw things at him, or least his group of bullies did. She shook her head, still unable to picture it. Jonah, a bully. It just didn't fit. But neither did the reason why he'd gone along with her lie and acted the part of her amnesiac boyfriend. She'd completely bought into every smile, touch, and sweet thing he'd said to her.

Shivering, she brushed her hands up and down her arms and hurried up the steps to the second floor.

"Paige hates coming in this way, too," Logan said. "I think she avoids it as much as possible and comes in the side and back entrances whenever she can."

"There're so many memories here," Tess agreed. "I don't know how she handles it."

"She's getting help." Logan paused behind her when she stopped at her door. "And she's working through it. I know what he did was awful, and he honestly tried to kill me." He ran a hand over his chest where his bullet wound was still healing under the cloth. "But he stopped himself before hurting Paige. I think that's what's hardest for her to deal with. Somewhere in his deranged little head, he remained her friend. Even though I know she doesn't want to, a part of her still feels bad for him and mourns him. It's hard to accept truly evil people have any kind of good, redeemable qualities in them."

"Or that good people have awful, unforgivable flaws," Tess murmured, wondering which category Jonah belonged to. Was he bad with a little bit of good, or good with a little bit of bad?

"It's easier when things are in stark black and white," Logan said as she opened the door to her room to reveal his girlfriend was inside, trying to calm a frantic Bailey.

"Where the hell have you been?" Bailey stormed forward the grab Tess's arm and haul her into their room. "It's already after supper, and you didn't answer any of the hundred and fifty text messages I sent you. Did you *want* to scare me half to death?"

Tess sighed while Logan went to Paige and drew her into his arms to murmur quietly into her ear. It was hard to watch them together. They had this connection, a connection she thought she'd formed with Jonah.

God, how could she have been so wrong?

Shoulders dragging and spirits drowning, she sent Bailey an apologetic wince. "I'm sorry," was all she found the energy to say.

"*Sorry?* I'm going crazy over here, worried out of my —" Stopping abruptly, Bailey sighed. Rolling her eyes, she folded her arms over her chest. "Well, it's obvious where you went. So…what happened on today's episode of My Fake Amnesiac Boyfriend?"

Tess swallowed and then let it all out. "There is no amnesiac. You were right. He lied about his memory loss. He *was* Einstein's bully. And it was his gun Einstein used to shoot all those people."

When Paige gasped, Logan took her arm and led her away. Tess knew he'd explain the rest to her, so she only had Bailey left to worry about.

But Bailey didn't explode with a series of I-told-you-so's. She stared at Tess with her mouth falling further open by the second. "What?"

Tess nodded, giving her best friend more fuel to start a lecture to end all lectures. "The police were there when I showed up, questioning him about the gun. And so was Coach Whitely. Jonah confessed his memory wasn't lost and told the police Einstein had stolen his gun."

"Holy shit," Bailey whispered.

Tess nodded. "He thinks I lied to him about the whole girlfriend thing to get close enough to exact some kind of revenge on him for bullying Einstein. Since I'm friends with Paige and all. Oh, and he also thinks I told Coach Whitely and the police where he was so he could get into trouble. God, he *did* get into trouble because I *did* tell the coach where he was. Not only did he kick him off the football team but the university expelled him from school completely. And he blames all that on me."

Rubbing her hands up and down the sides of her arms because she was chilled, she kept going. "But the best part. Oh, the best part is he went along with my whole girlfriend lie so he could hurt me. Somehow he figured out stringing me along so he could break my heart was the best way to get back at me for what he thought I was going to do to him. And since I did do what he suspected I would and he did pay me back, I guess that means we're all even now."

"Well…" Bailey blew out a breath, and Tess could see her mind spinning. But all she did was study Tess a couple of seconds before asking, "Are you okay?"

She couldn't imagine ever being okay again, but she nodded and turned away. "I'm fine."

A headache pounded at her temples. She didn't want to deal with this anymore. She just wanted to curl up in her boyfriend's arms, let him kiss it all better again, make silly ridiculous comments, and go searching for happy buttons. Except she didn't have a boyfriend. All she had was lies.

"But I'm tired," she murmured. "Didn't get much sleep last night. I think I'll go to bed."

Bailey didn't mention how it was only six in the evening or how silly she was behaving over some stupid crush she'd had on a fake boyfriend. She just stood there and watched as Tess crawled under her sheets without changing into nightwear and pulled the blankets up to her chin.

She must've willed herself to sleep, because they next thing she knew it was morning. No one had bothered her all night. Too bad she couldn't will away Jonah Abbott's existence. If she'd never met him, maybe none of this would've happened. Maybe she never would've felt so betrayed. But the problem with that was, lie or not, he'd given her some of the most precious memories of her life. She could never will those away.

Chapter Fifteen

When the nurse told Jonah his physical therapist was back and ready to try walking with him, Jonah could only snort out a hallow laugh.

Walking? As if he cared about whether he could ever walk again. As if he cared about *anything*. His life was totally and completely over. His best friend, the only person on earth who could put up with him, was dead. Football and college were both over. His future was shot.

And Tess was gone.

On top of that, there was Einstein. Not only did he have nothing and no one, but everyone hated and blamed him for what had happened with Einstein…with very good reason. Hell, even he blamed himself.

Lying in his bed and waiting for Frenchie to show up and let what little hope he had drown some more, he closed his eyes, wondering what would've happened if only he'd done everything different with his roommate, if only he'd taken that damn gun back to Sean's house the night of the target shoot. Why had he let the freaky kid get to him, why had he fought back every time Einstein had done something to piss him off?

Shit, why had he always fought back when his dad had hit him?

Maybe if he'd just sucked it up and let it all roll off his back, none of this would have happened. He just always had to fucking push back, didn't he? Especially yesterday when Tess had slapped him and yelled at him. He'd yelled back and let her make assumptions when—

"So, you ready for day two of the walking trials?" Frenchie asked, breezing into the room with a big grin, only to pause and glance around. "Where's the redhead today? I liked her."

Jonah's gut clenched. He'd liked her too. More than he should have.

The first day she'd come into his room, claiming to be his girl-friend, he hadn't known any better. The second day, when he did know it wasn't true, he'd played along because he'd wanted it to be true. Sure, he'd been mildly curious what her ulterior motive was, but most of all, he'd just wanted her to stay.

Over the course of the week, however, it had become true. She *had* become his. His girlfriend. His entire life.

That was why he'd confessed to not knowing her to the police. Afraid they might slap an accessory charge on him because of his gun, he hadn't wanted any of that shit to fly in her direction. No way was he going to let her feel any kind of blowback from *his* actions.

He'd already realized she wasn't guilty of the things he'd accused her of doing yesterday, not unless she was the best actress on earth. Every action, word, and breath she'd breathed had told him how genuine and altruistic she was. There was no way she'd made up the girlfriend story as a means to torture him. He still wasn't sure *why* she'd made it up, but no way had she meant anything nefarious by it. And even if she had told his coach where to find him, she couldn't have known it would go down the way it had.

So, why had he accused her of just that?

Because she'd pushed and accused and glared at him like the scum he already knew he was. The pain and betrayal in her stunning blue eyes when she'd asked him when he'd gotten his memory back had sliced into his guilt until he was running from it and lashing back with his own hastily thought up accusation.

But, Jesus, no wonder why he'd been such a great football player. If someone had shoved him on the field, he'd always had to shove back harder.

"Yo, Abbott." Frenchie snapped his fingers in front of Jonah's face, making him blink back to the present. "You check out on me, or what? I asked where your girlfriend was today."

Just hearing that word twisted something inside him. He had no idea how he was going to make it through without her.

Refusing to speak of her, he glanced at his PT. "Do you think I'll ever walk again?" he asked. "If not, I'd rather not even bother with this. There's no point."

Frenchie blinked a few times before he wrinkled his brow as if he considered the question ludicrous. "What're you talking about, man? Of course you'll walk again. The only question is how soon. After being in bed this long, due to the coma and all, it's going to take you longer than it usually would to get back onto your feet. But you'll get there eventually. Guaranteed."

The man seemed so certain of his claim that dizziness swamped Jonah. Five seconds ago, he'd convinced himself he didn't care if he would or wouldn't be able to walk. He didn't want to care about anything. Caring only got your heart broken. But learning that this was a certainty rocked his already unsteady world.

He couldn't quite believe it. After his hopes for everything else had been crushed, why would this one thing actually work out? But maybe...maybe if he could walk out of his hospital one day, he could also find Tess, convince her he wasn't the awful, awful person she thought he was.

"So, there's no question at all? I'll be able to walk again?"

Frenchie chuckled and shook his head. "Why would there be a question? You didn't suffer any spinal problems. I typically have people back on their feet within days of breaking their femur. I know I'm off my game not getting you up and around yet, but trust me, you will walk."

Mouth falling open, Jonah simply gaped at him. "But the nurse said..." Damn, what exactly had the nurse said?

"Said what?" Frenchie demanded, scowling with irritation. "Did someone *tell* you you wouldn't be able to walk again?"

"Well, no. Not in those words, but..." He glanced around for Tess to corroborate his story and remember exactly what the nurse had said before he remembered she was gone. Shit.

Frenchie gave an irritated sigh. "I bet this nurse, whoever she was, implied you might not be capable of walking to intimidate you into not trying it by yourself, probably so you wouldn't end up *hurting* yourself."

Jonah snorted and shook his head. "Figures," he muttered. That sounded exactly like something one of his nurses would do.

An hour after Frenchie left, Jonah stretched his toes, actually excited about the burning muscles in his legs. As soon as he was on his feet again, it'd only be days before they released him from this place. Days before he could find Tess and straighten this whole mess out.

Feeling slightly human and glad he had street clothes on instead of his hospital gown, he stared down the length of the bed at his toes, wiggling them through his socks. The sheets were tangled uncomfortably under his butt, but he didn't care. He'd taken ten steps today. Ten unbelievably amazing steps.

He was ten steps closer to getting out of here. Ten steps closer to finding Tess.

"So, I see you're a superstar," his least favorite nurse announced as she carried his supper tray into the room and thumped it ungracefully onto the rolling table beside his bed.

Jonah looked up from his toes, still riding the eager train. He thought she was actually going to praise him for his awesome walking skills until he saw her face. Uneasy about the smug smirk she flashed, he asked, "What do you mean?"

Pointing to the muted television on his wall, she snickered. "You made the national news."

Glancing up, he jerked back in his bed when he saw a photo of his football picture on the screen. "What the hell?" He scrambled for the volume buttons by his bed and turned up the sound just as the CNN reporter announced, "Police revealed the name of the gun owner today. Jonah Abbott, football linebacker and roommate to Anthony Morris, let the sixteen-year-old borrow his semi-automatic weapon—"

"*What?*" Jonah exploded. "I did *not* let him…Oh, Jesus." He brought his hands to his head and turned his beseeching gaze to the leering nurse. "That's bullshit. They're lying. I didn't let him anywhere near my Browning." And what was up with them calling it a *semi-automatic weapon* like it was some kind of assault rifle? It had been his freaking *deer-hunting* gun. Christ.

Looking too evilly gleeful that Jonah's reputation was being ripped to shreds on national television, the nurse merely turned away and strolled from the room, whistling.

"I'm not even a linebacker," he called after. "I'm a God damn tight end."

But she didn't seem to care. She wanted to believe the worst of him. And she obviously wasn't the only one. The news report recaptured his attention when they showed a clip of an interview with one of his teammates out on the football field, who actually *was* a linebacker.

"So, you knew Jonah Abbott?"

Benji Harmon gave a half-assed shrug. "Yeah, sure. I mean, we played ball together. I knew him just as well as anyone else."

Jonah rolled his eyes and snorted. He couldn't remember saying one word to this douchebag.

"He was kind of jerk. Thought he was better than the rest of us and kept to himself. And he picked on Einstein more than anyone I know. I heard he was still in the hospital from being shot during the massacre. If you ask me, I think he should've been on the fatality list."

Dry eyes burning, Jonah could only stare as the scene cut away from Harmon and returned to two reporters sitting at a desk.

"Shot with his own gun." The woman reporter shook her head and turned to the man. "Well, if that isn't justice, I don't know what is. Bob?"

Then the reporters suddenly sported bright smiles like they'd clicked an "on" switch, moving on callously to the next story, and Jonah muted the volume. But he could still see the two of them; they'd been pleased to hear that he'd gotten what he deserved.

This changed everything.

Jonah tore his gaze away. He tried to swallow, but it hurt, so he grabbed his water and took a sip through the straw to realize it was empty. The steam from his supper tray wafted up and made him physically nauseated from the smell.

Closing his eyes, he concentrated on breathing in and out through his mouth and not having a panic attack. But his chest heaved like crazy. When he heard footsteps as someone entered his room, he shook his head, unable to take anything else. He'd go insane, he'd freaking lose his mind, if he had to deal with one more problem right now.

A throat cleared, and he stole a couple of extra seconds, ignoring it, before he opened his eyes and lifted his face. "Oh…Jesus."

"Not quite." The girl next to his bed merely narrowed her eyes and set her hands on her hips. "You don't know me. My name's — "

"Bailey," he answered for her. He remembered seeing her with Tess the few times he'd ever seen Tess. The short, straight, multicolored locks that swung around her face and brushed the tops of her shoulders were almost as memorable as Tess's flaming red hair. "I know who you are."

That seemed to throw her off her game. She shifted, readjusting her pissed-off stance, and pinched her mouth up even tighter. "Then you know why I'm here."

"To put me out of my misery?" he asked hopefully.

She blinked. "What? No. I mean, *I wish*, but..." Frowning at him, she demanded, "What the hell is wrong with you? Your face is turning freaking purple."

"Panic...attack," he gasped, clutching his chest, and he tried to regulate his breathing, holding it for five seconds and then releasing. "Maybe a heart attack," he added on the next breath. "Hope it's a heart attack." Anything to stop this agony would be welcome.

"Well, stop it," Bailey demanded. "You're skeeving me out."

Gritting his teeth, he sent her a look of pure frustration. "I'm *trying*."

"Oh, my God," she muttered. "I came in here to chew ass, not play 'Kumbaya' to some asshole who hurt my best friend. Now *calm down*."

Even though it killed him to hear how hurt Tess was, hurt enough to send this girl storming into his room, he barked out a short laugh. "Jesus, no wonder she likes you so much. You can be as sour and sarcastic as — " When he realized he was about to say Sean's name, his eyes flooded with tears.

There was another issue he'd been refusing to think about. But he couldn't repress his sorrow any longer. His best friend on earth was gone, and it was his fault.

He hated crying in front of others, but after hearing those reporters on national news say he deserved what had happened to him, he was already in tatters. He shouldn't care if someone saw him sob. But he covered his face with his hands anyway, hiding his scorching hot cheeks as best as he could.

"How bad off is she?" he managed to ask.

He lowered his hands enough to see Bailey's mouth open and close a few times before she quietly answered. "She's devastated."

Another sob hurled its way up his throat. He sniffed back a couple tears and wiped at his face.

"Why did you push her away?" Bailey asked, her tone almost calm.

"What?" he blinked at her and frowned. "I didn't. She's the one who stormed off. And it wasn't like I could go chasing after her, now, could I?"

"Why the hell did you accuse her of all that revenge bullshit, then? If you've spent five minutes with Tess, then you know—"

"I know." He groaned and ran his hands through his hair as he closed his eyes, regretting pretty much every part of yesterday's conversation. "I messed up, okay? When she got mad, I got mad right back. I had to accuse her of *something* when she looked at me like I was...Jesus, I just wanted her to stop and think she wasn't completely innocent either. But compared to me, she was, and I should've just...I should've been honest."

"So...you never thought she purposely wanted to destroy you?"

With a snort, he shook his head. "Tess Simpson isn't capable of that kind of malice."

"Then why did you let her keep lying all this week? She *hates* to lie!"

"Why do you think? I liked the lie. I liked pretending I could be someone completely new, starting from fresh. I liked her being...mine."

Bailey let out a big, frustrated sigh and jerked her hands to her hips again. "Christ. You really do care about her, don't you?"

He nodded as he glanced away. "And if I was a completely different, better person who was worthy of her, I'd fight to get her back, too."

"Oh, there's no *if* to that statement, buddy. You *will* fight to get her back. In fact, I'm going back to campus right now, grabbing her ass, and dragging her back here so you can apologize and grovel and explain to her what an idiot you are."

"You can't." When she opened her mouth to argue, he motioned toward the television as it showed his picture again. "Just look."

Bailey glanced up and gasped. "What...? Why are you on CNN? Holy Jesus, you're on freaking CNN."

"Yeah. They know it was my gun. They know I bullied Einstein. And they all think it's only fitting I should be dead right now. I'm not just the most-hated guy in Granton anymore. It's spread nation-wide."

Swerving around with a look of disbelief, Bailey just gaped at him until he couldn't take it any longer.

"I know I deserved to be shot," he muttered. "I'm fully aware I should be dead right now. People that didn't even *know* him were killed. Completely innocent people died because I helped create a monster, and I'm still alive in this hospital bed, unworthy of my life. I know! You think that doesn't bother me every hour of every day?"

She opened her mouth but no words came out. When she closed her lips again, Jonah pressed his hand to his chest.

"I don't know how to deal with this," he confessed. "I don't how to say sorry and have it actually make a difference. I'm so fucked up right now, my life is basically over, and the only friend I ever had is dead, killed by Einstein. Now everyone in America hates me and thinks I should be dead too. No way in hell do I want Tess involved in any of that. And you *know* she would be. You know her better than anyone. She's so giving and big-hearted, if I apologized and managed to make up with her, she'd try to stand by me through all this. But it'd only drag her down too."

"Well, fudge," Bailey muttered. "I was all fired up to come in here and blast you a new one, tell you you had it all wrong, she didn't lie to you to get any kind of revenge. She honest-to-God just wanted to help the poor amnesiac in room three-twelve feel like he wasn't alone for one night. I was going to force you to talk to her."

"And now you see why I can't. I can't let her back in."

"Actually, Tess is a big girl and can decide with her own mind whether she thinks being with you is worth the risk. You should not get to make that decision for her."

Jonah held his breath and waited for her to reveal what she was going to do about it. When she didn't, he asked, "So...you're going to tell her I didn't really want her to go, then? You're going to let her know I actually do care?"

"Jesus, no!" Bailey exploded. "Are you insane? You're a fucked up mess, and everyone in America hates you and wants you dead. I'm not letting my best friend get within fifty miles of that."

He blinked, utterly confused. "But you just said—"

"Hey, just because you're wrong and shouldn't make a decision like this for her doesn't mean I don't agree with you. You need to straighten your shit out before you go anywhere near my best friend again."

His derisive laugh was harsh and bitter. "Yeah, if I could only figure out how to do that."

Bailey sighed again, scowling hard. "If you look at it from Tess's optimistic point of view, you'd see you can only go up from here. Right? So, stop whining over everything you lost. It's gone. Life sucks, and you have to start over from scratch, blah, blah, blah. I get it. But Tess isn't going to stop hurting until you fix yourself. So, find a way to get your act together, and then—only then—should you look up my girl again. Got it?"

That was not what he was expecting her to say at all. He'd been ready for her to warn him away from Tess forever. But to get a partial blessing from *the* best friend gave him a smidgeon of hope. "Why are you helping me?"

"Excuse me? Let's get one thing clear. I'm *not* helping you." She sent him a dirty look. "Why would I help *you?* I don't even know you. And what I do know, I don't like. To me, you're just that douchebag who's breaking my best friend's heart. This is all for Tess. Only Tess. And *she* likes you. She can open up to you as she's never opened up to any guy. I don't know what she was smoking when she chose you, but she did. I'm just here to make you pull your head out of your idiot ass and get my friend the guy she chose."

The crazy ball of hope in his chest that just wouldn't die stirred from the depths where he was so sure it had shriveled up into nothing. It pounded through his heartbeat until he heard it thrumming through his ears. Suddenly, he had something left to live for.

Nodding solemnly at Tess's unorthodox friend, he said, "I'll see what I can do."

Chapter Sixteen

A week passed. And then another. Tess didn't return to the hospital, not even for volunteer duty. Bailey called for them to say they wouldn't be in for their Sunday shifts any longer.

The days dragged on, and classes resumed. Tess went to each course lecture, continuing her regular routine…without any contact with a certain lying, deceiving, heartless gunshot victim. And on the weekends, Bailey drove them back to their hometown as she did every Friday, where they spent Saturdays and Sundays with their families.

Though her two older twin brothers, Marc and Eddy, still lived at home with her father, Tess rarely saw them anymore. They each worked odd shifts at the power plant near their farmstead and were usually asleep when she was awake.

But she did spend mealtimes with her dad. He took care of the cattle and came in whenever she texted him that she had lunch ready. She wasn't sure who cooked while she was away at school during the week, but it looked as if her father was gaining a little weight, so he must be finding food somewhere.

On the second weekend after everything fell apart with Jonah, her dad seated himself across from her at the family table in the kitchen, and they started a quiet meal together. He glanced over at her and finally noticed something was up with his only daughter because he frowned thoughtfully.

"You doing okay over there, little sparrow? Looking a little tired around the eyes this weekend."

He'd called her little sparrow for as long as she could remember. Their special time together had always been bird watching and identifying each type by song and appearance. Since Tess had always been so shy growing up and sparrows were typically social birds, he'd once told her—so she'd stop worrying that she'd be a public misfit—that one day, she'd spread her wings and turn into a sparrow.

Thinking about the origin of that nickname and how Jonah had managed to pull out the sparrow in her, then remembering how it had all been a lie, she grew even more depressed.

"I'm fine," she said, poking at the fake mashed potatoes she'd made from a box. At least the corn on the cob was real. A couple of Bailey's brothers had picked it last summer and bagged it for Tess's family to freeze. She lifted the corn and took a bite, but she realized she wasn't very hungry.

"Ever decide on a major?" her father asked.

She sighed, even more depressed about that. She just couldn't picture anything in her future. It looked like a miserable, gray blob. "No," she mumbled.

"Well." Her dad let out his own heart-felt sigh. "My shoulder's been bothering me again. After lunch, do you think you could rub it like you always do? I swear, no one works out a knotted muscle kink like my little sparrow."

She smiled softly. "Sure, Dad. I'd love to."

He didn't ask her any more about her troubles. He'd never been the type to push; he'd always let her go to him whenever she was ready to talk. But she didn't know what to say about this. So, when Bailey drove up her lane to pick her up Sunday afternoon and return them to Granton, she simply hugged him goodbye and climbed into the passenger seat of Bailey's car.

"Ready to return to hell?" Bailey asked.

"As I'll ever be." Tess pulled her seatbelt on and stared stonily out the front window. It only took five minutes of silence for her best friend to snap.

"Okay, enough of this. I'm sorry, all right? I'm sorry I love you and wanted to see you happy and protected and away from that asshole liar. He was and still is bad news. But I'm sorry it hurts you this way. I really am."

With a sigh, Tess closed her eyes. "I don't know why you're apologizing. None of this was your fault. You're the one who warned me away from him."

Bailey bit her lip, not looking certain about that. Then she hesitantly asked, "So...we're good?"

"Of course we're good. Why would we not be good?"

Blowing out a relieved breath, Bailey nodded quickly and said, "No reason." She began to talk then, about school and people around campus. About boring mundane things Tess listened to with only half an ear.

Inside, something was just...off. It was as if she was going through the motions of her life, but she wasn't really living it. All through classes on Monday, she sat and wrote notes, outlining the major points all her teachers emphasized, but she didn't really digest them.

When she walked down to supper with Bailey in the evenings, she heard the words her friend said and responded accordingly, but she still had no clue what their conversations were about. And as she ate, she rarely tasted the food. She just chewed and swallowed, eating enough to keep anyone from questioning her appetite.

Her numbness was still afflicting her when they stepped out of Gibson Hall and another countless supper together on the third week after meeting and losing Jonah Abbott. They'd no sooner taken two steps back to their dorm, than Bailey screamed, "*Cowboy!*" and took off sprinting across campus.

Startled from her funk, Tess gaped after her until she caught a glimpse of a white cowboy hat in the distance. Seeing her best friend race straight toward it, she kicked herself into gear, and took off after them.

Five minutes later, she finally caught up to a cursing, scowling Bailey who was glancing in a circle all around her. "I can't believe we lost him. I swear, if I hadn't seen him with my own eyes, I'd say this guy was a freaking figment of my imagination. I mean, you saw him too, right?" When Tess nodded, she growled. "How the hell does he just vanish like that?"

Still breathing hard from her run, Tess gave her a sympathetic pat on the back. "He can't escape us forever. Maybe we'll catch him next time."

Bailey didn't seem to want to give up and wait for a next time, though. She wanted to find him now. "I didn't even see which building he went into. Did you see?"

"No. Sorry."

"It must've been Hanley or Overmore."

"Or Echles," Tess put in, not so helpfully. When Bailey scowled at her, she shrugged. "What? It was also close to where we lost him."

"Damn it," Bailey muttered under her breath. "I'm beginning to think meeting this guy is not meant to be."

"Maybe he's just not meant for you *quite yet*," Tess said, thinking about Jonah, unable to stop wondering if they'd only met under different circumstances at a completely different time in their lives, would it have ended so awfully. Her throat went dry until it burned.

Damn him. When was she ever going to get over her stupid infatuation with a freaking liar?

"Hey, what's going on over there?" At Bailey's question, Tess followed the direction of her curious gaze until she saw an ambulance parked at the end of the block, right in front of their dorm building, where a crowd had gathering on the lawn around the main entrance.

"This can't be good." Grabbing Bailey's hand, Tess held on for dear life. "I hope Paige is okay."

"*Paige?*" Bailey sent her a brief incredulous glance. Tess shrugged because Paige was the first person, after Bailey, she'd worry about if something went wrong. And since Bailey was right here, her next worry went to Paige.

Face contorting into concern, Bailey took off running, dragging Tess along with her because they still had a death grip on each other's hands.

"What's going on?" Bailey demanded as soon as they reached the fringes of the crowd. Tess hopped up and down to see over all the people, but she barely caught a glimpse of half a dozen police officers barricading the front doors.

"They're not letting us in," someone answered. And then a murmured word whispered across the sea of people.

Suicide.

"Someone committed suicide?" Tess choked out. "In *our* building?"

She gaped at Bailey, who grimaced and patted her hand. "It might be something else."

But the word swept by again, the rumor gaining volume.

"Who would commit suicide?" Bailey asked, sounding completely perplexed. "Hasn't there already been enough death on this campus to last a lifetime?"

Tess let out a moan, one-third frustration and two-thirds pure fear. "Why does everything have to happen at *our* dormitory? Next year, we're renting an apartment off campus. That's all there is to it."

"Shit. Here they come." Bailey pulled Tess back as if to shield her from the view. But suddenly there were no more tall people standing in her way to block the entrance.

Two officers opened the door, and three EMTs rolled a gurney out into the bright day. A white sheet covered it, displaying the distinct outline of a body underneath.

"God." Bailey winced as she kept her focus on the stretcher. "Why didn't they put it in a body bag? It's not like we can't tell someone is dead under there."

"Bailey," Tess hissed in warning. "That dead body might have friends close by."

"Does anyone know who it is?" More people asked, but no one had a clue. Until the EMTs hit a crack in the sidewalk, jostling the stretcher. A limp arm dropped off one side and half the crowd screamed out startled yelps. Tess was one of them.

Covering her mouth, she stared at the dangling limb, or rather at the colorful tattoo of the Roadrunner on its forearm. Nausea welled in her esophagus. "Bailey," she choked out. "Oh, my God. It's that one guy."

"What one guy?"

"The *one!* The bully guy who was being harassed last month in front of the Ferdinand Hall. That's his tattoo."

"Oh, shit." Bailey's eyes were huge as she stared at the limp arm. "Damn," she breathed turned back to Tess. "The guilt must've been too much for him to handle."

Guilt? Tess blinked and stared back at Bailey as Logan's words echoed through her head.

If he's anything like I was, he's pretty upset with himself right now. And remorseful, and scared, depressed. Guilty. I'm sure he's full of a lot of uncomfortable emotions he doesn't want to feel. And I bet he's grasping for something to save him.

"No," she whispered.

You have no idea how much your visits help me, Jonah had once told her.

He'd been looking for someone to save him from the pain and guilt. And she'd walked out of his life and left him alone and abandoned. So, what was to stop him from doing exactly as the Roadrunner had done?

"Oh, God, no." She whirled around and took off, tearing toward the parking lot.

"Hey!" Bailey called after her. "Where're you going? *Tess!*"

But Tess didn't stop until she found Bailey's car and realized it was locked. Panic was thwarting all her thinking skills. She should've already known it would be locked and the keys would be with her friend. She spun back to find said Bailey when she jogged up, holding her side and panting like crazy.

"Too. Much. Running." She bent over and rested her hands on her knees as she sucked in oxygen.

"I need your keys. *Now.*"

"And where…do you think…you're going?"

"Remember what you said to me the day that bully was harassed for picking on Einstein?" Yeah, Tess just said *that name*. But at the moment, she was too panicked to care about bad juju or anything else. Jonah's life was in danger. "You said, 'at least he wasn't the head bully.'"

Bailey's eyes widened.

Tess shivered and hugged myself. "What if Jonah hurts himself?" She may want to hate him for using her and taking liberties with her feelings and her body, but no matter how much she could wish for a thing, it didn't automatically turn off her true feelings. And her true feelings didn't want to see Jonah hurt.

Bailey straightened, held up a finger to ask for a second to catch her breath. "I'm driving."

For once, Tess was glad her buddy drove like a madwoman. They made it to the hospital in record time. She didn't even wait until Bailey had thrown the car into park. As soon as it came close enough to a stop, Tess threw open the door and leapt out. She ran all the way to the front entrance and took the stairs because waiting for the elevator was more than she could handle.

The door to his room was closed, but she pushed her way in and was nearly to his bed before she realized it was empty. Tess skidded to a halt and stared at the spot where she was used to seeing him. Why wasn't he in his bed?

She was still frozen in the middle of his room, gaping at his stripped hospital mattress when a breathless Bailey blew into the room behind her. "Damn. I had no idea you could run so...Hey, where is he?"

Tess shook her numb head. "I...I don't know." She turned to look at her friend, and seeing Bailey's thoughts mirror her own worry made Tess freak. "Oh, God."

"Excuse me, ladies." A nurse poked her head into the open doorway of 312. "But this room had just been sterilized. I need you both to—"

"What happened to him?" Bailey asked, pointing toward the empty bed. "Where's Jonah, the patient who was in this room?"

The nurse blinked as if she didn't understand the question. Then she simply said, "He's gone."

Tess whimpered. *Gone?* When her knees gave out, Bailey lurched forward to catch her. The two clutched each other as a wide-eyed Tess whispered, "Gone?"

Bailey scowled over at the nurse while she propped Tess back onto her feet. "When you say gone, you mean...?"

Keeping up with the whole clueless expression she was perfecting, the nurse scratched her hair. "I mean gone, as in gone. He checked out this morning."

Tess's fingers gripped Bailey's arm harder.

"And by checked out, you mean released, right?" Bailey pressed. "He was free to leave the grounds? Not that he...died or anything."

"Why would he be dead?"

"Oh, my God, lady. It's a hospital! People die here. And he was shot three freaking times. Why do you think we were worried he might be dead?"

"Well, you don't have to get snippety with me, young lady. If you didn't know where your friend was, you should've kept better track of him. Now please get out of this room. We're already going to have to re-sterilize for the next patient because *you two* barged in."

"Where did he go? What time did he leave?" Bailey asked as she gently took Tess's arm and led her from the room. "Do you know how we can find him?"

Sending them both a bitter smile, the nurse said, "I don't know, and if I did, I still couldn't tell you."

"Let's go," Tess said, tugging on Bailey. She'd learned everything she was going to learn here. Relieved Jonah had been alive the last time the nurse had seen him and glad he'd been well enough to be released from the hospital, she started toward the elevator at a slow, sluggish pace.

"We'll find him," Bailey assured her as she pushed the button for the doors to open. "I'm sure — "

"No." Tess felt hollow as she shook her head. They wouldn't find him. Because they wouldn't even look. If he'd wanted anything to do with her, he knew how to find her. "He's gone, Bailey. He doesn't want to be found."

And he didn't want anything to do with her.

Chapter Seventeen

Jonah sat on his hospital bed, his feet flat against the floor as his fingers toyed with the cloth of his blue jeans. The nurses had bought him one more outfit to wear and had even asked him his size beforehand this time. But he must've lost weight because the shirt and pants fit him too loosely.

He didn't care, though. Today, he was being released from the hospital.

Tapping his new shoes — because the police had even taken the shoes he'd been wearing during the shooting as evidence — against the tile, he waited anxiously for the doctor to come tell him he could leave.

The woman in magenta scrubs who breezed into his room, however, was not his doctor. In her early to mid-thirties, she wore her pale blond hair pulled up tight in a perky ponytail. And she was a complete stranger.

But she smiled at him as if they were great friends. "Hello, Jonah." Then she paused with a slight frown. "It's Jonah, right?"

"Yeah," he said cautiously. "Who're you? You're not one of my nurses." After being here for as long as he had, he'd gotten to know who each and every nurse on this floor was. And none of them had ever smiled at him the way she was.

"No, I'm not. I actually work on a different floor." She held out her hand for a friendly shake. "My name is Samantha. I was sent here by the friend of a friend…" Then she frowned and shook her head, looking a little confused. "I think." Lifting her finger as if she needed to revise what she'd just said, she added, "Maybe it was a friend of a friend of a friend. I can't remember how far back the friend list went, but anyway, that's beside the point, isn't it?"

Jonah blinked. "Um…"

She sighed. "I'm sorry. I know I'm confusing you. And here I came to help, not confuse you more."

"Help?" He wrinkled his nose. "Help with what?"

"Oh, right." She covered her mouth as she let out an embarrassed laugh. "Outside my day job, my specialty is grief counseling. But I'm kind of kickass because I can actually help people with all sorts of emotional problems. Not just grief."

Licking his lips as a tremble of panic flittered across the back of his neck, he eyed the strange woman warily. "Who told you I had grief?"

With a secretive smile, she shook her head and waved her index finger at him. "Uh, uh, uh," she cooed in a warning kind of voice. "That's not what's important. The true question that needs to be answered, Mr. Jonah, is whether or not you're having trouble dealing with your grief."

Jonah stared at her a moment, looking deep into her clear blue eyes. Christ, why did she have to have blue eyes? Just like Tess's. They were so open and honest too, as if they held no censor or condemnation. They just wanted to help him.

He swallowed down the ball in his throat and gave a quiet nod. You could definitely say he was having trouble dealing.

"My best friend died in the shooting," he whispered, his voice gruff and raspy.

Samantha reached out and covered both his hands with both of hers. Her fingers were warm, and that look in her eyes was full of the same warmth and compassion Tess had looked at him with.

"Then I can help you. And I will. Whenever you're ready to talk, call me at this number." She let go of his hand to pull a bright yellow business card with a red smiley face on it from her scrubs pocket and held it out. "Just call, and I'll be there. You don't have to go through this alone. And I understand. I truly do. I lost my husband recently, and it was like losing a part of myself. It's not easy to get over this, but eventually you *can* pull through."

His eyes went moist. Jonah blinked repeatedly to dry them as he nodded his understanding. He slowly took the card from her, and the smile she gave him was so sweet and honest, he was once again reminded of Tess.

"Okay," he choked out. His fingers closed around her business card, holding onto it for dear life.

Samantha nodded and patted his hand. "I'll be waiting. Now, if you'll excuse me, I better check into my shift down in the E.R. Talk to you soon."

She was gone about as quickly as she'd come, her bright pink outfit disappearing from the room before he could say anything else. Wondering if she'd even been real, he glanced down at his hand and opened his fingers to read the proof of her existence off the card in his palm.

He was still a little discombobulated from his surprise visitor when his doctor entered the room. "You ready to get out of here, partner?"

Jonah lifted his face and took in the wheelchair a nurse was wheeling in behind his doctor. With a single nod, he murmured, "Yeah. I guess."

"Great." Still beaming as if happy for him, the doctor glanced at his clipboard. "Well, your release papers are signed, and since you said no one was coming to pick you up, we made arrangements for transportation. There's a cab waiting outside for you. You're a free man."

Joy. Jonah knew he should be happy, relieved, ecstatic. But he just couldn't summon the emotion. He had nothing, nowhere to go, and no future ahead of him.

He could walk, however. Pushing gingerly to his feet, he tucked his new crutches under his armpits and concentrated on holding himself upright before blowing out a breath and glancing at the doctor. His bad leg twinged, and he hobbled like a crippled old man, but by God, he was walking.

"Except you have to take the wheelchair to the front door. Sorry." The doctor motioned to the chair just behind him. "Hospital rules."

Hating the sight of that chair, Jonah rolled his eyes but limped toward it and eased himself down.

He took his one cab ride back to the university. A college representative had shown up last week to let him know they'd removed his things from his dorm room and boxed them up to keep them in storage until he could get out of the hospital. Jonah hoped he could find the keys to his truck in one of those boxes. And he really hoped the bank hadn't repossessed his beloved set of wheels because he was behind on his payment after his lovely stay at Granton Regional.

Just thinking about everything he needed to do to get his life back in order again gave him a headache.

An hour later, he'd found his favorite ball cap and slid it on, but he had no idea where his keys were. He'd left them on the hook by the doorway that last morning before he'd walked down to meet Sean for lunch in the food district. What if they were still there? Or... shit. What if they'd been packed away with Einstein's things? The hook had been on the kid's side of the room. Feeling a little sick to his stomach over that idea and weary from balancing all his weight on his crutches, he sat down on the dusty floor to collect himself.

He didn't like thinking about his things getting stored away with Einstein's. He didn't want to ever think of that boy ever again. But he knew there was no way in hell was that going to happen. Parts of both of their lives were now and forever more entwined together, a thought which didn't help the roiling in his stomach at all.

Refusing to believe his truck keys were not with his things, he stood up, limped back to the five boxes he hadn't gone through yet, and started searching with renewed determination. If he didn't find them after going through the last box, he'd just start over and look again.

But luck—or at least a small portion of luck—was on his side when he opened the third to last box and gleaming metal sparkled up at him. He almost wept as he snagged them to his chest and stole a minute to calm his rapid breathing.

He was doing that too much lately, getting so overwrought and emotional he nearly sent himself into a panic attack. Wondering if that woman, Samantha, could honestly help him with that, he dug up a warm Granton U sweatshirt, plus another pair of clothes. He stuffed them into his book bag, hoping that would keep him until he was able to get back and pick up everything else. After slinging the pack onto his back and pocketing his keys, he adjusted his crutches and limped away.

Sweat coated his face from the strain he'd already put on himself, and that worried him. All he'd done was look through a few boxes. Why did he feel so exhausted? Who cared if he'd only been released from the hospital a couple hours ago? He was heartier than this. He should be able to handle simply being upright for a while.

But he knew he didn't have much longer to go before he dropped.

His cell phone was one thing he hadn't found. Had he had it on him when he'd been shot or had he left it in his dorm room? Didn't matter. He hobbled along, not really caring because he didn't have anyone to call anyway.

Anxiety raced over his skin as he started down the block toward the parking lot where his truck had last been sitting. He'd have to walk right by Grammar Hall. Was Tess in class right now, or might she be in her room? He lifted his face to their shared dormitory and instead saw the crowd gathered outside the front doors. Police cars and ambulances with their lights flashing had him picking up his pace and peering around shoulders just as they wheeled a stretcher out the front doors.

Panic seized. Oh, Jesus. Who was under the sheet? If Tess—

When the attendants bumped into a rut in the sidewalk, a limp hand slid off the side to dangle lifelessly. Jonah nearly threw up. It wasn't Tess's arm, thank God, but he did know whose it was. He'd played ball with Jenner Treymore. Trey had been one of the people who'd always joined in when Einstein was being tortured. He had liked to hold the kid's head down against the floor and literally force him to kiss the ground.

As the word suicide floated past him, Jonah knew exactly why Trey had done himself in. Guilt was a mighty unbearable thing to carry. Jonah tucked his head down, hoping his hat concealed enough of his face. What would people say if they recognized him in the crowd? Would they wonder why he hadn't killed himself yet?

What the hell had he been thinking, coming here? He'd just been on national television as the only person alive left to blame for what had been done to this campus. No one would appreciate seeing him. He tried to back out of the crowd so he could find his truck and escape, but the horde around him seemed to thicken until he couldn't breathe, and panic laced his veins.

He wasn't sure how long he was jostled around among the other students, and no one seemed to care he was lame. The police waved to herd of people away, but the gawkers moved like molasses. Someone bumped into one of his crutches, and he nearly went down. He accidently put weight down on his leg to catch himself, which made his vision momentarily black out. Gritting his teeth, he repositioned and kept shuffling along with the flow, his head still lowered so no one would notice him.

Once he found a break in the crowd, he shimmied through and hobbled toward the parking lot. His good leg trembled from overuse, and his shirt was soaked with sweat.

He tumbled into the driver's seat as soon as he reached his truck. After catching his breath, he couldn't help himself; he had to check. He twisted in his seat without killing himself, biting back the pain, and lifted the rear seat only to blink repeatedly at the small padlock keeping his gun case closed. It didn't look as if anyone had tampered with it. Maybe…just maybe everyone was mistaken.

Praying for all he was worth, he unlocked the case and slowly lifted it, holding his breath, almost expecting to see his gun inside. If only this had all been a bad dream. But the padded interior was empty.

Sucking in a breath, he glanced away and slapped the case closed.

"Jesus," he muttered.

He wiped beading sweat off his brow and put the seat back down. After starting the engine, he sat there, wondering what to do now and refusing to think about what horrible things someone had used his beloved gun to accomplish.

Tess was the only person he wanted to see. God, he ached for even a glimpse of her smile, the echo of her laughter, a hint of her flowery scent. He glanced toward Grammar Hall, but he was nowhere near the man she deserved. He might be free from the hospital, but he didn't feel free at all. He felt trapped in a life that seemed to be spiraling straight over the edge of a rocky cliff. If Sean were still alive—

But, fuck, Sean was gone. And Einstein had used Jonah's property to take him away.

He fisted his hand and pounded the steering wheel before he brought his knuckles to his mouth and sucked in a noisy sob.

"Fuck." He needed to get out of here, off campus and away from these people before someone recognized him and made everything worse.

Even though his best friend was gone, there was still only one place he could think to go. Sean had offered to let him live at his apartment when he'd gotten it, but it'd only had one bedroom, so he would've had to bunk on the couch. Besides, it'd been cheaper for Jonah to stay in the dorms on his football scholarship. Now, he wished he hadn't said no.

Hoping no one had cleaned out Sean's place yet, but knowing no one probably had—Sean had come from the same trailer park as he had and had left behind the same miserable roots—Jonah found his best friend's key under the welcome mat and let himself inside.

He stood in the opened doorway, balancing himself on his crutches as he stared into the front room, trying to hold himself together. Sean's furniture was still there, just as it had been the last time Jonah had visited, with a rip in the couch cushion, a stack of magazines holding up the wobbly leg on the TV stand, and all. But it looked a little tidier, as if a maid had been by or something.

Jonah sniffed in a breath, refusing to cry, and limped over the threshold. The place didn't feel abandoned; it felt like someone was still living here. Even a light on down the hall welcomed him and let him know the electricity had never been disconnected. He could almost believe Sean would come loping down the hall and appear in front of him to demand to know why Jonah was standing there, gawking at his things like a total creeper.

His lips twitched at the thought. That was totally something Sean would say.

He moved deeper into the house, wanting to feel more of Sean's presence, needing that connection more than he needed his next breath. But as soon as he stepped into the hallway, something shuffled in the back room. Sean's bedroom.

Jesus. What was that? Rodent? Burglar? Ghost? Jonah put his crutches to work and limped as fast as he could, shoving open the unlatched door with the rubber sole of one crutch. The door bumped into something that screamed.

The shriek sounded like a woman's, but the guy quivering before him in the fetal position on the floor, protectively covering his head, was most definitely male.

"Don't kill me. Oh, God, please don't kill me. You can take anything you want, just—"

"I'm not going to kill you," Jonah muttered, nudging the trespasser in the ribs with his crutch as he narrowed his eyes. Who the hell was this, acting as if *Jonah* was the intruder?

Entire body shaking, the boy slowly uncovered his head to look up with bright green eyes that were outlined with thick black eyeliner.

"You're not?" the stranger asked before he gulped. "Oh, thank you, God. Thank you."

Irritation rising, Jonah just scowled. "Let me guess. You're the actor."

The cowering guy jerked back in surprise. "How did you—"

"It's Aubrey, right?"

Aubrey's mouth fell open. "Yeah, that's…that's right. How did you know?"

Jonah glanced around the bedroom. Yeah, it was in much too good of shape to have been abandoned for so many weeks. The two lovebirds must've been living together.

"I'm Jonah," he said.

Immediately, tears filled Aubrey's eyes. He covered his mouth. "Oh, my God. Oh…my God. He told you, then? You…know?"

Nodding, Jonah sank down to sit on the floor in the hallway because his leg was killing him. Staring at Sean's boyfriend through the doorway, he shook his head. "He was in the middle of telling me when…when it happened."

"And you were…okay with it? Please don't tell me he died thinking you hated him." Aubrey's bottom lip quivered. "You meant the world to that man."

Jonah closed his eyes and gritted his teeth, trying to combat the sorrow. "He died knowing I knew…and supported him."

"Oh, thank God." Aubrey waved a hand over his face as if to air dry his tears. "Oh, thank you, Lord Jesus. He wanted your acceptance so bad. This—thank you. Thank you so much."

He was definitely a grateful little thing, with a wiry, thin frame and extra short hair. Jonah wondered what the heck had attracted Sean to such a timid, quivering ball of gayness. Then he decided it didn't matter. Since he was into girls, he'd probably never get it. But it still itched at his craw that this complete stranger might've known his best friend better than he had.

"So, you were living here…with him?"

Aubrey stared at him from big, scared, green eyes. "No. Well, I *wasn't*. I guess I kind of am now, though. He gave me a key. So, I came here to feel closer to him, you know, afterward. And I just…I haven't been able to leave."

Jonah nodded, understanding the feeling all too well. "Yeah." He cleared his throat. "I don't blame you. The place still smells like him."

"Shit." Aubrey buried his face into his hands and began to sob uncontrollably. "You smell him too? You smell him too?" He made the phrase a litany as if relieved he'd finally found someone to share in his grief with him.

Cursing under his breath, Jonah rolled his eyes toward the ceiling and finally let it out. A tear slid down his cheek, quickly followed by another. Quietly, the two of them sat there crying with each other as they mourned the one thing that connected them.

Chapter Eighteen

Tess dwindled into a strange kind of depression. Two weeks had rolled by since the suicide of Jenner Treymore — more commonly known as Roadrunner among his friends, as she learned from watching the news — and her world only dipped to a new low. Food lost its flavor, the nights dragged on because sleep wouldn't come, and her attention waned even during the most stimulating of conversations. Yet, throughout it all, life around her kept chugging along, and she drifted with the current, continuing on without really participating.

When early enrollment for the Fall opened, she and Bailey registered for sixteen hours apiece. Tess was quickly running out of required classes to take, though. She was going to have to think up a major before entering her second sophomore semester. But planning her future just seemed so...blah.

She hated filling in the word *undecided* more, though, so at the very last second, she scribbled down physical therapy for a tentative major. With a gasp, she stared at what she'd just done. Holy crap. That was perfect. She had loved watching Frenchie help Jonah. And she loved that refreshing sense of accomplishment when she helped someone. She loved feeling needed, and she loved seeing the results of her labor.

Just like that, her tentative major became permanent.

She wanted to be a physical therapist. And it was all because of Jonah.

Ignoring the slice of pain that thought brought, she finished her online enrollment and declined to apply for a dorm room, since she and Bailey planned to rent some kind of place off campus during the next school year. It'd be nice to get away from this battle-scarred campus every evening after classes.

But the campus wasn't the only thing that seemed battle-scarred to her. She felt as if she'd lost a chunk of her life source. And it affected Bailey too. Bailey forced her out more as the weather warmed so they could take walks around the university in the evening and scout for a white cowboy hat and blue Wranglers. At least that's what her friend claimed they were doing. Tess noticed how Bailey had stopped scanning the crowd everywhere they went. She'd given up on her cowboy, just as Tess had given up on everything else.

As they were walking back to Grammar Hall one evening, Bailey chatted along, and Tess blocked most everything she said until Bailey blurted, "This Jonah guy totally messed you up, didn't he?"

Tess jerked to a halt and lifted her face. Her body responded at the mere mention of his name. "What do you mean?" How in the world had Bailey known she was thinking about him? She hadn't mentioned him aloud once since they'd rushed to the hospital to save him.

"You still behave like Tess, still smile like Tess, talk like Tess, but I don't know. It just seems like Tess is gone. You're this empty shell, going through the motions but not really living them."

Tess sighed and moved in closer as they walked along, resting her cheek on her friend's shoulder. "You're right. Lately, I feel…It just feels like something's…"

"Missing?" Bailey wrapped her arm around her shoulder and tipped her temple to the side until it pressed against Tess's.

Tess swallowed dryly. "Yeah." Something was definitely missing. Like half of her soul.

After a few seconds of silence, they turned a corner. As Grammar Hall came into view at the end of the block, Bailey murmured, "Maybe I messed up."

Since she never admitted such a thing, Tess glanced at her sharply. "What do you mean?"

"I went to see him."

When Bailey glanced at her with a please-don't-hate-me cringe, Tess pulled away abruptly. "Who? *Jonah?* Oh, my God, when? Why would you do that?"

"Promise not to hate me."

"Prom—oh, Bailey. What did you do?" Dread sank into Tess's veins as she covered her mouth with both hands.

"The day after his big reveal, when all the truth came out and he ended up on national television as a complete villain, I went to his hospital room."

"And?" Tess demanded. She couldn't believe Bailey had seen him more recently than she had and hadn't told her about it. She felt betrayed. But, dear God, Bailey had seen him more recently than she had! She grasped her friend's arm eagerly. Any scrap of news about him was like catnip to her. "What…what'd he say? What'd *you* say? What happened?"

"Well, I wanted to correct him on his thinking. I'm a hater of all things miscommunication, after all, so I was going to let him know how wrong he was about you, that you'd never had any bad ulterior motives against him and you never willing ousted him to the police, trying to get him into trouble."

Tess couldn't believe her friend had gone to so much trouble for her. Bailey had mostly been anti-Jonah in all their conversations. The fact that she'd gone to him to help repair Tess's relationship with him told her just how much her friend loved her.

But Jonah had only been using her, exacting his own revenge. She kept forgetting that part when good memories of him stole into her heart.

Her shoulders slumped. "Let me guess. He didn't believe you."

"Oh, he believed me, all right."

Shock pierced Tess's chest. She shook her head, certain she'd just misheard. "Wait. What?"

"The guy thinks you're a freaking saint and can do no wrong."

"Huh?" Heart beating madly inside her chest, Tess let the hope swell. "He does?" *Wait.* Her blooming smile faltered. If he truly thought that, then why hadn't she seen him since he'd gotten out of the hospital? Why hadn't—

"Never once did the thought cross his mind that you'd duped him."

"Then — " She choked on the question. Oh, God. Did this mean he'd cared about her all along? "Why did he accuse me of...of everything? Why did he...?" She shook her head. This didn't make sense. If he did care, then why hadn't he corrected her when she'd started assuming and accusing him of the worst? "I don't understand."

Bailey shrugged, a little too easily. "What's to understand? He's a guy. Does he need any more reason than that to be an idiot?"

"Yes! Dammit." Tess stomped her foot and glared at her friend with her hands on her hips. "Didn't you drag some kind of explanation out of him? God, Bay. Isn't that kind of your *specialty?*" What good was having a best friend who could be outgoing, rude, demanding, and forthright if she wasn't going to be outgoing, rude, demanding, and forthright when you needed her to be?

"Okay, if you think about this from his point of view — "

"*His* point of view?" Tess shrieked. She couldn't believe this. Bailey was taking *his* side? The outgoing, rude, demanding, forthright girl was *her* best friend, not his! She should be looking out for Tess's best interest, not —

"His life had just fallen apart literally thirty seconds before you guys exploded on each other. He had no future left to look forward to. On top of that, he was about to become embroiled in a huge scandal...on the national level. And let's face it, his physical capabilities were absolutely nil. You take that, add in a guy with typical macho protective tendencies, and of course he's going to want to keep the people he cares about the most as far away from that kind of mess as possible."

"So..." *Oh God.* "You're saying he just...he let me walk away to *protect* me?"

"More or less." Bailey winced and made a face. "Okay, yeah, that's it, exactly."

"But...oh, Bailey. You didn't agree with him. Did you?"

Dear Lord, she had.

"Hell, no. I told him you were a big girl and could decide for yourself which people you do and don't want anything to do with, and he had no right to make that decision for you."

"Oh, thank God. Thank — "

"Then I told him to stay away from you until he had his shit together."

"What? *Bailey!*"

"Well, what did you expect? You're my best friend; I feel protective of you, too, you know. And the guy was a freaking mess. He was crying all over the place and—"

Tess gasped and hugged herself. "He was *crying?*" Pain tore through her to even think of him getting emotional in front of Bailey. He must've hated that. "And you just—" Pressing her hand to her aching chest, she gaped at her backstabbing best friend. "You didn't tell me sooner."

Bailey began to wring her hands. "Now...don't look at me that way. Please, Tessie. If it's any consolation, I told him to look you up again whenever he feels worthy of you."

That only made things worse.

"You didn't. Oh...damn it, Bailey. Tell me, how do *you* feel whenever things can't get any worse for you and you think you're at rock bottom? Do you ever feel *worthy* of anyone? God, what if...what if he decides he'll never..." She couldn't even finish the question, bowing her head, she squeezed her eyes closed and prayed he came back to her. Soon.

"Tess..."

When a hand hesitantly touched her shoulder, Tess growled. "Don't." As she glanced with clenched teeth and flaring nostrils, Bailey snatched her fingers back, her eyes wide with shock. "I can't believe you! Once again, you interfered with my life and did something without my permission...on my *supposed* behalf. But this time...this time, you went too far."

"But—"

"No! It's my time to talk. Usually, I don't mind that you take over. I actually prefer it. You like to lead. I like to follow. That just works for us. But I do have my own thoughts, too, and I can make my own decision. Butting into my relationship with Jonah was one place you didn't belong. You weren't there when I went to visit him. You don't know what happened between us. What he made me feel. And...Jesus, Bailey how could you tell him to stay away? What if... what if I never see him again because of that? What if I can't find him? Oh God, what if I go through the rest of my life never feeling for anyone what he made me feel for him?"

As Tess's chest heaved from her fiercely given speech, Bailey gaped at her mutely. Then she shook her head slightly and drew in a sharp breath. "He hurt you."

"Yes, he did," Tess agreed. "But that's my pain to bear. Not yours."

Bailey snorted. "What the hell ever. You're my best friend. You can't just expect me to —"

"I can. And I do. I'm probably going to get my heart broken a lot in my life. I'm sure you will too. We can be there to console each other during the hard time and celebrate the great times. But interfering the way you did was wrong."

"Tess," Bailey whispered as she dragged in a shuddered breath. Her lashes blinked furiously and her chin quivered. "I did it because I love you."

"No. You did it because you feel the need to control me."

"*Control* you?" Mouth falling open, Bailey sputtered before hissing, "That's insane. I don't —"

"Yes, you do! Every time we do anything, it's always *your* idea. And on those rare occasions we actually do something *I* want to do, you bitch and complain the entire time…because it wasn't part of *your* plan."

Bailey threw her hands into the hair. "Okay, now you're just being irrational. You're upset and —"

"No, now I'm being honest." Tess dug her finger into her chest. "Brutally honest. Something I learned from you. I know this stems from watching your mom die when you were seven. You had no control over what happened to you then, so you feel the need to personally oversee every little detail over your life now and over the lives of everyone around you. But you went over the line this time. I mean, what if I never see him again because of *you?*"

When Bailey didn't answer, just stared with a pale, blank expression, Tess uncurled her fingers she hadn't realized she'd balled into fists. She took a few deep breaths to rein in her overwhelming emotions, and it finally dawned on her what she'd just blurted out.

She gasped and covered her mouth.

Bailey tipped her head to the side. Quietly and slowly, she asked, "What do you mean I saw my mother die when I was seven? I was *three* when she…" She didn't finish the sentence. She blinked a couple of times, then shook her head. "No."

"Bailey," Tess whispered. "I'm sorry. I'm so sorry. I should have —"

Holding up her hand, Bailey silenced her with a single look. She opened her mouth once, then closed it and turned away. As she walked off without a word, Tess whispered the worst curse word she knew.

Realizing she'd just done what she'd been so mad at Bailey for doing by interfering where she didn't belong, she hugged her waist and prayed for forgiveness.

This was bad, though. Bailey had never before walked away from a fight. She always stuck it out. When Tess was the one who wanted to crawl under a rock and hide from an argument, Bailey forced her to stay and talk it through.

Not sure if she should follow her friend and be the forceful one this time around or give her some space, she waited a second. Then another.

Since she was still wired from what she'd learned about Jonah, she decided to wait. Bailey probably wanted to confirm a few things with her family before—oh, dear Lord, Mr. Prescott was going to kill her. Bailey's father had always intimidated Tess with his gruffness, so she'd always been careful not to displease him. She had no idea what he'd do when he found out Bailey knew the truth.

Chapter Nineteen

Jonah wasn't sure what he was doing.

He'd gotten a job today as a short order cook in a greasy diner at the edge of town. But that by no means meant his life was back on track. Sure, no reporters had mentioned his name on the news in the past few days, and he'd found a place to stay, sort of, but he knew this wasn't what Tess's friend Bailey had meant by seeking Tess out only when he had his shit together. His shit was strewn around him so far, he still woke up in the middle of the night, gasping for air from nightmares and his muscles twisting in pain from his wounds.

Except he couldn't stay away.

Maybe if he just saw her once. Or if he could only talk to her. But, Christ, if he talked to her, he'd want to beg for her forgiveness, and then he'd beg her to give him another chance. Or would it be a first chance, since the first time around probably didn't count? Didn't matter. He shouldn't be begging for anything; he shouldn't be bothering her at all.

And he definitely shouldn't be on the campus of Granton, staking out her dormitory on the hopes of seeing her walk by. Because if he saw her, he'd want to talk to her, and then he'd start begging. From there, everything would just spiral out of control.

But he couldn't help it. He just had to see her, had to make sure she was okay. Happy. Healthy—

Damn it, okay, he wanted to see her because he craved it. One hit of Tess was all it would take. After that, he could deal with life again. And if she just so happened to see him back when he saw her, then maybe he could mention the whole job thing, his living arrangements, and maybe slip in that he was so far gone for her, his life felt purposeless without her in it.

He drew in a breath. No. He wouldn't talk to her just yet. Maybe after he got rid of the crutches, or when—

Someone walking up the front walk to Grammar Hall caught his attention. He peered out his hiding spot, which was in the shadows of a nearby copse of trees, and caught his breath. Bailey marched determinedly toward the front entrance. The urge to leap out at her and bombard her with questions about Tess was overwhelming. He actually took a step forward, nearly tripping on his crutches.

Maybe this would be better than talking to Tess herself. He could check up on her, make sure she was doing okay, get his fix, and not actually bother her.

But the way Bailey was walking made him pause. It was a fast, almost angry clip. She'd lifted her chin defiantly high as if she was pissed as hell, while tears streamed down her cheeks. Not sure what that was about, he hung back, hesitating.

When someone called, "Bailey! Hey, Bailey. Wait up," Jonah glanced over to catch some guy lifting his hand and waving to her down, trying to get her attention. But she was lost in her own world. She barely paused to unlock the front door and yank it open before darting inside.

Her pursuer broke into a run and reached out to catch the closing door but didn't make it in time. Staring at the locked entrance, he muttered a curse and ran his hands over his short crop of hair. Then he whirled away and paced toward a nearby bench to slump down. But as he landed with a plop, he winced and rubbed at a spot on the upper left-hand side of his chest, reminding Jonah of those times he hurt his bullet wounds, jarring them whenever he sat down too fast.

Wondering who this guy was, how he knew Bailey, and if that meant he knew Tess too, Jonah continued to study him. Contemplating if he should approach the stranger and ask about her, he sighed. This was bullshit. He should just—

Suddenly bench guy lurched to his feet. "Tess!" he called with a relieved kind of grin.

Jonah's innards shuddered as that name seared him in half.

He whirled until he spotted her. Unlike Bailey, she poked along at a slow pace, her head hung low with her long beautiful red mane covering most of her face. Swallowing dryly, he soaked in the view. God, just seeing her…he wanted to go to her, gather her into his arms, and pull her close until she realized every smile and touch and kiss had been the real deal between them.

But when she looked up at the stranger's call, it wasn't Jonah she saw. From his angle, he still couldn't see her face, which was slightly frustrating, but he didn't care. He could see enough. And when she darted forward, he saw her throw her arms around another man. She hugged him tight and buried her face in his neck as if she just couldn't get close enough.

Her "companion" seemed momentarily startled by the act, but then he eagerly drew his arms around her too and bowed his head to speak confidentially in her ear. As he led her inside, pausing so she could unlock the door for them, Jonah's world crashed around him.

She had someone else.

She'd moved on.

Hell, maybe she'd always had this guy. Jonah knew she'd lied to them about them being together, but he'd never thought she'd had someone else. She'd touched Jonah and kissed him, and…they'd talked like…Shit. Had she just been playing him all along, just as he'd accused? Maybe she'd even sent Bailey in to make him think she was innocent to really complete the act. Maybe—

He turned away, unable to concoct another scenario. It hurt too much. And besides, it didn't matter. Because he couldn't believe the worst of her. Maybe she'd moved on and had someone else now. But she hadn't when they'd been together.

This was good, he decided. Really. She needed to move on, find someone good for her. She needed to be happy.

It hurt, though. It hurt more than all the physical therapy sessions Frenchie had put him through. It hurt more than any of his bullet wounds or his head wound. In fact, he wasn't sure if he could survive from this kind of pain.

Stumbling when one of his crutches caught on an uneven piece of ground, he moaned out a sound of pain and kept hurrying away. By the time he made it to his truck, his leg was throbbing.

Pale and trembling, he fell into the driver's seat and panted, realizing he was probably on the verge of another panic attack.

"Damn it," he muttered, rubbing circles over his chest where the heart inside his ribcage kept chipping away shattered pieces.

He closed his eyes and rested his skull back against the headrest. He probably sat there for ten minutes before he fumbled for his wallet and yanked out a business card he'd kept for weeks but had yet to use. Hoping it brought about a miracle, he dialed the number and listened to the ring.

"Hey," a chipper-sounding woman answered almost immediately. "This is Sam."

He licked his lips. "I need—you said I could call if I needed help." Exhaling, he realized he was probably making no sense, so he started again. "I mean, this is Jonah Abbott. I—"

"Oh! Of course. I've been waiting for you, dear. I'm so glad you finally gave in."

She sounded relieved. For some reason, that calmed him. Running a hand through his hair, he gave a small smile. "Yeah. Well…" What now?

"Do you need to talk now?" she immediately asked, smoothing out all the awkwardness. "I have some time. But I'm starving. Do you mind if we meet for some pizza? There's a great pizza parlor on Grant Street."

Samantha had her light hair pulled up in another perky ponytail when Jonah managed to edge his way into the restaurant. He had a little trouble at the door because it kept wanting to close on his crutches, but once he was inside and hobbling her way, she finally noticed him.

Offering him a big smile, she waved him over before sinking her teeth into a large slice of pepperoni. "Sorry, I couldn't wait to order. I hope you don't mind." She gave him a guilty grin and dabbed at her face with as napkin as he propped his crutches on the wall beside their booth and hopped on one foot before sliding his way into his seat. "Hey, it looks like you're getting around well on those things."

"Yeah," he said, glancing at the food teasing his nostrils.

"Help yourself." She waved her hand toward the pizza. "And if you don't like this kind, I'm going to order another one anyway. My boys will kill me if I come home with pizza on my breath and don't bring them any."

"This is fine," he said and hesitantly picked up a piece. "Thanks." When he took a bite, his gaze met hers, and a strange kind of companionship filled him. He'd only met this woman once, and yet he instantly felt a comfortable easiness around her.

As they ate, she did most of the talking, telling him about her two sons and some of the crazy things they did. A couple things reminded him of his childhood in the trailer park with Sean, and he found himself smiling, despite the heaviness in his chest.

"So…" Sam patted her belly as they polished off all the pizza they were going to eat and the waitress went off to get her a box for the leftovers. "Why don't you tell me a little bit about…Einstein. Or did you call him Anthony?"

The name made him shudder. Not expecting this question, he shook his head. Why did she want to talk about Einstein? Didn't she specialize in grief therapy? He sure as hell wasn't grieving over Einstein.

"I've seen you on the news, you know," she murmured with a hint of sympathy in her brown eyes. "I've heard what they're saying about you. I thought you might like to start there."

No, he didn't want to start there. Actually, he didn't even want to go there. Truth be told, he didn't want to start anywhere. He'd kind of been hoping maybe she'd just hand over some miracle pill that would numb him to all pain and send him on his way. But, no, the woman wanted to talk.

It figured.

"What do you want me to say?" he croaked, already bracing himself and feeling defensive. "If you saw the news reports then you already know everything, right?"

She laughed softly. "Watching the news only confirmed that there was a lot more going on between you and Einstein than I originally thought."

The color drained from his face. He wasn't sure he could talk about this. It'd end up being his word against the freaking media. Why would anyone believe him after what they'd said about him?

Sam sighed. "Let me tell you a little story. My husband died in the line of duty. A drunken parolee had kidnapped his child and ex-girlfriend because he'd lost all his parent privileges. After hours of trying to negotiate with him to come out of the house where he was holding his family at gunpoint, the police finally sent in a SWAT unit. Frank was one of the first officers inside. When the crazy drunk opened fire, he aimed at his own family instead of the police. So… selfless man that my husband was, Frank dived in front of them and shielded them. He saved their lives that day. But not once in all the media coverage over the event did one reporter call him a hero or commend him for saving that woman and little boy. They were too busy degrading the other officers who used an excessive amount of bullets to return fire on the drunk. So, I know exactly how only one portion of the story gets told, or how some details are blown out of proportion, while others are completely neglected."

"They kept calling me a linebacker," Jonah muttered, his chest heavy and full with emotion over Sam's story and how it identified with his own. He wasn't sure why he said that. There were so many other more important issues. But focusing on that one small thing helped him keep himself under control. "I was never a linebacker. I was a freaking tight end."

Samantha chuckled. "Yeah. They kept calling Frank Fred, too."

"I'm sorry," he said. He was actually more sorry about her loss. But again, it was easier to apologize for the most insignificant detail.

She seemed to understand, though. With a nod and small smile, she reached out and covered his hand. "What else did they get wrong?"

He blew out a breath. Jesus, where to start. "I didn't give him the gun. I never would've done that. I didn't even realize he knew I had one. And I have no clue where he found bullets for it."

Warm fingers squeezed around his. "Where there's a will, there's a way. I've heard he was a very resourceful young boy. One way or another, he would've found something to kill Dorian Wade for what he did to Paige Zukowski. But I'd like to hear more about your relationship with him."

"You mean the part where I terrorized him?" Jonah bit out, every muscle in his body tensing. That was the part he wanted to talk about the least. His shame and guilt already attacked him enough every day. He didn't need this woman to do so too.

"Now, Jonah," she murmured in a soft, scolding voice. "Don't close up on me like that. I can just see you shutting down. Remember I know how the media plays things. Just tell me your side. That's all I ask."

"Why does it matter?" he demanded, scowling.

"Because I can't help you if I don't know what really happened."

"He bullied me first," Jonah finally said. "He hacked into my records and found out everything there was to know about me, and he used it all against me. He knew every grade I made and how to make me feel stupid and worthless. He knew how shitty my home life had been and made me feel awful. And he knew how to do it in the privacy of our dorm room, where no one else would see it. Then he knew how to run out into the hall when I retaliated, making *me* look like the asshole. *Every* time I went after him, it was because he'd done something to me first. But who the hell would believe that?... Who —"

He shook his head, feeling lost. Not only had everyone at Grammar Hall thought he'd tormented Einstein, but they'd congratulated him on it, and then followed him, helping him chase down the strange boy and harass him further. No one had once asked him why or what Einstein had done to deserve it.

Until now. Across the table from him, Samantha said, "*I* believe it. I do believe you, Jonah. I've talked to other students from Granton who had contact with him, and I completely believe what you say. Besides, I've seen my fair share of bullies over the years, and you are not one of them."

He shook his head, confused. She really did believe him. He could tell by the sincerity in her expression. But why did she want to help him?

The defensive starch drained from his bones, and almost exhausted from the force of relief he felt, he blurted, "He tried to kill me before. One time, I woke up to him suffocating me with a pillow. And I swear I came into my room when he was putting something into my bottle of Gatorade. But I threw it away because I didn't trust it."

"Holy hell," Sam squawked. "Did you tell anyone?"

Jonah shrugged. "I told my R.A. about the pillow incident, but she told me she didn't blame him. If I'd quit picking on him maybe he'd leave me alone."

"And there were other incidents?"

With a nod, Jonah began to tell her everything. And it felt good to let it out. He'd had no idea just talking would make him feel better.

He thought about Tess, and he wondered what would've happened if he'd been honest in the hospital, if only he'd told her the truth when he'd regained his memory. Would she have stuck around to remain his friend? If he'd just told her these things he was telling Sam, would she be with that other guy right now?

Chapter Twenty

After her argument with Bailey, Tess wasn't sure where to go. Finally, she decided to confess what she'd done to Paige. Besides, she needed some advice about what to do next. She was beyond relieved to find Paige's boyfriend waiting outside Grammar Hall for someone with a key to let him in. She nearly attacked poor Logan because her need for a hug was so great.

Though surprised at first, he finally hugged her back, and then promptly told her he'd take her to Paige. Without any questions.

But Paige was surprisingly unhelpful with her opinions.

"I don't know," she said. "I just don't know. You shouldn't have told her that way, no, but..." With a meaningful glance at Logan, she smiled softly. "I fully believe *not* addressing those kinds of issues never solves anything. She should've been told a long time ago, and maybe she could've gotten over it a long time ago. Now it may take a while for her to deal."

"But it was her dad who wanted—"

"I know, sweetie." Paige reached out and grasped Tess's hands. "I know. But on a totally different note, I'm kind of impressed you stood up to her like that. Bailey has always had this way of bulldozing over you, and you just let her. But, lately, you've really been coming into your own."

Tess didn't feel too proud over that, though. If standing up for herself caused her to hurt Bailey, she'd just as soon stay the meek, mild Tess she'd always been. She'd grown up with Bailey; she'd known what kind of person she was. And, most of the time, she loved Bailey for being exactly the way she was. It just seemed rude to push that behavior away now.

She needed to right things with her best friend. She made her way to her own room, but Bailey was gone, and the only thing she'd left was a hastily-written note on her unmade bed that said, *Went home. Be back later.*

Later lasted a week and two days. Bailey missed classes. She didn't answer any of Tess's phone messages or texts. She didn't even respond to Paige's attempts to reach her. Tess finally called her farm, braced to face the wrath of Mr. Prescott for letting the cat out of the bag about her mom. But, thank goodness, one of Bailey's brothers instead of her dad answered.

"I've never seen her like this," Brock — or maybe it was Bennett — confessed. "What the hell happened?"

Shocked he didn't know, Tess told him what information she'd leaked, and he cursed under his breath. "Shit, Tess. This could completely change Bailey as we know her."

Gulping down a rise of tears, Tess sniffed. "I hope not." And she meant it from the bottom of her heart. She missed her best friend, the filterless loudmouth best friend she'd known since birth.

Now it felt as if she had *two* gaping holes in her.

Eight days after Bailey had left, Tess was about to go crazy. Everything just…dragged. When a knock came on her bathroom door, rattling her from a test she was studying for but couldn't really concentrate on, she was beyond ready for a distraction.

"Yes?"

"Hey," Paige said a bit too timidly as she poked her head into the room. When Tess saw Logan hovering behind her, she sat up on the bed and smoothed down her shirt to look more presentable.

After clearing the cobwebs from her throat, she asked, "What's up?"

Paige glanced around, looking toward the other bed. "Is Bailey back yet?"

Tess sighed, sinking further into her doldrums. "No."

No Bailey.

No Jonah.

She felt completely abandoned.

"Good." Appearing relieved, Paige stepped fully through the doorway. When Tess's mouth fell open in outrage, Paige immediately winced and covered her mouth. "I mean, not good that she hasn't come back yet, but good that I caught you by yourself, because…" With a huffed sigh, she crossed her arms over her chest and sent her boyfriend an arched look. "Logan has something he needs to confess."

"Oh?" Tess glanced over to find his cheeks had darkened as he smoothed his hand over his hair in a nervous manner. In the past month and a half since the shooting, he'd filled out more, looked healthier, and had stopped wearing his arm sling. It was hard to tell he'd ever been shot.

When he lifted his gaze from the floor and sent her a tense smile, her stomach dropped.

"Is this about Jonah?"

When Logan winced, dread filled Tess's veins. "Oh, God. Not you guys too." Had every friend she knew interfered in her life? "What did you do?"

"Nothing bad," Paige assured her quickly, waving her hands in a placating manner. But then she, too, was wincing. "I mean, not too bad."

"Why don't I just explain?" Logan took Paige's hand as he blew out a long breath. "After you and I had that little talk a month or so ago…" He paused and sent Tess a look as if to make sure she remembered which talk he was referring to.

Since they'd only ever had one, she nodded. "Yeah?"

"Right." He nodded as well. "Well, after that, I wanted to help somehow. I knew you were worried about him, so I went to the counselor for my grief group. Samantha. She's helped both Paige and me in the most incredible ways."

When he glanced at Paige, his girlfriend shifted to his side and looped a supportive arm around his waist. He continued. "So, I thought she might be able to help Jonah as well."

"And I guess she did," Paige added. "After our meeting today, Logan and I were helping put the room back in order, and this terribly snoopy guy here came across a stack of files that belonged to Sam. One of them had Jonah's name on it."

"Really?" Tess popped to her feet, staring wide-eyed at her friends. "Did you open it?"

Logan and Paige exchanged glances. Finally, Logan spoke. "I know I shouldn't have, but you've been so sad lately. I just thought… if there was some kind of address inside, you could visit him and, I don't know, get some closure…or something."

Closure was the last thing she wanted. But an address that led her to Jonah…that would do nicely. "Oh, my God!" she rushed to Logan and grabbed his hands, unable to stop smiling. "Did you find one?" When he didn't answer soon enough, she started to tug on her grip. "Please, please, please say you did."

His face fell. Tess immediately dropped her hands from his and stepped back. "Oh."

"But I did find this."

When he pulled a folded sheet a paper from his pocket, Tess narrowed her eyes. "You stole from Jonah's file? What if that was some kind of important information that could help that Sam lady get him better? What if—"

"It's a letter addressed to you," Paige cut in.

When Tess stopped talking and gaped, Logan added. "I saw that it was to you and from Jonah so I took it. But that's all I read, I swear."

Tess glanced between the two to see if they were pulling her leg. Finally, she shook her head and focused on Logan. "You stole a letter for me?"

"He did." Paige bounced on her toes as a grin burst across her face. "Wasn't that so bad-boy of him? I swear, he just got, like, ten times hotter."

As Logan sent his girlfriend a heated grin, Tess leapt at him, clamoring for her letter. "Oh, my God, Logan. I love you."

"Hey, hey." Paige tugged him away just as Tess gained control of her letter. "That's my hot bad boy. Go read about your own."

But Tess was no longer listening to either of them. Her fingers trembled as she unfolded her letter and smoothed out the three creases in it. The heavy masculine scrawl that met her gaze made her heart thump hard in her chest.

"So, uh. I guess we'll give you some privacy to read that." Logan was already taking Paige's hand and backing her from the room.

Tess heard Paige mutter "Good luck" before the door shut between them. Not that she really took much notice. She was too busy reading.

Dear Tess,

Hi. I don't really know what to say. Sam just told me to write a letter to someone, and she kind of scares me, so I do what she says. Besides, her strange instructions actually help sometimes, so I guess I'll just keep writing, but mostly because she's watching me right now to make sure I don't crap out on her.

I should probably start at the beginning. Since I left the hospital, I've been meeting with a therapist lady named Samantha. She's a total pain in the ass and doesn't actually like to be called a therapist. She says we're just two people meeting for pizza every day, but she is really a therapist. I think she's a good one too. I don't feel as shitty as I did before I started "eating pizza" with her.

She's helped me deal with pretty much everything. Except maybe you. I still miss you. I miss you so hard it sometimes makes my chest hurt until I can't even breathe. I haven't felt right since that day you stormed out of my hospital room.

Shit. I can't believe I just wrote that. Pretty corny, huh? But Sam assured me no one — not even she — would read this. We're going to have some ritualistic burning of the letter after our next pizza session. So maybe that's why I'm being all lame and honest. I can "purge" as she called it and say any damn thing I want. I can say I LOVE YOU, TESS, in all bold caps, triple underlined and circled 5 times.

Wow, that did kind of make me feel better. What else can I tell you? There's so much. I want to tell you about Sean. He was my best friend who was killed right in front of me during the shooting. Then there's my parents. Einstein. Us. I want you to know why I was such an ass that last day in the hospital.

Now my mind is spinning, so I think I'll start over at the beginning again.

When I woke up in the hospital, I was confused, and lost, and scared. I really did have amnesia for the first few days. And I still had it the first night you came to my room. I knew something was off then, but I was so grateful someone was there to see me, I believed what you told me. Because I wanted to.

I must've wanted to remember you so much your visit jostled my brain into getting my memories back. But the only memory I had of you was from seeing you across an open courtyard walking down the sidewalk with who I now know was Bailey. Your hair is hard to miss, even harder to forget. But I knew I'd never talked to you, and I knew you weren't my girlfriend.

If you hadn't come back the next night to see me, I probably would've owned up to remembering everything then. But you did come back, and I just wanted to spend a little more time with you.

I did wonder why you were doing it, why you were lying and pretending to be my girl, but I knew without a doubt it wasn't for any reason with bad intentions. You were too good and sweet and innocent for that. With every visit, you made me better, made me fall a little bit harder, made me fake my amnesia just a little bit longer. Any extra time I could get with you was worth a few more lies.

I hope you don't hate me for all the liberties I took, but while we were together, you did become my girlfriend. You were the only thing I had and the reason I wanted to keep going.

When the truth came out and everything went down between us, I lied to you again. I didn't believe any of the accusations I made. I never thought anything bad about you. And everything we had shared was true. But I was scared, and not just for me. My life was shit. I was falling to rock bottom. When I hit, I didn't want you to land with me. I didn't want you to get hurt.

I knew you'd want to be there with me, though, while they laughed at me on national television and announced to the world that getting shot three times was the least of what I deserved. You didn't need that kind of attention on you. You deserve to be cherished and loved, not known as the infamous girlfriend of a national bully.

Yeah, I've been told—by a lot of people—that it wasn't my place to make that decision for you. I should've given you the opportunity to make it on your own. But it felt like it was the only thing I could do for you, to pay you back for saving me. I wouldn't have made it through these past few weeks if I hadn't had my memories of you. You've given me a reason to live. So I tried to save you from me.

Wow, Sam was right. Letter writing is pretty cleansing.

So, I'll start at another beginning. You saw where I grew up, in the Whispering Pines trailer park, right? I still can't believe you went there all by yourself to see them, just for me. But you were right about my dad. He's an abusive SOB. He would beat my mom all the time. When I got old enough to defend her, I did. So he'd turn on me and hit me, too.

In high school, I got big enough that I could actually take him in a fight. Near the beginning of my junior year, he started in on my mom one night for forgetting to pay a bill, which caused the electricity to go out. I thought he was going to kill her. When I came home from football practice, she was already bloody and curled up half-dead in the fetal position on the floor, but he still just kept kicking her. So, I took him down. Both my parents ended up in the hospital that night, and I was thrown in juvie.

When they released me, I went back home to pack my shit and get my mom. But she refused leave him and wouldn't go with me. It broke my heart that she chose him over me. As I walked away, my dad yelled at me to never come back. And that was fine with me. I haven't seen or heard from either of them since. You may think I'm awful, but I have no desire to visit or talk to them again. That door, for me, is closed.

I went to my friend Sean's place that night. He lived close, and we'd grown up together. His mom drank too much and barely kept a job, but she was cool with me sticking around until we graduated from high school.

After focusing all my attention on football, I got a scholarship into Granton. Sean's granddad had left him some money when he died, so he came along too and was able to rent an apartment off campus, but it was cheaper for me to stay in the dorms with my scholarship, so I went that route.

He was my best friend — only friend — since kindergarten. I've never been good at making friends. I always kept to myself on the football team, which no doubt made the other players think I was looking down on them. I don't know really. All I know is I've never been able to handle stupid people who do or say stupid things, and that's gotten me called a bigot more than once. But I never thought of myself as someone who hated groups of people in general. I just didn't care for some certain individuals. Though I have recently come to learn I've misjudged actors on the whole! They're really not as annoying as I used to think. Anyway…

Until this year, I'd never thought of myself as a bully either. I was too much of a loner to get involved in anyone else's business.

Einstein changed all that.

The first day of my junior year when his parents moved him into my dorm room with me, I was actually ready to be his defender. His mother was a hateful, nasty bitch. She kept saying things like, "I can't believe you came from my loins; you're such a freak." And his father didn't jump in to defend him. They were only in our room a couple minutes, dumping off all his shit before they left, but it was enough to tell me he'd probably had about as miserable a childhood as I had.

So, once they were gone, I tried to make a joke of it to make him feel better, to let him know he wasn't alone and that I understood. I said something along the lines of, "Don't you just wish you could exchange your parents sometimes?"

But I guess that was the wrong thing to say. He turned around and glared at me. I don't think he liked me knowing how miserable he was or how he was treated by his own family.

He already knew who I was. He must've researched me before moving in, because he went off, mentioning things about my life and my parents, my ball playing. He knew everything.

I probably should've brushed it off and not let his words affect me. But whenever someone pushes me, I push back. I can't seem to help it. Getting up in Einstein's face, I threatened him and told him to stay out of my business.

After that, things went from bad to worse. I'd catch him in my things and when I'd chase him away, he'd run out of the room, so I'd chase him down the hall, threatening to kick his ass. A couple times, I tripped him and he fell down, but I never actually physically touched him. I hope you know that. I never hit him.

He'd collected an entire crowd of haters, though. After my first couple of times chasing him from our room, other people would join in and help me. But they tormented worse than I ever did, calling him names and throwing things at him. The few times people actually caught him, I'd just turn and walk away, letting them deal with it.

Sometimes I have nightmares about my childhood. And one night, I had a dream about my mom getting beat. It was from back when I was young and too scared to try to help her. I was hiding under the bed and watching her cry and beg him to stop. I woke up calling for her. Einstein was standing over my bed, watching me. Totally creeped me out. I threw my pillow at him and told him to leave me alone.

The next evening, I came in from football practice to find jars of baby food and pacifiers and all sorts of infant crap strung all over my bed. Smirking at me from his side of the room, he told me he'd gotten those for me since I'd been missing my mommy. I grabbed up a handful of the stuff and chased him out of the room, throwing them at him.

He'd always watch me changing clothes, too, and once I caught him opening the bathroom door to peek at me in the shower. That shit creeped me out the most. I know I shouldn't have tortured him. I should've recognized that he had problems and needed help instead of me chasing him off and cussing him out, but I just couldn't stand him.

Sean liked to laugh about it and tease me that Einstein was going to steal his spot of being my best friend. But damn, some nights, I'd get so tired of his shit I'd go bunk on Sean's couch. I kept some stuff over there so Einstein wouldn't get into it. And Sean let me keep my gun there too, since there's a no-firearms-on-campus policy. That was fine by me. But I do like to hunt, and I compete in some shooting competitions.

The last one I entered, I didn't get the gun back to Sean's house that night. He was a photography major and had been helping the drama department get ready for their play, so he was gone a lot. I couldn't think of any reason anyone would need to look under the backseat of my truck, so I kept it locked in its case there until I went to Sean's again. And then I just kind of forgot about it.

I must've mentioned it to Sean in some phone conversation I had with him that I needed to get it back to his apartment. That's the only reason I can imagine Einstein even knew I had it. It wasn't even loaded. I have no clue where he found bullets for it.

The day it happened, Sean called me up and asked me to meet him down at the burger joint in the food district, saying he needed to tell me something important. They sold my favorite hamburgers there, so I went. I remember it being cold; I complained because we had to sit outside so he could smoke.

His big news was that he was gay. That completely blind-sided me. I felt betrayed because he'd waited so long to tell me. I seriously hadn't had a clue. It made me wonder what else he'd never told me, what secrets he didn't trust me to keep. And it hurt that he'd been afraid I'd feel any differently about him. But despite all that going on inside me, I knew I had to step up and convince him he could be whatever he wanted to be without losing me. That is one thing I actually did right. I'm glad I supported him in and told him he was still my best friend no matter what. Because ten minutes later, he was dead.

At least he died knowing I was still his friend. That's something Sam has helped me deal with the most. We've also touched on my parent issues. But we've also talked about you. You're the hardest to talk about.

I still think about those days you visited me in the hospital. They're the happiest memories I have. You talked to me and confided in me. I just wish I had done the same in return and let you see the real me.

My biggest regret is that I never really got to confide in you and that you probably hate me right now. It's a daily struggle not to go to Grammar Hall and just beg you to forgive me. I actually did a few months ago. I limped to your dormitory and waited outside for you. I knew you probably wouldn't give me the time of day, but I just…I had to see you. I had to do something. I was going crazy.

God, I should've stayed away. When I saw you with that other guy, I don't know, something inside me just broke. I had thought getting over Sean's death would be impossible, but this is almost worse. Because you're still out there somewhere. You're happy. With him. That just feel wrongs to me.

I keep telling myself I should be happy for you because you're happy now. This is exactly what I wanted for you. You've moved on. Not that there was anything for you to move on from. Being my girlfriend wasn't real for you. But it was real for me, and I'm not happy. I feel fucking gutted, and I hate him. He has what I want. He has you, and if he doesn't treat you like a queen and worship the ground you walk on, I may have to kill him. Not really, but maybe. Damn it, I really do want you to be happy. That's true. I wish it could be me with you, but I know that's not possible. So, I…fuck. I think I'm getting emotional. And Sam just ate the last piece of pizza. I don't think I can write any more.

I love you. I want you to have a good life. I want you to find reasons to laugh and be silly and carry on, because there IS good left in this shitty world. You're proof of it.

Forever yours, Jonah.

Chapter Twenty-One

A sob burst from Tess's lungs as she read the last word. She flipped over the last page, hoping to find more on the back. But that was all he'd written.

"No," she said, her voice frantic. "What other guy? There is no other guy!" Who the heck was he talking about? How could he say he loved her and write such beautiful things about his feelings for her and then drop such a confusing line about another guy?

If he was only staying away because he thought she'd moved on, then she needed to set him straight. Immediately. Scrambling for the bathroom door, she flung it open and raced to Paige's room.

"We need to find him," she blurted out as she exploded into her suitemate's den.

Paige and Logan were tangled together on Paige's bed, without shirts on, and not even that fazed her. Logan ripped his palm off his girlfriend's breast and jerked upright. The scar on his chest was an ugly purple pucker, but nope...not even that caused her pause.

"Well, put your clothes on," she said, helpfully bending down to scoop up their tops and tossing the clothes at them. "We have to find your friend Sam and get her to tell us where Jonah is. He has to be somewhere in Granton, right? If she's still talking to him."

Logan tugged his shirt back on, but Paige paused and sent Tess a sad cringe. "Tess, we can't go to Sam about this. Logan *stole* that letter from her. We'd get into big trouble if she knew what he'd done."

"But…" Tess shook her head. They were so close. They knew someone who could lead them to Jonah. They couldn't just give up now. "He said he loved me."

She thrust the letter toward Paige. Reaching out with an uncertain slowness, Paige hesitantly slipped the letter from Tess's hand and smoothed it flat before reading it. Logan leaned over her shoulder to read with her.

Tess chewed on her fingernails as she watched them, certain they'd love Jonah just as much as she did, just as soon as they saw his beautiful words. How could they not? She wanted to hug herself and laugh and cry and scream and smile and just spill out every emotion ever made because reading his heartfelt words made her love him hard. Her heart soared with how good his confessions felt. But being kept from him turned it all inside out until she ached.

Paige set her hand over her mouth. "Wow, this is just…wow. I want you to write me a letter like this."

Logan frowned and shook his head. "I'll work on it." Then he looked up at Tess. "What other guy is he talking about? I've never seen you around another guy. You can't even talk to them."

"I know!" Tess cried, taking the letter back to scowl at that part. "I have no idea what he's talking about either. That's why I need to find him. I need to set him straight. I need to tell him I love him, too. So, you guys have to help me find him."

When Paige and Logan exchanged wary glances, Tess growled. "You have to! You're the ones who brought me this letter. *You* gave me hope."

"We'll see what we can do." Paige bit her lip and glanced at Logan again. "But…"

Tess had a bad feeling Paige wouldn't do anything to get her boyfriend into trouble, so she held up a hand. "Wait. I have an idea." Turning on her heel, she raced back into her room.

With shaking hands, she scrambled for her bag and yanked out the first notebook she found. After writing, *I have no idea what other guy you're talking about. There's only you, so please come back to me. I'm waiting. I love you too*, on a blank page, she tore the sheet free of the binder, folded it into thirds and scribbled his name on the outside. Biting at a fingernail with chipped polish on it, she returned to Paige's room and thrust it forward.

"Could you give this to Sam? You don't have to tell her you know anything about the missing letter or how you know she's talking to him. Just…see if she can pass it along."

Paige hesitated, but then she nodded. "Okay." She took the note and looked at Tess.

Even though Paige's gaze was leery, as if she didn't think it would work, Tess gave her a watery smile of thanks. "I owe you, big time."

Tess wasn't sure how she made it through classes the next day. She only knew when they started because the professor began talking. And she knew when they ended because that was when everyone stood up to leave. But other than that, she wasn't aware of much else. She didn't realize she skipped lunch; she was too busy stalking Paige's room to hear back from either her or Logan.

She was lying on her bed, hugging Jonah's letter when the lock on her door clicked and the handle turned.

Sitting up fast enough to make herself lightheaded, she held her breath until the door opened and a hesitant Bailey stepped into the room. Gaze downcast, her friend didn't look up until she closed the door and leaned against it.

And even when Bailey lifted her face, Tess still held her breath, bracing for the yelling and accusations. Fearing she was going to lose her best friend forever, she covered her mouth with her hands and waited.

But her best friend shocked the crap out of her when she quietly murmured, "So…" She glanced away. "I'm sorry."

A huff of shocked air exited Tess's lungs. She dropped her hands from her lips, completely clueless. "*Sorry?* For what?"

"For, you know…" Bailey flailed out a hand, looking as stumped as Tess felt. "For doing everything that made you upset, for butting in, for visiting your boyfriend at the hospital. Just…for all of it. You were right; I needed to be reminded you are your own person, not just my best friend, here solely to love me."

"Oh, Bailey." Flying off the bed, Tess leapt at her, hugging her hard. "Of course I love you. And don't ever apologize for being you. I'm so sorry for yelling at you. I shouldn't have—"

"But you were right."

"No. I yelled at you for doing what you've always done, and—"

"You were right," Bailey repeated, more sternly this time. Tess opened her mouth to keep talking, but she looked into her friend's eyes and paused. Bailey looked tired and defeated, almost blank. Now wasn't the time. Bailey was here, and that was good enough for her. They could get to the in-depth opening up of their souls when they were ready.

Bailey pulled out of the hug and offered her a distant smile. "I'm glad you let me know I went too far." Then she shrugged and rolled her eyes. "And I'm kind of impressed you stood up for yourself. So, I will stand up too and admit I messed up as well. To make it up to you, I tried to find him. Jonah, I mean. But—" she shook her head "—that boy totally went off the grid. I couldn't find him anywhere. I even drove into Bristol and met his scary parents."

She let out a disgusted breath. "Thanks for warning me about them, by the way. That was one encounter I could've lived without for the rest of my life."

"You—" Pressure filled Tess's chest. Leaping at Bailey again, she gave her another hard, enveloping hug. "You're the best friend ever. I swear. You went through all that for *me?* You didn't have to do that."

Bailey tentatively hugged her back. "Um…not to get out of your good graces or anything, but are you forgetting the part where I pushed him out of your life in the first place?"

Tess pulled away to send her a watery grin. "You didn't. Not really. But, hey, you know me. Even if you had, it's fine. I can't stay mad for long."

"Obviously," Bailey muttered. "Your guy is a nationally recognized bully, and you got over that one before you even seemed to be…under it." Then she paused. "Not that I'm judging or butting in where—"

"You're not butting in." Blowing out a breath, Tess smiled. "He wrote me a letter."

Bailey glanced up. "A letter?"

Growing excited, Tess reached for it on the bed where she'd dropped it. After she explained Logan's thievery, Bailey scanned through it. The more she read, the deeper her eyebrows furrowed. "What other guy?" she finally said.

"I know, right?" Tess shook her head. "I have no clue what he's talking about. Paige and Logan are going to try to get me an address of where to find him so I can set him straight."

"Men." Bailey slung her arm around Tess's shoulder and walked them to Tess's bed so they could sit together. "What else did I miss around here?"

"Not much." After licking her lips, she leaned over to rest her head on Bailey's shoulder and took her friend's hand, squeezing warmly. "What about the other thing I said to you, though? Are you mad at me for telling you?"

Bailey cleared her throat the slid her hand out from under Tess's. "What other thing?" She shrugged away and stood up to return to her side of the room. When she began to clean, making her bed and picking up clothes off the floor, Tess knew something was definitely up. Bailey never cleaned.

"About your mom," Tess said anyway.

Without looking at her, Bailey merely shook her head. "Not sure what you're talking about." She tossed an armful of shirts and jeans into a nearby basket. "So, I'm like obscenely behind on my laundry. I'm surprised some of these dirty clothes haven't gotten up and run off on their own they're so rank. I'll be down in the laundry room."

Tess bit her lip and kept quiet as she watched her friend march toward the door. She hated to see Bailey in this much denial, but she wasn't going to push and butt in. She'd just be here when her friend finally faced it.

When Bailey opened the door, though, she almost collided with Paige lifting her hand to knock. Tess gasped and nearly shoved her roommate aside to talk to Paige.

"Did you give her the letter?"

Paige sighed and held out the letter Tess had written. "I'm so sorry. She lost contact with him. She has no idea where he's been staying, either. They used to meet every day at a pizza parlor across town, but a few days ago, he said he was doing okay and didn't need to meet with her again. She hasn't heard from him since."

"A few days?" Tess echoed hollowly, her hopes sinking. She told herself this was good news. He could be accounted for as okay and healthy up until mere days ago. But now...now she had no idea where he was or what he was doing or even if he was okay.

She glanced at Bailey. "Do you think I'll ever see him again?"

But Bailey didn't have an answer, so the question lingered in the air with a hollow, unsolved echo.

Where was he?

March passed into April, and before Tess knew it, May arrived. The new buds that had popped out on the trees around campus were now flowering in full bloom. Classes began to wind down for the semester, and students worked diligently to finish term projects and turn in papers for their final grades. Dead week was coming up in days.

Tess was beyond ready for the summer break to start. She needed time away from Granton and all the memories it had given her since January. She needed time to heal.

"Come on," Bailey said one day after their professor had let them out early from one of the classes they shared. "Let's go out to eat somewhere off campus for lunch. I want to get out for a little bit."

Since Tess felt the same restlessness, she agreed. Things between them had finally returned to normal again. It had been awkward at first. Bailey had been a lot more hesitant to be herself. And Tess kept having to bite her tongue not to bring up Bailey's mother issue, but after a few weeks, and one more cowboy spotting—where the slippery devil once more unknowingly evaded them—the old open, honest Bailey eventually returned.

As they left Grammar Hall and started for their car, they were intercepted by Paige and Logan.

"Hey, where're you guys going?"

"There's this burger joint on the edge of town I'm craving," Bailey answered. "Neither of us have a class until two, so we're going to hit it up for lunch."

"Oh, my God. Greasy food sounds so good." Paige moaned and rubbed her flat stomach.

After smiling indulgently at her, Logan took her hand and turned back to Bailey and Tess. "Mind if we tag along?"

"Sure. The more the merrier." But Bailey no sooner answered them than she glanced hesitantly at Tess. "Right?"

She did that more often lately—making a decision for both of them, only to realize what she'd just done and try to correct her mistake.

Appreciating how hard Bailey was trying, Tess hooked her arm through her friend's and grinned at Paige and Logan. "Right. We'd love to have you."

Chapter Twenty-Two

Aubrey St. Joseph was as verbose and dramatic as Jonah had feared the kid would be when Sean had first told him about the actor. But strangely enough, he was infectious. A freshman and into all things theatrical and dramatic, Aubrey had a freshness that managed to keep Jonah from the edge of depression.

After the day they'd met and shared their grief together, neither of them had left Sean's apartment. Jonah bunked on Sean's old couch, and Aubrey stayed in the bedroom. The next night, they did it all over again. When utility and rent bills began to show up, they paid them. And before they knew it, they were roommates.

The two of them had absolutely nothing in common, but strangely enough, they got along. Jonah totally blamed the link on Sean. The grief they shared drew them together with an unbreakable kind of bond. But at other times, Jonah had to admit the boy was damned entertaining, especially when something worried him.

As he finished a bowl of cereal before he had to head out to work, he watched Aubrey pace the length of the kitchen and wring his hands repeatedly. "Maybe this is wrong. We shouldn't be doing this." Rubbing his palms over his face, he turned and marched to the other end of the cramped room. Then he bit his lip and glanced at Jonah for reassurance.

"Of course you should." Jonah snorted and rolled his eyes. "This is the reason you're attending this college. To learn the fine art of dramatic performance. So, what's the point of continuing an education here if you don't *perform* anything?"

"But people are already protesting the play, saying it's too soon after—"

"And they're idiots," Jonah said sternly. He tipped his bowl up and drained the rest of the milk inside. Grabbing his cane, he began to stand, but Aubrey waved him back into his seat, grabbing the dirty dish from him and taking it to the sink so *he* could wash it instead.

It hadn't taken him long to realize Aubrey liked to stress clean. It was kind of comical, but this issue was really getting to him, so he didn't laugh.

Other students were protesting the end-of-the-year play, saying anything of such entertainment value shouldn't take place after the tragedy that had happened so recently on campus.

"I get that people are mourning," Jonah said, massaging cramped muscles in his leg before he had to stand again. "But you lost someone too. And you're *not* disrespecting Sean in any way by continuing your life and living it to the fullest." That was one detail Samantha had drummed into his head during their sessions. "Shit, you'd be disrespecting him if you didn't, if you curled up and died right along with him."

After Aubrey cleaned and put the bowl away, he returned to the table to wipe off the spot where Jonah was sitting. Grasping his arm to get his attention, Jonah waited until his friend looked at him.

"You know he'd want you to do this."

Eyes going moist, Aubrey managed a nod as he sniffed. "Yeah," he said and closed his eyes. "He would, wouldn't he?"

"Damn right, he would." Pulling his best friend's boyfriend in closer, he patted Aubrey's back heartily, proud of him. "I think you *have* to stick with this play...in honor of him."

"You know," Aubrey mumbled, glancing at him with puppy dog eyes. "If you weren't straight, I'd probably totally hit on you."

With a scowl, Jonah shoved him back. "Whatever. Cut that out."

Aubrey laughed, clutching his stomach. "Oh, my God. You should see the look on your face right now. You'd think I just grabbed your ass."

Glare only deepening, Jonah shoved to his feet. It was time to go anyway. "Don't say shit like that to me. You know it skeeves me out."

"Oh, come on." Aubrey playfully punched his arm. "You know I'm still hung up on Sean. And I would never risk our friendship by seriously coming onto you. I just…" He shrugged. "I thought we could use a little comedic relief. They do it in plays all the time when the angst begins to get a little too over—"

"Okay, okay." Jonah waved a hand to shut the guy up. "I get it. Next time, just…wait until after I'm done touching you before pulling out the gay humor, 'kay?"

Aubrey grinned but rolled his eyes. "Sure thing, sweetie. You know, I think there's still a little bit of homophobe left in you. But you're working through it very well. I must say, the way Sean talked about you, I never—*ever*—thought you'd even acknowledge me as a human being, much less pat me on the back with sympathy."

"Well." Jonah glanced away and shifted his weight more fully to his cane, uncomfortable with the conversation. "I guess I'm just a barrel of surprises."

It hurt to realize his own best friend had never known him well enough to realize most of his talk was just…talk. But it had also taught him he needed to watch what he said.

"Yes," Aubrey agreed, eyeing him thoughtfully. "That you are."

Hobbling past him, Jonah found his way into the front room where he picked up his wallet from the coffee table, which was doubling as his nightstand. Then he waved goodbye to Aubrey, told the kid not to take any more shit from anyone about the play, and he was out the door.

Cane in hand, he slowly trudged to his truck. Technically, he was supposed to wait four months after getting his femur broken before he transferred from crutches to cane, and it had barely been three since the shooting, but Jonah was getting antsy. He needed his mobility back. So, he'd made the switch a couple of days ago.

His crabby boss, Dale, already grumbled about his handicap. He hated how many breaks Jonah had to take and how often he slid a chair up to the grill so he could sit a second before regaining his feet. Jonah wasn't sure why it mattered; he'd yet to fall behind on his duties. In fact, Marla, a waitress who'd worked there for forever, said he got orders out faster and more accurately than any of the other short order cooks they'd had before. But he guessed some people just liked having something to complain about. Either that, or Dale had seen the news reports about Jonah and was judging him from those.

The diner might specialize in hamburgers, but Dale loved to cook pastries and pies the most. Jonah was always assigned the grill while

Dale worked the oven, which was fine by him. He learned how to make hamburgers that rivaled his favorite place in the university's food district. He was getting decent at fries too, cooking them to golden perfection every time.

Arriving about an hour before the lunch menu opened, he readied his station with one hand, gripping his cane with the other as he hopped on one foot back and forth between the fry grease he was heating up and the grill he was preparing.

He'd also been told he was the cleanest cook the diner had ever seen. But Dale found a way to complain about that too, saying Jonah threw out the grease too often and used so many cleaning supplies to keep his work station tidy. Deciding they needed more vegetable oil today, he set his cane aside so he could pick up a five-gallon bucket of lard and carry it out from the stock closet. It weighed a little over fifty pounds and wasn't the heaviest thing he'd carried around since breaking his femur, but it did give his leg some twinges the next day.

He didn't mind the added ache, though. This new life he'd started wasn't much — he would be the first to admit that — but Jonah found pride in his work. It felt honest, and he liked what he did. He'd found a purpose and a reason to get up each morning. He did his thing at work, then went home to see what new drama was happening with his roommate.

He tried not to think about Tess, but thoughts of her crept into his head anyway. Constantly. He hoped she'd completely forgotten him, because if she thought about him as much as he thought about her, he'd feel like a total snake right now for causing her pain. Because this hurt. It hurt, and yet it soothed to think about her, and it made him smile and want to weep at the same time. He wouldn't wish this kind of agony on anyone, especially Tess.

God, he missed her. Shaking his head, he tried not the think about the night she'd woken him at two in the morning when she'd crawled into his bed and demanded he cheer her up. But he did anyway, until a hot splash of grease from the fryer jumped up and bit him in the hand.

Cursing under his breath, he stuck his thumb knuckle into his mouth and sucked the sting away before adjusting the temperature.

"Ticket," Marla called as she clipped an order to the metal ring hanging in the small window separating the diner from the kitchen. "Time to start lunch, boys."

Jonah hopped over on his good leg, not wanting to overstress the bad one, and leaned in to read the order. As he did, the door in the diner opened and a bell jingled to announce a new arrival.

He couldn't see who came in from his vantage point, not until a pair of girls walked past his window.

He froze as he caught sight of blazing red, curly hair. He immediately ducked out of view. When he realized she hadn't seen him, he cautiously leaned back over so he could see out the window again.

His heart stuttered in his chest with longing. God, she looked good. Air swelled in his lungs until he was almost lightheaded from the rush. He reached for the edge of the window to brace himself as he openly gawked.

In the diner, Bailey chattered on, talking a mile a minute about something or other while Tess found them a booth and slid in. Instead of sitting across from her, however, Bailey sat beside Tess. Jonah frowned, wondering at that until another couple took the seat across from them. His breath caught when he recognized both of the new people.

Einstein's protector, Paige, cuddled into the booth with the very guy Jonah had seen hugging Tess in front of Grammar Hall. She wasn't hugging him today, though. And he was completely into Paige. He even leaned in to kiss her neck and whisper something in her ear before he closed his eyes and smelled her hair.

Returning his attention to Tess's face, Jonah felt pulverized. She wasn't smiling. Had that jerk dumped her to take up with Paige? But, no, that didn't feel right. She didn't seem at all bothered by the couple practically making out across from her. He knew he shouldn't feel hopeful about that, but damn, the hope rose up his esophagus anyway and filled his entire head.

She wasn't dating that guy and never had. Thank God.

That didn't explain her melancholy, though. Confused, he studied her a moment longer. What had happened to her? His Tess had been so adept at smiling. The first moment he'd met her, looking up to see her poised in his hospital room, he remembered how she had smiled at him. He'd always remember the happy curve of her lips.

So, why wasn't she smiling now? Why did she look so sad? Tess should never be sad.

Frustration gnawed at him as he tugged the order in front of him from its ring and hobbled back to the grill.

He couldn't see out into the diner at all from his work station, but he kept eyeing the window as he fixed his first meal of the day.

Working in Granton, even on the opposite side of town from the university, he should've known she might come in eventually. He'd seen some of his old football cronies a few times, not that they had noticed *him*, but he'd seen them. He'd grown out his hair and even started a beard in the past few months he'd been out of the hospital. He didn't look anything like the clean-cut Jonah Abbott he'd been in January.

He glanced over as the waitress clipped four new orders in the window. Hurrying to finish the last order, he piled everything onto a plate, grabbed up the ticket to slip under it and hopped on one leg to the window. After setting the plate down, he slapped the bell, letting Marla know an order was up, and he snagged the new ticket. When he saw it was for table number three where Tess had sat down, he shuddered out a shaky breath.

Three orders were the same, a cheeseburger with fries. But the fourth person wanted a bacon chicken ranch salad. He wasn't sure which one of them wanted which, but it really didn't matter. He was going to cook three of these meals. And they would be going to her table.

Unable to help himself, he leaned forward some more to peek out the window, knowing she probably wouldn't see him even if she glanced over. She wasn't paying a lot of attention to much of anything, actually, not even Bailey who was telling some kind of story as she flapped her hands madly, making the couple across from her laugh. Tess, however, focused a little too heartily on how she was idly stirring a packet of sugar into her iced tea.

An arrow of pain passed through his chest. This wasn't right. She should never look this depressed. Not his Tess.

"Hey, Abbott. We got another order or what?" Dale called from his station at the oven where he was taking out a fresh apple pie. "Why do you keep dawdling at the damn window today?"

"Sorry." Jonah jerked away from the window, hoping she hadn't heard his name, hoping she hadn't seen him. After calming his breaths, he glanced at his boss and nodded. "But, yeah, we have a new order. Three cheeseburgers and a salad."

Dale harrumphed, mostly likely put out because no one wanted any of his baked goods, and pointed to the grill. "Well, get to work then."

Jonah nodded. "Yes, sir." *With pleasure.*

Chapter Twenty-Three

"What the hell is this?"

At Logan's startled exclamation, Tess lifted her face from the salad that had been placed in front of her. Fork in hand, she watched him hold up the top part of his hamburger bun as he gaped in bewilderment down at the beef patty resting on the bottom bun as if it had grown two heads. Which it had. Well, one head anyway.

Tess's mouth fell open as she took in the smiley face drawn on the melted slice of cheese, ketchup making up its mouth and dots of mustard to create two eyes with a pickle slice in the middle to denote its nose. Even the tomato had been cut and set to either side of the hamburger in order to give it some big red, floppy ears. Just as her mom had always done it.

Gasping, she reached out and jerked the plate across the table, rotating so she could see the full face right-side up.

"Oh my God," she breathed, popping to her feet. "Oh my God."

She'd only told one person about her mother's smiley-face hamburgers.

Suddenly light-headed, she held out a hand to brace herself, but all she caught was air.

"Tess?" Bailey reached for her, but Tess shifted her hand, waving it to stop her.

"It's okay. I just have to…I have to…" This could only mean one thing. He was here. In the diner. In the kitchen of this very diner. "I have to go."

Nudging Bailey out of the booth so she could be free, she took off across the black and white tiled floor toward the two-way swinging silver door with a small round port-hole window in it. She'd never—ever—barged into the back of any kind of establishment before. But her brain was so scrambled she couldn't even think properly about what she was doing. She pushed through the doorway and was rewarded when she found herself in the back kitchen, a grill sizzling and the warm smell of food permeating her skin.

The middle-aged, pot-bellied guy sweating in front of the grill glanced up.

Skidding to a halt, Tess stared at him in disbelief and disappointment. Immediate tears throbbed behind her eyes as she licked her dry lips. "Did…did you cook my hamburger?"

He lifted an eyebrow. "There a problem with it?"

"No." She shook her head and sent him a tremulous smile. "Not at all. I just…I had a question about it, is all."

But where in the world had *this* guy come up with the idea to make smiley faces on his hamburgers, just as her mother had? It couldn't be a mere coincidence. Could it?

"The kid who made 'em is on his break," he said. He tipped his head to a door in the back. "You want to ask him, he's out in the alley there."

Tess nodded. Yes. Yes, she most definitely wanted to ask "the kid" about Logan's smiley-face hamburger. But her legs began to tremble. She swerved her attention to the door, almost afraid to approach it.

"Okay," she said, frozen in her shoes. "Thank you."

Still, it took her another five seconds to move. At first, she took a single step and then faltered. But with each step after that, she moved a little faster. By the time she made it to the exit, she was nearly sprinting. She shoved her way outside, spilling into the hot, humid alley, only to find Jonah hobbling along with a cane, his back to her while he rubbed a hand down his thigh as if kneading taut cramped muscles.

A whimper caught in her throat, but other than that, she couldn't speak.

He turned back slowly to shuffle the other way and finally caught sight of her in the doorway. When he jerked to a stop, she forgot to breathe. They stared at each other for a solid minute.

Then she swallowed dryly. "Y-You're walking."

He glanced down at his legs as if he just now realized, wow, he *was* walking.

She let the back door of the diner fall shut behind her and took a step toward him, only to hesitate. He lifted his face again.

"Yeah, I…" He drew in a breath and nodded. "I guess there was never a question of *if* I could or not. It was just a matter of when."

His eyes looked bloodshot as if he'd been crying, or maybe he hadn't been getting enough sleep. And he hadn't shaved in what looked like weeks. His hair had grown out, showing off some wispy curls that stuck out in places giving him a fashionable just-rolled-out-bed look. She wanted to sink her fingers into it and never let go.

With a forced smile, she said, "Good. I…" The words died on her lips. She didn't want to talk about walking. There was so much more she wanted to say. "I saw what you did to Logan's hamburger," she finally blurted.

He blinked. "Logan?"

"Yeah. Paige's boyfriend."

"Oh," he murmured as if realizing something big. Then he flushed and nodded. "Right. You've mentioned him before. I remember." He shook his head. "Sorry. The smiley face was meant for you."

Joy filled her chest. "Really?"

Eyebrows crinkling, he nodded again. "Yeah, you—I…" Running his hand through his hair, he closed his eyes briefly. "You looked sad, and I remember how you said your mom's smiley-face hamburgers always made you smile. I wasn't trying to draw you out here or anything. I just…I wanted you to smile."

She smiled now. She was unable to do anything *but* smile. "It worked."

His expression broke. Sorrow filled his features. "Tess." Her name cracked on his lips. It was an apology. A curse. A prayer. Thanksgiving. Elation. That one word was everything.

With a sob, she sprang into action, launching herself at him. He dropped his cane to catch her, pulling her tight against him as he buried his face in her hair and swept her off the ground. When his fingers cradling her scalp began to tremble, he turned his face in to kiss her temple.

"I got your letter," she whispered, clutching him for dear life.

"Letter?" Jonah pulled back to search her eyes, his eyebrows crinkled with confusion. "What letter? You're not talking about…" His face drained of color as panic flared across his face. "Oh God."

"The letter Sam made you write," Tess said, nodding. "The beautiful, amazing letter you wrote to me. Yes. *That* letter. A…A friend stole it from her for me."

He opened his mouth, his expression stunned. "You…Who? Bailey?"

Tess grinned and shook her head. "No, but it doesn't matter who. It matters that I got it, and it changed everything. I looked everywhere for you. Bailey and Paige and Logan and even Sam looked everywhere for you. I needed to tell you there is no other guy. There's only ever been you. I don't even know who you were talking about."

"It was Logan." When she wrinkled her brow, his lips tipped up in a grin. "I saw you hug him just outside Grammar Hall, so I stayed away. I didn't even think I might've been mistaken until he came into the diner with you today…with that other girl." His eyes searched her, and his breaths came a little faster. "So, you forgive me? Even after——"

"I forgave you months ago," she said.

She grabbed the front of his shirt and hauled him forward until their lips collided. A groan tore from low in his throat as he ground his mouth to hers. She made a sound against him but it wasn't any kind of resistance.

Spinning them until he pressed her back against the brick wall of the warehouse across the alley from the diner, Jonah took control, licking his tongue into her mouth and caging her face in his hands.

Tess climbed him, desperate for more, needing this connection more than she needed her next breath.

"I missed you." He broke away from her only long enough to murmur, "God, how I——"

"Oh…wow." A stunned voice broke Tess and Jonah's kiss apart.

Jonah whirled around, keeping Tess tucked safely behind him until they saw who'd surprised them. Then he slumped more against the wall, using his arm to catch himself and prop his weight against the warm brick.

Standing in the doorway to the diner, a guilty-looking Bailey raised her hands. "I...I thought this was the bathroom." She opened her mouth again, but then almost immediately clamped it shut. "Okay, fine. I was checking on you."

Tess rolled her eyes and grinned. "Go ahead. I know you're dying to demand answers."

Bailey crossed her arms over her chest. "Why do I have a feeling you left out a few details about your hospital visits, Tessie Ann?"

"Um..." Tess bit her lip and gave a guilty cringe. "Because I might have forgotten to mention a few things, maybe."

"Yeah, I'd say so." Bailey arched a skeptical glance at Jonah before returning her attention to Tess. "That was *so* not your first kiss with him."

After exchanging a silent glance with Jonah, Tess shook her head. "No. It wasn't."

"Oh, my God!" Tossing her hands in the air, Bailey began to rant. "How could you not tell me about this! We're best friends. I spilled every freaking detail to you about the time I lost my virginity, and you say nothing—*nothing*—about simply *kissing* him? Un-freaking-believable."

"Umm...I'm still a virgin if that makes you feel better."

Jonah tensed beside her. She looked up at him just as he skimmed him gaze down her body, the heat in his gaze making her burn in the most delicious places.

"Hey, stop looking at her like that, buddy," Bailey snapped. "She's going to stay a virgin, too. I haven't sanctioned this reunion yet. You may still be a—"

"Oh, hush." Blushing, Tess turned in toward Jonah to hide her embarrassment. "You have no authority to sanction *anything* between us. Butt out."

When Bailey didn't argue, but *did* heartily scowl at her, Jonah curled his arm around her and ducked his head so he could rest his cheek against hers. "You will not believe how much I missed you," he murmured in her ear.

Tess shuddered and grabbed a fistful of his shirt, inhaling his scent, afraid she might never get another chance to do so again. He seemed just as clingy, skimming his nose up her jawline and curling his torso in to create a little nest for her between him and the wall.

"Hel-lo," Bailey called from behind them, her voice making it sound like she was waving her hand to get their attention. "I'm still here."

Jonah's soft laugh was like a puff of breath on Tess's cheek. "You described her perfectly."

"A little too perfectly." Tess glanced over his shoulder to lift her eyebrows in question at Bailey. "What now?"

"I'm not butting in, but seriously? How can you two just start making out together after not seeing each other for two months?"

Probably because we haven't seen each other for two months, Tess was about to smart back. But her friend began ranting again.

"He lied. *You* lied. There's…stuff…that's kept you apart. Why isn't one of you mad, or hurt, or really freaking confused right about now? Personally, I'm riding the confused train over here. But, no, you two just look happy to see each other, which makes no sense. You spent, what, five days together, lying to each other, before you went your separate ways. That's not enough time for—" she waved her hand, motioning between them "—this."

"They were five very intense days," Jonah answered, turning back to Tess to gaze into her eyes with a slight, knowing smile.

Giddy warmth spread through her. Relieved he'd felt the same force of connection during their time together as she had, she grinned back. Her insides stirred with restless anticipation.

"Besides," she said to Bailey, not taking her eyes off him, "he explained everything I needed to know in his letter."

"But you didn't explain anything to *him,*" Bailey shot back. "Not why you claimed to be his girlfriend when you could've just as easily said—"

"It doesn't matter," Jonah cut in, taking Tess's hand and smiling softly at her. "She's here. That's all I care about."

"Well, then, *I* want to know why he stayed away so long, and why—"

"Oh, my God, Bay!" Tess gritted her teeth and set her a sidelong glance. "Can you give us a minute here?"

"Fine." Arms re-crossed firmly, feet braced in standoff mode, Bailey didn't move.

Jonah let out a breath. "She kind of has a point. We should probably talk before…" He smiled faintly and ran the back of his knuckles gently down Tess's cheek. "I need to get back in, anyway. My break should be about up."

No sooner had he said that than a voice spoke up. "Hey, kid. You coming back to work, or what? It's the busiest time of the day."

Tess glanced over, seeing his boss in the open doorway behind Bailey, spatula in hand and irritable expression on his face.

"Yeah." Jonah cleared his throat and stepped away from the wall.

When he bent in an effort to reach for his cane, Tess darted forward to fetch it for him. "Here you go."

Their fingers brushed, and he sucked in a breath, meeting her gaze. He cleared his throat. "Thank you."

From the achy desperate gleam in his eyes, she knew he wanted to see her again. "When do you get off work?"

His shoulders sagged. Relief cleared his face. "Six."

She nodded. "I'll be here."

He nodded too, his eyes igniting with a joyous sparkle that warmed her. "Thanks. I...we both have some unresolved issues we need to clear up for each other." Then he arched a look toward her best friend. "And for Bailey too, obviously."

Chapter Twenty-Four

She was waiting for him when he clocked off. Jonah caught his breath as soon as he saw her leaning against the far wall of the alley behind the diner, as if she hadn't left since he'd last seen her, though she and Bailey had gone back inside after their alley scene to finish their meal.

Stray pieces of red hair, glinting crimson in the waning sunlight, fluttered across her face. She looked picturesque and breathtaking.

"Did you drive?" She pushed away from the building to move toward him.

Every muscle in his body pulled taut with anticipation as he nodded. "Yeah. My truck's just around the block."

She reached for his hand. "Good. You'll have to give me a lift. I took the bus here."

Their fingers interlaced, and he gaped at their connection in wonder. Aside from Tess, he couldn't remember ever holding anyone's hand. Not even his mother's.

"Where do you want to go?"

Her answer was simple. "With you."

It tore into him to know she wanted to be with him, *really* wanted to be with him. Made him feel like shit for how he'd let her leave the hospital without clearing the air between them and for not going back to her these past few months. He'd stayed away for her, to help her, but she'd looked so miserable in the diner today. And now…now she didn't look miserable at all.

He'd messed up, big time. But he was going to fix this. Somehow.

"We can go back to my place. Aubrey shouldn't be home until late."

Color fled her cheeks and made the blue in her eyes stand out in stark color. "Aubrey?" she croaked as if the name physically hurt her to say aloud.

He paused. "Yeah. Did I not mention him in the letter?"

"Him?"

He smiled. "Definitely a him." Kissing her temple, he tugged her along. "He was the reason Sean finally decided to come out of the closet. He'd fallen in love, and Aubrey was…you know."

When he lifted his eyebrows, clarity sparked in Tess's eyes. "Oh. But, how did you two meet?"

"I went to Sean's apartment when I was released from the hospital. It was the only place I could think to go."

"Sure." Tess stroked his arm in sympathy. "That makes sense. You'd want to say goodbye."

Realizing he hadn't yet shared any of his Sean story with her except through his letter, he gulped. "Well, when I got there, Aubrey was also there, and we sort of…"

"Connected," she guessed softly.

"Yeah. Neither of us as has left since. So, we just sort of became roommates. He's not like any person I thought I'd ever like, but he grows on you."

With a knowing smile, she bumped her shoulder into his. "You like him."

He shook his head but couldn't hide his grin. "Don't tell him that. He'll want to hug or some kind of male bonding shit I'm not into."

Her laugh was outright musical as it filled the evening air. Jonah covered her hand with his as they approached his truck. He unlocked and opened her door, holding her hand and helping her up until she was safely inside.

On the short drive, she told him about her classes and how many finals she had to take the next week. "And the week after that, Bailey and I will go home for summer break. But we decided to rent an apartment off campus next semester. I think I've had about as much dorm life as I can handle."

Jonah glanced over, panic squeezing his lungs, as he pulled into his building's parking lot. "So, you'll be gone all summer?" He should rejoice that at least she was returning to Granton again in the fall. But thinking he might not see her for another few months was agony. These *last* few months had been bad enough.

Her gaze met his across the quiet cab. "Unless we find an apartment sooner," she said, hope lining her eyes.

He reached for her, and she leaned toward him willingly. As they kissed over the center console, he was a split second from crawling into the passenger seat to join her. But she broke away to say, "I'll make sure it's sooner."

"Good." Grinning, Jonah hurried from the truck and hobbled around with his cane to open her door, but she was already climbing out.

They met by the front bumper, and she took his hand again. He liked holding her hand. Her fingers were small and delicate and made him feel like her protector. He was freshly amazed by how much shorter than him she was.

Without talking, he led her up to his and Aubrey's apartment. Once inside, he pointed toward the kitchen, motioned down the hall to give her the mini tour, and then turned to study the couch across the living room. "And that's where I'm bunking."

Tess's brow wrinkled with worry as she studied the short couch and then turned to eye his large, tall frame. "There aren't two bedrooms?"

He shook his head. "No. But that's okay. This is better than I thought I'd end up with when I left the hospital."

Nodding slowly, she looked down to pick at her chipped fingernail polish. "And you never planned on coming back to me. Did you?"

He gulped, knowing they'd have to discuss this eventually. But he wasn't ready to leap right into it, first thing.

Grasping her hand, he lifted her fingers to touch the fading red polish, the same color they'd been when he'd last seen her. "Haven't you repainted them since..."

She watched him run his thumb over each nail. "No. I tend to only paint them when I'm—"

"Happy?" he guessed. She didn't answer, but when she glanced at him, she really didn't have to. Her expression told him he was right.

Bringing her telling fingers to his mouth, he kissed them desperately and then squeezed his eyes closed.

"I messed up." The confession tore its way from his soul. "I don't... I don't know." He glanced up through his eyelashes with a wince. "I'm still not...I mean, I'm better. Heaps better—emotionally—than where I was in February, but...it's still a work in progress. And I'm not anywhere near the kind of man who deserves you."

Her gaze clouded to a cool indifference. "So you said in your letter."

"And I know it wasn't my place to decide for you what kind of person you want in your life, but I also wanted—no, I *needed* to prove to myself that I could be apart from you without—" He shook his head, took a breath, and looked deep into her eyes. "I was in such a dark place when you walked into my hospital room that night. I was confused, hurt, angry. A total mess. And you saved me, saved me from losing myself to my own demons. You were like this angel, the only bright spot in my world. I latched onto you with both hands. So, I wanted to make sure that what I felt for you was—" he licked his lips and glanced away "—true. I didn't want this to just be a dependency for me. I wanted—"

When he looked at her, her blue eyes glittered with a restless anxiety. "You wanted what?"

"I want this to be real." He brought her hands to his mouth and kissed her fingers, his eyes begging for something that he couldn't voice with words. "I don't want you to be a crutch for me to lean on in my darkest hours. I want to be in a relationship where I give as much as I've already received. Hell, I want to give you *more* than I've ever gotten from you, but I know that's not possible because you've given me...everything."

"But you *have* given me things, Jonah. You—"

"I mean, more than just making you feel needed," he bit out. If only he could do for her half the shit she'd done for him.

"Listen to me." Her voice was as stern as it was soft. He had no idea how she managed it, but it was the kind of thing only Tess could accomplish. Casing his face between her hands, she smiled at him as if she cherished him.

"You have given me so much. More than you'll ever know."

He wanted her words to be true. But he just couldn't hope.

She must've seen the distrust in his gaze because she insisted, "You have. I told you about my stupid gene, right?"

"Yeah." He nodded and rolled his eyes. "But you've never said anything stupid to me, or acted—"

"No, actually, I have. But aside from that, for some strange reason, I can be more me around you than I can around anyone else, maybe even Bailey." Kissing him softly, she took a moment to simply hold her mouth against his. When a consuming need rose inside him, he took her bottom lip between his teeth and pulled her into a deeper kiss.

It was so easy to get lost in her. He would never be able to touch her enough, or kiss her enough, or love her enough. When she pulled away with a breathless laugh, he leaned into her and inhaled her hair, relishing every breath he got to spend with her, because he wasn't sure how long they'd have together.

"I am so awkward and clumsy and a complete dunce around any guy I find remotely attractive. That's why the whole girlfriend word popped out of my mouth when I first met you. I had it all planned to say we had a class together or were passing acquaintances, that we were just friends, and *that's* why I was coming to visit you. But then I saw this drop dead gorgeous stranger in the room, and everything in here," she tapped the side of her head, "went to mush."

A sudden thought struck him. He might have known she'd never had degenerate plans when she'd come to visit him, but he'd always assumed she'd at least known who he was. But she'd just used the word *stranger*.

"Why *did* you go into my hospital room that day?"

She flushed hard. "Bailey and I had volunteered to work as candy stripers one evening a week. I was supposed to make sure you ate." When she bit her lip and sent him a shy look as if bracing herself for his anger, he merely shook his head.

"So, you were assigned to me? You had *no* idea who I was at all?"

"None whatsoever. All I knew was that you hadn't eaten all day, you had amnesia, and no family or friends had visited you. I felt so bad for you. I just…I wanted to make things better somehow. And then, after you threw your tray against the door—"

"You were there when I did that?"

"I was standing right outside the doorway with Bailey, getting my instructions for the evening. No one was willing to help me get you another tray, so that's when I went to get you the tacos, and I decided to take off my striper apron to act like a friend…so you wouldn't feel so alone."

He chuckled and hugged her close. "Well, I'll be damned. You really are too sweet to be true."

She rolled her eyes. "Not hardly. Are you forgetting the whole stupid-gene thing? I outright lied to you and told you I was your girlfriend. But once I got to talking to you, the real Tess was actually able to come out." With a laugh, she buried her face to kiss his heartbeat before pulling back to grin up at him. "I was so afraid I'd have to settle for some guy someday that I wasn't attracted to in the least, because those tend to be the only guys I can talk to. But then you came along, or rather I came along to you. And you…saved me from that fate. Now I can even talk to Logan occasionally."

"And hug him too," Jonah reminded, still remembering how he'd thought Logan was with Tess. Unable to get the image of them embracing out of his head, he blurted, "God, I was such an idiot that day. I came to see you in the hopes of making my fake girlfriend into my real girlfriend."

Her mouth fell open. "Oh…wow. Really?"

He leaned his forehead into hers. "Would it…I mean, if I hadn't run off in a jealous pout, do you think it would've worked? If I had approached you and explained everything I had in my letter, do you think you would've taken me back that day?"

Cupping his face, she looked up at him, her blue eyes glittering with emotion. "Yes," she whispered. "Definitely."

"Will you take me today?"

Her breath caught as her eyes glittered with joy. "Definitely," she repeated.

He kissed her, sweeping her up off her feet and into his arms. As his mouth fed from hers, he carried her toward the couch. But after the first uneven, faltering stop, she broke off from his mouth, gasping. "Your leg! Oh, put me down before—"

He kissed her again, cutting off her argument, and carried her the rest of the way to the cushions. The tendons in his leg pulled, but it was good kind of stretching pain.

"You're too tiny to hurt me," he assured her.

With a self-derisive laugh, she shook her head. "I have always been short, but never tiny."

He kissed her again. It seemed to be the best way to hush her because he didn't like how she thought of her perfect figure. She was flawless and soft, and—"Tiny," he insisted. "Trust me, no one but you could fit on this couch with me."

He lowered himself, bringing her down with him and settling her into his lap. When her soft, rounded backside landed on his arousal, he groaned, clenching his teeth.

"What is—" She wiggled her bottom with a thoughtful crinkle in her eyebrows, until her face cleared. "Oh." Instantly blushing, she tried to crawl off him, but he caught her hip and swung them both around until she had her back to the cushions, her head resting on an armrest and his hips slotted perfectly between her thighs, where he was once again pressing the throbbing part of himself against the warm, soft, intimate part of her.

"Oh," she breathed again, her eyes wide with wonder. "We never quite did *this* at the hospital. I only ever felt you with my..." Realizing what she was going to say, she trailed off, blushing too hard to finish the sentiment.

Jonah chuckled and kissed her nose. "Mmm," he said. "That's my fondest memory of that place. But here, we don't have to worry about anyone interrupting us."

Her eyes twinkled with mischief as her fingers trailed down his shirt. Then she paused and cut a worried glance toward the front door. "Unless your roommate—"

"He's been out until after midnight every night this month, practicing for the play they're putting on next week. He's been pulling double duty. Not only does he have a major acting role, but he's helping build the set."

The two pink spots on her cheeks brightened. "So..."

"So," he repeated, his soul soaring with thoughts of all the fun they could have by themselves. "The only thing hampering us is this small-ass couch." He began to kiss his way down her throat. "Someday, I swear, I'm going to get you on a real bed that's at least a full size and—"

He cut himself off with a groan as her wandering little hand found him through his jeans.

"Damn." He panted, leaning his forehead against her shoulder.

"As I recall, you liked this. Right?" When she gripped him through denim, he made a strangled sound of assent from the base of his throat. She chuckled. "That's what I thought."

While her fingers examined him through his clothes, he toyed with a piece of her hair, smelling it and then winding it around his fingers, trying not to think too hard about what she was doing because it felt so good.

It'd been too long.

She glanced up at him coyly through the veil of her thick eye-lashes. "You won't believe how much I wanted to slide my hand under the hospital sheet that night."

He couldn't breathe. He literally—

Jonah looked into her eyes and sucked in air. "You just had to tell me that, didn't you?"

"Can I…can I do it now?"

When he saw temptation and desire on her face, it dragged him under.

"Anything," he said. "You can do anything you want, baby."

She bit her lip, and he lost it. Groaning when she flicked open the top button of his jeans, he closed his eyes, or maybe his lids naturally forced themselves closed because it was just too much to handle with all his senses firing this radically. But his hearing seemed to grow more acute with his vision out of the way, because the lazy rasp of his zipper had to be the most erotic sound he'd ever heard.

His juices flowed, and by the time her fingers touched the bare skin of his abdomen, he jumped from the overwhelming intensity of the contact.

"Jesus. I'm not—" He was going to freaking embarrass himself if he didn't cool it down. "You feel too good."

She grinned. "I bet this will feel better, though." As her warm, soft palm wrapped around his rigid column, his mind turned to liquid. Her touch was so shy and hesitant, he knew without a shadow of a doubt that this was the first time she'd ever felt anyone there. But, damn.

"Oh, Christ," he breathed. He watched her wide, amazed eyes as her fingers slowly slid their way down. When she paused and bit her lip, he blew out a strained breath. "You don't have to do this if you don't—"

"I *do* want to." She kissed him, and a split second later, her warm fingers slid back up. He jumped in her hand. She jumped too, as if startled, but then she smiled up at him, her face glowing with womanly accomplishment.

He sank his fingers into her hair and cupped her head, soothing her. "You okay?"

She nodded and looked down at him, though she could barely see the crown of his junk from the opening of his pants. "Wow," she whispered.

Fuck. He shouldn't. He really shouldn't. But he did anyway, easing his hand down so he could cover hers and guide her, showing her how to apply just the right amount of pressure and then move. When she got the hang of it, he let her go at her own pace and closed his eyes, concentrating on nothing but each warm, amazing glide of her palm.

"What does it feel like?" she asked, the awe in her voice making him open his lashes.

Jonah swallowed, trying to think of the right words to describe everything that was going on inside him. But the only word he could come up with was good. It felt good. Really good.

"Why don't I just show you?" he suggested as he found the waistband of her jeans and slipped open the top button.

Her eyes widened. "Jonah?"

He met her gaze. "Can I touch you there too?"

She gulped. "Okay."

"Are you sure?" He hesitated, squinting as he studied her. "If I'm going too fast—"

"No! I mean, yes, I'm sure. And no, you're not going too fast."

"Okay. We'll just...we'll go one step at a time, though."

He eased open her pants, and they both lifted up so he could slide the cloth down her legs. She sent him a shy yet excited grin. He wanted to bring her to so much pleasure in that moment, he almost couldn't control his own libido. Gently squeezing the hand she still had around his penis, he pried her away, saying, "We'll get back to that later. I want to concentrate on you for a while."

Tess nodded, absolute trust glimmering in her eyes. In fact, feeling the weight of that trust almost stopped him in his tracks. But he could see the anticipation as well. She wanted to know what this felt like. She was eager and curious.

He couldn't let her down.

Grasping the waistband of her panties, he eased them away from her. Their gazes met and locked. She bit her lip and pulled in a breath as if to say, *Here were go.* He couldn't seem to look away as he removed her underwear and distractedly dropped them over the side of the couch.

"You are so beautiful," he said. He lowered his gaze to take in the scarlet curls between her legs.

Her fingers clenched at her sides. "You have no idea how much effort it's taking not to cover myself right now."

He caught both her wrists and pinned her hands to her sides. "Don't even think about it. You're so amazing right now, Tess. I can't even…" He looked up and met her gaze, but that only turned him on even more. "It's taking everything I have to keep from…Oh, screw it."

He leaned down and kissed her. There.

Her hips arched off the couch as she yelped in surprise. But the move only made her push deeper against his mouth. "Jonah! What're you…oh…you shouldn't…it…*God.*"

He let go of her hands to catch her waist and ease her back down. Then he licked her again.

She lurched under him once more and grabbed handfuls of his hair. "Omigod, omigod. That's…wow. Wow."

He almost came.

Holding her steady, he began to feast. He'd only intended to touch a little tonight. Get her used to the feel of him. This should probably stop here and now, because he was only going to want more when she finished. He knew she was inexperienced; he shouldn't rush too much in one night, but damn…He didn't want it to end. And now that he'd had a taste, no way was he stopping until she was falling apart under his tongue.

Besides, he could tell she wanted him to keep going from the way she writhed in his arms, begging him with her gasps and the grip she had on his hair. Which only made it that much more impossible for him to keep himself under control.

When her breathing told him how close she was, he pushed a finger inside her and almost wept from the snug, wet fit.

Her body went rigid, and he knew this was it. Throaty cries filled his ears as she came against his mouth. Concentrating on nothing but her, he stroked her through her completion, overcome by how perfect she was. When her thighs loosened from around his head and began to tremble while she petted his hair with shaking fingers, he slid his fingers free and looked up.

"That was…that was…" She paused to lick her lips.

He slid up her body to snuggle with her. "Are you okay?" Hugging her, he grinned as she burrowed close against him, quaking as if cold.

"No, I'm…not okay. Okay is so tame for what I am. God. Amazing is too tame for what I feel right now."

Hearty male satisfaction filled him. "Good," he said and kissed her hair. Then her cheek. Her neck. "That's all I needed to hear."

Chapter Twenty-Five

Tess had to be floating at least a foot off the ground. She wiggled into Jonah's T-shirt and wasn't at all surprised to find the hem fell nearly to her knees. He paused to grin at her after he slipped on a pair of track pants.

"God, you're adorable," he murmured, shaking his head as if he couldn't believe such an adorable woman was in his apartment with him.

But what was more, he made her *feel* adorable. She loved that about him, just as she loved pretty much everything else about him. He was just so…Jonah.

Needing to escape the intensity of everything he did to her, she took his hand and dragged him toward the kitchen, because both of their stomachs had been growling for the past ten minutes.

She'd assumed they'd graze on whatever snack they could find, but Jonah wanted to cook her his cheeseburger specialty since she hadn't gotten to taste it at the diner. Tess protested, not wanting him on his feet for longer than he should be. He did too much without his cane, hopping around on one foot as it was. Sometimes, he even stepped down, putting his weight on his bad leg. She sucked in a breath and cringed every time he did that. But he didn't seem to be in much pain, so she tried to calm herself.

Still, she insisted on helping him, to speed up the process, so they could sit and eat.

Jonah did the smiley face on her hamburger again, and grinned bashfully when he handed her the plate. "Since I know it's actually coming to you this time," he said.

She rolled her eyes as if the gesture was silly, though, honestly, it touched her deeply. Over supper, he told her how he'd spent his last few months, and she told him about all the changes that had happened around campus.

"After the suicide—" She started, breaking off with wide eyes. "I mean, did you know...?"

"Yeah." He laughed softly, lowering his gaze. "I was there when they brought the body out of Grammar Hall. I can't believe Roadrunner would do that. But I guess if he was feeling as guilty as I was..." He shrugged and looked up to catch her expression.

She reached across the table and took his hand. "I worried about any guilt you might feel."

Jonah nodded, squeezing her fingers. "Yeah." He blew out a breath. "I always wondered if people thought I should've done what he did, since I was—"

"What?" Tess surged to her feet to gape down at him with her hands on her hips. "You absolutely shouldn't have done what he did. No way. No how."

Jonah bit his lip a let out a breath he'd been holding. "I kind of felt like a coward because I couldn't even consider the idea."

"Oh, my God." Her anger drained away instantly, and she slid into his lap to sit on his good leg. Wrapping her arms around his neck, she cuddled her face into his neck. "I'm so glad you *couldn't*. Because I don't know what I'd do without you, Jonah Abbott. Do you understand that? You cannot leave me."

He buried his face in her hair. "I kept holding on to life, even though I was sure the world would be a better place if I wasn't in it. I kept holding on because I had this piece of hope stuck in my head that maybe, one day, I could be with you again, like we are right now. Even after I saw you with Logan, I just...I couldn't give up."

She shuddered and clutched him tight, overwhelmed by the thought that she'd given anyone a reason to fight for their own life. "The world would not be a better place without you, Jonah. It would be dark and gloomy, and I don't know if I'd ever smile again if you left it."

Their supper officially over, he picked her up and carried her back to the couch. She didn't complain about his bum leg this time because he seemed determined to carry her everywhere despite how much she objected. And besides, it made her feel as tiny as he said she was.

Back on the couch, they held each other, and eventually turned on the television to watch a sitcom as they lay wrapped together.

At some point, Tess fell asleep, only to wake up to a voice screeching, "Oh, sweet holy hosanna, you have a naked woman in bed with you."

"She's not naked." Jonah slurred out the half-awake argument as he yawned and shifted under her.

Tess lifted her face from his chest to see the silhouette of a guy from the open doorway of the apartment. When the silhouette stepped inside and shut the door, she decided he must be Aubrey.

He pointed to her pants and shirt wadded on the floor by the couch. "Not naked, huh? God, Jonah. I can't believe you brought home a woman. You are such a whore. You're supposed to still be hung up on—" As he swaggered closer, he took in Tess and halted in his tracks. "Well, glory be. Curly red hair, big blue eyes, innocent face. You must be Tess."

Tickled he knew her name just by looking at her, she twisted to sit up and grin at Jonah as he settled beside her. "You talked about me?" And enough to warrant Aubrey's recognition of her at first sight, too. How amazing.

Jonah rolled his eyes with a moody harrumph. "He forces me to talk. It's a pain in the ass."

"Oh, whatever." Aubrey gave a tickled squeal and rushed forward. "You love me. Now scoot." He plopped down between the two of them, forcibly wedging them apart so he could sit in the middle.

Tess scrambled to smooth the hem of Jonah's T-shirt down her thighs, because it wasn't uncomfortable at all for a complete stranger to sit by her and throw his arm around her while she was wearing nothing but a huge shirt and panties. Yeah, not uncomfortable at all.

But Aubrey didn't seem to notice. He grinned and touched her face with fingers that were stained with what looked like every color of spray paint. "You have such a clear complexion. I love this skin. It's like alabaster. Jonah, don't you just love her skin?"

"I doubt she'd be sitting here in nothing but my shirt if I didn't."

Aubrey rolled his eyes and snorted as if that answer was simply too male. Then he turned back to Tess. "Sweetie Pie over here has gushed about you so much I feel like we're already sisters."

Tess glowed. She loved hearing how he'd gushed. "I don't have any sisters," she admitted. "But I've always wanted one."

"Then you're adopted." Aubrey gave her arm a squeeze. "We're going to have to go shopping together now and rent lots of movies with Channing Tatum in them and eat popcorn while staring at nothing but his perfect little tush and glorious abs for a solid two hours."

While Jonah groaned and rolled his head onto the back of the couch, Tess laughed. "Sold. It's a date."

"Great. You bring the popcorn. And I'll whip up some margaritas and—"

"Hey," Jonah cut in, shoving his roommate off the couch. "If you'll excuse us, you're interrupting what is technically *our* first date."

"*Oh!*" Eyes going wide, Aubrey slapped his hand over his forehead, highlighting the fact he had a touch of blue paint on his jaw. "You're right. I'm so sorry, honey. You two continue. I'll just adjourn to my room, plug in the iPod, and stay there for the rest of the night. Enjoy him, sweetie." He tapped Tess's knee and winked at her. "He's a good man."

"Yes, he is," she said softly. She waited until he was gone and heard the soft click of his bedroom door before she turned to Jonah. "I like your roommate."

He snorted. "I've had worse."

When they both realized how much worse of a roommate he'd had, Tess shivered. He pulled her close and tucked her head up under his chin. "How've you been holding up with all that lately? If you've decided to come back next semester, I'm guessing you're not so scared of campus anymore."

"No," she admitted. "Not *as* scared, anyway. There are still moments I feel like I'm tramping over someone's grave, like whenever I'm in the food district, but I've worked through a lot of it."

He kissed her hair and smoothed his hand up her arm. "Good. I knew you'd pull through."

She spent a second just listening to his heartbeat before pulling away and looking up. "I should probably get back. Bailey will worry."

That was meant to be a joke, but Jonah said, "Or you could just call her. Tell her I'll get you back in the morning in time for your first class."

He wanted her to stay the night? Tess almost leapt to her feet to dance around the living room in excitement. But she bit her lip, holding back.

Nudging her shoulder, he winked. "We've already proven we can sleep together in a small space."

The hope in his brown eyes tipped her decision over the edge. After texting Bailey, she turned off her phone and settled down on the couch with Jonah.

"Wakey, wakey." An unfamiliar voice dragged Tess from pleasant dreams.

Under her, a warm, solid Jonah stirred, grumbling something about shutting up and leaving him alone.

"But it's time to rise and shine, you two love birds. You've got work. She's got school. So...up and at 'em, kiddos." When Aubrey clapped his hands with way too much enthusiasm, both Tess and Jonah groaned.

Thank God Jonah obviously wasn't a morning person either. That might've actually been a deal breaker.

She lifted her head, strands of red hair falling into her face. Instantly worried how she must look first thing in the morning, she scrambled off the couch.

"I'm just going to...visit the bathroom real quick." She deserted the two guys, scooping up handfuls of her clothes and hurrying down the hall until she was locked inside the lavatory.

Though she dreaded looking into a mirror, it was the first thing she did. A groan later, she began to finger-comb her wild locks. If Jonah decided to stay with her after this, it was definitely true love.

By the time she exited the bathroom, she was a quivering mess inside. Hands trembling, she folded the shirt she'd slept in and gingerly stepped forward to hand it to him where he was still sitting shirtless on the couch talking to Aubrey.

"Thanks," he said, his smile warm. But when his gaze drifted over her hair, he frowned slightly. "Oh, man. You combed it. I liked it all sleepy and wild."

After he struggled to his feet with his cane, he limped to her and paused with a long, chaste morning kiss. He tasted like orange juice, telling her he'd already been up and in the kitchen.

She melted into a gooey ball of adoration as he stepped back and smiled at her. "My turn," he murmured. He hobbled around her and headed down the hall to the bathroom.

She gnawed on her lip as she stared after him. Was he limping worse now than he was yesterday? Dang it, she knew she shouldn't have let him carry her last night.

"His limp is always worse first thing in the morning," Aubrey said from beside her as if reading her mind. Or, crap, maybe she'd said that aloud. "I think it just takes a bit for him to stretch and warm his muscles back up for the day."

"Thank God." Tess turned to him with a relieved smile. "You really don't think I made it worse somehow?"

"Nah. And I doubt he'd care if you did. He looks happier and better rested than I've ever seen him. And with that, I need you to come with me, girlfriend."

When he held out his hand with a mischievous wink, she reached for it, curious as to what he wanted to do. He bound their fingers together and dragged her down the hall until he reached a door, which he shoved open and pulled her through.

Not sure what was going on, she initially resisted when she realized they were in an immaculately clean bedroom.

"So, Sean was a great organizer," Aubrey started as if he didn't notice any of her apprehensions while he tugged her to a calendar tacked to the closet door. "He wrote everything on this damn thing. And this…is what he had penciled in for today."

Stabbing his finger at the date, he turned to scrutinize her with an arched, so-what-are-you-going-to-do-about-this stare. Tess shrank back from the expectant look, but he didn't care. He continued to watch her. Clearing her throat quietly, she leaned in and took her eyes off him to look at the date in question. When she saw the words *Jonah B-Day* written in, she caught her breath.

"His birthday's today," she breathed out in wonder.

"Exactly," Aubrey said. "And he has no idea I know, so I was going to come home early from rehearsal to surprise him with a cake or something. But now that you're here…there are two of us to plan. So, we need something big and splashy and—"

"Whoa, whoa, whoa." Tess lifted her hands to stop him. "I'd be all for that. I don't even care what it would take to get it planned and ready by this evening. But…are you sure *Jonah* wants something big? Or splashy?"

Aubrey's expression crumpled. "But he *deserves* big and splashy. I'm telling you, that man has been here for me to help me through this. If it hadn't been for him, I would've fallen to pieces by now. He's my rock. My friend. And I don't have the luxury of making a lot of real, true, honest-to-God friends. He should have…He needs…"

When he blinked rapidly, his eyes glistening with tears, Tess made a sound of sympathy and pulled him in for a warm hug.

"I know. He deserves the best. And we should do that. But *his* way. Small, intimate, meaningful."

After staring at her with wide eyes for a good ten seconds, Aubrey smiled. "That's perfect," he whispered. "You know, after he talked about you, I was worried you might be—" He wrinkled his nose, making a face as if he'd just tasted a tart lemon. "But you're nothing but heart and soul. And you actually know my boy and care about how he feels. I am *so* relieved you're back in his life." He hugged her and then let out a giddy squeal as he pulled away.

"So, you're going to arrange something for tonight, right? Small, intimate, and meaningful. We can have it here. Just the three of us, you think?"

"Actually…" Tess tapped her chin thoughtfully. "What would you think about six or seven of us? I know of a few more that might make the evening perfect."

Chapter Twenty-Six

Jonah drove Tess back to campus, rubbing his sore thigh as he turned down the street that led to Grammar Hall. He hadn't been back here since the day he'd seen Tess hugging another man.

It felt different. And he was more nervous now than he'd been that day. That day he had still been in so much pain, too lost to care much about everyone else's opinions, and utterly overwhelmed by the turn his life had taken. This morning all he could wonder was how many people might notice him. Would they say anything to him if they did? Would they say anything to Tess?

Shit. He hadn't thought of that. She *would not* suffer from being associated with him. He didn't care what he had to do; no one was allowed to hurt his girl.

Tugging his ball cap lower on his head after he parked in a visitor's parking space, he glanced around, feeling a measure of security from his beard and longer hair.

"You ready for this?" he asked, blowing out a bracing breath as he killed the engine and opened the door.

But Tess caught his arm before he could get out. He glanced at her, and she sent him a sympathetic smile. "You don't have to walk me up. Aubrey told me your leg bothers you more in the mornings. And stairs can't be any fun with a cane. I'll be fine."

Double shit. Now he felt like a total tool for not walking his girl to her door after spending the night with her.

"It's okay," he said. "I want to see you to your door."

She opened her mouth, no doubt to argue, but she must've seen the determination on his face because she stopped whatever she was going to say and drew in a breath.

"I'd like that," she said brightly. "Thank you."

He felt royally exposed as he limped slowly toward the entrance of her dorm building. People glanced over, but they were so busy looking at his cane, they probably didn't even notice his face. But he stayed braced for the moment when someone yelled out an insult and called him a murderer, a bully, a bigot, or a coward. They'd lost interest and stopped calling him that on national television, but he doubted the local crowd would forget so quickly.

Leaning down toward Tess, he murmured confidentially in her ear. "If anyone gives you any flak about being seen with me, you'd tell me, right?"

She abruptly stopped walking and glanced up at him with a sharp, irritated frown. "If anyone gives me any trouble, I'll call them an idiot."

He wanted to smile and dance and cheer that she was so fervently willing to defend him, but the point of the matter remained. "I'm serious, Tess. I know how people around here can pick on someone. I've been right there in the thick of it, remember. If someone gives you a hard time, I want to know about it."

"And I'll make sure you will," a new voice answered.

He and Tess looked over to find Bailey, a book bag slung over her shoulder, strolling down the sidewalk toward them.

When she flashed him a thumbs-up sign, letting him know she wouldn't let anything happen to his girl, he sent her a grateful nod. "Thanks."

Tess, however, gritted her teeth and flashed her best friend a scowl.

Then she turned to him. "I am proud to be seen with you, and I don't care who knows we're together." Sweeping off his hat to reveal the parts of his face he'd been successfully shadowing, she wrapped her arms around him and kissed him long and passionately.

She had the power to pull him under and sweep him along the current of her desire; before he knew it, Bailey was clearing her throat. "Tess needs to get to class sometime today. You can see her later, Romeo." She slipped his hat out of Tess's grip and thrust it at him. "Bye-bye now."

As she hooked her arm through Tess's, Tess sent him her sweet, angelic smile and mimed putting a phone to her ear as she mouthed the words *Call me.*

He chuckled and waved goodbye as Bailey herded her inside Grammar Hall.

As he drove to work, he couldn't stop smiling. Then he began to whistle under his breath. At the diner, he ditched his cane entirely. The endorphins surging through his system gave him a pretty damn good high, because he barely felt a pinch in his leg at all.

He was humming along to the song playing out in the diner when Dale scowled over at him. "That redhead must've gotten under your skin good. I've never see you so jolly."

The word jolly gave him pause, but then Jonah decided he liked it. Jolly was a nice thing to be. Made him think he was turning into Santa Claus or something, but who cared? He could be a lot worse than jolly.

He sent Dale a smile. "Yes, sir."

His boss cracked a grin — the first Jonah had ever seen him give — and shook his head. "Yeah, those petite little redheads will get you every time. I was married to one for fifteen years before I lost her to cancer. She was the love of my life."

When a distant look entered his gaze, Jonah drew in a breath, wondering what it would feel like to lose the love of his life. Losing Sean had nearly cut him in half. But a partner, a soul mate. Tess.

They hadn't known each other as long as he'd known Sean, but already he knew she'd become an integral part of who he was. Losing her would be like losing himself.

"How long has she been gone?" he asked quietly. He'd never discussed anything personal with his boss before, but now he felt a kinship with the man.

"Let's see…today's the third. So, it'll be three years next Thursday."

Jonah began to nod with understanding until he realized what Dale had just said. "Today's the third? The third of May?" Spinning toward the nearby calendar hanging by the wall next to the employee time clock, he gaped at the date. "Holy shit."

"What? What's the third mean?"

"Nothing." Jonah turned back to his grill and flipped the burger, which had been a breath away from burning. But, Jesus. Last year, he and Sean had been planning on how wasted they were going to get on each of their twenty-first birthdays. Sean's had passed a month ago, and Jonah's…hell, the last thing he cared about today was finding a bar or buying all the legal beer he could afford.

He couldn't believe it was his birthday and he'd completely forgotten it. His parents had never made a big deal about it. Only Sean had ever remembered and bought him presents, and even then, it had been pretty low key. But without Sean around…

A fresh wave of grief filled him, making him miss his friend all over again. Sean probably would've gotten him some kind of corny gag gift, like he usually did. He'd gotten a box of tampons last year. But it had been the thought, the knowledge that someone remembered his one special day, that had always counted.

The rest of his afternoon mellowed from there. He still had an overdose of euphoria flowing through his veins from spending the night with Tess and having her tell him to call her before he'd left campus. But that was now tempered with a dose of reality. It was his birthday, and probably no one would ever recognize it as such again.

Still, as he finished his shift, he was looking forward to calling Tess once he reached his apartment. Being able to talk to her would make the day complete.

Before leaving work, he purchased a bag full of Dale's cinnamon rolls. No one else might know what date it was, but at least he could celebrate by himself. He used his cane to hobble his way to his door. Then he rested his shoulder on the frame, so he could hold his bag of baked goods with one hand and dig his hand into his pocket for his house key with the other. But as soon as he slotted the key into the lock, the knob turned from the inside, and the door was flung open.

He nearly tripped in his haste to get out of the way as Aubrey came flying out to greet him with a crazy, happy smile and a huge bear hug.

"What the hell?" He caught the kid with one arm, unintentionally hugging him back by bracing them both so they didn't spill to the floor. "What're you doing home so early?"

"I took the evening off from rehearsal." Aubrey grabbed his cane and bag and hooked their arms together to help him into the apartment.

"Why? What's going on? Is everything okay?" If someone else was giving Aubrey any more grief about this damn play, he was going to have to kick some ass.

But Aubrey just grinned. "Everything's fabulous. I just wanted to spend a couple hours with my favorite roommate on earth to help him celebrate his birthday."

Jonah jarred to a halt. "How did you——"

"Know?" Aubrey sent him a saucy wink. "Well, someone had it written on his calendar in his bedroom."

Mouth falling open, Jonah could only gawk. He couldn't believe it. Someone had recognized his special day after all. Emotions overwhelmed him, and he opened his mouth to thank his new friend for his thoughtful consideration. He probably would've totally embarrassed himself by hugging the kid, but half a dozen voices shouted from the darkened kitchen, scaring the holy hell out of him.

"*Surprise!*"

Tess was the first to pop forward, racing to him and hugging him. Shocked to see her, he hugged her back, pulling her close and breathing in her hair.

Bailey was the next to spill out of the kitchen, then Logan, followed by Einstein's friend, Paige. But the last person to fill the front room startled him the most.

"Sam?"

His counselor hurried to him to give him a hug as soon as Tess pulled away. "Happy birthday! I wasn't sure if you wanted any, but I brought you some beer, since you're legal now, though I think you, me, and Logan are the only ones here old enough to actually partake."

He shook his head. "You have to be the most unorthodox counselor I've ever known."

"But you love me for it." She gave him a motherly pat on the cheek.

"Yeah, yeah. So do I." Bailey waved her hand to get their attention. "Now can we *finally* eat this pizza I've been forced to smell and not touch for the last half hour of waiting on Abbott's slow ass to make it home?"

"I've got paper plates and napkins." Aubrey led the charge back into the kitchen. As everyone filed off, Jonah lingered behind with Tess.

She glanced up at him and bit her lip. "Is all this okay? I know you don't know Bailey and Paige and Logan all that well, but——"

"They're you're friends." He drew her fingers up to his mouth so he could kiss her knuckles. "That's good enough for me."

She smiled and lifted up onto her toes to kiss him.

"Oh, please." Bailey groaned as she strolled back into the living room with a half-eaten piece of pizza in her hand. "Do you guys ever stop doing that anymore?"

"Not if we can help it," Jonah said into Tess's hair.

When she laughed, Bailey scowled. "What? What did he say?"

"Nothing." Tess ducked closer to him to hide her embarrassment.

He held her face to his chest and couldn't stop grinning, especially when Bailey rolled her eyes. "Damn, you guys are already making inside jokes. How sickening. Pretty soon, you'll be as bad as ol' Paige and Xander."

"What about Logan and me?" Paige's question was muffled by her mouth full of pizza. When she paused to pat the side of her lip with a napkin, Logan walked into the living room behind her, only to lift his eyebrows with interest at her half-eaten slice.

"Ooh, you got supreme. Is it any good?"

"Here." Turning to him, Paige lifted her piece. "See for yourself." After he opened his mouth, she fed him, then dabbed his lip with her napkin.

Bailey pointed at them. "Exactly."

Paige and Logan glanced at her with matching expressions of cluelessness. "What?"

Together, Jonah and Tess burst out laughing. Then they looked at each other because they both knew they were laughing about how funny it was to watch Paige and Logan speak simultaneously. Realizing they were doing the whole synchronized laugh thing, they laughed even harder.

"Oh, Jesus! *Sam! Aubrey!*" Bailey set her hand against her forehead. "Get your single asses in here. I'm being invaded by the couple-palooza."

Chapter Twenty-Seven

The birthday party went better than Jonah thought it would. At first, he was wary of how Paige would treat him. All he remembered about her at college was how she'd scolded him to leave Einstein alone. If anyone blamed him for what had gone down on that campus, it would be Paige Zukowski. But she was Tess's friend, and he'd been prepared to bend over backward and kiss the ground she walked on to make his girl happy.

Except, Paige seemed surprisingly open to receiving him on friendly terms. He wondered for a moment if she even remembered who he was, though he couldn't see how it would slip her mind. No way was he ever going to forget the way she'd twisted his finger and brought him to his knees in a split second. Total humiliation. But that was in the past, and he decided he was going to delete it from his memory banks along with a million other things he wanted to forget.

Bailey, on the other hand, apparently wasn't a fan of letting tense issues or huge elephants in the room go unnoticed. They'd all found places to sit around the living room, on the floor, couch, and rocking chair while Tess, the slowest eater, finished her meal.

Bailey waited until there was a lull in the conversation before she struck. "So, are we going to talk about Einstein and the shooting and find out where everyone stands, because I've had to bite my lip about fifty times tonight to keep from mentioning something that relates to all that."

When Paige went sheet-white, Logan grabbed her hand. "Maybe we shouldn't—"

But Samantha broke in over him. "Sure. Let's talk about it. I think it'll be good for us."

Great. Get the counselor involved, and they were all going to have to open up and talk about their freaking emotions. Couldn't they just stick needles in his eyes for the evening's entertainment?

Bailey blew out a loud, relieved breath. "Thank God, because Paige—" She twisted in her spot on the floor to face her suitemate. "I never know what I'm allowed to say around you, what will trigger some kind of downward spiral or put you in tears. I mean, am I allowed to say I hate Einstein, and I hate what he did, and I hate how it affected every single one of us?"

Logan scowled like he might want to strangle Bailey, but Paige nodded. "You can absolutely say that. I hate what he did too and how we've had to stumble through the aftermath of his actions. As for Einstein himself, it was always an effort to be his friend, but after he turned the gun on us and shot Logan, it's been even harder for me to forgive him. I don't want to hate him, but I definitely do blame him."

Next to him, Tess began to run her hand soothingly up and down Jonah's arm. "So, you never blamed Jonah?"

Every muscle in his body tightened. He glanced at her, thinking she was crazy for putting that question out there. Of course, they blamed him. He—

"Why would we blame *Jonah?*" Paige asked, wrinkling her brow in confusion. "I don't remember him there, holding the gun and showing Einstein how to pull the trigger. That was one hundred percent Einstein. Besides—" she flashed him a small smile "—weren't you a little too busy bleeding from your own wounds and falling into a coma right around that time?"

She hadn't even paused to give that answer. Jonah shook his head. "But what about the bullying?" he asked, his voice raspy with emotion.

Paige shrugged. "I'm sure the way you treated him didn't help the situation. But Einstein was messed up long before he came to Granton."

"Amen." Samantha spoke up from her own cross-legged seat on the floor. "I never had the opportunity to speak to or meet the boy, but from listening to everyone talk about him, he came from a family who didn't understand his differences and probably didn't deal with him in a way that helped him emotionally. I'm not blaming his parents, per se, but his problems stemmed from way back. They didn't start after he arrived on campus."

Jonah glanced at Tess when she squeezed his knee. They shared a relieved smile until Bailey said, "Well, I blamed you. I pretty much blamed anyone and everyone I could. The world had gone to shit, and I was ready to start pointing fingers. And after Tess got mixed up with you, and you turned her world upside down, I was ready to aim a firing squad at you."

"So, what changed your mind?" Tess asked, as if she were just learning this little tidbit about her friend as everyone else was. "Because I know you don't still blame him, or you wouldn't be sitting here right now, supporting my relationship with him."

"You're right. I wouldn't. I think I stopped blaming him the moment I visited him at the hospital to majorly bitch him out, and he ended up bawling all over me."

"I didn't bawl." Jonah scowled as he leaned against Tess and squeezed her knee right back. But if Bailey went on any longer, he was likely to strangle the girl tonight.

"Well, what about you, Aubrey?" Samantha asked, scooting toward the rocking chair he sat in to pat his thigh. "You're being awfully quiet over here. What do you think about all this?"

"I think I totally love you guys," he said, covering his eyes with his hands. "My family never talked about this stuff or opened up about their feelings. I just had to keep it all repressed down deep until I felt like I was going to explode. I've been asking myself for months and months why this all had to happen, why God had to take such a beautiful person like S-Sean. But sitting here with you people and listening to you talk makes me realize something beautiful can actually come from something ugly and awful." Jonah glanced at Tess and had to think Aubrey was right. The most amazing thing in his life had indeed come from the worst thing.

Paige and Logan were the first to leave the birthday party, and Sam wasn't far behind, kissing Jonah on the cheek and telling him she had two kids to get home to. Then Aubrey hugged him good night and disappeared down the hall. When only Bailey, Tess, and Jonah remained in the living room, Bailey shuffled her feet and reached into her back pocket and yanked out a small wrapped package.

"Here." She shoved the gift at him, nearly stabbing him in the chest with it. "Happy birthday." She didn't look too happy about delivering her well-wishes, but he was coming to learn she liked to be moody and sarcastic.

"Wow. Um…thanks." He took the box and slowly unwrapped it. He couldn't remember the last time anyone but Sean had given him anything.

His chest hurt thinking of that, making him miss his bud all over again. But he flashed Tess's best friend a grateful smile as he tore away the last of the wrapping paper. Then he looked down to find a flashlight in his grasp.

"It's not a flashlight." Bailey scowled as if she could read his mind. Yanking the item out of his hand, she turned it on.

It totally looked like a flashlight to him when a bright yellow beam blared out one end. He arched his gift-giver a curious glance. "Okay," he said. If she wanted him to call it a blue-horned pig, he would. But it still looked like a flashlight to him.

Bailey huffed and rolled her eyes. "Okay, but it's not *just* a flashlight." She pressed the button again and a piercing red light shot out above the flashlight's ray. "It's also a flashlight with a freaking laser beam on it!"

"Oh…cool." Genuinely intrigued, Jonah yanked it out of her hand to play with it himself and aim it at objects around the room, after clicking the button to toggle between flashlight, laser beam, and both.

"I know, right?" For once in her life, Bailey looked excited. With a proud grin, she nodded. "I designed it myself."

"Bailey's an electrical engineering major," Tess said, sounding like a bragging parent, which reminded him she'd told him this information before. "She's always creating cool electronic doo-hickeys."

"Whoa. You actually *made* this?"

When he glanced up, Bailey blushed—the first time he'd ever seen her do anything like that. "Well…" She cleared her throat and glanced toward the door. "It's kind of my thing."

"This is so boss." He glanced back at the object in his hand and brushed his thumb over the plastic surface. "I love it. Thank you."

She nodded and shuffled a step in reverse. "Yeah, well…this is about all the gratitude and nice crap I can handle, so I'm gonna jet." Glancing at Tess, she winked. "Don't do anything unless you can totally give me every detail about it tomorrow."

And then she was gone. He blew out a breath and fiddled with the button on his new present, hoping Tess didn't make him confess he how much he thought the loud-mouthed Bailey was okay after all.

But instead of needling, she clasped her hands together and grinned. "So…are you ready for part two of your present from me?"

Jonah instantly forgot about the flashlight-laser in his hand. "Part two? Jesus, Tess this is already more than enough. The whole supper, inviting everyone over, and a laser flashlight. Really, I don't need—"

"Well, I think you're going to like part two anyway." Her grin was almost too bright, and her eyes were a little glassy as she lifted up onto her toes. Realizing she'd done that toe-lift thing before at the hospital when she'd been nervous, he blinked, wondering what would make her nervous. "Because you're the first boyfriend I ever had, and—wait. It is okay to call you my boyfriend, right?"

He blinked. Had she really just asked that? "Yeah. *Yes.* My God, Tess. I hope so." Because he'd been feeling pretty proprietary of her. She was his now, and he wasn't sharing her with anyone.

Her bright grin returned. "Great. So…as your girlfriend, I want this birthday to be special. Better than special."

Oh, Jesus. She wasn't thinking to do what he was beginning to think she was going to do. Because the very idea—remote as it was—that she might possibly want to give him birthday sex thrilled, excited, and downright scared the shit out of him.

"But it's already—"

"You're not seriously going to decline this, are you?" Her big blue eyes pleaded, and suddenly she looked as scared at he felt. "It's the most important one yet."

He gulped loudly and caved. "Of course I won't. I'm just saying—"

"Great." She clapped with joy and bounded to him, holding out her hand. "Come along then. We're going to have to leave the apartment for it."

Jonah couldn't help but grin back as he pushed to his feet and took her hand, looking forward to his most important birthday present yet. His nerves eased a little as well, thinking if she had to take him somewhere to give him his gift, it must be a physical object and not her virginity.

"Is it a pony?" he couldn't help but ask.

Tess laughed and swept herself against him for a hug. "Better."

"Better? What's better than a pony?" He kissed her hair, inhaling the soothing, familiar scent of her shampoo, thinking he knew exactly what would be a million times better than a pony. When his hormones stirred, he tried to convince himself he wasn't disappointed it wasn't sex after all. But damn, he *was* a guy, and once sex entered his head, it didn't want to leave.

Tess pulled back from their hug just enough to grin up at him. "Let's find out, shall we?"

They walked to his truck hand in hand. He could become addicted to handholding. As he paused at the passenger side of his truck, he lifted her knuckles to his mouth for a quick appreciative kiss before he opened her door for her. And he loved that she was so short; it gave him the perfect excuse to grasp her waist and lift her up into the cab so she didn't have to try to crawl in by way of the running board.

She gasped from the unexpected boost but grinned back at him once she was nestled in her seat. "Thanks."

He winked and shut the door.

"So, where to?" he asked, once he was behind the wheel and had the engine started.

"We need to get to four twenty-four East—" She paused a moment, opening her mammoth purse and pulling out a scrap of paper. She unfolded it and turned it up-right to read. "—Poplar Street. Do you know how to get there?"

Jonah squinted at her. "What's at four twenty-four East Poplar Street?"

This time, she was the one to wink at him. "Why don't you drive us there and find out?"

He rolled his eyes but had to bite his lip to keep from grinning. "Okay, four twenty-four East Poplar Street it is, then."

Ten minutes later, he strained forward in his seat to read the numbers on the businesses on East Poplar Street. When he came to a fairly fancy hotel with a beveled glass atrium and brick-laid circle drive curling around to the front door, he glanced over at her. "A hotel?"

Oh, shit. Now the thought of sex was never going to leave his head.

Tess bobbed her head, smiling uncontrollably as she pulled a key card from her purse and flashed it at him. "We're in room two twenty-five. It has a Jacuzzi, fifty-inch television, and a king-sized bed. Won't it just be *awesome* to sleep in a real bed that's larger than two feet wide? I'm so excited."

"You—" His mouth went dry, and his hands froze to ice chips. With his heart thumping madly in his chest, he pulled into the parking lot. Once he had the engine off, he turned to face her fully. "Tess…"

What if she only wanted to rent a real bed for him to sleep in for the night, while he was over here with all his dirty, presumptuous thoughts?

"And the best part," she went on as if she had no clue he was about to have a nervous breakdown. "I bought a new bra and panties I think you'll like." When she tugged down the side of her jeans to show off a peek of pale blue silk fringed with black lace, he croaked out a whimper, his mouth falling open.

"Plus…these." When she pulled a box of condoms from her purse, he blanked out for a second.

But it was all…everything was just too…fuck. He didn't know how to process this. He'd wanted to go slow with Tess, give her time to adjust and possibly even back out of their relationship once her reason caught up with her, because, seriously, soon she was going to realize being with him was awful.

Except, with the only woman he'd been daydreaming about lately offering herself to him, saying no seemed impossible.

"So…" She let go of her waistband, and her shirt fell back down over her jeans. When he still hadn't responded, she bit her lip. "Why do you look like you're going to throw up?"

He could only shake his head. "I think I just experienced my first taste of performance anxiety. But, Jesus, Tess." He looked at the hotel and back to her. "This is big. This is huge. Are you sure—"

"I am *so* sure, it's not even funny. So, please, please don't say no. My confidence will plummet, and I'll probably never have the nerve to do something like this again if you turn me down tonight."

After a speech like that, there was no way he'd be able to turn her down. But he was too moved to speak immediately. No one had ever done anything like this for him before.

No doubt taking his non-answer for hesitation, Tess clicked off her seatbelt and crawled toward him. "I just want to make this the best birthday you've ever had."

When she cupped his face, he gave a shaky laugh. "It was already the best."

She kissed him, a simple press of her lips against his. Surging into her, he sank his fingers in her hair and opened his mouth, trying to show her how much all this meant to him.

But it wasn't enough, would never be enough. "I love you," he said as one long drugging kiss bled into the next. "I love you so much. It's crazy to love someone this much, but you're just…you're… Jesus." He crushed his mouth back to hers. He was better at showing than telling.

When Tess broke off to laugh breathlessly, she curled her fingers around his neck and pressed her cheek to his. "I love you too. And it *is* crazy, but it's still amazing."

"Crazy amazing," he agreed, caressing her soft cheek with his beard.

She hummed out her pleasure and ran her fingers over his facial hair. "Have I told you how much I like this?" she asked, slipping her fingers up his beard and into his hair. "And this new length you're growing this out to. It's rugged and sexy and…" She shivered. "Maybe we should go inside, and I'll show you just how much it turns me on."

He came a little in his pants, but her words were just that powerful. Kicking open his door, he dashed around his truck with a one-legged hop, putting weight on his bad leg every two or three steps. Once again, she didn't wait inside the cab for him to come around and open her door but met him at the edge of the curb.

"You left your cane in the truck," she immediately noticed.

He took her hand and nearly dragged her into the first entrance he saw. "Later."

Chapter Twenty-Eight

They undressed next to the king-sized bed, facing each other. It started out as a race, Jonah ripping his shirt over his head, Tess kicking off her shoes, and both of them laughing at their eagerness.

But when he realized he was rushing through one of the best parts, he paused, his hands hesitating on his fly. She seemed to understand because she slowed her pace too, dragging out the process with the most seductive moves he'd ever seen. She brought her shirt up and tugged it over her head. There was second when the hem caught on the swell of her breasts, and he had to hold his breath until the cloth popped free, showing off the pale silk and black lace cups hugging her perfect breasts and making them bounce.

"Lord have mercy," he murmured, forgetting what he was doing so he could just stare.

"Hey, don't stop." Scolding playfully, she motioned to his hand stalled out at the top button of his pants. "You were just getting to the best part."

He shook his head. "This entire night is the best part." But he freed the button to please her and drew the zipper down with the least amount of haste he could manage.

Her eyes grew a little glazed as she watched. When she unconsciously licked her lips, he hit a snag because he swelled even larger. With a wince, he pulled the tab down and let his erection fill the gap.

Tess's mouth dropped open. "Oh…my…God. You're not wearing underwear."

Jonah shook his head, giving her a slow smile. When his girlfriend shuddered from pleasure, he was suddenly grateful he was nearly two weeks behind on laundry and had had no clean boxers today.

She stepped toward him, her gaze fixed on his swollen dick. He tensed from the anticipation, impatient for her touch. When she reached out, he had to hold his breath.

"You painted your nails again," he noticed, doubly turned on by the flash of bright red polish highlighting the tips of her fingers. Imaging them on him was—Shit, he didn't have to imagine anymore. He could only gape as he stared down, watching her envelop him with her tight, warm grip.

"God, you are so hot," he choked out. Swooping in, he kissed her hard and thoroughly.

She backed toward the bed, literally leading him by his erection. He growled against her mouth and picked her up by the hips to lower her onto the mattress as he followed her down, covering her completely.

"I just can't stop touching you," she admitting, trailing her fingers from his neck, down his chest, pausing every few inches to kiss the warm flesh she stroked.

"Ditto." He started at her hips and worked across her smooth, flat belly.

Cupping her breasts, he took a hard peak into his mouth, coaxing her to cry out and arch her back. After licking and sucking on one, he moved over to roll the other nipple with his tongue and bit her lightly.

She was so responsive. She grabbed fistfuls of his hair and writhed under him. And that was it; he had to feel her. Running his free hand down her hips while he cupped her breast with the other, he grinned against her nipple when she lifted up her hips as soon as he trailed his fingers across her abdomen and toward their destination. Burying his digits in soft red curls, he held his breath and slid two fingers in the warm, wet hollow of her womanhood.

"Jonah," she breathed. The caress of his own name on his ears did him in. He abandoned her breast to kiss his way down her ribcage, across her abdomen and into those curls. His tongue found her most intimate nub and batted it gently. But her response was anything but gentle. She cried out her pleasure and nearly yanked him bald.

Growling against her, he licked her harder and moved his fingers faster.

Under him, she mewed and twisted and begged. Her breaths came in rapid bursts that made him match his pace with each pant. He didn't mean to rush, but he was sucked into her pleasure. The insistent thrust of his fingers and swirl of his tongue had her coming way too soon. Not that he was complaining, but it made him want to go even faster and forget about savoring every second.

"Here," Tess said.

He glanced up to find her holding a condom. He stared at it—when had she pulled the box from her purse? He transferred his gaze to her.

How could she look so sure of herself when he was all torn up inside—nervous, and scared, and as excited as he was afraid. What if she regretted it as soon as it was over? That was not something he could handle.

"Aren't you scared?" he asked, hoping she didn't see his own worries lingering in his gaze.

She bit her lip and then smiled softly, cupping his cheek. "I'm not exactly sure what to expect, but there's no one I trust this with more."

He closed his eyes. When he opened then and blew out a breath, she finally appeared concerned. "Why? Are *you* scared?"

"Only shitless." His laugh was shaky, almost as shaky as his hands as he took a piece of her hair and wound it around his fingers.

Concern wrinkled her brow. "Is...is this your first time too?"

He shook his head. "It is with you, and that's all that matters." Pressing his brow to hers, he leaned in to nip a quick kiss to her lips. "I want it to be amazing for you, Tess."

She smiled and closed her eyes. "It already is."

He took the condom from her and put it on. She sat up to watch curiously.

"You are too cute, you know that?" Kissing her, he stretched her back and positioned himself above her, settling most of his weight on his right side and lowering his hips to rest his body against hers.

When she pulled in a breath, he kissed her cheek. "You doing okay?"

Bobbing her head immediately, she swallowed loudly. "I'm doing great."

So brave, though he could sense her apprehension beginning. He interlaced their fingers before drawing her knuckles to his mouth and kissing them, then let his hardness press against her opening so she could get used to him.

"The first time I saw you in the hospital when I didn't have my memory back yet and I had no idea who you were." He paused until she lifted her face and he knew she was listening. "I thought you were an angel. The light from the hall made your hair glow in this almost halo effect, and I wanted to touch it so bad, just to see if it was real."

Smiling softly, he leaned in to kiss her hair. "And when you said you were my girlfriend, the idea was so thrilling I could barely believe it. I couldn't imagine how someone who looked so angelic and beautiful could be mine. What amazing thing have I done to deserve you?" Closing his eyes, he rocked an inch inside her.

Tess gasped under him. Her nails dug into his back as he paused to let her adjust some more.

"Oh, my God, Jonah," she sobbed. "You don't even... You have it all wrong. I'm the one who doesn't deserve you."

"Impossible," he countered, and this time when he began to push deeper, he didn't stop. He knew it had to hurt her, but it felt so damn erotic to him, and when her nails gouged his back, it was the best pain he'd ever experienced.

"I love you," she whispered, burying her face in his neck as she clung to him.

"I love you more."

When he moved again, she moved with him, wrapping her legs around his waist and shifting her hips to meet his next plunge.

"Does it hurt?" he asked, his voice strained as he tried to keep it slow and easy. He'd never been with a virgin and had no idea how bad the pain was or how long it lasted.

"It's...different," she managed to answer. Then she met his gaze with wide eyes. "How the hell do strangers do this with each other? It's so...intimate."

"Not always," he admitted. He'd never felt this bonded to any other girl while he was inside her before. But mentioning the fact he'd been inside anyone else to Tess at this moment seemed sacrilegious, so he leaned in close and whispered into her ear. "It's only like this when you're with someone important."

With his next thrust, Tess ground her heels into his spine and gave a surprised yelp. "Oh!"

He froze solid. "What? Are you okay? Did I hurt you?"

"No, no. Not at all. That actually felt good. I just wasn't expecting…I mean, from stinging to feeling uncomfortable to actually feeling…Oh, wow. Do that again."

"What? This?" He shifted angles and slid deeper with a sure, solid plunge.

She arched her head back and moaned.

"You are so…beautiful." Focusing on nothing but her pleasure, he pumped her again with nearly similar results. Discovering her sweet spot, he took advantage and made sure to hit it with every thrust he made.

Her nails dug deeper into his back, and he gnashed his teeth because he wanted to come so bad, but not until—

"Jonah," she gasped, gaping at him from wide, surprised eyes. "Jone… Jo…" When she fell apart under him, that was it. He pushed into her one last time and found his own release within the bonds of hers.

Unlike Bailey, Tess was usually a solid sleeper. But for some reason, she stirred when the mattress shifted beside her at some point during the night. Vaguely aware of Jonah leaving the bed, the hush of his bare feet shuffling an uneven hobble across the floor, she roused even more. But she didn't fully waken until a small stream of light flickered on inside the bathroom and moved across the walls, alternating between red and white.

Smiling because he was using the gift Bailey had given him, she sat up and shoved unruly hair out of her face. The blankets pooled around her waist, brushing cool air across her bare shoulders. It had to be the first time in her life she didn't feel completely self-conscious to be without a stitch of clothing. After what she'd just experienced with Jonah, she was still feeling as beautiful as he'd insisted she was.

A sniff came from inside the bathroom. The flashlight's beam shifted slightly, and she frowned, pushing the covers the rest of the way off. When she stepped on a piece of clothing in the dark as she tiptoed forward, she paused to pat around the floor until she discovered she'd stepped on Jonah's shirt. Quickly slipping it on over her head, she finished making her way to the bathroom. Afraid to find him upset for any reason, she clutched the frame and cautiously peered around the corner.

He sat on the closed lid of the commode in just his jeans, toggling the laser of his new flashlight on and off.

"Jonah?"

He lifted his face with a startled expression and sat up straighter. "I'm sorry. Did I wake you?" He didn't appear to have any tears in his eyes, but he didn't exactly look like he was full of joy, either.

She let go of the doorframe and approached him. "What's wrong?" As she slid into his lap, he wrapped his arm around her and pulled her close so he could bury his face in her hair.

"Tonight was the best night of my life."

Tess didn't smile over the announcement as he kissed her hair. She touched the scruffy beard on his cheek and pressed her forehead to his. "Then why do you sound so sad?"

"I don't…Jesus. What the hell am I doing, Tess?" he asked in a tortured whisper. "Why am I having the best night of my life — being this happy — when my best friend on earth is cold in the ground and has only been gone a few months? When it's *my* fault he's gone? It's my fault they're all gone."

"Oh, Jonah," she started, wanting to cry for him. "Please don't —"

"I know, I know." He shook his head. "Samantha went over and over this with me. It's supposed to be natural to feel guilt every time I smile for a while. And, shit, I even said something like that to Aubrey just the other morning — that it's okay to move on. But actually dealing with it head-on, moving on and being happy…It's hard. It's so fucking hard." He began to run his fingers through her hair and then curling red ringlets around his finger. "I'm sorry I woke you. I didn't want to bother you with this and ruin your first time because of my personal shit —"

"Jonah Abbott," she scolded before he could finish his apology. "Don't you dare. I'd be bothered if you *didn't* share any of this with me. I want to be able to experience all of your life with you, especially the hard parts." She leaned in to press her cheek to his heartbeat and just hold him.

"I don't deserve you." He gulped loudly as if swallowing back tears. "I don't deserve to be this happy. All those people died, and I'm here with you. It's not fair."

She smiled softly, relaxing against him. "If you think about it, none of us deserve true happiness. We all have our sins and selfish ways and bad thoughts."

"But some of us deserve a lot less than others."

Tess sighed, realizing she needed to come at this from a different angle. "Did you know Logan killed Paige's brother?"

Geesh, if she didn't have a point to that statement, one might've thought her stupid-gene was returning. Or maybe it was.

Jonah glanced at her sharply. "What?"

"Yeah. I guess he was a big basketball star in high school. But one night he got into a fight with some guy from a rival team. One punch, and bam, Paige's brother fell over and hit his head on something. He died instantly."

"Shit," Jonah breathed, reaching up to touch the area on his own skull where she remembered he'd had a bandage from hitting *his* head and falling into a coma. He could've had the same fate as Paige's brother so easily.

Tess shivered and held him a little tighter. "Afterward, Logan's parents kicked him out, and he was forced to live on his own. He ended up in Granton and started college. But a few years later, Paige enrolled there as well, and on her first day of class, she realized she had a class with her brother's...well, you know."

Jonah blinked. "And now they're *dating?*"

Tess nodded. "It just goes to show you that things aren't always as they seem. Logan never thought he deserved to be happy again either. But Paige — *Paige*, of all people — saw something in him that was redeemable." She paused. "I know you're working through a lot of things, not just Sean's death. But I see something very redeemable in you. And I know someday you'll see it too. Until then, I hope you continue to let me hold you and be with you through these dark parts."

Pulling in a sharp breath, Jonah nodded and squeezed his arms tighter around her. "Always," he promised her. "With you, I know I can make it through anything."

Their lips met, and fingers skimmed over bare skin. Jonah set his flashlight on the counter of the vanity beside him so he could free up his other hand. He slid it up her thigh and under the hem of his too-large-for-her shirt. When his fingers discovered she wasn't wearing panties, he groaned. She followed with her own gasp of pleasure as he sank a thick digit inside her.

Stroking her slowly, he kissed her deeper. Her body grew warm and taut and unable to help herself, she began to ride his hand, undulating against each masterful thrust.

Breath going shallow, she bit her lip and met his gaze. "Can we... again?"

He let out a strained laugh and gave a bemused shake of his head. "I don't know how you do it, but you always know how to draw me back up whenever I get down." Then he winked and dug into his pocket to pull out a single foil package.

Tess blinked at the condom between his fingers. "Hey, that's not the same brand I bought you."

Flushing in the beam of the flashlight, he admitted, "I slipped this one into my pocket before we left tonight."

Her eyes grew big. "You mean..."

He nodded. "I had hopes." Bringing it to his mouth, he tore the package open with his teeth and drew out the condom inside. "Want to get my zipper?"

Oh, boy, did she. Suddenly giddy, she scooted back on his lap toward his knee, making sure to reposition most of her weight on his good leg. Once she had him free, she pulled him into her hand and pumped him as he'd taught her to do only the night before.

"God, you're a quick learner." He moaned, throwing his head back. "Jesus, babe, you..." Suddenly, he was there with the prophylactic, batting her fingers aside so he could sheathe himself.

Realizing where they were and how they were going to do this, Tess experienced a rush of bashfulness. "Are we really going to do it here, *like this?*"

He glanced up, and she could see the anticipation his brown eyes. "Don't you want to try it?"

"I..." She gulped, and then bobbed her head, still nervous but beginning to let her curiosity get the best of her. "Okay."

"Okay," he agreed, his grin growing as he pulled his shirt over her head and flung it across the hotel's bathroom. "Bring this lovely thigh over here, then, and straddle me."

She began to move, then paused. "What about your leg?"

A frustrated groan rumbled from his throat, and he caught her thigh, leading it where he wanted it to go. "That's the last thing on my mind. Trust me."

"But—"

"It's fine," he assured her. "I swear. It doesn't hurt any more with you there than it does without you there. And I much prefer you there. Right…there." Gnashing his teeth, he caught her hips as she began to lower herself.

When she felt him at her entrance, she paused, but he kept pulling her down. Clutching his shoulders, she gave in, and he pushed up inside her.

"Oh…*oh!*" Seated on him fully, her red fingernails bit into his shoulder blades. "Whoa, you…you feel a lot bigger this way."

"Yeah. And you feel a lot more…Jesus."

He choked out a gasp as she squeezed her inner muscles around him. Fingers bit in her waist, and he lifted her and brought her right back down. This time, they both moaned. Following her body's natural instinct, Tess began to ride, undulating her hips. Lifting and falling. The slide and thrust of their bodies worked in tandem, rubbing at the most sensitive spots at the most sensitive moments.

Jonah leaned down and plucked one of her nipples between his teeth, and she grasped his head and held on for dear life as he brought her to the pinnacle of her pleasure. Once she plummeted off the edge and dove straight into her completion, he joined her, arching his hips up and making it that much more intense by the way he slammed their bodies back together.

Drifting back down from the plunge, he continued to leave small kisses around her breasts, and she patted his wispy strands of hair.

"I love you so much." He lifted up to kiss her mouth. "I swear, God made you just for me, to fight away my demons."

As she held him close and soaked in his love, Tess realized this wasn't just a simple first love kind of affection. This was flat out forever love. Jonah Abbott was her soul mate.

Chapter Twenty-Nine

"I can't believe school's almost over." Jonah leaned against the wall beside Tess's dorm room entrance to rest his leg a second while she dug inside her huge purse to find her key. "This is going to be the longest damn summer of my life."

Tess bit her lip but didn't admit she felt the same apprehensions because she didn't plan on leaving. She had a week to figure something out, and she would, come hell or high water. After last night, being apart from him for the summer was impossible.

But how did you tell the guy you'd just started dating how badly you wanted to be with him…all the time…without looking like a total stalker?

"We'll figure something out," was all she could say.

He nodded but didn't look too hopeful.

When he didn't notice two girls who'd come out of a room halfway down the hall and stopped to stare at him, then whisper amongst themselves, Tess breathed a sigh of relief.

Tugging her room key free, she ignored her door and instead rested her head on his shoulder. She stroked her fingers up his arm, keeping his attention on her so he could continue being oblivious to the girls still gossiping about him.

"Have I thanked you for last night yet?"

He seared her with a surprised look. "You have it backward. I owe you the huge thanks." Then he leaned in and smiled devilishly. "It was *my* birthday sex, after all."

She flushed because hearing the S word aloud always made her uncomfortably hot. Except today, the uncomfortably hot part was a little too delicious. She wanted to molest him, right there in the hall.

As if reading her mind, Jonah's grin grew, and she decided what the hell. She grabbed a handful of his shirt and kissed him hard on the mouth. She paused only long enough to say, "I love you," before going back up for seconds.

He groaned against her lips, and his warm body melded to hers, reminding her all over again how much he'd lit her up last night… and this morning…in the shower.

"When's your first class?" He buried his fingers in her hair and kissed her jaw, then her throat.

"In fifteen minutes. So, sorry. No time for hanky panky."

"Damn." He blew out a breath. "That's what I thought." With a last peck to her nose, he stepped back. "Okay, then. I'll let you go for now. But I'm returning for you this evening."

Tess swerved back to him, a thrill rising inside her. "You are?"

"I only have *days* left with you before you're gone for the entire summer. Hell, yes, I'm spending every available second with you until then."

She was such a goober; the college freshman in her emerged, his announcement making her giggle and blush. "Okay. I'll see you tonight, then."

"Yes, you will." His gaze promised her a whole heap of deliciousness. Then he turned away to hobble off.

Tess would've stared after him all the way back to his truck, but Bailey opened the door, grabbed her arm, and yanked her inside their room. "At least tell me you've had a shower this morning, unlike yesterday."

Remembering her shower, in detail, Tess let out a dreamy sigh. Oh, how she'd had a shower. "Yes, I took a shower at the hotel, *mother*."

"Good." Bailey didn't say another word until she shut the door, locked it, and spun to Tess. "So?" she demanded, eyeing her roommate up and down, just as she'd done the morning before when Jonah had brought her back. Then she repeated the same question she'd asked yesterday. "Are you still a virgin?"

Today, however, Tess had a different answer. Her face lit up, and she squealed, "No!" Jumping up and down, she was unable to control her enthusiasm. "I'm not. Oh, my God, I'm totally not."

"Holy shit." Bailey joined in, holding her hands and jumping with her. "I can't believe you actually did it. This is so big."

As they were hollering and twirling together in a giggling circle, a tap came on the bathroom door, and their suitemate popped her head into the room. "What? What'd I miss?"

"Paige!" Bailey cried, letting go of Tess to drag Paige into the room. "Get your ass in here. Tess isn't a virgin anymore. Can you freaking believe that?"

"Whoa," Logan said from still in the bathroom. Lifting his hands, he immediately skipped in reverse back toward Paige's room. "TMI."

Before she'd met Jonah, Tess would've buried her face into her hands and died of mortification to learn that Logan knew what she'd done last night. But the new, Jonah-improved version of her could handle it.

Paige captured her attention, grabbing her hands and squeezing. "Oh, my God. Are you okay? Did you like it?"

"Did she *like* it?" Bailey slung an arm over Tess's shoulders and pointed at her face. "Just look at this girl's smile. Her cheeks would burst if she spread her lips any wider than they already are."

Tess tossed back her head and laughed, feeling so very alive and euphoric.

"Well, my goodness," Paige murmured, beaming at her. "Congratulations."

"I know. It's about time she joined the rest of us dirty sinners. Ever since I've fallen off the wagon, she's been way too pure for my taste."

"And now I've actually done it *more* than you," Tess teased, bumping her hip into Bailey's. "Who's the pure one today?"

Bailey swerved her head around to gape at Tess. "What? How the hell many times did you two little humping bunnies go at it last night?"

"Last night?" Tess asked. "Twice. This morning?" She gave a modest little shrug. "Only once."

"*Three* times?" Her best friend gasped and stepped away from her so she could stare her up and down. "Oh my…why you dirty ho.

I'm so proud." She wiped away a non-existent tear. "But wait. Just how many orgasms did *lover boy* manage to give you, huh?" With a snarky grin, she folded her hands over her chest and nodded as if she knew she had Tess in a corner now.

But Tess only preened. "Four."

"F —" Bailey's mouth was too busy hanging open to finish the word. She whirled to Paige. "How do you have *four* orgasms from *three* rounds of sex?"

Paige sighed and patted Bailey's arm sympathetically. "You obviously haven't had any decent experiences with the subject if you don't know the answer to that."

"Well, that's for damn sure. The one and only time I let a guy do me, it was less than stellar. I'm talking zero fireworks. It's no wonder I haven't been all eager to try it agai — wait. Wait, wait, wait. Are you trying to tell me even *Xander* has gotten you off more than once in a single round?"

Turning all kinds of red, Paige discreetly cleared her throat. "His record's three so far."

While Bailey was too speechless, what with her jaw bouncing off the floor from dropping so far, Tess made a contemplative face and wrinkled her nose. "Three, huh? Jonah and I will have to try for four then."

A male snort came from the other side of the partially closed bathroom door. All three ladies glanced at it, then at each other. Bailey marched over and yanked it the rest of the way open, exposing an eavesdropping Logan who jumped back in surprise.

"Well, well. Looks like Mr. Perfect Xander is quite the peeping Tom."

"*Logan*," Paige gasped, darting around Bailey to reach his side. "I can't believe you just listened in on our private conversation."

"You were talking about sex," he mumbled, scowling no doubt to hide the flush in his cheeks. Then he leaned in close to his girlfriend and hissed, "And why did you tell them only three times?"

Paige blinked, clearly stumped by his question. "Because I wanted to be honest?" She phrased it more as a question than an answer.

"You still should've said something like five. Made it sound really impressive."

"Yeah." Paige snorted out a laugh. "But who'd believe *that?*"

"I still don't believe three," Bailey spoke up, raising an eyebrow as if to question his abilities. "You must have some kind of talent with—"

"And I think that's my cue to leave again." He was gone before anyone could stop him. The loud click of Paige's room door closing signaled that he was gone for good this time.

Paige, Tess, and Bailey exchanged arched glances before they burst out laughing.

Tess realized this was one of the happiest moments of her life. She had two amazing friends, a non-fake boyfriend who made her insanely happy, a future to look forward to, and a life worth living. It was strange how much good had endured through so much tragedy. But it helped her realize that, if she could just survive through all the hardships, she might come out okay on the other side.

"I don't see why the hell you two had to drag me along to this crap. I don't *do* musicals."

"Because," Jonah told Bailey as he turned around to send her a smirk. "If I have to sit through this shit, then so do you."

She snorted, turned around to scowl at some poor girl who'd bumped into her from behind, then whirled back to finish glaring down Jonah. "As if I care what you think. You're not *my* boyfriend, pal. I don't need to please you."

"But you do care what Tess thinks, and *she* wants to please me. So, if you want to please her, you better start pleasing me too, woman."

As she sputtered back a string of obscenities, calling him every dirty, male chauvinist name in the book, he chuckled and shook his head. But damn, it was way too easy to rile her up. Next to him, Tess squeezed his hand and bumped her shoulder into his. When he glanced down, she rolled her eyes.

"I think you get too big of a kick out of teasing her, sometimes."

He loved how she only shook her head and smiled, amused, instead of reprimanding him for purposely ticking off her best friend. But yeah, he did totally love saying inappropriate stuff to Bailey just to see her completely overreact.

Pulling Tess's knuckles to his mouth, he kissed them softly. "But I need some kind of entertainment to me get me through the next few hours." Because sitting there, watching Aubrey's end of the year play was going to drive him batty for sure. The first time some guy in tights started singing soprano, he was probably going to detonate from the agony.

But he seemed to be the only person dreading tonight. The performing arts center was packed; they'd already been shuffling along behind the crowd for five minutes just to get into the auditorium to find their seats. When someone squeezed past Tess, knocking her off balance, Jonah caught her around the waist just as she tumbled into him. Straightening her back upright, he glared at the kid cutting in front of them and nudged the guy—probably a little harder than he needed to—with his cane in order for Tess to regain the personal space she'd just lost.

"Watch it!" he and Bailey barked at the same time, Bailey appearing at Tess's other side to help him flank her and keep her protected.

Hearing each other say the same thing at the same time, Bailey and Jonah grinned at each other over Tess's head, and Bailey held out her balled hand for him to fist bump. As he clashed his knuckles with hers, pleased she was as protective of his girlfriend as he was, Tess gave a weary sigh.

"It's like going out in public with two bodyguards."

"Hey, own it, princess." Bailey lifted her chin regally. "Only the truly important get more than one bodyguard."

And Jonah had to agree Tess was one truly important person. Grinning, he pulled her even closer to kiss her hair. He loved her so much it was ridiculous.

As they shuffled along and entered the main arena, a pre-show singer stood on the stage in front of the closed curtains and sang an upbeat ditty next to a single piano which accompanied her performance.

Bailey moaned. "God, shoot me now." When the people in front of them glanced back and sliced her a dirty look, she returned it with one of her own. "What?"

Tess elbowed her silently while Jonah rolled his eyes, unable to contain his grin. Waving his cane in her direction to remind her what had happened to him, he said, "Ixnay on the ooting-shay."

"Oh, whatever. If people are going to be so sensitive about it, they need to—"

"*Bailey!*" Tess squeezed her arm as she hissed out the warning. "Filter, remember?"

Bailey huffed but shut up. "Fine." She was silent the rest of the way to their seats.

Jonah figured the turnout had been so big *because* of people's sensitivity, though. With protestors waving signs outside to warn everyone away, it had only gained the play more attention. There were even two news vans parked outside, interviewing individuals over whether or not they thought the play should continue.

Flopping down in the seat corresponding with her ticket, Bailey glanced up at Jonah and Tess. "There better be vendors walking the aisles, selling drinks and popcorn and shit, because I'm already starving."

"It's not a ball game. And I told you to eat a snack before we left." Tess sat beside her. "It's going to be at least three hours before the show's over. *Then* we're taking Aubrey out to supper, remember? We're supposed to meet him forty-five minutes after the curtain closes at the side entrance he told us about."

Jonah silently groaned as he eased down next to her. But three freaking hours in these snug little seats with cushions that would no doubt be killing his back before the curtains even opened sounded about as fun as going to the dentist for a root canal.

As Bailey begged Tess to dig through her huge purse to look for a snack for her, Jonah rubbed his thigh and propped his cane in the space between him and Tess. He turned his attention to the singer and watched her for a moment. She wasn't half bad. There was a certain soothing quality about her performance, easing the tight nerves in his chest. Blindly reaching for Tess's hand, he squeezed warmly when she immediately took his fingers.

Life was good, he decided. It wasn't the same as it had been a year ago. But it was almost better. He'd give anything to have Sean back, but adding Tess, Aubrey, Bailey, and even Paige, Logan, and Samantha to his life had filled it with a love and friendship he'd never realized he'd craved.

When his phone vibrated in his pocket, he pulled it out to see Aubrey's number and immediately smiled. "Aren't you supposed to be getting ready, or something?" he asked.

"Omigod, Jonah. It's a bust. Did you see all the protestors out front? No one's going to show up."

"Well, I see all the people crowding into the auditorium right now, and I'd say you're dead wrong. It took us damn near five minutes to reach our seats."

Aubrey gasped. "You're here? Right now? You really came?"

Jonah shook his head, not sure why his friend sounded so shocked. "I said I was coming, bud. And it's about two minutes until the play starts, so…where else would I be? This place is packed."

"It is?" He could tell Aubrey was beaming by the awed tone in his voice.

"Yeah. Now get off the phone and get into character or whatever. You better give me a damn good show for making me sit through this."

Aubrey laughed. "Yes, sir. Oh, wait. What do you think of my background? I swear there are at least twenty layers of paint on that thing because I just couldn't find the perfect color. Do you like it?"

"The curtain's still closed. I can't see it yet."

"Oh. Right." Sounding disappointed, Aubrey sighed. "Well, tell me afterward. You're still picking me up—"

"At the side entrance," Jonah repeated dutifully since Aubrey had gone over it with him about fifty times already. "Forty-five minutes after the show. Yes, we got it. Now go break a leg."

Bailey snorted as he hung up. "Yeah, because wouldn't it be *so* cool if both of you were hobbling around on canes."

"Shh." Tess tapped her knee as the lights dimmed and the curtains opened.

All three of them gasped when they saw the castle prop background Audrey had been raving about. It took up the entire width of the stage, and the turrets rose until they disappeared into the valance curtain.

Heaps of tulle fabric had been used at the base of the castle to give it a foggy—or maybe cloudy—dreamlike look. And obviously-fake but artistically-designed tree props made a little forest on the right side, which Aubrey would call stage left.

Ugh, after listening to so much of the kid's babbling, Jonah was actually beginning to learn theater terms.

"It looks like a fairy tale," Tess breathed next to him.

"Or like a medieval wedding threw up on stage," Bailey said.

Both Jonah and Tess hushed her just as a girl appeared in the open tower window of the castle.

And the play began.

Two hours later, Tess nudged Bailey, who'd fallen asleep, and the three of them stood to applaud with the crowd.

Jonah shook his head, wondering how the hell he was supposed to tease Aubrey and pretend he'd hated every minute of this damn play. It had actually made him smile and laugh and ache in places because of all the freaking singing, dancing actors.

And Aubrey…who knew his own roommate would be such a sensation?

"He stole the entire show," Tess leaned up to tell him.

He nodded and grinned as Aubrey stepped forward next in the line of actors and actresses on stage to take his bow. Jonah could honestly admit he was happy for his friend. The roar of the clapping and whistling rose throughout the auditorium, and pride swelled in his chest as a beaming Aubrey straightened and waved giddily to his adoring fans.

"Yeah," Jonah agreed. "He did great."

If only Sean had been able to see it.

After the last person took a bow, Aubrey stepped forward again.

"And now to honor our fallen friends and classmates who were taken so tragically from us only a few short months ago, we'd like to have a candlelight vigil in memory of the eleven souls who lost their lives on this very campus. Eleven very important people who were adored by so many of us…" He paused when he got a little choked up. "Tonight I burn my candle for Sean Thompson, who taught me how to love and be loved. His life was cut short too soon, but he'll always live on in my heart."

With a watery smile, he turned to an assistant who approached him with a basket full of candles. As he picked one out and lit it, he turned to light the candle of the next actress who'd taken one from the basket. They went down the line, spreading light and hope across the stage. Once every person on stage had a lit candle in their hand, they began to sing.

The music was more gripping than anything they'd played all night. It held every member in the audience enthralled. Jonah glanced at Tess just as she turned to look at him. When she mouthed the words, *I love you*, he followed suit, whispering it right back. Then he turned his attention back to the stage as the melody came to a crescendo.

But just as the last note of the song rang through the auditorium, a handful of people stood up in the front row of the audience and began to shout, "Hypocrites. Frauds. Phonies." Then they began to throw—

"Holy shit. Are those tomatoes?" Bailey turned to gape at Tess and Jonah. "They're actually throwing *tomatoes*. People really *do* that?"

Jonah shook his head, confounded, and turned back to stare up at the protestors as they kept slinging vegetables at the actors. This certainly hadn't been part of the plan.

When one girl on stage was hit and bright red juice exploded in her face, she screamed and retreated further back into the stage. The rest of the performers scrambled backward to safety with her, shielding their faces with their arms.

Jonah stood up, as did half the audience. He wanted to rush forward and help Aubrey, somehow stop the tomato-slingers. But then one of the actors dropped his candle—right into a fluffy ball of tulle at the base of the homemade castle, constructed of wood, cardboard, and at least twenty layers of paint.

Chapter Thirty

It happened so fast.

One second, the actors were screaming in fright, and protestors were shouting insults while audience members bellowed at them to stop. In the next, the stage ignited, and fire sprinted up the tower of Aubrey's beautiful castle.

A pregnant pause followed as everyone seemed to freeze, held horrifyingly captivated by the sight. But then reality kicked in, and pandemonium reigned.

"We're getting out of here. Now!" Jonah grasped Tess's hand and yanked her to the aisle.

Thank God he had an end row seat because the doors were already crammed with people, shoving and fighting to get through when he looked toward them.

"Oh! Your cane." Tess tried to jerk away from him and return to their seats. But he wasn't having any of that.

He tightened his clamp on her fingers. "Forget it."

But Bailey popped up behind him, waving it triumphantly. "I got it."

When it found its way into his hand, he didn't use it as a crutch but as a cattle prod, fencing people off when they crowded in too close. More screams and cries of terror filled the auditorium; the air was layered with the acrid stench of smoke. Behind him, something popped and sparked as if the fire reached the stage light cans, making them explode. A second later, half the lights went out. And a breath after that, the fire alarms went off, producing another round of hysteria throughout the crowd.

Pulling Tess in closer until her front was molded to his back, he made her wrap her arms around his waist and hook her fingers through his belt loops. "Do you have a hold of Bailey?" he shouted back to her over the rising sounds of chaos. When she told him she did, he nodded. "Bring her in close."

After they passed through the bottleneck of the door into the lobby, they still had the front doors to fight their way toward. Jonah was used to being shoved and shoving back, though he usually had on hefty shoulder pads when he was doing it. But this was exactly why he'd gotten a scholarship to Granton, so that was what he did now, bowing his head and plowing forward, ignoring every stabbing pang that throbbed up his bum leg.

A girl about five people ahead of him went down and was trampled under the stampede.

Jonah, Tess, and Bailey reached her all too soon because the momentum of the crowd behind them pushed them forward so fast. Stopping to help her was like fighting a wave in the ocean. He could barely manage not to trip over an already bloody leg as he was swept along toward the entrance.

"That girl." Tess sobbed against him, her entire body trembling. "Oh, my God. Someone needs to help that girl."

"Jesus," Jonah uttered. He glanced over his shoulder and barely caught sight of some hero lifting the battered body off the floor and throwing her over his shoulder. But looking back might've been a bad idea because Jonah was shoved hard into the person in front of him, where he accidentally knocked another girl to the ground.

"We gotta get out of this place," he muttered, bracing his body with all this strength to keep from being pushed forward anymore. Gritting his teeth, he reached down and grabbed the fallen girl's arm to help her back to her feet.

He, Bailey, Tess, and the girl he'd swiped off the floor couldn't reach the open warm night soon enough, but when they did, they all sucked in their own lung full of fresh air.

The crowd kept surging, urging them along, away from the building. As soon as they hit a free pocket of space across the street, Jonah stopped his group to check all three girls over and make sure they'd come out okay. But Tess was too busy hugging him as soon as he turned around for him to look her over very thoroughly.

"Are you okay?" she demanded, patting him down. "How's your leg? You're not using your cane to walk with."

"I'm fine. It's fine," he assured her. He glanced over her shoulder. The stranger he'd picked up off the floor was already rushing away, finding someone in the crowd she knew, so he turned his attention to Tess's best friend. "Bailey? You okay?"

"Oh…hell," Bailey murmured, too busy staring back at the performing arts center to answer him.

He looked over, and his chest dropped into his stomach. He almost expected to see big orange flames licking out the roof of the building, but there was nothing, not even smoke escaping yet, just a frenzied mass of people pushing and shoving and trampling each other to escape the front doors.

"I can't believe we were just a part of that." Tess clutched his arm, as she echoed exactly what he'd been thinking. How the hell had they come out of that place alive? He clutched her close, glad she was alive and in his arms. So very thankful…until she went and added, "I hope Aubrey got out okay."

Aubrey? Jonah jerked a sharp glance her way. "*What?*"

He'd been so concerned with getting *her* to safety, he'd completely forgotten about his roommate…his roommate who'd been mere feet away from the castle when it had caught fire.

"Shit." He scanned the crowds. When he didn't spot anyone in costume, he began to panic. Big time.

"I don't see him," Bailey said, sounding freaked.

It was her sense of alarm that set him off, because, damn, if Bailey was losing her cool, then things had just gotten real.

He let go of Tess and started limping-slash-jogging back toward the center.

"Jonah!" she cried.

He could tell she was following, so he held up a hand. "Stay here. I'll be back."

People were still flooding out the front doors, a mass exodus of panicked proportions. No way could he get back in that way. But no way could he leave Aubrey inside alone.

Remembering the entrance where they were supposed to meet his roommate, he fought his way through terrified, confused, and sobbing people so he could round the side of the building. It was fairly crowd-free here. Able to move more easily up the alley, he really put his cane to work, skipping the last few feet to the side door just as three coughing, hysterical actors shoved their way outside.

He caught the door before it closed, because he had a feeling it was locked from the outside. "Did you guys see Aubrey? Do you know if he's still inside?"

When no one claimed to know where his roommate was, dread clutched his heart. He couldn't lose another friend. He just couldn't. Since he and Aubrey had found each other, Jonah had always figured Sean's ghost had somehow brought them together because he'd wanted Jonah to look out for his boyfriend. Well, no way was Jonah about to let Sean down.

But someone crying out his name made him falter and glance back. "I told you to stay back," he shouted just as Tess and a panting Bailey reached him.

"What do you think you're doing?" She tried to manually pull his arm away from the door he still held open. "You are *not* going inside there, Jonah. No. No way."

"I have to find Aubrey."

"What if he already got out somewhere else?" Bailey said. "There's so many people; he could be anywhere."

Jonah merely shook his head. "He's still inside. I know it." His instincts were going crazy, screaming at him that his friend was in trouble.

"Then wait for the fire department," Tess pleaded, her eyes filling with tears as she tugged on his arm again without any success. "Listen. You can hear the sirens. They'll be here in just a few minutes."

But what if Aubrey didn't have that long? He couldn't explain how he knew his roommate needed him; he just knew it. He couldn't wait; he couldn't just stand here, doing nothing. He had to find Aubrey.

"Keep her out here," he told Bailey. Her eyes flared, but she bobbed her head without complaint.

Tess wasn't so easily persuaded, though. "No!" she screamed, grabbing for him again, except her friend had already hooked an arm around her waist and was dragging her away. "No. Jonah, please. Don't do this. Don't go in there."

He slipped inside to keep from seeing the terror on her face, hoping to God that wasn't the last time he'd ever see her. But as soon as he entered a narrow back hall, a haze of smoke started to make him cough.

Shit. This wasn't going to be good. How the hell was he supposed to see where he was going, let alone find his way back out?

Lifting his shirt, he used the cloth to cover his mouth and nose. Then he yanked his keychain from his pocket to find the flashlight Bailey had given him for his birthday. Clicking it twice until the light and laser beam both came on, he started to move away from the door. But he was scared to let it shut and possibly not be able to get open again. So, instead of keeping the flashlight with him, he plugged it into the doorjamb, letting a small stream of fresh air filter in behind him.

Then he rushed further into the burning building, his cane clutched in one hand and thumping ominously against the floor.

First thing he did when he turned a corner was run smack into a sobbing, hacking girl dressed as a medieval wench. He grasped her arm hard to get her attention when she did nothing but cling to him. Screaming in order to be heard above her crying and the blaring fire alarm, he shook her once.

"Hey! Have you seen Aubrey?"

"He's trapped," she finally babbled, the only understandable thing she'd said so far, and the only thing to put the fear of God into him. "I couldn't help him. He's trapped."

"Jesus. Where?"

He had to shake her again before she pointed. "Down there. Oh my God, they're going to die. I couldn't help them. We're all going to die."

"No. We're not." He shoved her around the corner, pointing at the red laser beam through the smoke. "Follow that red light. It's the door to outside, okay? You'll be fine. Now, go!"

She nodded and took off running.

Jonah didn't wait around to make sure she got out okay. He limped down the hall, yelling, "Aubrey! *Aubrey!*"

His throat burned and eyes watered. He had no idea what he was doing. This had to be the stupidest thing he'd ever attempted. But he couldn't give up, couldn't turn around and head back to the exit. She'd said his friend was still alive...*trapped*.

Sean would never forgive him if he left now.

"*Aubrey!*"

Just as his head went dizzy and he didn't think he could go on, he heard a faint call. "Here! We're here."

He dashed forward, gnashing his teeth when his leg tried to give out on him. He could barely make out a doorway, which he charged through to find himself on the wings of the stage. The water sprinkling system had gone off in here, and it immediately doused his hair and clothes and made the floor under his cane unbearably slick.

But the fire still crackled ahead, refusing to die completely where the water assault didn't quite reach. A few lasting flames tried to finish off the incinerated castle. What was worse, Aubrey lay only a few feet away, trapped under some fallen set trees along with two other people while those few flames crept closer.

"Help us. Please help us," wailed a guy with his entire chest pinned.

Jonah knelt next to Aubrey and took his hand, shaking uncontrollably.

"I think...I think my leg's broken," Aubrey said, gagging on his own tears and coughing.

Jonah nodded. "I'll get you out," he promised. He dropped his cane and grabbed the thick tree trunk. But, shit! Were these things made of steel filled with concrete or what?

Gritting his teeth, he roared through the pain in his straining muscles, braced the foot from his one good leg against the wet floor and shoved with all his might. When metal groaned and barely budged, the three trapped underneath gave a relieved shout and began to push with him, crawling free as best as they could.

His adrenal glands must've suited up and gone to work, because in the next instant, he pushed the tree away from them and shoved it to the side. The booming sound of it landing again was loud enough to rattle his teeth in his head.

After managing to ground himself after the release of all that weight against his shoulder, he reached for Aubrey. But his friend resisted. "No! Them first."

Oh, you gotta be kidding me. They didn't have time for him to save three people. But Aubrey was right. No way could he just leave them here.

Glancing at the other two, he gulped. Both were just as bad off as Aubrey was, mangled and bleeding profusely. None of them would be able to walk. They were all doomed, except he refused to admit defeat.

Declining to think through the impossibly of it, he simply started loading bodies into his arms and, settling them over his shoulders, two on one, one on the other. They were fairly small, but still, the bulk piled on top of him bore down on his bad leg. It buckled under him once. But he gritted through it and kept walking, one slow torturous step at a time. They might've made it away from the fire, but the smoke was just as deadly.

The first hall they came to was so congested with smoke, he couldn't even see down it. Breathing hard, he sucked nothing into his lungs but thick, choking soot. He tried to pick up his pace, but the faster he attempted to go, the slower he actually went. It felt like he was moving through lung-collapsing sludge.

When he turned the last corner, he spotted the thin ray of red light from Bailey's laser flashlight, and he literally started to weep. Tears flooded his cheeks, and sobs wracked his chest. He wanted to tell the people piled on top of him they were almost there, but the effort seemed to take too much of the strength he didn't have left.

He knew he was crushing Aubrey as he leaned heavily against the wall, but he figured it was better than tumbling all four of them to the floor. After a second to rest, he pushed away and took another step. Pure stubborn willpower was the only thing making him move forward, because he was out of oxygen, out of strength, and his leg was screaming with agony.

But he refused to give up. Just ten more yards. Five. Three.

His knee buckled. White-hot pain shot up his entire body. All four of them went down in a heap.

"No!" The girl sobbed, clinging to his shirt. "No. Please."

"It's okay," he panted, patting her hand, wishing he could get a good, clean lungful of fresh air right about now. "It's…"

Coughing, he pushed them off him so the four of them could all crawl with nothing but their arms. He trailed behind so he could push them forward when one of them started to give up.

"The door," he wanted to say and ask someone to open for him, but he was too busy hacking to form the words. His head fogged up as if smoke had seeped in through his ears and made his entire brain fuzzy. If he didn't get the door open and drag these people outside before he lost consciousness, none of them would survive to see tomorrow. They were only a few yards away. Surely, they could make it the last few feet.

But, fuck, those feet felt like miles.

A vision of Tess filled his head. He wanted to see her again, more than anything. He wanted to hold her, marry her, and start a life with her.

He wanted to live.

A tear slid down his cheek. "Tess," he choked out just as his world went black.

Chapter Thirty-One

Tess's heart stopped in her chest as Jonah disappeared into the performing arts center. Screaming his name, she clawed at Bailey's arm to break free.

"Please. Don't do this to me." She'd just found him again. Losing him one more time wasn't an option.

"He'll be back." But Bailey's reassuring tone was so calm it actually had the opposite effect.

Rage boiled inside Tess. Bailey had been the one to keep her from following him inside. Bailey had been the one to tell him to stay away from her at the hospital. Bailey was keeping her from him right now.

Rearing her elbow back, she slammed her best friend in the ribcage. Bailey cried out and lost her grip, and Tess scrambled forward, going down on hands and knees before she regained her footing. She actually got close enough to the door to reached out and open the handle when her best friend tackled her from behind.

Blacking out for a second from the pain of her concrete landing, rough gravel biting into her hands and knees, Tess shook her head, and then screamed in frustration, trying to buck Bailey off her back.

But Bailey was just as willing to fight dirty. She grabbed a handful of red hair and yanked. "You are *not* going inside that building."

"Get…off…me!" She screamed again and managed to fling Bailey off, losing a chunk of hair in the process. But just as she reached for the door handle, it came flying open, smacking her in the arm. She cried out and clutched her elbow as a terrified girl careened into her.

"Oh my God. Oh my God." Tears tracked through the black soot on the girl's face. "I thought I was going to die. I thought I was dead." Clinging to Tess, she hugged the first person she saw. "He saved my life."

"What? Who?" Tess demanded. "Did you see my boyfriend? Is he okay?"

"I don't— " Pausing to cough and cry some more, the girl shuddered. "I don't know. I was lost. It was so smoky. I couldn't see where I was going. And suddenly there was this big guy with a cane. He pointed me toward this laser beam and told me to follow it to the door. And it did. It did…I think he was an angel."

When she broke into more sobs, Tess met Bailey's gaze over her shoulder.

"Oh my God. My laser flashlight is *saving lives.*" Bailey streaked toward the door where her flashlight had spilled to the ground after the girl had plowed her way into the alley. It was still cracking the door open an inch.

Swiping it up, she began to kiss it in praise. "Oh, you good amazing flashlight, you. I knew you were wonderful. You did good. You did so good."

"Put it back!" Tess broke free of the terrified girl and yanked the flashlight out of Bailey's hand. "Jonah needs that to find his way out." She opened the door further to tuck the leading light safely in the doorjamb, but a plume of smoke spilled out, making her cough.

Oh, dear God. How was Jonah supposed to survive for a single minute in there? She covered her mouth and began to cry in earnest. Bailey slipped the flashlight from her limp fingers and reverently wedged it back into the door for her, but Tess couldn't see how he'd ever find his way through *that.*

She doubled over, bawling for all she was worth. "He's not coming back. Oh, God, Bailey. I can't lose him again. I just got him back."

"It's okay. It's okay," Bailey reassured her, hugging her close and stroking her hair. "Abbott's a survivor. He made it through three bullet wounds and a coma. If anyone could make it out of there, he can."

If? Why was she saying *if? If* was totally not acceptable.

Pushing away from Bailey, she went back for the door. "I have to get him out. Now."

This time when Bailey wrapped her arms around her, Tess wasn't playing around. She rammed her foot down on her friend's instep and pounded her elbow backward. Bailey doubled over with a groan.

As soon as she was free, Tess yanked the door open only to hear his voice...calling her name.

"He's right there," she cried, surging forward.

"Tess!" Bailey screamed, following her inside. "No!"

But Tess had already tripped over what seemed like a pile of bodies. When she felt at least three arms, she moaned. "Help me, Bailey. Dear Lord. How many of them are there? Help me get them outside."

Both girls grabbed arms and legs and started dragging. As soon as they reached fresh air, Tess sucked in a breath, only to discover she and Bailey had saved Aubrey and some stranger. Both were unconscious.

She and Bailey exchanged glances. "Jonah had to be right there with them. I heard his voice."

With a nod, Bailey followed her back inside. The next round and too much coughing later, they found one more guy. But still no Jonah.

"Where *is* he?" Growing frantic, Tess started back inside, hacking madly, her lungs heavy with smoke. But a shout cut her short.

"Hey, don't go into that building, miss."

When she saw a pair of firefighters jogging her way, she pointed into the opened door. "My boyfriend's right there. I *heard* him."

"We'll get him, then. You just stay put." After they radioed for paramedics to come help the three people Bailey and Tess had brought outside, they disappeared into the burning building, only to reappear a half-second later, toting a limp Jonah.

Tess launched herself at him. "Is he alive? Oh, please. Tell me he's alive."

"He has a pulse," one of the firefighters assured her. "But we need to get him on some oxygen right away."

That was all she needed to hear, because Bailey had been right. Jonah was a survivor. If he had half a chance, he'd make it through this.

Jonah came to with something strapped over his mouth. But at least there was fresh air moving through his lungs. He coughed anyway, choked up by stray pockets of smoke still trapped inside him.

"Easy." A strange but sturdy hand clasped his shoulder and re-adjusted his facemask. "Just breathe deeply and relax. You're going to be okay, kid."

Something shifted against his other side, and he realized it was a body. A trembling, curvy, feminine body. Tess. When her fingers grabbed ahold of his, he finally did relax and tried to turn her way.

Her beautiful blue eyes appeared with tears streaming down her cheeks, and it struck him that he'd messed up. He'd left her outside. By herself.

But she must've already forgiven him because all she did was smile. "You came back to me."

Jonah nodded, wanting her to know he always would. As long as his heart kept beating, he'd find his way back to her.

He glanced around. They were sitting on the ground leaning against a tree while paramedics, police, firefighters, and news media milled around the area between crying, shocked bystanders. Noticing the paramedic who'd been lingering at his other side, he nodded to the man, silently thanking him for his help.

The EMT nodded back with a smile. "Looks like you're in good hands with your little ladies here," he said, nodding toward Tess and then Bailey, who Jonah hadn't noticed before. "I'm going to go check on some of the others. If you need anything, just wave us over."

When Jonah gave him the thumbs up, the guy took off, half-walking, half-jogging to help more people. Staring after him, Jonah felt the itching need to stand up and assist someone too.

"Damn, Abbott, you totally scared the shit out of us, you know that?" Bailey plowed into him and clamped her arms around his chest. He wasn't sure how to apologize, so he patted her shoulder, and she gave a watery laugh before slugging him. "Thanks a lot, asshole."

He rolled his eyes. Only Bailey.

Across the way, more firefighters led a few coughing people away from the building. A cool evening breeze, smelling of charred wood, wafted over him, sticking his damp shirt to his chest.

"We need more oxygen over here," a desperate voice called. "Are there any tanks left?"

Jonah fumbled to rip the mask off his mouth. "You can use this one."

"No!" Tess squeezed his arm and sent him a warning scowl. "You still need it."

"Don't worry. I feel better already. Besides, I can't hold you how I want with this damn thing on."

When she finally relented, he handed it over to the waiting fireman. "Thanks, man."

Jonah nodded and yanked Tess into his arms. She clutched him hard and buried her face into his chest as he burrowed his nose in her red curls and hugged her back. When he smelled smoke in her hair, he pulled away.

"We're going to have to take another one of our special showers as soon as we get out of here. You smell awful."

She blurted out a laugh before bursting into a fresh wave of tears. "I love you so much. I can't believe I almost lost you again."

"Never," he promised. "Never again. I love you too much to go anywhere."

"Hey, there's Aubrey," Bailey cut in, pointing.

Realizing he'd forgotten all about his roommate, *again*, he zipped his attention up and saw Aubrey laid out on a stretcher that sat outside next to the open back door of an ambulance.

When he struggled to rise, Tess clung to his side and kept her shoulder under his arm as if she knew he needed to use her as a crutch. But what surprised him more was when Bailey appeared at his other side to do the same thing. Wrapping his arms around both girls, he limped with them to his friend.

Tears streamed down Aubrey's blackened face. "You saved my life." As he sobbed between wheezes, he reached out and grasped Jonah's hand. "I love you, man. I love you."

Jonah nodded. "Yeah," he said as he tugged Tess closer to him. "You too."

She pressed her cheek to his shoulder and set her hand over his heart.

"There!" A girl's voice called, breaking into Jonah's reunion with his roommate. "That's the guy who saved my life."

Jonah had no idea he was the subject of her attention until a male voice interrupted. "Young man." Jonah glanced up just as a bright light blinded him. "I'm Charlie Martin with Channel Nine," the voice continued, "and this is my daughter you saved tonight. Can we have your account of what happened?"

Jonah lifted his hand to shade his eyes before he noticed the microphone in his face with the logo of a nearby television station on it. The hand wrapped around the microphone led up an arm until he focused on the face of a man he'd seen on the evening news almost every night.

"I'll tell you what happened," Charlie Martin's daughter spoke up, stepping in front of him and straining onto her tiptoes so she could be included into the frame. "This guy was a hero tonight. A straight-up, risk-his-life-for-other-people hero. When I fell down just feet from the exit, he immediately swooped in to lift me back up before I could get trampled."

"No," Jonah started modestly, remembering her from the front foyer of the arts center. He lifted his hand to silence her. "I'm actually the one who accidentally knocked you down in the first place."

"But you had to fight against the crowd to stay there and help her back up," Tess said.

"He was amazing." The girl patted his arm. "I was so sure I was going to die. But he saved me."

"He saved me too," Aubrey called from his stretcher.

The microphone and light from the camera instantly shifted away from Jonah to swerve his roommate's way.

"Three of us were trapped under this tree prop that had fallen on stage, when suddenly I heard Jonah calling my name. Then he appeared like an angel from the smoke and pushed the beam off us. None of us could walk so he carried us, and, oh hell. Your leg's broken. How could you carry all three of us?"

The camera and reporter whirled back to Jonah. "Your leg's broken?"

Jonah shrugged. "My femur's still technically mending from being shattered in the massacre."

"Wait!" Charlie Martin waved his hand with an incredulous air. "You were wounded in the school shooting, you had a broken femur, and you still carried *three* people out of a burning building?"

"Well…" Hmm, he had, hadn't he? That was strange. It sounded almost noble when phrased that way. But still…"It's practically healed. I've had over three months to—"

"He was amazing. Totally amazing." Tess wrapped her hands around his arm and squeezed. "We were screaming at him, begging him not to go back inside. But he was so determined and brave."

"Then he used the laser off my flashlight to wedge in the doorway so he could see his way back out," Bailey felt the need to add with a self-congratulatory nod.

Charlie Martin's jaw dropped. "So, you'd already escaped outside after the fire had started, but you went *back in?*" The light from the video recorder shifted and the cameraman moved to get a better shot of Jonah's face. "Weren't you scared?"

"Of course." Jesus, who wouldn't be scared? Was this guy for real? "But my friend was still in there. I couldn't just leave him."

"And another girl came running through the doorway while he was inside because she'd been able to follow the line of red laser right out the exit." Bailey preened, obviously still proud of her invention. "So, there's another life he saved tonight."

"What's that up to, then?" Aubrey asked. "Five people who might've died if not for him?" He gazed up at Jonah with complete adoration. "You really are a hero."

But Jonah shook his head. "No. My leg gave out on me about ten feet from the door. I dropped all three of you guys, and—" he glanced at Tess "—I don't know who, but someone else got us all outside."

No one seemed to care that he hadn't done it all by himself. Charlie Martin shook his head with amazement. "What did you say your name was again?"

Jonah paled. "I didn't—"

Aubrey talked over him. "His name's Jonah Abbott. That's Abbott with two b's and two t's."

Mouth falling open, Charlie Martin gaped at him before stuttering, "Did you say...*J-Jonah* Abbott?"

"Oh, so, you remember totally lambasting him a couple months back, do you?" Bailey smirked cheerfully as she hooked her arm through Tess's. "Just because he owned a gun, which a really bad person stole to do really bad things with. No, I guess a hero with a bum leg risking his life and rushing inside a burning building to save his best gay friend from certain death doesn't quite fit the mold of evil bullying bigot all you friendly media people made him out to be, *does it?*"

"Ooh…burn," Aubrey said. Bailey laughed and fist-bumped him.

After gaping at the two of them for totally defending him, Jonah looked incredulously at Tess. Had she just heard the same thing he'd heard? Maybe too much smoke to the brain was making him hallucinate.

But Tess merely grinned at him and lifted up on her toes to kiss his cheek. "Reason number one why having Bailey for a friend kicks ass," she murmured in his ear.

Um…yeah. Definitely.

As the news reporter stammered for an apt reply, a trio of firemen approached them. From the sweat and soot streaming off their faces and uniforms, they'd all just come from inside the building.

"Hey, man. We heard what you did. Carrying three people out of there all at one time was pretty heroic." They gave him a solemn nod.

Staring at them in awe, because firefighters—freaking firefighters—were commending him for a job well done, he began to stutter profusely. "I…I…" Hell, he had no idea what to say to firemen who saved lives on a daily basis while they were looking at him as if impressed. "I…played football," he finished lamely. "I'm used to carrying a lot of weight on my shoulders."

The guys chuckled. "Well, you did good, kid." One slugged him companionably on the shoulder. "You ever need a job, come see us."

Jonah gawked after them as they walked away.

Tess curled her arms around one of his and rested her chin on his shoulder. "And I bet you still don't feel as if you redeemed yourself tonight, do you?"

A small smile played across his face as he glanced at her. "Stop reading my mind, woman."

Grinning, she kissed his cheek. "Take me home, handsome. Some very brave and gorgeous hero just told me I needed a shower."

Chapter Thirty-Two

Tess and Jonah didn't actually make it back to his apartment until the wee hours of the morning. He'd been required to go to the hospital to get checked out, so they'd been forced to sit around for hours, waiting until he was released. Then, they had showered together, soaping each other's hair three times before they gave up and decided they were just doomed to smell like smoke for a while. But after lying down for a few hours of shut eye, they were both up again, unable to sleep.

After another shower, Tess lingered in the bathroom to blow-dry her hair. Wrinkling her nose, she smelled one of her pungent locks as she strolled back into the living room where she caught sight of Jonah sitting on the couch, hanging up his cell phone.

"Well, Aubrey has a broken leg," he announced with a heavy sigh. "The prop that fell on him busted his femur, just like mine."

"Oh, my God." Covering her mouth, she let out a small, horrified laugh. "And you told him to break a leg."

Jonah groaned. "Don't remind me. Seriously, the two of us hobbling around here for the next half a year is going to be hell, especially with the drama queen. He got a paper cut once and literally cried. With tears."

Tess sobered immediately and winced. "Oh, boy. Poor Aubrey. But at least he wasn't hurt any more than that. He could've been crushed to death. Or burned to a crisp."

"Amen." Wrapping his arms around her waist when she came close enough for him to touch her, he buried his face in her stomach. "All that matters is he's alive."

She stroked his hair as he rested his face against her.

"I'm going to go see him in a little bit, here. But I think I'm going to dig out my crutches first. My leg's killing me."

Tess eased out of his grip so she could sit beside him. Silently, she dug her fingers into the muscle he'd been trying to loosen when she'd walked into the room.

He groaned out a sound that told her her ministrations were the good kind of pain. Throwing his head back to rest it on the back cushion of the sofa, he closed his eyes and breathed deeply through his mouth.

"Thank you. That feels…God…amazing."

"How bad did you hurt it?" she asked quietly, already knowing it wasn't good.

He cracked open one eye to give her a why'd-you-have-to-ask-that glance. "Let's just say my PT is going to be pissed when I see him for my next checkup."

She bit her lip and dug a little deeper into the twisted mass of tissue. He sucked in a breath and grabbed the armrest to brace himself. "God, that's perfect."

Emotion rose in her throat. She wanted to tell him how much she loved him, how amazed she was by all the heroism he'd shown last night, and how scared she'd been when she was sure he'd never make it out of that building alive. But it was all right there, too, close to the surface. She didn't want to cry any more, and if she said anything that was on her mind, she knew she'd lose it. So, she decided to keep it light.

"I decided on a major."

He opened his beautiful brown eyes to study her. "So, you finally realized physical therapy was your calling, huh? Good."

"Wait, how'd you know—" Her shoulder fell as she smiled and shook her head. "This is scary. Are you supposed to know me quite this well yet?"

He just smiled at her. "Couldn't have happened fast enough for me." Taking her hand, he played with her fingers as he looked into her eyes. "Speaking of moving fast, I was going to ask you to move in with me so we don't have to be apart this summer, but that might not be a great idea. I think this apartment is cursed. Whoever stays here ends up with a broken leg."

Tess caught her breath and unconsciously squeezed his hand as she gaped at him. "You mean, you...you really *want* me here?"

He snorted out an incredulous sound. "Of course I want you here. But—"

"But what?"

He flushed and glanced away. "But, I don't know. Jesus, Tess. We just started this. I know it's too soon to go asking if we can live together. Isn't it? I mean, after all the shit that's happened this year, last night included—"

Setting her fingers over his lips to silence him, she gave a soft, thrilled laugh. "After everything that's happened, I'd think we'd have learned by now that every second we have is a gift we shouldn't squander by worrying about things happening too fast. If we have a chance to be happy, then we should grasp it with both hands and hang on tight for as long as it lasts."

Jonah gazed at her, his eyes suddenly glassy. Then he reached out and gripped her face with both hands, bringing her in close. "In that case, I don't want you to go home for the summer. I don't want to spend a day without you. Stay here, with me."

The joy that welled inside her bubbled up until she was laughing and crying and throwing her arms around his neck to hug and kiss him. "Okay." She sniffed away the happy tears. "Okay."

Tess drew in a deep breath. When Bailey had learned that she and Jonah wanted to go see Aubrey, she'd decided to tag along. The three of them took Bailey's car, since Jonah wasn't really in any condition to drive.

Flanked by her best friend and her boyfriend, Tess recalled a few months earlier when she'd made this very same walk up the front sidewalk to Granton Regional's entrance. She'd had no idea her life was about to change forever.

It felt strange, entering the same building today, as if everything had come full circle. Except, now, as she glanced at the ornamental trees lining the sidewalk, she realized the branches weren't as frozen and bare as they'd been in February. Green buds had popped out fresh leaves, signaling a new beginning.

With all the metaphorical optimism literally springing up around her, she took Bailey's hand and squeezed Jonah's forearm to let them both know how much they meant to her.

"Oh, God." Bailey groaned. "You're remembering the first night you met Abbott, aren't you?"

Tess merely grinned at her before she leaned up past his crutches to kiss his cheek. "Of course. It's a great memory."

Bailey snorted. "Yeah, I'm sure the fact that you lied to him the entire evening is something to pass along to the grandkids."

Tess merely shrugged. "Best lie I ever told."

"Amen." He grinned back at her.

"Gag me," Bailey muttered. She let go of Tess's hand and led the way into the hospital.

They found Aubrey's room a few minutes later. He was resting when the three trooped quietly in. Bailey, Tess, and Jonah exchanged a glance, wondering if they should bother to wake him or come back later, when he stirred and slowly blinked open his eyes.

"Hey," Jonah said softly, approaching him. "How're you feeling?"

Aubrey was pale and had cuts all over his face and arms; some of them had even been stitched back together. But he smiled from dry, chapped lips. "I feel great," he slurred, his voice so hoarse Tess had to wince because she could actually hear how raw his throat must be after so much smoke inhalation.

She glanced worriedly at Jonah. He wasn't as hoarse, but his esophagus had to be sore after being inside the building for as long as he'd been. She knew he was keeping how much his leg hurt from her; she kept catching him rubbing it. But what other pains wasn't he mentioning?

"Drugs are a beautiful thing." Aubrey's eyes glazed over as he gave the girls a goofy grin. Then he reached for Jonah's hand. "Almost as beautiful as you."

Jonah jerked his arm back and shook his finger at his roommate. "Damn, Aub. How can you be half-dead, doped up on painkillers, and still manage to freaking flirt?"

The loopy patient merely grinned. "Talent," he said and blew Jonah a kiss before turning his attention to Tess. "And there's the only girl who could make me go straight." When he held out his hand to her, she took it eagerly, squeezing with a gentle warmth.

"I don't know if anyone's told you this yet, but your performance last night was…amazing. You were by far the best actor on that stage."

Tears glittered in his eyes. "Actually, no. No one's talked to me about the play at all. They've only mentioned—" Too choked up to continue, he slid his hand away from Tess's to wipe his damp cheeks. "Did you guys watch the news last night?"

When Jonah gave a loud sigh, Tess met his gaze. He sent her a weary look. "No. We haven't." From his tone, it was obvious he didn't care to know what he'd missed. "So, what'd they have to say about me?"

"They called you a hero," Bailey answered.

When Tess and Jonah sent her a startled glance, she and Aubrey nodded. "They showed the same picture of you they'd showed back when they were calling you the anti-Christ, and they even brought up your involvements with the shooting."

Jonah groaned, and Tess stroked his arm in sympathy, until Aubrey took up where Bailey had left off. "And they damn near apologized for turning you into a public menace. They said after tonight's events, your true colors came out and showed off the amazing person you really are."

"They *what?*" Jonah glanced at Tess as if to see if she'd heard what he'd just heard before he turned back to Bailey and Aubrey. "They didn't really say that."

Bailey just nodded. "Oh, yes, they did. Practically verbatim."

"Wow." Jonah sank into the chair by Aubrey's bedside.

He was still sitting there looking stupefied when his cell phone rang. After digging it from his pants pocket, he wrinkled his face at the number.

"Hello?"

Tess touched his shoulder when he pulled back his head, obviously experiencing another shock. "Yeah…" he continued. "Okay… but there's no way I could play by next semester. Oh. I see…well… wow. Thank you. Okay. Thanks."

When he hung up, he sat in silence staring at the phone as if he didn't know what to do with it.

"Well?" Bailey finally said.

He lifted his face. "That was Coach Whitely. He called on behalf of the university." Hand trembling, he covered his face. "Jesus."

"What?" Tess demanded, worry gnawing at her gut.

He looked up at her. "They saw me on the news last night. Crap. When I heard that, I thought I was going to get reamed out for being caught on campus. But…they're rescinding my expulsion. I can enroll in classes again for the Fall semester."

"Oh, Jonah. That's amazing."

"I know." He hugged Tess back, still sounding dazed by the news. "Coach even knew there's no way I could play ball my senior year, but he still wanted to be the one to call me personally so he could… apologize for the way the university treated me."

When he glanced at Tess, she could only grin. With a happy squeal, she hugged him hard. "That's great."

"And about freaking time." Bailey gave a vengeful sniff. "You never really did anything wrong."

"I brought a gun on campus," he reminded her. "If I hadn't done that, none of this would've happened."

"Oh, I'm sure it would've happened," Aubrey said. "Just not in the same way. And it probably wouldn't have brought you and I together. You've become one of my best friends, Jonah." Tears leaked down his cheeks. "Which is why what I have to say next so incredibly hard."

When Jonah's face paled, Tess grasped his hand.

"What?"

Aubrey glanced away. "After everything that's happened this year, I'm not coming back next semester. I'm going home."

Jonah blew out a shaky breath, his grip on Tess's hand never losing its strength. "You're leaving?"

His roommate nodded. "I'm not strong like you. I can't deal with all the tragedy this town has delivered me. I just need to go home."

After blinking a few times, Jonah gave a short, jerky nod. "It's okay," he assured. "I completely understand."

Aubrey wiped more tears away. "The apartment's all yours. We both know Sean would've wanted you to have it. Do you think you'll be able to afford the utilities by yourself?"

Jonah glanced at Tess. "Actually, I might have another roommate already lined up."

Bailey glanced between them with a suspicious frown. "Wait. Are you *moving in* with him?"

Tess bit her lip. "Um…" When she cringed, her best friend narrowed her eyes.

"Holy shit, you are."

"Bailey, I —" Tess floundered and glanced to Jonah for help.

"I just asked her this morning," he said, rushing to defend her. "And she never answered." It was a lie — a loving lie. "I think she wanted to discuss it with you first."

Bailey nodded before cursing under her breath. "Okay, fine," she finally said. "Here's the deal. I found an apartment for us, a really amazing, beautiful, nice, spacious place in a good neighborhood, close to campus. But it's three bedrooms and a little out of our price range. So…I asked Paige if she wanted to chip in and take the third room. But, of course, she's in the same boat as you. Physically attached to her man, so it seems."

With a muttered sigh and roll of her eyes, she continued. "She wants to stay wherever Logan stays and was only willing to join us if he could live there too. So, what I'm saying is…God, I can't believe I'm saying this. But if you two want the third room, you can take it. I can stomach being Fifth-Wheel Bailey to make my two best friends happy. Except I'm taking the master bedroom because *I* found the place."

Her sniff challenged everyone to contradict her, which they didn't.

Tess glanced at Jonah, who shrugged and made a face, letting her know he'd be okay with whatever arrangement she wanted. She whirled back to Bailey, smiling big. "Sounds like you're going to have four roommates instead of one."

"Yeah." Bailey groaned loudly. "The joy." She scowled at a grinning Tess and Jonah. "I better freaking find that cowboy quick, because being around both you and Paige with your icky, cuddly boyfriends without having my own icky cuddly boyfriend is going to drive me insane."

The End

(The next Granton University book will be Bailey's story.)

Acknowledgments

Thanks so much to my first draft readers: Cindy Alexander, Nancy Crumpacker, Kayla Crumpacker, Morgan Gilmore, Jamie Hixon, Sandra Martinie, Alaina Martinie, as well as Ashley Morrison from the Book Labyrinth, Pepper and Michelle from All Romance Reviews, Andrea Reed, Lindsay Brooks, Ami from Romance Readaholic, and authors Mary Crawford and Ada Frost.

A huge thank you to the entire team at Omnific Publishing who took care of everything else.

As always, I appreciate Kurt and Lydia for putting up with me on the day to day. And the best for last, thanks to the good Lord who loves me no matter how much of a big, fat sinner I am! You're all the best!

About the Author

Linda grew up on a dairy farm in the Midwest as the youngest of eight children. Now she lives in Kansas with her husband, toddler daughter, and their nine cuckoo clocks. She works a day job in the acquisitions department of a university library and feels her life has been blessed with lots of people to learn from and love. Writing's always been a major part her world, and she's thrilled to finally share some of her stories with other romance lovers.

Young Adult Romance

The Ember series: *Ember & Iridescent* by Carol Oates
Breaking Point by Jess Bowen
Life, Liberty, and Pursuit by Susan Kaye Quinn
The Embrace series: *Embrace & Hold Tight* by Cherie Colyer
Destiny's Fire by Trisha Wolfe
The Reaper series: *Reaping Me Softly & UnReap My Heart* by Kate Evangelista
The Legendary Saga: *Legendary* by LH Nicole
Fatal by T.A. Brock
The Prometheus Order series: *Byronic* by Sandi Beth Jones
One Smart Cookie by Kym Brunner

Paranormal Romance

The Light series: *Seers of Light, Whisper of Light & Circle of Light* by Jennifer DeLucy
The Hanaford Park series: *Eve of Samhain & Pleasures Untold* by Lisa Sanchez
Immortal Awakening by KC Randall
The Seraphim series: *Crushed Seraphim & Bittersweet Seraphim* by Debra Anastasia
The Guardian's Wild Child by Feather Stone
Grave Refrain by Sarah M. Glover
The Divinity series: *Divinity* by Patricia Leever
The Blood Vine series: *Blood Vine, Blood Entangled & Blood Reunited*
by Amber Belldene
Divine Temptation by Nicki Elson
The Dead Rapture series: *Love in the Time of the Dead* by Tera Shanley

Romantic Suspense

Whirlwind by Robin DeJarnett
The CONduct series: *With Good Behavior, Bad Behavior & On Best Behavior*
by Jennifer Lane
Indivisible by Jessica McQuinn
Between the Lies by Alison Oburia
Blind Man's Bargain by Tracy Winegar

Erotic Romance

The Keyhole series: *Becoming sage* (book 1) by Kasi Alexander
The Keyhole series: *Saving sunni* (book 2) by Kasi & Reggie Alexander
The Winemaker's Dinner: *Appetizers & Entrée* by Dr. Ivan Rusilko & Everly Drummond
The Winemaker's Dinner: *Dessert* by Dr. Ivan Rusilko
Client N° 5 by Joy Fulcher

← ⟶ Anthologies and Sets ← ⟶

A Valentine Anthology including short stories by
Alice Clayton ("With a Double Oven"),
Jennifer DeLucy ("Magnus of Pfelt, Conquering Viking Lord"),
Nicki Elson ("I Don't Do Valentine's Day"),
Jessica McQuinn ("Better Than One Dead Rose and a Monkey Card"),
Victoria Michaels ("Home to Jackson"), and
Alison Oburia ("The Bridge")

Taking Liberties including an introduction by Tiffany Reisz and short stories by
Mina Vaughn ("John Hancock-Blocked"),
Linda Cunningham ("A Boston Marriage"),
Joy Fulcher ("Tea for Two"),
KC Holly ("The British Are Coming!"),
Kimberly Jensen & Scott Stark ("E. Pluribus Threesome"), and
Vivian Rider ("M'Lady's Secret Service")

The Heart Series Box Set (*Beside Your Heart, Disclosure of the Heart* &
Forever Your Heart) by Mary Whitney
The CONduct Series Box Set (*With Good Behavior, Bad Behavior* &
On Best Behavior) by Jennifer Lane

← ⟶ Singles and Novellas ← ⟶

It's Only Kinky the First Time (A Keyhole series single) by Kasi Alexander
Learning the Ropes (A Keyhole series single) by Kasi & Reggie Alexander
The Winemaker's Dinner: RSVP by Dr. Ivan Rusilko
The Winemaker's Dinner: No Reservations by Everly Drummond
Big Guns by Jessica McQuinn
Concessions by Robin DeJarnett
Starstruck by Lisa Sanchez
New Flame by BJ Thornton
Shackled by Debra Anastasia
Swim Recruit by Jennifer Lane
Sway by Nicki Elson
Full Speed Ahead by Susan Kaye Quinn
The Second Sunrise by Hannah Downing
The Summer Prince by Carol Oates
Whatever it Takes by Sarah M. Glover
Clarity (A *Divinity* prequel single) by Patricia Leever
A Christmas Wish (A *Cocktails & Dreams* single) by Autumn Markus
Late Night with Andres by Debra Anastasia
Poughkeepsie (enhanced iPad app collector's edition) by Debra Anastasia

coming soon from
OMNIFIC PUBLISHING